AUTHOR'S

I first decided to rally to the defence of the cruelly maligned Emperor Nero when the glaring mistakes of Tacitus and Suetonius led me to read between the lines and embark upon research of my own. Nevertheless, this work would not have been possible but for the meticulous research and biographical skills of both Tacitus and Suetonius, who, though biased, were nonetheless gifted for gathering quotes and stories.

Though fictionalised, this book is more than simply 'based' upon a true life. Wherever possible I have included genuine quotations from Nero and those he knew; and if an event or conversation was not historically recorded and factual, then it was not included. Every person within these pages existed; every action within the book involved them some nineteen hundred years ago; every event really did take place, exactly as written.

For the ability to do this I must thank Epaphroditus, the emperor's secretary, who must have been as compulsive a scribe as I; and to the historians of the era, Cassius Dio, Tacitus and Suetonius, who meticulously collected up his work and used it to throw in the face of his employer wherever the chance arose!

I could not bring Nero to life without his own words and, in recognition and honour of that fact, I devoted the final chapter - the final hours of his memorable life - to those very words. Unlike the remainder of the book, it contains none of my own fanciful input. Every spoken word was originally voiced and recorded in AD68, from the salute of the soldiers as they called from within the Guards' Camp, to the final words of Nero himself.

The story, then, is not mine; the research one of love and no labour at all; and credit, if it is due, must go to my four previously mentioned literary partners; Jerome Carcopino, whose book 'Daily Life In Ancient Rome' proved invaluable; and Michael Grant, whose biography of Nero was the most perfect I have yet come across.

But the true acknowledgement must go to Nero himself. With his ideals, his extravagance and his family, he is truly a god's gift to an author.

This, then, is his book; his work; his life.

Lissa Oliver

Introduction

The Nero known by academics is not the Nero perceived by the general public.

Times have changed since the First Century. The vilest crime of that era might well be considered a virtue in today's society; just as things currently frowned upon were encouraged two thousand years ago, when morals were virtually at the reverse end of today's spectrum.

And yet, when we read two-thousand-year-old history, we can only equate it with the society and morals we currently understand. If we are told a man is a monster because of his crimes against humanity committed in the amphitheatres of Rome, we immediately conjure up visions of the worst forms of arena death. Without knowledge of that Roman society, how can we realise that the man's crime was to ban death from the arena?

When the Roman biographies of emperors, written in the first and second century of Rome, were first translated and read by nineteenth century scholars, those scholars had no concept of first century life, society or morals. Gradually, over the next hundred years, archaeologists pieced together something of that period and lifestyle - but by then, the lessons already learned from those first translations had become ingrained in modern history. Even today, while scholars agree that the truth is far removed from the basic history we have come to know, it will continue to take many decades to correct the misconceptions.

Biographies that were understood a century ago to be just that are now recognised as mere works of political propaganda - negative in some instances, and overly positive in others. Politicians have always had their spin-doctors, even in ancient Rome. Unfortunately, we have based much of our historical studies on the works of those spin-doctors, only in recent years realising our error. And so academics have been forced to rethink old attitudes and re-evaluate the evidence left by those Roman writers.

Which brings us to Nero in particular, as great a victim of this propaganda as Julius Caesar has been a fortunate recipient.

The principal aim of a Roman emperor was to leave behind a legacy - a memory of his reign to ensure immortality. The first emperor, Augustus, laid foundations that would never be equalled or bettered. Successive emperors looked to monuments and public amenities to secure their place in history. Nero somehow contrived to surpass all predecessors and to set standards that would be insurmountable by his own successors. In so doing, he earned such respect and adulation from his people that no subsequent emperor could hope to fill his shoes.

Monuments and public amenities can be torn down and built over. Reputations are somewhat harder to destroy. The emperors who succeeded Nero not only destroyed his great public works, but successfully destroyed his reputation - not in his own day, when he was still mourned some thirty years after his death, but for the future generations, who could not remember the success of his reign.

Nero's death resulted in civil war. The first three emperors to succeed him each survived for less than four months. The public longed for Nero's return and was ready to accept any trickster claiming to be their former emperor, who had somehow cheated death and returned to save them. Not only the Roman public, but dependant and allied states such as Parthia, Greece and Armenia - all major forces who time and again backed the claims of yet another new Nero impostor and once more raised the hopes of the Roman populace and reminded them of the emperor loved and lost. This was the ghost subsequent emperors had first to overcome before being accepted into power.

Biographers such as Tacitus and Suetonius were encouraged. The public needed to be reminded of former glories, of Augustus and Germanicus. These two, in particular, were so coloured by positive propaganda that they became legendary heroes, far over-shadowing Nero. Julius Caesar himself, something of a despotic villain in his own day, began to acquire heroic status. Similarly, those more closely linked with the last of Caesar's family - Nero - were dealt more sinister press. Full-blown character assassinations were made on Tiberius, Claudius and Nero himself. The Caesar family was portrayed as an ever-degenerating gene pool finally culminating in Nero and merciful destruction.

In biographies written long after Nero's death, therefore, the crimes laid at his door were often completely false. Events were portrayed out of context; every death purported as murder. A list of murder victims by Tacitus and Suetonius were in truth the names of conspirators found guilty of an assassination attempt. Both authors perversely condemned the emperor's apparent thirst for blood, while at the same time mocking his distaste for bloodshed.

Eventually, this was enough to win back public respect for the emperors who succeeded the House of Caesar, with no dynastic birthright themselves but gaining an opportunity to found their own dynasty. And so, the success of their propaganda campaigns has coloured our own view of history, even without such minor incidentals as changing concepts of good and evil. And the concept of good and evil has changed drastically, radically, in two thousand years.

We wonder now at the lack of respect for life in Roman society. We see re-enactments of gladiatorial fights and wild animal hunts in the amphitheatres of ancient Rome and we conclude that life then was cheap. But values have changed and our conclusions could not be any further from the truth.

Life in ancient Rome was very highly prized. The children of Rome were taught to value and respect life by the very life and death battles they witnessed in the arena. How better to understand such values than to witness a trained gladiator using every skill at his disposal to fight for that very life?

But gladiators were the highlight and featured late on the bill at the arena. The value of life was taught by their death, but the total lack of value of such citizens as criminals and prisoners of war was also presented, as appetisers to the main bill. These people were thrown to their sordid deaths without any display of skill or will to live. They were torn apart by wild dogs, the display of death as worthless as their existence. Few people bothered with this spectacle, until in later years, long after the death of Nero, it was enhanced with the introduction of more exotic creatures such as lions, tigers and crocodiles.

The arena was a source of public entertainment - competing only with horse racing - on the 159 days a year of state-funded public holidays. Though the arguments in its favour were moral - the teaching of respect for life - it was fundamentally a good day out for all. Not only were there a vast number of public holidays in Rome, there was also a vast number of unemployed - almost a third of the population receiving weekly dole. The leisure industry was as important as it was fruitful. Something had to keep the masses in its place and prevent unrest.

But the amphitheatre was also important for another reason. It was a rung in the political ladder for those seeking office. Not only were there state-funded shows, but many privately funded shows, too. Senators outdid one another to stage the most elaborate and memorable show. Would-be senators strove to attract supporters by hosting even better shows. The battles out of the arena were often greater than those within it.

The problem for the general public was that the financial burden of the shows hosted by local governors invariably fell on them. The trend of elaborate shows started by Julius Caesar was eventually ended by the last member of his dynasty. Nero felt that the financial burdens imposed by provincial shows was unacceptable and banned them. He felt that the lives of even criminals and prisoners of war had some value and forbade their deaths, setting them to work, instead, on civic building works. He felt that the skills of gladiators were admirable enough to warrant the end of fighting to the death. So he banned that, too.

In short, he dealt a severe body blow to both the public, whom he sought to protect, and the nobility. Public affection towards him was such that any minor injuries were quickly forgiven and forgotten. The nobility, however, were already plotting his downfall and were ready to name him Enemy Of The Public.

These are just a few examples of why contemporary and historical portraits of 'a monster' may differ. The remainder will be told within the pages of this book, largely in Nero's own words and those of his contemporaries. The salient point to remember here is that it is unwise to regard Nero as a monster simply because history tells us so. When biographers of his day listed Nero's bad points, the ending of provincial shows and deaths in the arena figured high on the list. However, when forced to include a redeeming factor, they conceded that his putting to death of some three hundred Christians was certainly a particularly worthy action.

Times change.

Chapter One

ROME 22ND DECEMBER A.D. 37

The baby's cries reverberated through the marble loggia as it kicked uncomfortably within the unfamiliar arms of its mother.

'Dash its brains out against a pillar,' Gnaeus Ahenobarbus advised his beautiful young wife.

She handed the child roughly to him.

'It's your son; you do it.'

He held the screaming infant at arm's length until Agrippina finally relented and took back her first born.

'I would have been thanked, you know,' Gnaeus reflected. 'Any child born to you and me is bound to have a detestable nature and to become a public danger!'

'On the contrary; you forget that you address the daughter of Germanicus,' she reminded him sarcastically. 'If public opinion is correct, any bearer of his blood is bound to be deified!'

'Like your baby brother?' Gnaeus sneered.

'Huh! Caligula will be deified - if he has to do it himself!'

Gnaeus came to a halt in the anteroom and looked with disdain upon an immense gold statue of the emperor, positioned with distinct purpose in front of the family shrine, welcoming all visitors to the Palace.

'He appears to be making moves in that direction already. Are you certain he didn't declare himself a god while we were in Antium, awaiting our own 'blessed' event?' He flicked a glance at the tiny infant, whose cries still went unheeded. 'It has already been a week, to the day, since the wretched creature's birth.'

Agrippina smiled. 'My dear little sibling was arranging immortality even at the conception of our 'blessed' one. As we created one life, so Caligula was joyfully snuffing out another.'

'You mentioned nothing of this! So Tiberius did not willingly concede to age, then?'

'It was of no consequence. But I'm afraid my family are destined to meet death prematurely. Even my own dear father was taken in his prime; and who could be less deserving than he? Not the emperor Tiberius, the besotted guardian of my poor, fatherless brother! His fatal mistake was to name him as his heir - at which point Caligula lovingly administered a pillow to his face!' She laughed at such a vision. 'To think, Gnaeus, that as we writhed and fought in bed, so did he!'

Gnaeus laughed too and allowed his son to grasp his finger.

'What a pity,' he said, 'that we could not have had so successful a result as Caligula.' He jerked the finger easily away and clapped to summon a slave.

Agrippina looked up thoughtfully at the golden face of her brother. Had he not at an earlier age found murder so simple he might not have been heir to an empire at all. It had been taken for granted that such an honour would fall to the venerated Germanicus; and the public's pain at his demise was now eased by the solace of his young son's succession.

She smiled inwardly at her own private joke. Poor, superstitious Germanicus - driven to an early death by thoughts of witchcraft. How sorely the public still wept for him. And how they loved their Caligula, the living embodiment of their idol! How touchingly blind they were to his faults! And what if they knew what she knew?

She looked down at the baby in her arms, remembering, vaguely, Caligula in such a position, when she was no more than a child herself. She remembered, too, that sharp and cruel mind; so akin to her own. Two children who could do no wrong; gleefully hiding, beneath their family home, the rotting carcasses of animals they'd killed. Watching, with morbid fascination, as their doting father faded rapidly before their eyes; eaten away by fear. He was young; Tiberius was not. And the temptation of the empire was one that could not wait.

'I will rule through my brother,' she told the baby softly, 'and then, my son, it will be your turn to dance to my tune.'

'You! Slave!' Gnaeus called across the anteroom. 'Tell the emperor that his sister and her husband are here, to present their new-born son at Court.'

The slave led them through to the great banqueting hall and formally announced them.

'Gnaeus! Agrippina!' cried the senator Vitellius, with genuine pleasure, as he hurried to their side and inspected their offspring admiringly. 'Congratulations to you both!'

'Huh! Congratulations indeed!' Gnaeus sneered; reiterating his views on the character of his son.

'A public danger?!' Vitellius laughed at the joke; but suspected its truth.

At twenty-three, he bore the cynicism and bitterness of an old man, his youth long gone - if, indeed, it had ever existed. He had been brought up on Capri as one of Tiberius' boy prostitutes, where he had earned the desultory nickname of Spintria. A sexual invert by nature, he seemed to make no objection to the title; and his cruel vagaries appealed to Caligula as much as they had appealed to Tiberius, making him as popular at the new Court as he had been at the old.

'Spintria, how is my precious young brother?' Agrippina enquired somewhat sarcastically, passing the infant in her arms to a wet-nurse. 'I trust he is treating you well?'

'While I continue to lose to him at the gaming tables he treats me as his own brother!' Vitellius replied.

'I don't doubt it!'

She crossed the marble floor of the great hall to where a small collection of couches were assembled, in a horseshoe pattern. A tall, heavily-built young man, with a powerful jaw and sharp unyielding eyes, lay sprawled across the centre couch, flanked on either side by two scantily-clad young women, who were laughing in turns at his amorous touches. As though unaware of Agrippina's presence, he continued to fondle the two girls and did not look up.

'Ah, dear brother, I see that you have remained unaffected by the burdens of State.'

He looked up at her and grinned broadly. 'My darling, darling Agrippina! A delight to see you!' His eyes strayed swiftly to her heavy breasts and lingered there. 'Childbirth suits you.'

'Indeed it does not,' Agrippina retorted, turning her gaze to the two young ladies, 'I urge you, my dear sisters, to avoid it at all costs. The scrawling brats are not worth the pain.'

Her two younger sisters and brother laughed heartily; Drusilla the more so at her own private joke. She suspected that she already carried Caligula's child.

Lesbia raised herself up on one elbow and said with a smile, 'but the point is, dear sister, was Gnaeus worth the pain and the scrawling brat?!'

She and Drusilla flopped back down on their couches, laughing convulsively. Agrippina did not smile, but met the steady eyes of her brother.

'Perhaps.'

Caligula smiled slowly.

'So, what is my nephew to be called?' he asked.

'You are the emperor. Let it be for you to decide.'

'Ha!' Caligula sat up and looked about him with wicked delight. 'Then let the child be called Claudius, after our esteemed uncle!'

Lesbia and Drusilla laughed all the more, but Agrippina's face remained stern. 'I expected nothing less from you. As it happens he already bears a name. Lucius Domitius.'

'Very fine, my love, but my choice was much more appropriate, do you not think? Does the child not dribble like Claudius and twitch its limbs in the same ridiculous fashion?!'

It brought forth a smile even from Agrippina, who clapped her hands and summoned the nurse.

'Well, here he is,' she announced, 'judge that for yourself.'

Lesbia and Drusilla gave him cursory glances, while Caligula studied him in fascination. 'By the gods, it even smells like Uncle!' he declared.

The subject of their derision, having been arguing silently with himself for the past ten minutes, chose that moment to walk across to them. He had no real wish to pay his respects to the child and its mother, but feared the consequences of not appearing to willingly do so. The nerves that had urged him to stay away until summoned now made him more awkward than ever.

'Dear Uncle Claudius!' Caligula said loudly, as though his uncle were deaf, jumping up from the couch and grasping him by the shoulders, 'we were just remarking on the close family resemblance!'

Claudius twitched his head violently, aware of the joke. He looked at the young baby held by the nurse and smiled warmly, his eyes softening and his mind temporarily released from the strains of perpetual wariness. There lay the first grandson of his beloved brother Germanicus; how proud he would have been. Claudius' eyes moistened at the thought.

'Your dear parents would have been so proud of you,' he said softly, his pronounced stutter controlled, for once, by his rare ease.

'Nonsense!' mocked Agrippina. 'You are, as always, deluded by sentiment. They would never have bothered to make the trip to see him.'

Claudius shook his head wearily, knowing better. Germanicus may have acted always for the good of the State, without a thought to his own needs and safety, but his family had always come first and foremost, prized above all else. Agrippina senior had borne all of her children at the army camps where she had been stationed with her husband, never once allowing the commander to be separated from his family, no matter how great the danger. How else had the infant Gaius earned his endearing nickname of Caligula - 'Little Boots'; appearing before his father's troops in the miniature boots of a soldier and being immediately adopted as their mascot.

'Even at this early stage, one can see that he will be a bright child,' Claudius remarked, 'see how alert he is.'

Caligula laughed sneeringly. 'Well, of course, Uncle, to you a week-old child would seem bright!'

The baby gurgled and allowed milk to escape from its mouth.

'You see!' Caligula mocked, 'He is already a good deal more articulate than you!'

They all laughed; Claudius included, which made Caligula laugh all the more. Head twitching furiously, Claudius slipped away unnoticed at the first opportunity, joining Lucius Otho and his wife Albia, who viewed proceedings from a safe distance. Their noble birth compelled their presence at Court, but their noble bearing invoked an abhorrence at such a necessity.

'How is the child?' Albia enquired, with only faint interest.

'A delightful baby! Very fair and very alert. Let us hope that the noble qualities of his great family have merely skipped a generation.'

'We already have the proof that they have missed one generation,' Lucius Otho remarked coolly, his eyes fixed on the decidedly un-brotherly embrace Caligula was now bestowing on Agrippina, 'and we can do no more than hope that they will not skip a second.'

Albia said with obvious concern, 'What does it matter? Whatever qualities he is born with, can he hope to retain them when raised in such surroundings?' She reached out her hand and instinctively drew her own son close to her; five-year-old Marcus Otho, the youngest of her two sons.

Lucius glanced at her fiercely. 'While I am their father their surroundings will count for nothing. They will do as I say, not as they see others doing.'

The severity of his tone left Claudius with little doubt as to his sincerity. He reached out and patted young Marcus fondly.

'You are a good man,' he assured Lucius, 'and your sons will reflect that.'

The nurse passed by them, taking the now noisy young baby away to its room. The mother of the child paid it no attention, lying beside her sisters and sharing confidences as the wine flowed freely. Caligula had deserted his sisters in favour of a new playmate, whom he treated with no less intimacy; sprawled on a couch with Vitellius, their ultimate intention unashamedly there for all to see.

A.D. 40

Claudius was throwing dice with Lucius Otho and Vitellius when the news arrived that Gnaeus Ahenobarbus was dead. In the three years that had passed since the birth of his son, Gnaeus had rarely been in Rome; his final resting place being Pyrgi, where he had died of dropsy. Agrippina, in contrast, had rarely left the Palace and the incestuous relationship between herself, her sisters and her brother was the talk of Rome. Caligula's male lovers were no doubt also shared between his sisters, but such sexual decadence was the least of his failings. The Reign of Terror of Tiberius paled in comparison.

'Young Lucius Ahenobarbus is now a very rich child,' Vitellius remarked, 'I wonder how long he will survive.'

'He is a mere child of three!' Claudius protested, 'Caligula will not need to put an end to him in order to steal his inheritance. I'll warrant the boy is safe enough. For the time being, at least.'

'I hope you are right,' Lucius said, throwing three ivory dice, each coming to rest on a six, 'my youngest has taken quite a shine to the little fellow. He has him tagging along with him most afternoons. I think he enjoys the power of having small children looking up to him. Young Claudius Senecio must be a year or so younger than him and they seem fairly close, too.'

'How old is Marcus now?'

'He was eight in May. How the time flies, eh, my friend?'

Claudius took his unsuccessful turn with the dice. 'Perhaps we should worry for the boy's mother, rather than for the boy himself,' he suggested.

Lucius Otho considered the remark. 'She must see her son's new found wealth as her own; she will not readily part with it. But will the emperor readily part with his sister?'

'Since taking Drusilla as a 'wife', Lesbia and Agrippina have fallen out of favour,' Vitellius pointed out, 'have you not noticed?'

'I prefer not to notice anything that goes on at Court since our emperor declared himself to be a god and therefore above our laws and morals. His poor daughter. What chance does she stand?'

Claudius snorted in disgust. 'That 'poor child' as you call her spent yesterday morning torturing a kitten while her father looked on indulgently - even shouted words of encouragement! I know toddlers can be rough and unintentionally cruel, but that little monster Julia Drusilla is frighteningly spiteful. She frightens me.' He laughed at Lucius' mocking smile. 'No, really - I mean it, she frightens me!'

'Only the idea that one day one of his offspring will be ruling us frightens me!' Lucius laughed.

'But our beloved emperor is a god - an immortal!' Claudius teased. He threw again, without success. 'Damn these dice, they must be weighted wrongly!'

When next they met, some of their previous fears had already been realised. Having seized the entire estate of three-year-old Lucius Ahenobarbus, Caligula had promptly banished Agrippina, who was now apparently earning a living by diving for pearls off of her bleak island home.

'She always was a strong swimmer!' Claudius laughed, when he heard the news. 'How has your son's little friend taken the events?'

'Bitterly; as one would expect. But between you and me, my friend, I think it's the best thing that could have happened to him. Lepida, Gnaeus' sister, seems to be caring for him far more ably than his mother ever did. I wonder only at his education.'

'Oh?'

'The dear lady, though no doubt full of good intent, is on so tight a budget she has hired only her barber and her freedman, the dancer Paris, to tutor him!'

'Your young Marcus will play tutor, no doubt! There'll be no living with him, with such power swelling his young head!'

'Huh! He so lacks ambition that I wonder if he plays with infants merely because it is less taxing than mixing with children of his own supposed intellect. Power-hungry he most certainly is not.'

'In that case he is a sensible young fellow.'

Lucius regarded him sharply. 'You do not need to be the Court buffoon to survive this bloody reign.'

Claudius sniffed and wiped the slight trickle of saliva that habitually escaped from the corner of his mouth. 'Perhaps not.' he agreed. Then he forced a nervous stutter and exaggerated twitch, 'but it helps, my friend. It helps.'

Chapter Two

A.D. 47

Claudius sat in the position of honour reserved for the emperor and surveyed the vast circus, filled with the young Roman boys of high rank. His own son, Britannicus, sat in the seats below him; at six too young to compete. Exceptions could have been made for his fourteen-year-old companion, Marcus Otho, had he been good enough to take the field. But Otho considered it better to abide by the rules and accept that he was too old to compete, thereby allowing himself the comfort of sitting back to watch others. Sitting back to watch others had become his prime objective in most spheres of life; although there was one newly discovered pastime that he considered to be more fun as an active participant than as a mere spectator. The young ladies at the brothel seemed readily to agree to that view, though he could expect another rod broken across his back if his father ever found out. Lucius Otho was a strict disciplinarian and young Otho didn't quite fit in with his moralistic expectations.

Claudius rose up out of his seat and was greeted with a hush. He stumbled over a few brief lines, his stutter at its worst and rendering his speech all-but unintelligible. Drawing a breath and twitching his head in an effort of supreme concentration, he finally declared the Troy Games to be open.

The future noblemen of Rome stepped forward to show off their skills in a variety of sporting and military exercises. Nine-year-old Lucius Ahenobarbus looked up at the emperor and his party and waved cheerily, ignoring those around him who voiced an opinion that he should remain respectfully still and silent until called into combat.

Claudius watched the spectacle commence and thought back on his own brother's exceptional performance, so many years before. Neither of them then would have guessed that he, Claudius, would now be opening the Games, as emperor of Rome. In fact he still found it hard to believe himself, in this, the sixth year of his reign. His accession had been traumatic, to say the least, and the whole experience had seemed to dull his wit, as though he subconsciously wished to blot it out.

But even now, he could still remember hiding in terror behind a curtain as troops filled the Palace. Less than a year after banishing his sister and stealing the inheritance of his nephew, Caligula had been hacked to death by assassins, his mind so deranged that he was a public danger. He had murdered vast numbers of citizens and most of his own family; Claudius surviving only because he was too useful as the butt of the Court and supposedly too poor and stupid to be considered a threat. Agrippina, too, had slipped by unnoticed in exile.

From his position behind the curtain, Claudius had listened as the soldiers picked up by the ankles the infant daughter of the murdered emperor, swinging her against a wall until her brains were dashed out. No one who knew the child shed a tear. But his own terrified sobs betrayed his presence and the soldiers had quickly turned on him. One of the few surviving members of the imperial family. Brother of Germanicus. The soldiers lifted him high on their shoulders and presented him to the throng of people waiting outside the Palace. The citizens of Rome had greeted him as their new emperor. The Court buffoon had survived the four year reign of Caligula.

'Have I missed anything?'

Claudius looked up sharply, startled from his thoughts. Vitellius limped towards him, to take the seat reserved for him beside the emperor.

'I was afraid I would miss the equestrian events,' Vitellius continued, sitting down, 'my hip is playing up badly today and I have had to make no end of stops.' He rubbed the offending joint and stretched out a leg. His good friend Caligula had deliberately run him down whilst driving a four-horse chariot and had left him with a partially crippled hip. Vitellius had wisely accepted the incident as a high-spirited prank and had survived the reign without further injury. It was enough to have survived at all.

'That young Ahenobarbus is a fine horseman, is he not?' Vitellius remarked. His own passion for horses and his skill at driving in chariot races had ensured his favouritism with horse-mad Caligula. 'Is Agrippina not here to watch him?'

'No, unfortunately not. I restored his inheritance and I restored his mother, but both went by unnoticed by him. Agrippina seems to take no interest in him whatsoever. A pity. He's a bright boy.'

'Certainly a fine horseman, anyway,' Vitellius repeated, admiringly.

The Games moved on swiftly, Lucius continuing to wave to his friend Otho between each event and to accept the tumultuous applause from the crowd with equal enthusiasm.

'He seems to have rather a taste for it,' Claudius observed dryly.

Lepida Ahenobarbus' choice of tutors for her nephew made their mark in the fencing, as Lucius' graceful technique met with a certain amount of derision from the crowd. His blond curls flying, he looked, as Vitellius pointed out, more like a ballet dancer than a swordsman. But those who mocked his grace could not deny its efficiency - he beat all challengers, as he had done in the equestrian events.

The emperor's party broke up and got ready to leave as the Games ended. Narcissus, one of the emperor's most powerful freedmen, though deceivingly soft in manner and genteel, escorted Britannicus and his older sister Octavia across to their father. His natural authority and power kept the high spirits of the excited children in check, but Claudius lost all control when once they were released into his indulgent care. They bounced on his lap and re-enacted one of the sword fights.

'Their mother could not make it?' Vitellius enquired, for the first time noticing the absence of the empress Messalina. She and Claudius were so rarely to be seen together that it was easy to forget her.

Narcissus shot Vitellius a heavy glance, but Claudius merely looked about him vaguely.

'No. She had promised to join us here later; though she was having a lie down when we left. Her health has never been good since the birth of Britannicus, you know. Well; of course you do. Yes; yes, of course you know.' He continued to look around him vaguely, rambling aloud about her headaches and lack of energy.

Vitellius made sympathetic noises, concealing his embarrassment. It was widely known by those at Court that Messalina had no shortage of energy when it suited her.

'You imbecile!' Narcissus hissed, 'You should have more sense than to mention the empress.'

'I suspect he must know fully what goes on behind his back,' Vitellius retorted in a whisper. 'The woman turns the Palace into a one woman brothel in his absence! She surely cannot conceal her tracks that well!'

Narcissus drew him grimly to one side.

'Claudius will hear no wrong of her, and to discredit her would destroy him. Yet she has made a vital slip; and I must denounce her, if only for the sake of young Lucius.'

'It is true, then, that she sent two Guards to kill him while he slept?'

Narcissus nodded.

'It is rumoured they were frightened away by a snake which slept beside him! A ludicrous idea, which made the whole tale sound preposterous!' Vitellius laughed.

'I would have agreed. But when I woke the boy from his siesta, we found a snakeskin shed beside his pillow. Agrippina had it set within a gold bracelet for him; he wears it now as a charm against ill luck. Messalina's men told the truth.'

Vitellius looked at Narcissus doubtfully. 'Why should she wish to kill the boy?'

'He commands great respect, particularly from Claudius. The emperor is not a young man; and already Messalina schemes the accession of her own son. She sees Lucius as a threat to Britannicus.' He hesitated and looked anxiously towards the emperor and his children. 'And I'm afraid, Vitellius, that I see her as a threat to Claudius.'

Claudius took the news of his young wife's infidelities badly. He ordered her immediate execution; though later claimed to have had no part in her death and often spoke of her as though she were still alive. His mind wandered increasingly and his short temper increased with the impatience of celibacy.

Elsewhere, the news was received with greater pleasure. Vitellius wasted no time in meeting with Agrippina privately, in her apartments at the Palace. She welcomed him with a degree of suspicion.

'Claudius is anxious to take a new wife immediately,' Vitellius told her, as she studied him assessingly.

'And?'

'Well I could not help noticing that you are more than aware of that fact yourself.'

Agrippina considered his unvoiced suggestion.

'As the emperor's niece,' she said carefully, 'I have the unique advantage of a certain amount of intimacy. I could, quite easily, while seeming to console the emperor, arouse more.'

It seemed to Vitellius to be a ridiculous understatement. Agrippina had been openly seducing Claudius without shame.

'There are the laws of incest to overcome,' he said pointedly. 'Our emperor is not a god and the people would not tolerate a sacrilegious ruler. Not again.'

'So what do you propose?'

Vitellius smiled and took a seat. 'I propose to call upon the senate to amend those laws, in favour of a marriage between a man and his brother's daughter. I have great influence in the senate, as you well know, my Lady, and my orations bear heavy weight. They are nearly always met with a favourable response.'

Agrippina inclined her head somewhat in agreement. 'And in return?'

Vitellius rubbed his hip, more from habit than to ease any discomfort. 'In return, you will be in a position of supreme power. Past events have shown that Claudius is easily influenced by his wives - in fact, more often than not, he is blind to any sanctions they may make. Seemingly on his behalf you may exert such power as you wish.'

'And my wishes will be?'

'Will be mine, Agrippina.'

She laughed appreciatively. 'You are obviously a man of ambition, Spintria. In what manner may I aid those aspirations?'

'Simply eliminate some rivals; some enemies. Those that pose a threat, of one form or another.'

She nodded her assent. 'Then, Vitellius, if you will be so good as to keep an ear to the ground for dissidents, I shall be happy to receive your information and to ensure that prosecutions are brought about; without the need to trouble the emperor. And I wish you every success with the senate.'

Satisfied, Vitellius stood up to leave.

'One other thing,' Agrippina added casually, 'I missed much during my exile. Messalina's behaviour, when I returned, was something of a surprise to me. I had not remembered her as being quite so wayward. But I did recognise certain influences. Tell me, Spintria - you were close to my brother; did his affairs include Messalina? I ask only out of interest, you understand.'

Vitellius understood perfectly. 'Messalina was one of his mistresses right up to the time of his death.'

'Even when pregnant with Britannicus?'

He grinned. 'Particularly when pregnant.'

Agrippina bade him farewell, showing no reaction to his information. It meant very little to her; but could, perhaps, prove to be a useful lever in the future. She stowed it away, alongside a multitude of other 'possible levers'.

Though Narcissus was violently opposed to the marriage, it went ahead anyway. He sensed that Claudius was aware of Agrippina's ambitions, but the old emperor was happy to accept her on any terms. He was done with love. He had married Messalina for love, and look where that had got him. For too long he had been sexually deprived. He now wished only to have a wife permanently in his bed. In return, she received the title of empress, and all the wealth and luxury that went with it. He was too dull of wit to suspect that she wanted more.

Pallas, Minister of Finance, however, was not so shortsighted. Like Narcissus, he recognised Agrippina's lust for power; and he saw her as a useful ally. It was quite clear that his position made him equally desirable in her eyes and he was quick to offer his services.

'You seem remarkably forward for an ex-slave,' Agrippina remarked coldly, as he offered to take her on her first tour of the household accounts. She smiled at his offended reaction. 'Perhaps you have been used to Messalina for too long. Unlike her, my infidelities are limited to the advantages to be gained from them.'

Pallas smiled. 'I believe you have some influence with Vitellius - and therefore the senate. Your hold over your devoted husband cannot be doubted. As I see it, you require only one additional tool to secure your position. And, dare I say it, my Lady; I am - and have - a most suitable... tool.'

Agrippina did not smile, though she accepted him into her bed.

'Just remember,' she warned, 'that I expect the discretion and loyalty worthy of an empress. Lose either, and we will both lose a tool.'

She stared blankly at the ceiling as he made love to her; satisfied only that she had gained a further hold over the State. Pallas was at least more tolerable than Claudius, which set her in mind of the future provisions to be made for.

'My darling,' she told Claudius one evening, after supper, 'Lepida was kind enough to take charge of Lucius for me during my exile and I have hardly dare step in since and criticise her. But since he is now your stepson, I really think that more suitable tutors should be found for him.'

'Of course, my love. Let him take his lessons with Britannicus.'

'Oh no! That would not do at all!' Agrippina protested. 'My son cannot sit alongside the emperor's heir!'

Claudius laughed. 'Why ever not? They are of the same blood, are they not?'

'But there are practical considerations to take into account. Britannicus is only just seven. Lucius keeps company with older boys and is far more mature as a result. He is of advanced intellect for his age. The boys would naturally compete, which would place unfair pressure on Britannicus.

'No; Lucius needs a tutor of his own. Perhaps Senecio and Otho could study with him, to provide competition. I thought that Annaeus Seneca would make an ideal candidate for the position.'

Claudius kissed her cheek, grateful for her good sense.

'That is an excellent idea, my love,' he agreed, 'Seneca has been in exile for six years now - ample punishment for his adultery with my sister Julia, wouldn't you agree? I shall have him recalled immediately.'

Agrippina smiled with silent satisfaction. It would win her a great deal of public popularity, she knew, to be responsible for Seneca's return to Rome, where he was much admired for his literary talents.

In addition, he would make a most suitable tutor for a young heir to an empire.

Chapter Three

A.D. 49

Lucius casually etched a portrait of a horse onto his wax tablet, while Annaeus Seneca read a final piece from Menander. As the details on the tablet became more precise, so the young boy's concentration increased, until he was oblivious to the existence of his tutor altogether.

Seneca was engrossed in his subject as he launched into a critical analysis of Menander, proud of the fine rhetorical skills he was displaying to the three pupils seated before him. It was only when he sought admiration from their intent faces that he realised his skills were being wasted. Otho and Senecio were quite clearly engrossed, but not in Menander. Their attention was held by Lucius, whose excited whispers were suddenly audible to Seneca.

'...it's not as marshy as the Circus Maximus and his fall wasn't cushioned at all. He must have been dragged two hundred yards at full racing pace; all his face was bloody and dirty, and his hands were almost hanging off with the reins cutting right through them, and his arms were all wet and red with blood...'

'And to which particular passage would you be referring?' Seneca enquired with loaded sarcasm, pulling Lucius up to an abrupt halt.

The boy turned to face him, without a moment's hesitation, and met his stern gaze with bright, alert eyes.

'I was comparing him with Homer and recalling Hector's fate in The Iliad.'

'Ah, yes! Hector. Whose fate was so remarkably similar to that of the unfortunate member of the Green team at the Circus Flaminius yesterday. I understand the poor fellow fell from his chariot during the fourth race.' Seneca allowed himself a smile at Lucius' self-assurance, and his own ability to crush it. 'However, I cannot see why Menander would invite comparison with Homer, particularly when you were absent for yesterday's class, when we dealt with Homer in detail. You, apparently, were too sick to attend. May I see your tablet and read the notes that you have been so diligently making?'

Showing no remorse at having been caught out, Lucius handed over the tablet and awaited his punishment without concern. It seemed to Seneca that nothing could curb Lucius' happy-go-lucky attitude, nor win over that perilously short attention span. He studied the fine portrait of a racehorse in harness, then returned it to its owner.

'Perfectly drawn, my boy, but unfortunately it bears more resemblance to a modern day racehorse than an ancient warhorse. I doubt that Homer would recognise the beast. Wipe that smirk from your face, Otho, I seem to remember that your attention was not fully on Menander either. Perhaps I should hand out two punishments instead of one? Lucius, you will write for me an essay, in Greek, on the influence of Homer on latter day writers, in addition to the critical analysis I have requested on Menander. Not less than a thousand words on each.'

He knew that it was wasted on Lucius, who could dash off essays with ridiculous ease, faultless in their content despite his lack of attention in class. But

Seneca had no faith in the power of corporal punishment, believing that it induced only hypocrisy and cowardice among pupils. The three young noblemen entrusted to his care made only half-hearted attempts to lie their way out of laborious extra essays. Lucius himself was incapable of deceit, simply because he had never known any need for it. Seneca had been employed by the empress Agrippina to groom a future emperor and he was more than satisfied with his results. The strong foreboding that had accompanied him into his new job had been quickly replaced by optimism for the future.

He looked proudly at the three boys seated on benches in front of him. As close friends now, Marcus Otho and Claudius Senecio were likely to grow up to be influential, and their grooming was as important as that of Lucius. Thirteen-year-old Senecio was the least bright of the three, content to be led along and yet a little too ambitious. Not a happy combination of traits, but one well manipulated by Otho and Lucius. That pair were birds of a feather, uncomfortably alike in character and attitude. Except that Otho was unnecessarily proud. Seneca was loath to consider pride a fault; not if one had accomplished enough to be justifiably proud of. But Otho was not the country's leading stoic, not the empire's most admired rhetoric and historian; not the tutor of a young heir to an empire. Otho's vanity was distinctly offensive. And yet he accepted anything dealt out to him with good grace, he was patient and un-ambitious. Lazy. Yes, that was Otho's saving grace, laziness.

'Right, now then, boys. A legal case for you to debate. Otho, you are prosecuting. Lucius, you shall defend.'

'But I was a barrister in the last legal case,' Otho protested.

'I always have to defend,' Lucius complained.

'Otho, when I feel that you have acquired a sufficient grasp of law and legal procedures, I shall allow you to retire from the bench. And Lucius, you may choose whichever of the parties you wish to represent. First, listen to the case. Then tell me which party you favour and whether you will be defending or prosecuting.

'Imagine this: a man is out for a stroll, when he comes across a fisherman. He agrees to buy the contents of the fisherman's net for a set price, but when the net is brought in it is found to contain a gold ingot.'

'I don't want to stay in the Palace,' Lucius said, kicking a pebble, as they left the classroom and wandered across the main courtyard. 'Mother and Claudius will be drunk by now.'

'Let's go to the port,' Senecio suggested, 'and watch the fishermen catching gold ingots!'

'Gold ingots!' scoffed Otho, 'Where does he dream up these cases?! Pompous old windbag!'

'Let's go to the market by the Forum and see the fish,' Lucius decided, and the others readily agreed.

The market was crowded that afternoon, particularly the fourth floor, where the weekly distributions of money and food were made. The poorer citizens, with no other income, eagerly accepted the all-too-few sesterces and as quickly parted with them in one of the hundred-and-fifty booths, which sold food, drink and clothing. The three boys darted through the crowds, weaving their way across the ground floor, taken up wholly by booths selling fruit and flowers. Lucius snatched at an orange as he passed by one stall and had blended back into the crowd before the theft was even noted.

Up the short flight of steps and into a loggia of vast arcades, whose long vaults served as storehouses for oils and wine. These held no interest for the boys, who paused only to hurl abuse at another group of young boys lurking behind a pillar. The insults echoed round the vaults as Lucius and his companions fled from any further trouble and continued upwards to the next two storeys, which housed rarer, more expensive products such as silks and spices from the distant East. The three boys lifted the lids of the large wooden tubs and dipped illicitly into the spices with licked fingers, the strong scents blending into a single, over-powering aroma. Every so often a stallholder would shout angrily at the boys, sending them scurrying hastily into the crowd. The shouts were soon lost amid the general noise of people shopping and the cries of the stallholders, advertising their goods.

Lucius hesitated as they passed through the fourth floor, disturbed by the sight of so many people accepting the meagre handouts of the State. He recognised a great many of the faces, having passed them daily in the street. The majestic private houses and squalid apartment blocks were built side by side, in terraces, along every narrow street. Not even the imperial family could be blind to the poverty intermixed with the wealth, but they could comfortably ignore it. Lucius found it impossible to ignore, and the sight of so many people dependent upon the state raised a multitude of questions in his young mind. He resolved to tackle Seneca about it and took one last look at the familiar faces in the crowd before chasing after Otho and Senecio, who were already on the top floor amid the many fishponds.

An aqueduct filled one set of pools, which were linked by channels, with seawater from Ostia; while another set of pools was supplied with fresh water from the main city aqueduct. The three boys preferred the sea fish and splashed their fingers in the crowded pools, marvelling at the beautiful colours and patterns of the occupants. They daringly teased a host of crabs and lobsters, plunging their fingers into the clear, flowing water and swiftly avoiding the menacing claws. In the freshwater pools, Senecio pointed out the brightly coloured perch and gave a yell when a sharp fin stung him. Lucius stroked the huge carp that splashed tamely on the surface, awaiting food.

Tiring of the fish at last, Senecio still nursing the red weal on his hand, the boys left the market and wandered through the tangled web of streets, in the general direction of the theatre. The narrow, winding lanes were closed in on all sides by the uniform blocks of flats, rising five or six storeys high. Some were not divided into apartment blocks, but were private dwellings, owned by the very wealthy. Still more consisted of a luxurious ground floor villa, with over-crowded apartments on the upper floors. The private homes were easily distinguished from the apartments by their bare walls. All the windows and doors opened onto courtyards, off of the street, keeping the noise and smell of the street at bay. The apartments themselves were a mass of windows, each one underlined by gaily-planted window boxes, even in the most poverty-stricken blocks.

Where the ground floor apartments were not a single dwelling they were divided into shops, opening out onto the street their full width. One of these was a particular favourite with the boys and they hurried eagerly in through the high arched doorway. The counter before them was laden with sweetmeats of every variety; crystallised fruits, and sweet pastries baked in wonderful forms. The three boys poured over the display, each taking time to make their careful selections. A glorious smell of cooking flooded the shop, as sugars and oils melted in a pan in the loft above them. Lucius paid for his small basket of pastries, then waited for Otho and Senecio to make their purchases. He glanced across at the stone steps in the far corner, six in all, which were continued by a ladder up to the tiny sloped loft above the shop.

'Can I see how you make the fruits?' he asked keenly, recognising the scent drifting out from the loft, arousing his insatiable curiosity.

The shopkeeper took in the fine clothes, bordered with the distinctive purple and gold of the imperial household, and nodded his head in assent. Lucius eagerly climbed the ladder into the tiny, low-ceilinged loft, lit only by a long, rectangular window, pierced above the centre of the shop's doorway. In the dim light he saw the charcoal fire in the centre, its fumes filling the room, over which stood a large pan of bubbling brown mixture, sweet-smelling and sticky. A woman stood over it, unaware of his presence. A variety of pots and crockery stood along the floor beside her and the only other furnishing-of-sorts was a long wooden shelf, stretching the full length of the longest wall. With slight disbelief, Lucius recognised it to be a bed - or several, to be more precise - and realised that the rough wooden pallets were expected to accommodate all of the residents of the shop. There were no counterpanes to offer warmth or comfort, simply rolled sacking on which to rest a head. Four children sat on the floor packing freshly made sweetmeats into baskets, while an older girl helped her mother wrap pastries in clay and set them in the fire. Forgetting the interest that had led him there, Lucius quickly climbed back down to the shop and rejoined Otho and Senecio.

'Did they let you have a taste?' Otho enquired, as they left the shop and approached the theatre.

Lucius shook his head. 'I didn't ask. They all live there, you know; the whole family, in that one tiny room.'

'All those lofts are the same,' Senecio said, 'I've been in some. More than one family shared some of them. My father had to evict a complete block of tenants once, because they kept allowing their fires to get out of hand. We had to have some of the apartments rebuilt. They sleep on a shelf, Lucius, did you see it? What a lark! I'd like to see your mother getting up to it on a little wooden shelf! Can you imagine it?!'

'What's that supposed to mean?' Lucius snapped indignantly.

'Your mother and her fancy men! Come on, Lucius, everyone knows about it, you don't have to get so high and mighty about it.'

'Drop it, Senecio,' Otho warned sharply, 'I've heard a few rumours about your father that you wouldn't like to hear us repeating.'

'Don't tease him,' Lucius said lightly, 'he's right about my mother, anyway. Claudius is such an old drunk you can hardly blame her, can you?' He laughed, as though not caring, and Senecio fell silent; annoyed that he had failed to provoke Lucius and even more upset by Otho's rebuke.

They crept into the back of the theatre and stood against the wall, looking down on the tiers of stone seats to the stage. Some pantomime actors were in full swing, but their performance was being interrupted by abuse from the wings, as a rival troupe awaited their turn. Such rows were frequent and were often the main attraction for the audience. They were certainly popular with Lucius and his friends, who liked to add to the abuse and encourage more aggressive disputes. The fighting on stage often spilled over into the audience and several of the cheaper wooden seats at the back were badly damaged. As the pantomime actors ground to a halt and the two troupes began to argue on stage, Lucius pulled at the broken slats of the back row seats and armed himself with some short lengths of wood.

The members of the audience down at the front began to jeer loudly and threw fruit and rubbish at the fighting actors. Lucius took his cue from them and hurled the wooden slats down at the stage, Otho and Senecio following suit with enthusiasm. Fast running out of ammunition, Lucius picked up one of the sturdier lengths of wood and hurled it forcefully at the stage. It fell short, landing amid the row reserved for praetors. The heavy missile struck a praetor neatly on the back of the head and he fell forward, his hair quickly glistening with blood. All heads turned to face the three boys at the back. Lucius, in the clothes of a young prince, his bright blue eyes wide in horror and his blonde curls clear against the marble wall, was only too easily recognisable.

'Run for it!' hissed Otho, and they fled from the theatre as though pursued by all the Furies.

'You're in for it now,' Senecio pointed out gloomily, 'there isn't a praetor who doesn't know you, and you've killed that one for sure.'

They split up at the Palace gardens, Otho and Senecio making their reluctant way to their families' apartments, while Lucius attempted to sneak into the Palace unnoticed. Rather than await impending disaster in his room, he hid himself outside the dining hall and listened to the conversations within. All too soon they were interrupted by the arrival of a messenger, who informed the emperor and his wife that their son had just fractured the skull of a praetor at the theatre. The news was greeted by laughter from Agrippina and exaggerated concern from a drunken Claudius.

'I had better deal with this,' Agrippina said at length, a note of seriousness returning to her voice. 'He's my son; you leave him to me.'

Otho wandered along the vast corridor, not bothering to creep silently at such a late hour. Many of the imperial slaves were still at work, but they paid him scant attention. Narcissus, working late, as always, in his capacity as the emperor's advisor, approached and looked at Otho reprovingly.

'The empress has given word that Lucius is indisposed and not to be disturbed,' he told Otho. 'Are your parents aware of your absence at this hour?'

Otho grinned and shook his head.

'No, I thought not. Off you go, then. And take this in to him, would you? I'll see to it that I am the first one to look in on him in the morning. And don't keep us awake with your incessant chatter all night!' Narcissus smiled indulgently and watched as Otho slipped into Lucius' room.

A polished bronze bed, with ornately carved ivory feet, dominated the sparsely furnished room. Lucius lay across it, his face buried in his pillow, muffling his stifled sobs. The richly embroidered counterpane covered only his legs, leaving his body open to the air. The cuts and wheals of a whip had left his back raw and even his arms bore the marks of a brutal flogging, as he had sought in vain to protect himself. Agrippina would have taken as much pleasure in the punishment as she had done in the crime.

'Narcissus gave me this pitcher to fetch in to you,' Otho said casually, sitting down carefully on the edge of the bed. 'I think he's put fortified wine in it. Do you want some?'

Lucius lifted his head from the pillow and managed to turn to face Otho. He raised a smile.

'Did you fetch anything else? I've had nothing to eat.'

Otho pulled out a basket of sweetmeats, a chicken drumstick and some grapes, from the folds of his tunic. Lucius brushed away the last few remaining tears and took the drumstick.

'Hurts like the Furies, doesn't it?' Otho said with empathy, making a start on the basket of sweetmeats.

'As though I've been dragged behind a chariot at the races!'

The two friends were soon joking cheerfully about the events of the day, and before the household slaves had retired for the night Narcissus had to remind the boys on three occasions to be a little less noisy. As he looked in on them for a final time he was greeted not by noisy conversation, but by the sight of them curled up tightly together in the bed, sleeping peacefully.

Chapter Four

A.D. 51

'Hey! Ahenobarbus! Home from school? Was there no racing today, Lucius?!'

Nero stopped in his tracks and turned slowly to face Britannicus, who hovered outside his chamber, ready to duck in at the first sign of retaliation. The younger boy knew well enough that Nero now regarded his former title as a bitter insult, having been adopted by Claudius the previous year and receiving both a new life and a new name in the process. And, for a year, Britannicus had hurled his past back in his face, until his stepbrother hated the very sight of him.

Nero felt that he owed no allegiance to his paternal family. He had merely been born an Ahenobarbii, which had brought him no particular good fortune; while his present position, as son of the emperor of Rome, owed nothing to chance of birth. He had been *chosen* by Claudius and had been honoured, too, with the emperor's choice of name. Britannicus, who had only been born to the emperor, not chosen by him, obstinately refused to accept his new brother; and his continual rejection of the new name was seen by Nero as an insult not only to himself, but to the emperor who had bestowed the title.

Nero seethed with anger, as he did every time the accursed brat taunted him with his old family name, but now revenge was in his grasp; and it tasted sweet.

'Did your tutor recognise you, Ahenobarbus, after such a long absence?! Or did he ask you for your advice on tomorrow's racing?!'

Nero smiled. 'At least I can afford to miss lessons,' he said carefully, leading Britannicus into his firing line, 'I do not struggle to keep up, as you do, little brother.'

'You're no brother of mine, Ahenobarbus!' Britannicus snapped indignantly, 'my father only adopted you to stop your mother nagging him.'

'*Your* father?' Nero inquired sarcastically. 'Claudius has only one son - the one he chose personally! *Your* father died ten years ago, *cousin*.' He turned swiftly and retreated to his own room, leaving Britannicus to stew on the implication.

Otho was waiting for him in his room and looked up at him questioningly as he entered.

'What was all that about?'

Nero grinned broadly and sat down beside him. 'His mother slept with Caligula more often than with Claudius! It's doubtful that Claudius is even his real father!'

'Where did you hear that?!'

'Mother told me. I complained to Aunt Lepida about his constant taunts, but she just said I should ignore him. So I thought I'd chance my arm with Mother. She might have even complained to Claudius about it and secured the wretched brat a flogging for his insolence. But anyway, she just told me that he was jealous, because Claudius is more my father than his!'

'And she would know, of course.'

Nero regarded him carefully. 'Caligula is not my father. He was on Capri with Tiberius when my parents were first married.'

'I suggested nothing!' Otho protested, laughing at Nero's solemnity, 'but Britannicus might. Be prepared for it.' He playfully ruffled Nero's hair, who pushed him down onto the bed, then stretched out beside him.

'I'm ready for anything he can come up with,' Nero assured him, 'I'll make him squirm and hide at the very sight of me.'

Otho smirked. After a while, he said, 'I went down to the stables this morning and the Blue team have a new horse, just in from the Spanish stud of Tigellinus. You should see it, Nero - a real beauty of an animal. They're fetching it out for tomorrow's racing.'

Nero sat up and cursed bitterly. 'I dare not miss classes again this week. Seneca reports my every move to Mother and she is less lenient than he.'

Otho sat up too and put an arm around him reassuringly. 'She must have softened slightly to feed you the gossip on Britannicus. Make the most of her current good mood. I'll pay one of the freedmen to give Seneca a reasonable excuse. Perhaps we could say that Claudius requires your company. Seneca never reports to him and your mother might not necessarily recognise the deception. I believe she will be with Pallas all day tomorrow, going through the household accounts.'

'Then it's a day at the races!' Nero declared cheerfully, 'my cousin got that one right, at least!'

*   *   *   *   *   *   *   *   *   *

'Claudius! I want a word!'

Claudius was just on his way to the baths as Agrippina called to him and he stopped beside an impressive bronze statue, leaning against it as he awaited the approach of his wife.

'Finished with the accounts already, my love?' he asked, as she joined him.

'For today. But they will keep me busy for all of tomorrow as well.'

'You have Pallas helping you?'

'Yes; thank you for sparing him. I trust his absence has not left you short of help yourself?'

'Not at all, my love.' He looked up at the bronze image of his friend Lucius Otho and patted the cold foot admiringly. 'It looks well, does it not? A fitting tribute and one not out of place here in the Palace. He is a descendent of the Etruscan royal house, you know. I must speak to him about my fresh work on the subject. I keep meaning to, but it slips my mind.'

Agrippina interrupted him impatiently before he rambled still further. 'We must discuss Britannicus. His education leaves a great deal to be desired and his manners are appalling. I have tried to speak to his tutors, but quite frankly their attitude is little better. No wonder that he is so insolent, with such examples being set.'

Claudius looked shocked. 'I had no idea there was a problem?!'

'At the moment it is minor, but without check it is liable to escalate. I suggest that the first thing we do is replace his tutors.'

Claudius nodded solemnly, relieved to find that Agrippina already had everything in hand. He had not even perceived a problem, let alone considered its solution. 'Well obviously that is imperative,' he agreed, 'can I leave the matter in your capable hands, my dear? You are far more expert in these matters than I. Nero is an exemplary student, far ahead of other boys his age. If you can work such magic with my own son, I shall be a happy man indeed.'

Agrippina's face clouded. 'Yes, your own son. Perhaps that is something else we should discuss. I think that you need to have a fatherly talk with Britannicus. He seems upset by rumours he has undoubtedly overheard. You would think that the household would be more careful in the hearing of vulnerable children. It's quite probable that his behavioural problems even stem from such tittle-tattle.'

'What rumours? To what do you refer?'

'Oh, well, of course! There are so many! The Court thrives on gossip!' Agrippina laughed, clearly not one to take any of them seriously herself. 'Britannicus seems concerned about his mother's liaisons with my brother. As though they give rise to doubt about his parentage.' She noted Claudius' horrified expression. 'Who knows where he picked it up! Messalina slept with all and sundry, why anyone should centre on Caligula alone I don't know!'

'I had no idea...' Claudius muttered, disbelieving.

'To be honest, I didn't realise he knew about it myself until I heard Nero throwing it in his face. You know how boys are; Nero knew it was the one thing to hurt him and Britannicus was not undeserving. He can be most cruel to Nero at times. Nero is so vulnerable where you are concerned. You are the first real father he has ever known and he worships the very ground you walk on. But even so, he is only adopted. He is not your real son, as Britannicus is, and he feels it deeply. And I am very much afraid that Britannicus abuses those emotions cruelly.'

'My goodness!' Claudius mouthed some words speechlessly, unable to digest all that he had heard. 'My goodness!' he repeated, beginning to stutter. 'I shall certainly speak to Britannicus - on both matters. My goodness, I had no idea... simply no idea.' He leant weakly against the statue, trying hard to curb his stutter. 'Do you know, my concern was that I may have been showing Nero a little *too much* favouritism. I simply did not realise, my dear...' He took a deep breath, twitching violently now as more of her words sunk in. He glanced up at the statue, requested by the senate to honour his friend, and shook his head in bewilderment. 'One whose loyalty I can hardly dare hope my children will emulate,' he remarked, patting the bronze foot for some sort of reassurance.

'Loyalty to you unites your own children,' Agrippina assured him, 'while the children of poor Lucius Otho bring him nothing but grief and hardship.'

He smiled at her warmly. She had mocked him in her youth and ignored him in later years; to the extent that he had questioned her motives in marrying him. But there was no doubt now that she was good for him. Her keen interest in politics was infinitely more preferable than Messalina's scandalous hobbies. Messalina...

Claudius thought of Britannicus; and as he pictured his son he saw his dear brother Germanicus. The boy had always been so uncannily like him. The great likeness had always given him pleasure; but now... he was not so sure. Could it be that the family resemblance was all the stronger because Germanicus was the boy's grandfather, not his uncle? He shuddered.

Of course, he had heard no such rumours himself. Half of Messalina's activities had been deliberately kept from his ears, he knew; the hushed conversations ending abruptly at his approach, the whispered names always eluding him. He felt a sudden nausea. The others... the others he could take. But Caligula...

He was no longer heading towards the baths. He had forgotten his original intention and could think only of Britannicus. Of Caligula. Of the relief he had felt when Caligula's daughter had been slaughtered. Deservedly so. His own little Britannicus, showing new sides to his character, insolent and cruel towards his brother; the result of a union between Caligula and Messalina.

Claudius fought to contain his nausea and entered his son's room. Britannicus was seated at his desk, studiously working on his homework. The sight of him evoked a sudden feeling of repulsion within Claudius. It wasn't the boy's fault. One couldn't take it out on the boy. But it was too soon to come to terms with the sudden tumult of feelings. Claudius regretted his inability to talk to the boy, but couldn't yet overcome it.

'Britannicus,' he said coldly, 'it has come to my notice that you treat Nero insultingly. He is my son. He is my eldest son; and therefore my heir. You would do well to remember that and treat him with reverence accordingly.'

The sudden decision to make Nero his heir surprised Claudius as much as it surprised Britannicus; but not until much later, when the words were remembered and absorbed for the first time. Only Britannicus showed his shock and horror.

'But father...'

'But nothing! If you wish to be treated as a prince you must first start behaving as one. Your brother has conducted himself with honour even before joining our family. He has shown himself more worthy to be my son than you, who hold that position through accident of birth.' Claudius stopped, though there was so much more he wanted to say. Britannicus was crying, and the boy's tears triggered his own. He turned abruptly and hurried out of the room, rushing to the sanctuary of his own chamber, where he wept bitterly for what might have been.

The Circus Gai buzzed with the noise of an excited crowd, pressing forward to gain the best possible view of the start of this, the twenty-fourth and last race of the day. Nero and Otho watched in hushed excitement, having pushed their way down to the very front. Four chariots were lined up before them, each pulled by four horses. Two mares were harnessed to the shaft in the centre, while a stallion, loosely attached by a trace, stood either side of them. Each chariot depended on the strength and handiness of the two outside horses; the off-side stallion swinging out to the right on each turn without giving away valuable ground, while the still more vital near-side stallion acted as a pivot on the tight bends.

The horses pawed the ground, laurel branches on their heads, tails held high in the air by a tight knot. Their manes were threaded with pearls and they wore breastplates and collars studded with decorations. Each team wore round their necks a ribbon dyed in the colours of their faction. There were only four factions - the Whites, the Greens, the Blues and the Reds - but each had their enthusiastic supporters.

Nero looked from the beauty of the horses nearest him to the splendour of the charioteer, who stood upright in his chariot, helmet on head, whip in hand, leggings swathed round calf and thigh, clad in the blue tunic of his faction. The long reins were bound round his body, and at his side was the vital dagger that would sever them in case of a fall.

Nero linked his arm through Otho's and pulled him close. 'I wish...' he began, but Otho interrupted him, already guessing his wish.

'Don't we all! Riches untold, women untold! There's not a man in Rome who does not wish to be a charioteer!'

'Even so,' Nero continued, undeterred, 'I wish I could drive in the races.'

'I think I'll just wish for the women and the money!'

The presiding consul was perched high above them in his tribune. Over his scarlet tunic he wore an embroidered Tyrian toga, and on his head a heavy wreath of golden leaves that was supported by a slave beside him. He carried an ivory baton surmounted by an eagle on the point of flight, and in his other hand he held a white napkin. As the excitement intensified, he stepped forward and dropped the napkin into the arena. This was the signal for the trumpet to sound the start - and the race was on.

The dust flew up from the wheels and the crowd roared. Every time a chariot safely negotiated the tight turns the audience cried out in relief. As the four chariots raced into the final circuit, having already completed thirteen laps, the cheers of the crowd reached epic proportions. The Blue team ran wide at the final turn, narrowly avoiding the path of the challenging Greens. As they straightened up, the Green team passed them, gaining a decisive victory as they swept through to the finish.

'YES!' Otho cried out, punching the air in triumph and turning to embrace Nero joyously. Their excitement was mirrored by several others around them. It had been a popular victory.

'Let us go and collect my winnings!' Otho said cheerfully, 'they will be well spent this evening!'

Nero grinned. 'As they were last night?'

'Last night we had barely enough on which to get drunk. But for a little sport out on the streets we would have had no fun at all. We happened upon a particularly drunk and elderly wretch and we tossed him in a blanket! You should have heard him howl! He was convinced we intended to murder him!'

'Your usual idea of a practical joke,' Nero said, feigning disapproval but taking delight from visualising the scene. Otho had fallen in with a rough crowd, but they were not yet bad. Lucius Otho considered them to be so and dealt out frequent beatings to his son in a vain effort to keep him away from his friends. But the rod only served to drive Otho to them. It was a phase and it would pass before the gang matured into violence; and Nero listened to Otho's tales with envious reverence. He longed for Otho's maturity and above all else his freedom.

'Tonight,' declared Otho, as he sorted through his coins, 'we will visit a tavern to become outrageously drunk; then a brothel, for outrageous relief; then a spot of blanket tossing on our way home - always supposing we're up to it by then, of course! And my dear father may raise a thousand rods to me - I shall be too numb to notice!'

Nero shivered involuntarily and Otho put an arm around his shoulder, squeezing him genially. 'You are thirteen, an exemplary student - so my father keeps reminding me! - and you're the emperor's favourite. Britannicus is unpleasant, his parentage is in question, and your mother has had his tutors executed and replaced by a pitiful collection who haven't the intelligence of a simpleton between them! I ask you, my friend - who is more likely to incur a beating? You? Or your shameful little brother?'

Nero smiled. 'And if he attends his classes, while I slip out to the races?'

'When even Seneca admits that there is little more he can teach you, you have surely earned the right to skip school occasionally. Does your mother really take enough interest in you to dish out punishment?'

'Not any more.' Nero shuddered again and Otho hugged him lightly. 'But she shouts,' Nero pointed out, beginning to smile, 'and that can be fairly unpleasant!'

Otho grinned. 'Unpleasant, but not unbearable.'

Nero's smile faded. He looked up at the eighteen-year-old for whom he felt such love and respect; such complete adulation. 'I fear for you, too.'

Otho's embrace tightened. 'I'm not easy to hurt, don't worry about me. The rod is a small price to pay for the enjoyment of one's leisure time. And you! You are in an enviable position, my friend! You have a licence to do just as you wish! You are the emperor's heir!'

Nero smiled resignedly. 'But I am not free, Otho. I am not free.'

Chapter Five

APRIL A.D. 52

Nero had been betrothed to Octavia for three years, but had never given it thought until now. His mother had arranged the betrothal before his adoption, determined to establish him as the emperor's son-in-law should her hopes for his adoption fail to materialise. It had meant nothing to him at the time and had, on the whole, been forgotten. But just recently certain experiences were causing him to think of Octavia and to consider the implications of their betrothal.

In the past weeks he had been thrown into a turmoil of confusion, only to be followed by the frustration of enlightenment. The mere glimpse of a pretty young slave girl at the end of the hall left him in an embarrassing and uncomfortable predicament, and even academic concentration often left him similarly afflicted in the classroom, so that he dared not rise to leave the room until Seneca's sharp rebuke had cured him.

He wasn't at all sure what was happening, but was aware that it was not happening in the company of the twelve-year-old Octavia. The mere mention of a pretty girl's name was enough to send him warning signals, yet thoughts of his future wife had little affect. He imagined, delightfully, the fully clothed girls he saw around the Palace; yet failed to stir himself further about his naked bride-to-be. His imagination lacked the all-important ingredient of knowledge; he simply didn't know what lay beneath her clothes. He was familiar with the female form and of late had made quite a study of the various portraits of naked women that adorned the Palace walls. But try as he would, he could not put Octavia's face to the bodies.

They were to be brought together again for today's festivities, their father tactfully allowing Nero to partner Octavia rather than the ever-hostile Britannicus. But Octavia's company was no less frosty; sharing, as she did, her brother's view that Nero was no more than a usurper, who had stolen their father's affection and her brother's birthright.

Nero dressed for the day's Games at the Fucine Lake, pulling on the triumphal robes allowed to him only a few months earlier and not looking out of place in the adult costume, despite his obvious youth. Satisfied with his appearance, after much assistance and artistic arrangement by his slaves, he finally stepped out into the anteroom and ventured out into the courtyard to meet the rest of his family.

His parents were not yet out, but the other members of the emperor's party were quietly assembled in the gardens, seated around the carp pond. Lucius and Albia Otho, together with their son Marcus; Vitellius, with his recently adopted daughter Octavia; and Seneca, in company with the acclaimed writer Petronius. Octavia had distanced herself from Vitellius, regarding his adoption of her as no more than a simple observance of protocol. She had been betrothed to Nero when he was still only her step-brother, and his own adoption by her father had necessitated hurried arrangements to overcome the legal technicalities.

Seeing Octavia alone, Nero merely waved in greeting to Otho, but neglected him in preference to his bride-to-be.

'How are you, Octavia? It is a fine day for the spectacle, is it not?'

She regarded him, with starched indifference. Whatever she might now be on paper she was still the emperor's natural daughter and considered herself to be above the flamboyant youth who was no more the emperor's son than she was Vitellius' daughter. The contrivances of his mother had split her family asunder and opened a breach between her father and brother that neither she nor Britannicus could understand.

'I believe your friend is signalling to you,' she said with distaste, turning away from him to trail her fingers in the water and summon the brightly coloured tame carp, imported for her from the Orient.

Nero turned to see Otho beckoning to him and readily left her to the company of her pet fish.

'Nero!' Otho embraced him heartily, overcome with the excitement of the news he had still to impart. He drew Nero to one side, away from his own parents, and threw a glance towards Seneca and his companion. 'You see who that is? Petronius! The writer of adult satires. And I mean *adult*!'

Nero looked across at him with interest. 'And poetry?'

'Enough. But his satires would interest you more, my friend! As bedtime reading they raise the blood most satisfactorily!'

'Then let us gain an introduction.'

They crossed to Seneca, who introduced them formally to his companion, who was clearly no more than that. Mutual respect seemed more evident in their manner than friendship and Nero detected the faint disapproval in Seneca's attitude, giving him an instant regard for Petronius.

'Petronius, allow me to introduce you to Marcus Otho, son of Lucius and Albia, of course, and a former student of mine.' Seneca made the announcement with pride, much to Otho's amusement. 'And this, of course, is Nero, Prince of Youth, whom I am honoured to have as a student.'

Petronius regarded them both with obvious interest.

'Have you read any of my work?' he asked.

'I am a great admirer of your satires,' Otho declared.

'And you, my Prince?'

'Nero has more of an interest in poetry,' Seneca stepped in, 'he can dash off verses enthusiastically without the least effort. A quite remarkable scholar! And more than gifted musically, I might add. He excels in the Arts.'

'Indeed?' Petronius met Nero's eye, and his own twinkled mischievously in return, as they privately mocked Seneca's self-gratified pride. 'I have written some serious poetry,' Petronius told Nero, 'but I'm sure they hold no interest for your friend here.' He grinned at Otho.

'Perhaps you could supply me with some of your work?' Nero asked, to which Petronius readily consented.

'He is a hard critic to please,' Seneca warned, 'I hope your poetry is as serious as you claim.'

Petronius smiled, exchanging amused glances with Otho and Nero. He recognised in them a free spirit, uninhibited by protocol and un-smothered by etiquette. His satires were written as a form of fanciful escapism for his readers, but here was a pair who could happily live them.

'I too am a hard critic to please,' Petronius told Seneca admiringly, 'yet your student here has already won me over. I speak, of course, of his maiden speech in the Forum. His eloquence was a credit to you, Seneca.'

'Well, of course, I cannot take all the credit,' Seneca admitted, 'but you are not alone in your opinion. When Nero qualified for an official career last autumn it was the proudest moment of my life, I must confess. To see him prematurely assume adult dress and to receive his title, Prince of Youth - well, that was the pinnacle of my career. There was no prouder man in Rome than I, as Nero led the ceremonial march past of the Guards, shield in hand, from the Forum to the senate.'

'Oh, that I don't doubt, Seneca,' Petronius quipped, to the amusement of his two new young friends.

'Of course, you missed his speech to the senate,' Seneca observed somewhat cattily, 'but the House was so impressed that it was proposed he should hold a consulship at nineteen!'

'The speech I missed,' Petronius agreed, 'but the result of it is common knowledge. Thanks to the young consul-designate here I have never attended so many celebratory dinner parties! You must allow me to host one in your honour, my Prince.'

'Granted; on the condition that I am allowed to attend!'

'Young men such as yourself would find dinner parties tedious,' Seneca pointed out.

'Not so!' Petronius argued, 'You obviously don't attend the right ones!'

'Yes, well; perhaps Nero can look to you for advice on those matters in due course,' Seneca said with obvious disapproval, 'but for now I fear he must take his leave. The emperor is here.'

Claudius had entered, unobserved by the animated group, and Nero hurried over to join him. The emperor, wearing a splendid military cloak, was accompanied by Agrippina, dressed strikingly in a mantle of gold silk; by Pallas and Narcissus; and by Britannicus.

Riding in the ceremonial golden coach, Claudius and his immediate family led the way to the mountain between the Fucine Lake and the River Liris, to unveil the culmination of one of his most ambitious projects. A tunnel had been built through the mountain, to link the lake and the river, and Claudius had long awaited its completion. By way of celebration, he now staged a naval battle on the lake.

He had equipped warships manned with nineteen thousand combatants and surrounded them with rafts to prevent their escape, leaving enough space in the centre for all the action of a sea-battle. Double companies of the Guard and other units were stationed on the rafts to shoot catapults and stone-throwers. The remainder of the lake was covered with the decked ships of the marines.

The coast, the slopes and the hilltops were covered by people who had come from far and wide to witness the impressive spectacle. The coach passed still more, making their way belatedly to the lake, as it threaded its own way through the throng.

Upon arrival, the emperor was met by Sextus Burrus, the newly appointed Commander of the Guard, who escorted the imperial party to their places of honour. Until a year ago, the Guard had always been maintained by two commanders, most recently Lucius Geta and Rufrius Crispinus. But Agrippina had set about removing all sympathisers to the plight of Britannicus, to whom Geta and Crispinus were known to be loyal. She had convinced Claudius that the Guard was split by the rivalry of the two commanders and recommended unified control to obtain stricter discipline. On her recommendation command was transferred to Burrus, who was fully aware of to whom he owed his appointment.

The battle commenced and the fighters - all criminals - fought bravely; so much so that after a particularly bloodthirsty battle the survivors were spared death. Claudius sat on the edge of his seat throughout, raising himself from his chair with the occasional force of his encouragement. Nero regarded him disdainfully, having little taste for the bloodshed before him, and even less for his father's pleasure in it.

Following the display, Claudius made a short speech and the waterway was opened. But it became immediately evident that the opening ceremony was premature. The tunnel had not been sunk to the bottom of the lake, nor even half way down, and it was clear that time would have to be allowed for the deepening of it; this time with more careful construction.

The party returned to the Palace, the high spirits of the day unimpaired by the failure of the project. The atmosphere in the great dining hall was particularly relaxed that evening and the emperor and his guests enjoyed a boisterous dinner party, overflowing with wine and revelry.

At the behest of Otho, Nero spent the evening at one of the higher tables, away from that usually reserved for the young princes and the children of the noblemen at Court. He failed to match Otho's cups, but nevertheless far exceeded his usual intake of wine and was distinctly animated as he retired, with Otho, to his bedchamber.

'That wine has gone straight to my head,' he complained, as he flung himself down on the bed. 'Pass me the pitcher, Otho, I have an unquenchable thirst. It's so warm tonight.'

Otho poured some water into a goblet and flicked the spillage from his wet fingers at Nero's face and neck. The gesture, though not intended as any form of relief, was welcomed. With a groan of reluctance, Nero sat up and accepted the water.

'Is it genuinely humid, or is it the wine?' he asked.

'That I cannot answer,' Otho admitted with a grin, 'I myself am over-heated by your mother's companion. Did you see the way Junia Silana flirted with me? That woman is shameless! Beautiful and shameless! What a wonderful combination!'

'I can't say that I've ever paid her such attention. She is simply one of Mother's friends.'

'And so to be strongly avoided. Who does take your eye, then? Or do you have eyes only for Octavia?!'

Nero snorted in disgust, but made no reply.

Otho watched him for a moment as he sipped without satisfaction at the water. Even now, as Nero blossomed towards maturity, he still retained the feminine features of boyhood, the blonde curls, the startling blue eyes, the grace of movement that would always see him labelled pretty rather than handsome. Otho was more classically handsome; and knew it. There was nothing particularly eye-catching or out of the ordinary about him, but he was fastidious about his clothes and toilet, and his mild conceit showed in his appearance.

'I myself have a fancy for any number of the slave girls in our household,' Otho said, lying back on the bed alongside Nero, 'but I fear my father would flog me yet if ever I strayed beyond the realms of fantasy. Senecio's father takes a more traditional view. He actually gave Senecio his choice of slave girl for his fourteenth birthday. If you were so fortunate, you kept uncharacteristically quiet about it, my friend. Any possibility of such a gift for this year, do you think?'

'Not a hope! Octavia is Father's pride and joy; we may as well be already married for all the free rein I am allowed.'

'You are missing out on a pleasurable pastime, my poor young friend; as, indeed, am I for the most part. There are brothels in this city that can offer you a taste of the most exquisite delight imaginable - ecstasy beyond description.' He sighed with a mixture of pain and pleasure. 'Ah, the dear gods, what I wouldn't give to be there now. What say you to slipping out now and visiting a particularly discreet house that occasionally welcomes my custom?'

'I dare not.'

'Then let us take up the dice as distraction. Your father lost heavily to Vitellius this evening. Given the practise he has, he is not a good loser, is he?'

'He has become a little morose in his cups of late. He and Mother are not the best of companions at the moment; I do not know if that is the cause or simply the result. But I suspect that he is aware of her infidelities.' He glanced at Otho. 'Is sex really so wonderful as to warrant the problems it causes?'

'Oh, better than that, Nero! There are no problems when you're with a beautiful woman, no worries at all. In the name of the gods, boy, throw the wretched dice and change the subject! This heat is stifling.'

Using far-fetched dares instead of gold pieces, they gambled heavily on each winning pip of the dice and collapsed with laughter at the consequences. Neither was expected to fulfil their tasks, but the visions conjured up by the bizarre situations appealed to their humour.

They sat, as always, wrapped in each other's comradely embrace. The close physical contact had always been a mark of their friendship, serving to cement their relationship and, at the same time, excluding Senecio and others of their less-intimate friends. But this time they were both aware of something different; a new strength in the embraces.

Nero was less content simply to lean languidly against Otho, their faces brushing as they joked and laughed. Instead he took advantage of each opportunity and bestowed chaste kisses upon his friend, who did nothing to stop him. Soon the ever-increasing intensity of Nero's kisses had aroused Otho and their frenzied passion quickly carried them beyond the realms of simple friendship. They stopped short of the ultimate act, but as a sexual experience it was far more fulfilling than anything they could have achieved alone.

Narcissus was the first to enter in the morning, armed with paperwork and documents from the emperor. As he arranged the papers in order on the desk he paid the boys only scant attention, but hesitated as he approached them to wake Nero. They were somehow no longer the boys he had treated with such indulgence in the past. The smell and stains on the tangled mess of covers were little more than he had been accustomed to finding over recent weeks, yet still seemed to convey a new loss of innocence. Narcissus shrugged it off as mere supposition and shook Nero by the shoulder.

'Come, my young Prince, the sun has risen without you this morning.'

'Then let it set without me, too! Go away and leave me in peace.'

'Remember the strain of working by candlelight throughout the winter and make the most of daylight while you have it.'

'It would seem that I am left with little option, Narcissus! You are intent on preaching to me until I am dressed and seated at my desk!'

'You will be even less eager when you see your workload. The emperor feels that you are becoming mature enough to take on greater responsibility,' Narcissus glanced at the still sleeping Otho, 'and I am inclined to agree with him. And awaiting you is the heavy price to be paid for such confidence.'

Nero groaned and began to dress, then went straight to his desk and sifted through the documents. 'Is Seneca aware of this increase?'

Narcissus shrugged. 'Probably not. But don't complain about having two masters - you will have far more than that in a few years time!'

'Huh! Britannicus regards me as a usurper, let him step in and take his rightful place.'

Narcissus smiled, but not without mixed feelings. His loyalties lay with Claudius; and therefore with Britannicus.

'Just do the work!' he said lightly, and took his leave.

For the second time that year a vast crowd assembled at the Fucine Lake, this time to witness an infantry battle fought by gladiators on pontoons. But when the completed waterway was opened the force of the out-rushing water swept away everything in the immediate vicinity, and the sheer noise caused shock and widespread terror far afield.

The only celebration in the Palace that evening was a private one, in memory of the first failed opening of the ill-conceived waterway and its sensual result.

Afterwards, Nero sat up and reached across for the volume of work given to him by Petronius, quoting from memory one of the verses as he did so.

' "Find me any man who knows
Nothing of love and naked pleasure.
What stern moralist would oppose
Two bodies warming a bed together?
Father of Truth, old Epicurus
Spoke of bodies, not of soul,
And taught, philosophers assure us,
Love is life's sovereign goal." '

Chapter Six

A.D. 53

Nero had made his first appearance on the tribunal as City Prefect during the Latin Festival in April, presiding over the court that sat in the Forum of Augustus. Eminent lawyers had given him a number of important cases to try, instead of the usual trivial cases that were normally reserved for such an occasion.

Claudius, having expressly forbidden this, was annoyed at the unnecessary pressure placed on his son, who was still a mere boy of fifteen, after all. But Nero had come through with flying colours. The stifling atmosphere of the tightly packed Forum failed to unnerve him and he listened patiently to each advocate, unruffled by the clamour of their hired admirers, paid to clap and cheer after every speech or clever sentence. The sessions had opened at dawn and gone on until dusk, with brief adjournments allowed for refreshments, and Nero had finally returned to the Palace exhausted, but exhilarated.

'How did it go?' Otho and Senecio enquired the following day, as they met up at the Circus Maximus for the day's racing.

'It was marvellous!' Nero enthused, 'I envied the advocates. You should have heard the applause they received!'

'They pay for the cheers,' Otho pointed out, 'it's no reflection on their skills.'

'Their skills as orators speak for themselves,' Nero argued, 'and the paid admirers only help to spur on the rest of the audience. No, the adulation was merited.'

He smiled happily to himself, still savouring the events of the previous day.

Trick riders passed by, standing on the backs of a pair of horses, jumping from one to the other, sometimes swinging under their bellies. The crowd roared in appreciation and Nero glowed, as though fed by the applause.

'Still want to do that?' Otho asked, casting him a glance.

Nero shook his head. 'I couldn't do it as well as they can. If I can't be the best then I can see no point in competing. Do you remember the Troy Games, Otho?'

'Vaguely. You excelled then, if I remember rightly.'

'I did. And I earned applause that day, Otho. That's what I want. Charioteer, actor, advocate - it doesn't matter which. Just so long as I excel.'

'And emperor?'

Nero glanced at him ruefully.

'As emperor you can chase any pipe dream you wish,' Senecio remarked, 'You can have the applause without the talent.'

'And what is the use of that?' Nero asked.

Senecio shrugged. 'I don't know; it's your pipe dream.' He watched the riders complete their display. 'The point is, the emperor holds the ultimate power. He can use it as he wishes. He can have it all.'

Nero snorted disparagingly. 'Using power in such a way only devalues the things one obtains. Renders it all worthless, and therefore not worth desiring. The emperor has no power of any real value.'

'No power?!' Senecio laughed. 'Do you expect to be no more than a puppet in the hands of your ministers?! I ask you this, Nero - who has the power to execute those very ministers at will and to control the senate?

'That's not power, that's simply position,' Nero argued. 'I will be no one's puppet. It will be a job, and I shall carry it out. No more, no less. I am speaking of personal things, not of a public career. Position is of no importance in such matters, talent is the only requirement.'

'That's true,' Otho agreed, 'win public adoration and your power can easily match that of the emperor, however humble your background. Look at Mnester. Greatest comic actor of our time. He could ask any favour of any statesman. He could hold the political reins as strongly as the emperor himself.'

'He *slept* with the emperor himself!' Senecio argued, 'his power came not from the stage, not from his talent - but from Caligula! There is only one power. One ultimate power. And it serves only one person. Others are raised up or dropped at his will.'

'Some can raise themselves up without the influence of the emperor,' Nero said sharply, 'and then they need not fear a fall.'

'So who will your influences be, Nero?' Otho teased.

'The emperor should have no influences. It is his duty to influence the senate. But Senecio's theory of an ultimate power is suited only to tyrants and despots. The state itself thrives on shared power, with the emperor no more than a chairman, an overseer.'

'Your noble intentions match those of each of our previous emperors,' Senecio sneered, 'but only Augustus saw them through to the end.'

'Augustus was no better than his successors,' Nero retaliated. 'The state prospered right up to his death and beyond, but did his subjects? Of what benefit was his Golden Reign to them? They paid a high price for the success of the few. The state is self-preserving. It survives the bloody reigns just as it prospers in the Golden Ages. My concern will be for the people. They are the ones on whom the state is built, and they alone suffer the mistakes of the emperor. The Golden Age of Augustus was more harmful to the ordinary citizens than any of the cruelties of Caligula.'

'Yes, well I forgot that all the Caesars are Republicans at heart,' Senecio said sarcastically. 'Every one of you has preached Republican views while reaping the profits of the empire.'

'And you are a Republican, Senecio?'

'No more than you, Nero. Republicanism is the biggest pipe dream of them all.'

'The Republic fails because of greed and power-lust,' Nero argued, 'a figurehead un-swayed by such faults can work to the same ideals.'

'How can the emperor exhibit greed and power-lust,' Otho agreed with a grin, 'when he already has everything?! He has nothing to covet and nothing to connive for!'

Nero clapped an arm across Otho's shoulder and grinned at Senecio. 'Thank you for the debate, my friend, but as usual it takes one of Otho's apathy to supply the final answer! You and I take too keen an interest in our subjects, we drown ourselves with knowledge! Otho pays such scant regard to anything that he can always be relied upon to come up with the pure facts and nothing more!'

'Then tell me, Otho, your views on the next race?' Senecio joked, lightening once more.

'Alas, my friends, there are no pure facts on a racecourse! Form, pedigree, the well-being of the stable, the skill of the charioteer - there is enough knowledge to drown us all, and I sink as quickly as the next man!'

'There! You see! Another of your ideals crushed, Nero!'

Nero mounted the seven steps leading up to the impressive marble portico of the Basilica Julia, taking the next two steps in a single stride to bring him in to the vast hall, divided into three by immense marble-faced columns. The central section was by far the largest, some two-hundred-and-fifty feet in length and over fifty feet wide. Yet even that was insufficient to accommodate the volume of spectators crushed into the Basilica; those less fortunate having to crane their necks from the tribunes on the first storey in order to follow the court proceedings below.

As consul, Claudius himself was presiding over the hearings, seated on a curule chair, on an improvised dais, with some ninety assessors seated either side of him. On the benches at their feet sat the various parties to the suits, their defenders, friends and prosecutors. Nero took his place among them, joining Seneca and Petronius who were in attendance as advisor and observer, respectively.

Nero was to plead two cases that day and already had a well-earned reputation as a learned and eloquent advocate. He had, earlier in the year, successfully backed Ilium to be exempted from all public burdens, having fluently recalled the descent of Rome from Troy and the Julii from Aeneas as a precedent. He owed much to Seneca, who supplied most of his information and even went so far as to draft the speeches. But the speeches were nothing without their orator, and Nero played his audience with a skill and delight that was extraordinary for one so young.

The morning's proceedings opened, just as the sun broke through in earnest, and Nero took the platform on behalf of the people of Bononia, devastated by fire. By the end of the session his advocacy had secured them a grant of ten million sesterces.

Accepting the congratulations of Seneca and Petronius, Nero slipped outside with them and sat on the marble steps to the Basilica while the court took a brief recess. They sat among the hired applauders, who had chalked rough boards onto the steps and were playing a variety of games. Most only entered the court when paid to do so and filled the rest of their time out on the steps, awaiting their call.

'A remarkable speech,' Petronius said, watching one of the games in progress, 'but on which of you do I confer the praise?'

'Since Nero rewrote most of my script anyway, I think he deserves the full credit in this particular instance,' Seneca pointed out graciously.

'In this particular instance?' Petronius queried. 'So you aim to take full credit for the second session?'

Seneca raised his hands in mock defeat. 'I imagine the young Prince will ignore my efforts again, but you can excuse me for attempting to bask in his reflected glory!'

'That I overshadow yours is my only regret,' Nero insisted. 'Your groundwork is essential to me and I merely alter your work, not rewrite it.'

'I trust you would not dare to alter mine,' Petronius remarked.

'I have yet to find a word out of place,' Nero assured him.

'Well I hate to break up your mutual appreciation society, but it's time to return to court,' Seneca said lightly.

'So soon? My father generally takes his time where food and drink are concerned.'

'He must be anxious to get through the day,' Seneca observed. 'Is all well at home?'

'No worse than usual. He and Mother seem to regard one another with a healthy suspicion, but without open hostility.' He grinned. 'He believes that he knows far more than she gives him credit for, but my money is on Mother!'

They returned to the stifling courtroom and took their places once more. The acoustics were appalling and the voices of the advocates were as strained as the hearing of the listeners. Claudius had clearly taken sufficient refreshment to give up the unequal struggle and sat back for the second session as though tired and uninterested. He would rely, as usual, upon the prompting of the assessors when judgement was called for.

This time Nero spoke on behalf of the Rhodians, continually liberated or subjected, according to their services in foreign wars or their disorders at home. He put forward their case in fluent Greek and won for them their freedom. Then he sat back and listened to another successful advocate, before securing a five year remission of taxes for Phrygian Aramea, overwhelmed by a recent earthquake.

'Do you not regard it as a portent?' Petronius asked of his two companions as they left the court in the early afternoon.

'Regard what as a portent?' asked Nero.

'Why, all these earthquakes, of course! Last year they were constant throughout Italy, and the trend looks set to continue. One is forced to consider them as a sign.'

'I have never heard such superstitious nonsense in my life!' snorted Seneca.

'Mark my words,' Petronius insisted, 'these disasters will not abate until a great event quells them. And we cannot be far from that event. Before the year is out we shall have something to celebrate, of that I'm certain.'

Nero grinned. 'I am to be married in December.'

'There you are, then!' Petronius declared triumphantly. 'An apt portent if ever there was one!'

'In that I fear you are very much mistaken!' Nero said with a wry smile, 'your portent could not be more inappropriate.'

He thought, not for the first time, of his impending marriage and his unsuccessful attempts to avoid it. His mother appeared to have no special fondness for Octavia, yet remained fiercely adamant that the wedding should take place. He knew that there must be some underlying motive and therefore didn't dare to oppose her.

But he couldn't help wishing that one of Petronius' natural portents would open up beneath his bride-to-be and put an immediate end to his mother's plans.

Chapter Seven

DECEMBER A.D. 53

Octavia rose on the day of her wedding, having lain awake for most of the night, uncomfortable in the strange surroundings of Vitellius' house and unhappy at the prospect of her marriage. It could have been avoided - though not without difficulty - but Octavia had long ago made the decision to consent to the wishes of her father. The idea of the marriage pleased him and she liked nothing better than to see him happy. Relations had been so strained within his own marriage that her future happiness was his only source of comfort. And, in the face of things, it was a small price to pay. As much as she loathed Nero, he in turn regarded her with no more than indifference. It would be a marriage of convenience, and no more. She hoped that he would have the decency to respect that.

She sat back now, without interest, as her slaves attended her. Dressing as custom dictated, she wore a tunic without a hem, secured round the waist by a girdle of wool fixed by a double knot. Over the top she wore a saffron cloak, matched by her sandals. Her hair had been confined with a crimson net the evening before and was now adorned by six pads of artificial hair, separated by narrow bands, such as the Vestal Virgins wore. Around her neck she wore a metal collar; and the entire costume was completed by a veil of flaming orange that covered the upper part of her face. The veil was secured by a wreath of myrtle and orange blossom.

Having been dressed for the ceremony, she went out to greet her family and to await the arrival of the groom. But, for Octavia, there was no family to greet. Her father had been claimed by Nero, and Agrippina's presence offered no consolation.

'Oh, she looks fetching does she not, Spintria?' Agrippina declared, not bothering to rise as Octavia entered the room.

Vitellius smiled warmly and grasped her by the shoulders. 'I almost wish I were marrying you myself, my dear.'

Agrippina laughed. 'Coming from you that is a compliment indeed!'

Vitellius released Octavia and went across to the door. 'I think I hear them coming!'

The groom and his party were indeed on the doorstep and were quickly ushered in. They consisted of Nero's immediate family - Claudius and Britannicus included - his friends and his relations. Octavia looked upon them all with a sudden, renewed bitterness. With the exception of his Aunts Domitia and Lepida, Nero had claimed as his own her entire family and circle of friends. He stood before her now, dressed in the fine toga of a prince, while her brother languished in his shade, still dressed as a minor. She hated Nero as a usurper; but pitied him as a puppet. He had been brought here no more willingly than she; yet she was here for the love of her father, while he was driven only by fear of his mother. Though still only fourteen and two years his junior, she considered herself to be his superior, in both maturity and propriety.

When everyone had been welcomed, they all adjourned to the entrance hall, where the family augur awaited them, in front of the shrine of the Household Gods.

There the augur sacrificed a ewe; and ten members of the wedding party, chosen as witnesses, stepped forward to put their seals on the marriage contract. As they solemnly fulfilled their roles, the augur examined the entrails of the ewe and finally declared the auspices to be favourable. Without his guarantee of the approval of the gods the marriage would have been invalid. Nero and Octavia then exchanged their vows, to become as one, and the marriage rite came to its close.

The respectful silence of the guests broke with a sudden tumult of congratulations and best wishes. Agrippina kissed Nero warmly, satisfied in the knowledge that his union with Octavia would overcome any remaining prejudices against him. Those who doubted his right to succeed Claudius could not doubt the right of the emperor's own daughter to sit beside him as empress.

'I am so very happy for you both,' Claudius said with genuine warmth as he paid his respects to the bride and groom.

Octavia glowed under his praise, looking happy for the first time that day. Nero watched her, taking note of her reaction. He admired her affection for the father they both loved and shared, and he resolved to make her happy, if only for the sake of Claudius. He reached out a hand to take hers, but she drew back from him sharply. He shrugged it off, unperturbed, and went across to join Otho and Senecio. They joked coarsely and enjoyed the lavish festivities, until it was time for the groom to take his bride to his own home.

'Good luck,' Otho said, casting a glance at Octavia, who was deep in conversation with her brother, 'I have an idea you'll need it.'

Nero looked across at his wife. 'I think we shall be all right.'

'And, if not, the Palace is a large place!' Otho added.

Nero looked at him, then smiled.

'Get going,' Otho told him lightly, 'you're expected to be at least somewhere near the front of the procession! At this rate you'll be bringing up the rear!'

Outside, the guests had arranged themselves in readiness for the wedding procession, flute players leading the way and five torch bearers following in their wake to light the group. In a jumbled mass the party set off for the Palace, voices raised in cheerful and licentious singing. Octavia was accompanied by the customary three young boys, one carrying a torch of hawthorn twigs, the other two holding her hands. Nero followed far behind, his arm slung across Otho's shoulder, their voices singing out above the rest. A handful of children, on hearing the wedding procession, ran out and followed along with them, collecting up nuts thrown to them by the guests.

At the Palace, the main doorway was strewn with laurel leaves and other luxuriant greenery, lying upon a carpet of white cloth. Nero stepped forward and carried Octavia over the threshold, her three bridesmaids following behind. One of the bridesmaids carried a distaff and another carried a spindle, as emblems of virtue and diligence. In the final rituals of the ceremony, Nero offered Octavia water and fire, then the maid of honour led Octavia through to the nuptial bed and Nero invited her to lie down. He slowly removed her cloak, then began to undo the knotted girdle, whereupon the wedding guests retired hastily and left the newlyweds to the privacy they deserved.

The door was closed and the cheery voices faded into the distance. Nero succeeded in untying the girdle, but Octavia sat up and drew away from him.

'Please; I'd rather you didn't.'

He tried to smile reassuringly, but couldn't mask his true lack of feeling.

'Would you like me to blow out the candles?' he offered.

'I'd prefer them left burning. Do you have a screen? I wish to undress.'

He looked about him uncomfortably and gestured towards a screen by his toilet things. Octavia scooped up her cloak and walked across to the far corner, disappearing behind the screen and re-emerging with the cloak wrapped firmly round her.

'If you would care to leave just one candle burning, I think I should like to retire for the night. It has been a strenuous day,' she said, climbing carefully into the bed and giving up the cloak only in exchange for the all-concealing counterpane.

Nero did as she requested, then undressed and joined her. She kept her back to him, the counterpane clutched tightly under her chin. He could see her eyes, still open, in the candlelight, and reached out hesitantly to touch her.

'I'd rather you didn't, if you please,' she said stiffly.

'But...'

'Women's things, Nero, which I would prefer not to discuss. I'm afraid that our wedding was rather ill-timed.'

'Oh.' Nero swallowed. He didn't altogether believe her, but hardly dared argue. After a moment's silence he said hopefully, 'There are other options, you know - other... methods.'

'Exactly what are you suggesting?'

He knew at once, by her tone, that he had made a mistake, but pressed on, regardless. 'I mean that we can work around this; find some other form of relief.'

'How dare you! How dare you even suggest such a thing!' She pulled the counterpane even more tightly around her, her voice relaying her abject horror at his proposal. 'Father assured me that he had kept you away from those innocuous establishments your friend Otho so frequently inhabits. But you are no more than an animal! To ask such a thing of a decent woman - of your wife!' She shuddered with disgust. 'If you measure all women by the standards set by a prostitute then you have sadly erred. I will thank you to refrain from touching me again until such time as our marriage can be consummated in a proper and rightful manner.'

Nero was disconcerted by her unexpected outrage at what he and Otho considered to be wholesome pleasure. He had intended no offence and was irritated by her reaction.

'If our marriage is to be consummated then it ought to be now,' he declared rather hotly.

'If you dare lay one filthy finger upon me I shall scream.'

'You may scream all you care to, for it will not summon help. Not tonight. It is the custom for a bride to scream on her wedding night, is it not?'

Though his words were lightly mocking, his tone was sharp and Octavia could not doubt his intention.

'Very well,' she said stiffly, 'it is best to get the deed over with.' Yet she made no move to encourage him.

The futile frustration she had thrust upon him spurred him on. He was determined to banish the icy lack of feeling, even if it meant replacing it with passionate hatred. Any communication was better than none at all.

He pulled roughly at her shoulder until at least the seemingly immovable obstacle of her tightly covered back had been overcome. She lay now flat on her back beside him, her head turned towards the flickering candle that held the un-flickering attention of her eyes. Nero struggled briefly to release her undergarments, only at the last moment remembering her earlier attempt to avoid his touch. It came as no surprise to him to discover that she had lied, her virtue as false as her pride. His determination increased.

It was not an easy task; devoid of love, and hampered by ignorance and disgust. She yielded only to the inevitable, refusing to allow any other unnecessary touch. Neither of them understood how necessary such caresses really were. They both struggled against discomfort until the unobtainable had been suddenly vanquished, leaving them both sore; and more distant than ever.

It was not the experience Otho had described and Nero lay awake for a long time afterwards, questioning his feelings. The cold act of sex was far removed from the warm passion he had shared with Otho and he found Octavia's dismay disturbing. If either of the acts were to be described as unchaste and unnatural then it would have to be this evening's encounter. Yet decent society, apparently, did not agree. Perhaps Octavia was right; and he and Otho had been wrong to assume the escapades of prostitutes were general of all women. Or perhaps the problem went deeper.

Nero looked across at his sleeping wife and felt nothing for her. Neither did Otho confess to such feelings when in the company of a prostitute; yet still he enjoyed the experience. Love did not appear to be a prerequisite for pleasure. With or without encouragement he had performed the act to its climax, so why had he not felt the elation that Otho had spoken of? Were his private fantasies really so grotesque and perverted; or was Octavia too unreasonable?

He lacked the knowledge to answer the question himself, and was too full of self-doubt to ask it of anyone else.

He turned over on his side and closed his eyes. But he did not sleep.

Chapter Eight

A.D. 54

Agrippina reclined on the couch alongside Pallas, their morning's work of household accounts quickly turning into an afternoon of passion in the absence of Claudius. He was attending the amphitheatre, to watch the usual bloodbath of fighting and animal hunts that so set his pulse racing. He would sit, riveted, from beginning to end, even foregoing breaks for refreshment. While Agrippina mocked his passion to his face, she privately welcomed the opportunities it presented.

'Nero is much involved in official matters these days,' Agrippina remarked as she sipped from a glass goblet, 'he has certainly won over that old fool.'

'That old fool, as you call him, is neither stupid nor infirm,' Pallas warned, 'he has come to rely increasingly on Narcissus and I can do little to sway him. Nero, too, is beyond my reach.'

'Beyond mine, too, of late.' Agrippina turned the goblet slowly in her hands. 'He spends a good deal of time with Lepida. More so than with me.'

'Understandable enough,' Pallas concurred, 'for she has had as much involvement in his upbringing as you - if not more.'

'No involvement at all!' Agrippina snapped angrily, 'She merely took charge of the boy for a short time. And she has certainly not provided him with anything of lasting value. She does nothing but spoil and indulge him. He might run to her with his childish problems, but it is I who command his respect. She gave him dancers and barbers, while I gave him Seneca. She gives him no more than kind words and indulgence, while I shape him and create a future for him.' She twisted the goblet more violently with her anger.

Pallas sat up and poured some wine into his own goblet.

'I do believe you are jealous of her, my dear!'

Agrippina shot him a venomous glance. 'Jealous indeed! She has nothing that I do not myself possess. It is she who envies me, because I am succeeding in the position that her own daughter Messalina failed to keep!'

'She is wealthy, she is beautiful, she has a great deal of influence over your son,' Pallas pointed out, much to Agrippina's supreme aggravation. 'Is there any way of putting that influence to our own use, do you suppose?'

'What influence?! Indulgence breeds only contempt. She has no hold over the boy. He can refuse her any request without fear of a rebuke. But he would not dare to cross me.'

'Perhaps that is so,' Pallas agreed, 'but when exactly are you given the chance to exert that influence? If he is not with Claudius and Narcissus then he is with her.'

'Umm.' Agrippina rested the glass against her lips thoughtfully.

With a sudden decisiveness she said, 'go and fetch him. Tell him I wish to speak to him on a very important matter. Tell him I am much distressed.'

Pallas regarded her disdainfully. 'I am not your mere messenger boy. Without me your plans amount to nothing. If I am to be a party to this ploy then you must first tell me what it is in aid of.'

Agrippina smiled. She admired his arrogance that so annoyed everyone else. 'I plan to be rid of Lepida,' she told him simply, 'and I intend to use Nero to destroy her.'

'Well I don't see how,' Pallas retorted, 'nor do I see any need to involve the boy.'

Agrippina's eyes glinted with the pleasure of a new scheme to occupy her mind. 'He will destroy her, you need have no doubts on that score. And as to why; simply because it suits me, Pallas. You doubt my control over the boy. Well, you shall doubt no more.'

Pallas smiled and went off to do as she asked, returning some time later with an anxious-looking Nero.

'You wished to see me, Mother?' Nero asked nervously, his mind racing through all the possibilities, deeply afraid that he might be the cause of her distress and terrified of a reprisal.

Agrippina touched her eyes, as though to make sure that no tears remained.

'Leave us, if you would,' she told Pallas gently, then, to Nero, 'be seated; here, next to your mother.' She patted the couch beside her and placed a hand on his leg as he sat down. There was no affection in her touch.

'My darling, you are fond of your Aunt Lepida; you spend much time with her, do you not?'

'She likes to listen to my poetry,' Nero said, somewhat defensively.

'Well of course,' Agrippina agreed, 'I only wish that I had the time to enjoy your recitals, too. Or even just your company. But, as you know, my position brings with it so many pressures; so many other commitments. One day, Nero, you will take your father's place and I will be free of the burdens of empress. And then you and I can become close, as I would like.'

Nero smiled, wishing for nothing more than that himself.

'Does your aunt ever speak of me?' Agrippina asked.

'Often,' Nero told her truthfully, but declined to mention that it never involved pleasantries. Agrippina already seemed to know, however.

'But she does not like me, you will agree?'

Nero smiled ruefully. 'I think she is a little jealous of you.'

'And I of her,' Agrippina admitted frankly, 'for she has won your affection.'

Nero patted her hand warmly. 'You know that is not so, Mother. I understand that you can spare me no time, but that does not make me any less fond of you.'

Agrippina smiled and kissed his forehead. 'You are sweet, my child. But if it came to an ultimate choice, which of us would you choose?'

'Why you, of course.'

'Oh; my dear. That choice may have to be made immediately. Are you so certain of your answer?

'You are my mother,' Nero insisted, 'but why do you ask this of me?'

Agrippina withdrew her hand from his. 'I must be frank with you, Nero; though it grieves me to hurt you so. Your aunt is indeed jealous of me and - more to the point - wishes me dead. Your father and I do not get on so well together these days, and Lepida sees an opening for herself, with your influence, should anything happen to me. And so she has taken to practising witchcraft, and I am to be her victim.'

Nero was horrified and protested his aunt's innocence.

'I am thankful that she has at least had the decency to keep it from you,' Agrippina said in a choked voice, 'but with or without your knowledge, her witchcraft continues. She has already caused me no end of pain and discomfort with her magic, and ultimately she intends to kill me. Yet I cannot bring charges against her. It is my word against hers. I am a doomed woman and quite powerless to prevent my fate.'

Nero grasped her hand, as much to reassure himself as to offer her comfort.

'I am sure you must be mistaken,' he insisted.

'You have seen her with her potions?'

'Well; yes. But they are herbal remedies that she brews for the slaves. Their ailments never vanish over night, but nor does she seem to do them any harm.'

'Of course not, you little fool! Because the brew is neither for their cure nor their death - she blinds you with her good intentions to mask the real use for her potion!' Agrippina's voice rose in panic and Nero held her hand tightly in alarm.

'It is not a poison that she brews,' Agrippina continued, 'but a spell. She casts a spell as she mixes, I have seen magic of this sort practised before and there is no avoiding its outcome.'

'But Aunt Lepida wouldn't! She wouldn't!'

Agrippina made no attempt to hide her anger. 'Defend her, then, and suffer the consequences! Because it will be to the two of you that fingers will point when I die!' She jerked her hand away from his and turned her back to him.

'What do you wish me to do?' Nero asked weakly. 'I'm certain I could reason with her; dissuade her from these intentions.'

'When you didn't even know of her magic in the first place?!' Agrippina snorted in disgust. 'You will only realise that she has deceived you when I am placed on my pyre!'

'Then what am I to do?!' Nero cried in consternation.

'You must prosecute her, Nero. You must bring charges against her, for conspiring to use magic to take my life, and for failing to keep her Calabrian slave-gangs in order - for they, too, are a public menace, as well you know! She must be prosecuted and condemned. It is her or me, Nero - her or me.' Agrippina began to weep bitterly and Nero embraced her.

'I will do whatever is necessary,' he said quietly.

He took his charges to Claudius, feeling that the entire Palace was against him, abhorred at his betrayal of the aunt he so loved. He doubted the allegations himself, but didn't doubt his mother's belief in them; and to her he owed his allegiance. Claudius heard him solemnly and set a date for the trial. Lepida was taken into custody to await her hearing, and so Nero was spared the ordeal of having to face her.

It was to Lepida that he would normally turn, in such times of distress. Narcissus, his ally in all matters but this, vigorously opposed the charges and no mention could be made of them in his presence. Nero was completely alone. Alone with his conscience.

He stood in the Basilica of Iulia, even more crowded than usual due to the nature of the charges and the parties to them. Lepida sat, in chains, to one side of him, defended by a barrister new to his profession and conscious of his own shortcomings. Agrippina had seen to it that no one else dared take her case. Only Narcissus spoke in Lepida's defence, but against Nero's eloquent prosecution his arguments were worthless. Lepida, who sought in vain throughout the trial to catch Nero's eye, was found guilty of attempting to kill Agrippina by magic, and for failing to keep her Calabrian slave-gangs in order. In the excited hush of the Basilica she was sentenced to death and led away to await her fate.

Agrippina smiled with grim satisfaction and reached out an arm to comfort Nero; allowing him to sob uncontrollably against her breast, while she exchanged a triumphant glance with Pallas. Narcissus watched them, his expression controlled by only the most supreme of efforts.

'Well might he feel sorry for himself,' Claudius remarked, following Narcissus' gaze, 'if she is offering any comfort at all then it will be for the first time. He might have done better to say nothing at all and let Lepida follow through with her murderous intentions. What do you say, Narcissus? Umm?'

'I have no doubt of the murderous intent,' Narcissus said coldly, 'but, like you, I believe the wrong woman went to her death.' His tone said it all, but it was lost on Claudius, as he knew it would be.

They travelled back to the Palace in sedan chairs, wheeled vehicles not being ordinarily allowed on the crowded streets of Rome during the hours of daylight, even for the emperor himself. Claudius stepped down and hurried through for his evening meal, agitated at having missed lunch. Narcissus waited for the next chair, to watch Pallas and Agrippina alight, supporting Nero between them.

'The boy is completely insensible!' he protested, stepping forward hurriedly to assist them, 'Why did you not summon his nurses? A runner could have been sent from the Basilica.'

'Nurses!' Agrippina scoffed, 'he is a married man! Sixteen in December, or did you not notice?!'

Ignoring her, Narcissus instructed a slave to fetch Ecloge and Alexandria, the two Greek nurses who had attended Nero since his birth. He took the place of Pallas, who was happy to escape his burden, and helped Agrippina escort Nero to his bedchamber, where Octavia sat writing at the desk. She looked up without interest, disturbed only by the commotion caused by their arrival.

'What ails him?' she asked, turning back to her letter.

'No more than a fit of nerves,' Agrippina assured her, 'though Narcissus flaps about as though the attack were fatal!'

Ecloge swept into the room, ahead of Alexandria; filling it at once with her matronly presence. 'Leave him! Leave him!' she demanded, 'This noise does him no good, no good at all. Come on, out with you!' She clapped her hands and ushered Narcissus and Octavia out into the corridor, much to the irritation of the latter.

Nero clung to Agrippina tightly and was reluctant to be separated from her, only switching his embrace to Alexandria with the utmost force from Ecloge. Ecloge then escorted Agrippina to the door and closed it firmly behind her.

'This really is most irksome,' Octavia complained, 'I was midway through a letter to a friend.'

'If it is of any interest to you,' Narcissus said sharply, 'your husband's aunt was condemned to death.'

'And are we to congratulate him, or console him?' Octavia asked sarcastically.

'Little wonder he spends so much of his time with Otho,' Narcissus muttered distinctly, under his breath.

'Little wonder that I am happy to allow it,' Octavia retorted spitefully, 'rather him than me.' She looked at the uncomprehending face of her mother-in-law and smiled bitterly. 'So there is at least one secret which has escaped your notice within the Palace. I confess to being both amazed and gratified by your unexpected fallibility.' So saying, she turned on her heels and walked haughtily away, to retreat to her brother's room.

'And before the cogs start to turn within your mind,' Narcissus said, turning at once on Agrippina, 'your scheming will be in vain. This shall be the last atrocity you slip by me. I am ready for you, Agrippina. And so is the emperor.'

Agrippina's eyes narrowed. 'No, Narcissus. I am ready for you. So watch your back; for all the good it will do you.'

Chapter Nine

SEPTEMBER A.D. 54

Narcissus sat with Epaphroditus, the emperor's secretary, drinking fortified wine to relax his nerves. Gone was the vigour and confidence of earlier days; he looked tired and frail, his face pale from the pressures of work.

'You are pushing yourself too hard,' Epaphroditus observed, 'the emperor is well aware of Agrippina's actions. He is on the verge of dealing with her.'

'He is on the verge of considering her actions,' Narcissus corrected him, 'but he is still a long way from dealing with her. She may well deal with him sooner.'

'Oh, now, come, Narcissus! Your suspicions run away with you! Granted, she has excelled herself when it comes to contriving the succession of her son. But is that really such a bad thing?' He took a drink and emptied his glass. 'Nero takes a far healthier interest in politics than Britannicus; I personally have more confidence in him.'

'That is only because Agrippina has destroyed any chance Britannicus has of securing a good education.'

'Oh it goes beyond that. Nero is altogether more energetic, enthusiastic. Zestful! Why, you yourself are fond of him. His succession would suit you far more than that of Britannicus.'

Narcissus shook his head regretfully. 'Whether Britannicus or Nero comes to the throne my destruction is inevitable. But Claudius has been so good to me that I would give my life to help him. The criminal intentions for which Messalina was condemned have re-emerged in Agrippina. With Britannicus as his successor the emperor has nothing to fear. But the intrigues of his stepmother in Nero's interests are fatal to the imperial house - more ruinous than if I had said nothing about her predecessor's unfaithfulness. And once more there is unfaithfulness. Agrippina's lover is Pallas. That is the final proof that there is nothing she will not sacrifice to imperial ambition - neither decency, nor honour, nor chastity.'

Epaphroditus drank in his words. 'You seriously think that Agrippina would be prepared to push Nero forward sooner than is necessary?' He topped up his glass, offering the jug to Narcissus, who merely shook his head. 'And she is sleeping with Pallas? You have proof?'

'Not enough to present to the emperor.'

'Pallas has always backed her. He instigated their marriage, not to mention Nero's adoption. It certainly explains a great deal. But still, I had no idea! But tell me, Narcissus, why do you fear for your own safety? Nero would not willingly lose either of us.'

'Not willingly, no. But his mother holds the reins and he will do nothing to obstruct her. The prosecution against Lepida was entirely without foundation. The charges were fabricated by Nero himself. He stood in that courtroom and lied convincingly to condemn the woman he has loved since infancy. It matters not that he was left insensible with grief for two days - he is as dangerous as his mother, for they are one and the same.'

'A chilling thought.' Epaphroditus summoned a slave and called for more wine, privately unconcerned by his colleague's morose pessimism. Narcissus was inclined to brood on his suspicions, which were easily aroused but never so easily allayed. His tales rarely alarmed anyone but himself.

'You need a holiday,' Epaphroditus said, 'why don't you take a short break, go to the country for a while? It will do you good to escape the intrigues of Court.'

Narcissus sighed. 'I suppose I am looking too far ahead, for dangers that don't yet exist. Lepida's trial distressed me far more than I can tell you. Perhaps a holiday would not be such a bad thing; at least until I get my strength back. I have a villa in Sinuessa...'

'There you are, then!' Epaphroditus declared cheerfully, as though the matter were settled. 'I must confess to being frankly envious, Narcissus. For there is nothing I would like more than a break from official business. I have rarely known a busier year; and the year is not yet over!'

'Eventful, yes' Narcissus agreed, 'and you, as secretary, have felt it more than most, I imagine.'

'Quite so!' Epaphroditus warmed to his drinks and emptied his glass far quicker than the last one.' Appointments alone have taken up most of my time; there seems to have been no end to them!'

'I was, of course, instrumental in the final selections,' Narcissus reminded him, 'and it took much effort on my part to over-ride the arguments of Pallas.'

'His candidates having been selected by someone else, of course,' Epaphroditus observed. 'But if you only knew the paperwork such appointments entail! No end of documentation. Do you realise that within the space of summer alone we have filled a position in every official post, from consul down to quaestor! Quite incredible, is it not?'

'There is one higher post yet to become vacant,' Narcissus observed darkly.

'The emperor has many a year left in him yet. Relax, and enjoy your holiday! Here, let me top up your glass.'

Claudius slumbered noisily on the couch at the head of the table, a collection of empty wine pitchers grouped around him to testify to his deep sleep. Agrippina watched him disdainfully.

'What were you discussing during dinner?' she asked Vitellius.

'Nothing of consequence.'

'I chanced to overhear something that I consider to be of great importance, and I should be grateful if you would repeat it.'

'Are you referring to gladiators, horses or the pattern of consecutive throws of a die?'

'I am referring to a remark he made about his wives,' Agrippina said in agitation, remembering the look he had given her as his voice had risen above her own.

'I am afraid I know nothing of any such remark. I have heard his theories on the throwing of dice a thousand times and this evening he lost my interest after the second account of the third race at the Circus.'

'I heard him,' Pallas said.

Agrippina glanced across to where Nero reclined with Otho, and beyond them to Britannicus and Octavia, engrossed in a board game. All were safely out of earshot.

'He said it was his destiny first to endure his wives misdeeds, then to punish them,' Pallas told her.

'And what do you suppose he meant by that?'

Pallas smiled without humour. 'Exactly what he said.'

'But he can't possibly know!'

'He knows nothing of us. And probably very little of anything else that has occurred. But enough, nevertheless, to warrant such a remark.'

'And Narcissus? Narcissus all but threatened me earlier in the year. Is he behind Claudius' sudden malevolence?'

'He is suspicious, certainly. But as yet he has voiced none of his suspicions to the emperor.'

Agrippina fidgeted on her couch nervously, her eyes coming to rest momentarily on Nero and Otho. They were laughing loudly at some private joke of their own and were oblivious to the others in the room.

'How close they are,' Agrippina remarked, almost to herself.

'They always have been,' Vitellius said casually, 'I wouldn't read too much into it myself.'

'I am not happy about any of this,' Agrippina said, her thoughts returning to the subject uppermost in her mind, 'Claudius is plotting something; I feel it in my bones. He knows too much. It is all Narcissus' doing.'

'Narcissus knows nothing!' Pallas retorted scornfully.

'And yet I am to be punished! Claudius as good as told me!'

'He was drunk!' Pallas argued, 'it was probably a reference to Messalina. Half the time he forgets that she is dead!'

Agrippina was not to be reassured. 'Within the past few months there has been a death in every official post - a quaestor, aedile, tribune, praetor and a consul. It is a portent that I am to be next. From consul to one of the imperial house. Claudius intends to do away with me.'

'Mere coincidence,' Pallas said soothingly.

'Coincidence? That they should each die within weeks of one another? And what of the other portents? Soldiers' tents set on fire from the sky! Deformed children born throughout the country! And a swarm of bees settling on the Capitoline temple! If that is not a sign from the gods then I don't know what is!'

'You over react,' Pallas assured her, yet she could not be pacified.

It was the following morning that she finally found relief from the months of anxiety that had plagued her. As she dressed and prepared to visit the baths for the morning Pallas entered and told her of Narcissus' departure.

'Narcissus leaving? For how long?'

Pallas sat down on a stool. 'He isn't certain. He says he will retire to Sinuessa to recover his strength.' He sounded scornful. 'Apparently he has been under immense strain of late.'

'Haven't we all!'

'Some of us soon will be, with this sudden extra burden of work.'

'Oh, don't complain so, Pallas! Don't you realise what this means? Whether in favour or not, you have been thrust upon the emperor and he must involve you in all his plans.'

'And you are still convinced that they include your elimination?'

Agrippina laughed at the very idea. 'He will make no move without Narcissus. He lacks the brains and the initiative.'

'So, then, you are safe for the time being.'

Agrippina grew thoughtful once more. 'For the time being.'

Pallas left her to mull over his news while he went about the day's business. As soon as he had gone, Agrippina hurried through the Palace in search of the eunuch, Halotus. She found him out by the pond, watching the carp as they fed on the breadcrumbs he threw to them.

'A fine morning, is it not?' Agrippina said in greeting, sitting beside him on the edge of the pond.

'Oh it is, my lady.'

'You wait for Nero?'

'Yes, my lady. He is taking me to the stables to watch the horses prepare for next week's racing.'

'Do you go racing often, Halotus?'

Halotus shook his head regretfully. 'No, my lady. I am always required throughout the day, my lady.'

'Oh yes; of course. Does the emperor never spare you? Surely he will allow you the occasional day at the races?'

'Oh no, my lady.' Halotus was shocked at the suggestion.

Agrippina trailed her fingers in the water. 'I regret that the emperor does not treat you fairly.'

Halotus made no comment.

'But still, he must pay you well.'

Halotus proved her wrong by his silence.

'Good grief! You surprise me, Halotus! You are his food taster - you risk your life for him! And he does not reward you for such loyalty?'

'The emperor is good to me,' Halotus said non-committally.

'Good morning, Mother,' Nero said cheerfully, joining them, 'you'll forgive me if I don't stop for a chat, but I promised to take Halotus to the stables with me.'

'So he was just telling me. I trust you treat him more generously than your father appears to. Halotus was just saying that your father's meanness does not extend merely to you and me.'

Halotus fidgeted with embarrassment, having said nothing of the sort. Nero simply laughed, clapping Halotus on the back. 'Don't worry, Mother, I take good care of him; as I do all of my friends.'

'I am very pleased to hear it, my dear. I would hate you to follow the example of your miserly father. Generosity comes from the heart, Nero, and costs nothing but money - of which you have plenty. Your father has money; but he has no friends.'

Nero smiled at her, surprised by her sentiment.

She returned his smile. 'Hurry along now, I wouldn't want you to be late.'

Her smile fell away sharply as she watched them depart. She disapproved of Nero's familiarity with the slaves, but in this instance it suited her plans well.

She returned to her room to fetch her cloak, then set off from the Palace, threading her way through the cobweb of city streets to an apartment in the Esquiline district, where lived an expert on poisons.

Keeping her cloak pulled up around her head, she banged at the door, until it was opened by a dark, slender young woman who ushered her inside.

'You are Locusta?' Agrippina enquired, glancing at the surprisingly smart apartment.

'And you are?'

Agrippina lowered her cloak. 'I am the empress Agrippina. I require a poison.'

Chapter Ten

OCTOBER A.D. 54

'Halotus, I want a word.'

Dinner had ended and the musicians had made their entrance, the imperial household settling back to allow their meal to settle before retiring for the night. Halotus approached the emperor, unconcerned.

'It has come to my attention that you spend much time in the company of my son. That you take him to the stables of the various factions and encourage him to gamble. That you allow him to mix with the many undesirables who frequent such places and that you address him with contemptible familiarity. What have you to say for yourself, Halotus? Hmm?'

Halotus was too stunned to say anything, but his lack of explanation only served to irritate the emperor more.

'You appear to be preying upon an impressionable youth,' Claudius complained sternly, 'I am told you have accepted gifts from him. Is this true? Hmm? Can you deny it?'

'N...no, my Lord,' stammered Halotus.

'Have you no more to say for yourself but that?'

'N...no, my Lord.'

'So be it. Outside with you.'

Claudius emptied his glass as Halotus left the dining hall. He glanced across at Agrippina, who steadfastly ignored him, aware that the intended punishment did not meet with her approval. It gave him all the more pleasure.

Nero seemed to be overly familiar with most of the household slaves and his casual generosity was limitless. Ordinarily Claudius would have ignored the complaints of Pallas, who was no doubt irritated that a slave should receive more than he. It was only when Agrippina, over-hearing, had complained at Pallas' tale telling that Claudius was provoked in to action. He so hated the thought of being manipulated by his wife that he resolved to make an example of Halotus, and perhaps teach Nero a little propriety in the process.

He set his empty glass down on the floor beside him, then gestured to Nero, who looked across at him enquiringly.

'Outside with me, please, Nero.'

Nero shrugged at Otho and followed Claudius out into the anteroom unhurriedly. There he was greeted by a nervous-looking Halotus and grim-faced Claudius.

'Is there a problem?' Nero asked, alarmed by the obvious signs. 'Halotus has done nothing wrong, surely?'

'I suspect that you are as much to blame as he is,' Claudius said sternly, 'but you are above punishment and he is not. That is a lesson that you need to be taught, Nero. A matter of position, which you seem frequently to disregard.'

Claudius clapped his hands and summoned a slave, demanding that a whip be fetched. Nero flinched.

'But Father, what warrants this?'

'Halotus has failed to treat you with the respect you deserve and examples must be set, for the sake of the other slaves.'

'But it is my fault! You know that it is my fault!'

'Then you will accept this as your own punishment.'

Nero's continuing pleas were lost on Claudius, who solemnly dealt out ten lashes of the whip. As the emperor handed the whip back to a slave, Nero stepped forward to offer Halotus assistance, but Claudius put out an arm to stop him. 'Let the slaves tend him; he is hardly hurt.'

Nero glared at him and attempted to push past.

'Aid him, and your familiarity will earn him a more severe flogging.'

Nero hesitated and backed down, admitting defeat. He shot Claudius a defiant glance, his lip glistening with blood, bitten through in the agony of the moment. Feeling its sting for the first time, he flicked his tongue across the barely visible cut.

'I am no more your son than Britannicus.'

He watched the words register in Claudius' eyes, then stepped round him, bristling with rage and frustration, to retreat to his own room. But he found no sanctuary there.

Octavia reposed on the bed, reading through a letter. He had not even noticed her absence during dinner and recoiled at her unwelcome presence.

'Can you not read elsewhere? I wish to retire.'

She said nothing, but moved to the desk.

He flopped down wearily onto the bed, but was not tired and could not think of sleep.

Otho entered without knocking, not expecting to interrupt man and wife. He nodded to Octavia with no more than obligatory politeness, which she ignored, then sat down on the bed.

'What did the emperor want? I was expecting you back straight away.'

'It seems that I am not to be allowed to talk to the slaves. I must issue written orders, as Pallas does, should mere hand signals be insufficient.'

'Ouch! Such bitterness!' Otho teased, surprised by Nero's tone.

'It is no joke,' Nero said, raising himself up on one elbow, 'I had to witness Halotus' flogging, for which I am entirely responsible.'

'Why? What had he done?'

'He had accompanied me to the stables and accepted my gifts. For which he received ten lashes.' Nero raised his voice and looked across at Octavia. 'These are the actions of the father you so love.'

Octavia did not turn round. 'Since you have done no more than marry into the imperial house, I cannot expect you to have any understanding of propriety and the maintenance of position it entails. I pity you for your ignorance.'

Otho swung round. 'Forgive me, Octavia, but I was of the belief that it was you who had married in to the imperial house?! My friend here has the distinction of being the emperor's son, while you are no more than the daughter of an emperor's prostitute!' He grinned at Nero as Octavia stiffened visibly. She gathered up her papers with unseemly haste and left the room without another word.

'I wonder that you don't give her a room of her own,' Otho remarked.

'I would gladly do so, but Mother will not allow it.'

'Ah yes! The happy union between the Prince Of Youth and the emperor's beloved daughter, that has brought so much joy to the hearts of the commons!'

Nero smiled. 'It is too early for sleep, and yet I cannot face Claudius this evening.'

'Senecio and I were waiting for you to sit down to a game of cards in my room.'

'Then I shall!'

Nero rose with sudden, forced cheeriness and made an effort to forget the troubles of the evening. He did not return to his own room until the following morning, entering as Octavia was dressing. She hurriedly pulled on her tunic, irritated by his lack of decency.

'It is customary to knock before entering a lady's room,' she complained icily.

'It is my room; and, as my wife, you have nothing to hide from me.'

'Wife in name only!' She thought back to the insulting words of Otho the night before and her eyes narrowed. 'But that sort of wife suits you, does it not? For then you can spend your nights with Otho.'

Nero was not to be riled. He smiled without concern.

'Who says I spend my nights with Otho? Perhaps he is a little too old for my tastes. I may even look for a younger boy to satisfy my needs.' His blue eyes burned into her. 'If the sister will not oblige me, perhaps the brother might?'

She swallowed, unable to voice her hatred. Furious at her own failure to retaliate, she snatched up her toiletry case and stormed out of the room, to visit the baths. His smile haunted her; teasing and provocative. She hoped that he intended only to tease. He was too casual by nature to exhibit any real vindictiveness. And yet he had callously prosecuted his aunt, and those cold blue eyes shone only too frequently with spite. She shuddered at his words. But that, of course, had been his only intention. To hurt her, and not Britannicus. She tried to reassure herself, but the doubt lingered.

Agrippina was just leaving the baths as Octavia entered. They ignored each other with their usual frostiness, although Agrippina detected a sharper edge in her daughter-in-law's coldness. But it was not enough to spoil her own good mood. She was never happier than when watching people fall into her schemes unwittingly, her subtle manipulation making puppets out of them.

She put her toiletry case into her room and exchanged it for a basket of sweetmeats and fruit, together with a small purse of gold pieces. Then she hurried down to that part of the Palace occupied by the slaves, where she quickly located the room Halotus shared with some of his colleagues. Halotus was fortunately alone, his services not yet required, but he jumped up from his bed hastily as Agrippina entered.

'Please, please - be seated,' Agrippina assured him, herself taking a seat on one of the other beds. 'I have fetched you a small gift from Nero. Obviously he cannot come here himself, nor extend his deep regret to you personally. But he hopes that this small token will make amends for the distress he has caused you. It was never, of course, his intention.'

Halotus accepted the basket. 'You may assure the Prince that I was not caused distress; nor do I hold him in any way responsible.'

Agrippina smiled regretfully. 'No; of course you don't. We all know the person responsible for these distasteful events. I only hope that he does not intend to come down any harder on my son.'

Halotus said nothing, uncomfortable in her presence and hoping that she would leave. Agrippina sensed his discomfort and stood up.

'Well, I have other tasks to attend to. But Nero was most insistent that I should visit you first thing. I will not take up any more of your free time, Halotus. I wish you well.' She smiled graciously and left him to examine his gift.

Her next stop was at Nero's room, where he reclined on his bed going through the paperwork Claudius had given him.

'I hope you have not fetched me more work, Mother,' he said, glancing up to smile in welcome, then quickly returning to the task in hand.

'No; I merely came to tell you that I chanced to meet Halotus this morning. He is well and suffering no ill effects from his beating, which he assures me was minor. But he sends you his apologies, for he will no longer be able to associate with you.'

'What brought it on, do you suppose?'

'Your father's sudden strictness? Britannicus, I believe. He is still only a child, and you know how spiteful they can be. He runs to his father with tales at every available opportunity.'

'It is not my fault that he is jealous of me,' Nero complained, 'his own father shuts him out and favours me. Or, at least, did until recently.'

'Sometimes I cannot fathom your dear father at all,' Agrippina said with fondness.

Nero looked up at her and smiled.

'Anyway,' Agrippina said, turning to leave, 'I have much to do. But please remember to behave with more decorum, for a little while, at least. For you came dangerously close to a beating yourself.'

She returned to Halotus' room later that night, when the Palace was quiet and most of the household had retired to bed. Claudius' own late night had kept Halotus up later than usual and his roommates were already sleeping soundly as he prepared for bed. Agrippina tapped at his door gently and gestured to him to speak with her outside. He followed her to one end of the hall, hesitant and full of puzzlement.

'Halotus, I am here to throw myself on your mercy,' Agrippina confessed, her voice heavy with fear. 'If you refuse me, then I beg only that you do not betray me, for the sake of Nero. I can bear to see his suffering no more.' She thrust a purse and a small jar into his hand, much to his bewilderment. 'The purse contains twenty gold pieces,' she told him, 'and the jar contains a powder from the poisoner, Locusta. If you accept the purse, I ask that you sprinkle the contents of the jar onto Claudius' mushrooms tomorrow at dinner. The taste will not be apparent and the affect, I am assured, will be immediate.'

Halotus stared at her in amazement. His fingers closed around the heavy purse.

'It will not have to cover the price of your freedom,' Agrippina added, 'for that is assured to you as a gift, should Nero become emperor.'

Halotus' grip tightened. He lowered his eyes, unable to face Agrippina. 'Thank you, my lady,' he said simply, and turned away.

Agrippina could barely contain her delight as she hurried back to the bed that she would share with Claudius for the last time.

Chapter Eleven

OCTOBER A.D. 54

The family meal was no different than normal. Britannicus reclined at one of the lower tables, with the other children of the Court. Octavia was in the company of Albia Otho, while her husband reclined with Albia's son. Agrippina lay at the head table, on a couch alongside the emperor. He was drunk, as usual, and had commandeered the unwilling attention of Vitellius.

Halotus, as always, served the emperor personally, having first sampled the food himself. He took one of the lesser mushrooms from the plate, taking care to save a particularly large and succulent mushroom for the emperor. Claudius cleared the plate with relish and flopped back down on the couch, his speech exhausted and the trickle of saliva from his mouth turning to a torrent. Agrippina watched him expectantly.

'Is he all right, do you think?' she asked Vitellius, after a while.

Vitellius glanced at him. 'Just a drunken stupor.'

'He looks a little glazed to me,' Agrippina said doubtfully, 'I think it might be as well summon Xenophon.' She rose from her couch, telling Vitellius that she had no wish to alarm the slaves unduly and that she would therefore fetch the emperor's doctor herself. She looked down at Claudius as she passed him. If the poison had had any affect at all then it was lost in the general affect of the alcohol.

She found Xenophon in his quarters and came straight to the point.

'I have reason to believe that the emperor has been poisoned,' she told him calmly. 'He appears to be in no more than a drunken stupor. I want him taken to his room, where you will administer a second dose. In return, you may ask anything of me that you wish. A country estate, money - the choice is yours.'

Xenophon considered the offer.

'If you refuse, then I shall be forced to find a different use for the lethal dose,' Agrippina added, impatient at his indecisiveness.

Her final argument swayed him. He followed her to the dining hall, where he feigned great concern at the emperor's digestive system.

'He is merely drunk,' Vitellius told him, amused by his antics.

'The drink does him no good at all,' Xenophon announced to anyone who would listen, 'it has no doubt precipitated this collapse.'

'Very astute, my good doctor!' Vitellius laughed.

'You and you!' Xenophon ordered, pointing to two of the slaves, 'Help the emperor to his bedchamber.'

'Try two more,' Vitellius advised, grinning.

'Shut up, Spintria!' Agrippina snapped, looking concerned, 'this is no joking matter!'

Claudius was carried to his bedchamber and Xenophon pulled out a feather and a potion from his box. 'I must make him vomit,' the doctor declared, 'to expel the bad humours that disturb his stomach.' He dipped the feather into the bottle Agrippina had earlier given him and slid it down the emperor's throat, applying the poison thickly. Claudius gasped and shuddered violently, then lay still.

'Clear the room, clear the room!' Xenophon cried, ushering out all but Agrippina.

'Is he dead?' Agrippina asked, looking at the still body.

'He is, my lady. On top of what has already been administered, death was instantaneous.'

'Stay with him. I have arrangements to make. He is not yet dead, Xenophon. I need him alive for the time being. I will see to it that no one enters.'

Agrippina swept through the Palace and into the dining hall.

'The emperor is gravely ill,' she announced, her voice trembling, 'Xenophon is with him, but no one is to see him; he is not to be disturbed, under any circumstances. His life depends upon it.'

Octavia rose from her couch. 'I must go to him at once!'

Agrippina hastened to her side and embraced her, the tears beginning to fall. 'No, my child; even I cannot be permitted to see him. He needs peace.'

'I will just sit by his side!' Octavia protested, crying.

'Let her go, Mother,' Nero pleaded, 'she can surely do no harm.'

'I wish that I could!' Agrippina sobbed, 'But Xenophon insists. He is treating my poor dear Claudius. Let the poor man have his dignity and be tended in private. Xenophon will call us in at the first opportunity, you may be sure.' She pulled both her children close to her and fought to control her own tears. 'Claudius will be well again; don't fret so, my dears. I have every faith in Xenophon. Why, Claudius fetched him to Rome as the best that money could buy and has trusted him all these years! Of course your dear father will live. Of course he will.'

Halotus began to wail loudly, convinced of Claudius' recovery and of his own doom. Agrippina let go of Nero and Octavia and attended him at once.

'He's dead,' she hissed, under her breath, then said gently, 'Please don't fret so, Halotus, you'll only distress the others. The emperor is gravely ill, but we must hope for his recovery. We cannot give way to tears as though he is already dead.'

Octavia took comfort in her words and made a visible effort to compose herself. Nero was no less upset himself and made a hesitant attempt to embrace her and offer what comfort he could; but she pushed him away roughly, her tears turning to rage.

'It's a wonder you can contain your pleasure! Isn't this what you have longed for? To be emperor!'

Albia hugged Octavia to her breast and shook her head at Nero, to let the remark go. He felt the wound deeply, but gestured towards the lower table where Britannicus sat, sobbing in bewilderment. Albia nodded and led Octavia down to her brother, who at once clung to her.

Vitellius sat in silence, regretting his earlier flippancy.

Otho stood up and wandered across to Nero.

'Are you all right?'

Nero nodded, the shock of the occasion abating slightly.

'Come on; we'll go and wait in your room,' Otho suggested, looking round. 'Where is your mother?'

Nero glanced around him. 'I don't know. I didn't see her leave.'

'She is probably with Claudius; I can't see her accepting orders from Xenophon!'

Nero smiled.

They walked back to his room in silence, slaves bustling to and fro in great agitation. The whole Palace seemed prepared for the worst. Otho pulled the door shut and sat on the bed. Nero simply stood, for a while; deep in thought.

'If he dies, then I am to be emperor,' he said at last, his voice concealing whatever emotion he felt.

'That cannot be a bad thing,' Otho pointed out realistically.

Nero said nothing.

'What is there to dread?' Otho asked. 'You already have too much work to do. As emperor, you will have a large staff at your disposal. Narcissus, for one. If anything, your workload should decrease. You will be thrown under the control of the senate, of the freedmen here in the Palace, of the people. But you will hold the reins. Not your mother. Not Claudius. Life, in general, can only improve.'

Nero sat down beside him.

'Hold me.'

Agrippina sat in consultation with her astrologers, not at all happy with their advice.

'It will be soon,' they assured her for the second time, 'very soon, but the time is not yet right.'

'This cannot continue for any length of time,' Agrippina insisted.

'Nor will it need to, my lady. The perfect time is almost within sight. But to present your son as emperor before then would be a grave risk.'

'Well, thank you,' she said grudgingly, 'there is little more that can be done this evening. We will meet tomorrow.' She stood up and left them to their charts.

She entered her own room without knocking and looked with distaste at the body on the bed.

'We may have to keep up the pretence tomorrow. I had hoped it would be for this evening alone,' she told Xenophon as she gathered up her belongings to take to a guestroom. 'I will look in on you in the morning. Don't look so dismayed, Xenophon - you will be paid handsomely for this.'

The following morning she summoned the senate and announced that the emperor's condition was grave. Priests and consuls offered prayers for the emperor, while Agrippina appeared throughout the day, issuing frequent and encouraging announcements about his health.

She returned to her astrologers, to be told that the following day, at a precise hour, she should present the new emperor. Delighted with this news, she immediately summoned Burrus, the Commander of the Guard.

'Burrus,' she began gravely, 'I have been told by the imperial doctor that the emperor is unlikely to live through the night. We must therefore prepare for the worst.'

'I am sorry to hear that, my lady,' Burrus said respectfully, though he suspected that she did not share his sorrow. 'Has the emperor indicated as to who will succeed him?'

'Many hoped he would finally favour Britannicus, I know. But his mind has for long been set on Nero. I rely upon you, Commander, to ensure that that choice is a popular one.'

'You have my assurance of that, my lady.'

'I would like you to spend today with Nero. Prepare him for what is to come. Seneca will join you and discuss speeches and procedures. Between you both I have no doubt that Rome will accept her new leader.'

'Yes, my lady.' Burrus bowed to her courteously, then took his leave.

He had been waiting for this summons since he was first appointed Commander. He had known then that he was to be an ally to Nero; having replaced known sympathisers to Britannicus. The fact that Nero was now sixteen, proven in maturity to handle matters of State, married to Octavia in what was a very popular union, and now suddenly coming to power, seemed to be something more than happy coincidence; too convenient and far too contrived.

He didn't go instantly to Nero's room, but instead to the room of Seneca, where he was welcomed with a caution that mirrored his own.

'You have spoken with Agrippina?' Seneca asked.

'I have indeed. Her conviction that the emperor will not live through the night raises a great many suspicions. I felt, from her manner, that the old emperor is already gone and a new one in his place.'

'Sit down, Burrus. There is much to discuss.'

Burrus did as he was directed, sensing that he had found a friend and ally in whom he could trust. 'If Nero's succession has been contrived,' he asked cautiously, 'is he himself aware of it?'

'No; and nor must he ever be,' Seneca said with conviction.

'I have met the boy on a number of occasions and I have never failed to be impressed by him. But you will know better than any - is he up to this?'

'Most assuredly so. But he will need help.'

'And who do we have to fear?'

'Ah! There now is the hub of the matter, eh?'

'I was instructed to go straight to Nero. But I needed to know his position first.'

'Quite.' Seneca considered his words carefully. 'You will enjoy working with Nero; and it is imperative that he should enjoy your company and trust you implicitly. Provided Narcissus returns to us promptly and in good health we will not be working alone. But everyone else - Nero included - is under the control of Agrippina. And she is the one we have to fear.'

Burrus nodded, his own instinct now confirmed.

'Are you happy about this accession?' Seneca enquired as he showed Burrus out.

'Very much so. It marks the beginning of a new era.'

'I'm glad you think so, for I share that view. The old emperor and I never did see eye to eye and I have groomed Nero for this role since my return to Rome.'

'Well it certainly marks a new era for ourselves, my friend,' Burrus said with sincerity, 'I will go and meet with our new emperor now. And I look forward to you joining us later.'

At midday on 13th October the Palace gates were thrown open and Nero stepped out, accompanied by Burrus. The battalion on duty immediately acclaimed him as emperor, as he stood on the Palace steps. Required to give a password to the Colonel on duty, he gave 'The Best Of Mothers'. Overawed by the occasion, he allowed them to put him in a litter and take him to the Guards' camp, where Burrus announced his accession. He was hailed as emperor by the delighted troops, whereupon he delivered a brief speech, warming to the response he received and taking immense pleasure in addressing so adoring an audience.

Having received the support and loyalty of the Guard, he was taken to the Curia of Julius Caesar, where the senate sat. The three hundred seats, rising up in three tiers, were insufficient for the members who had pressed into the Curia at the first indication of a change of emperor. It was a far cry from the half empty house Nero had first addressed three years earlier.

He remained at the Curia until nightfall, doing nothing but accept the variety of senatorial decrees voted to him. The only honour he refused was 'Father Of The Country', which seemed to him to be laughingly inappropriate for a boy of sixteen. Throughout the afternoon, the provinces sent messages of congratulations, showing no hesitation in accepting him as emperor.

Having begun the day with trepidation, still mourning the father he had so suddenly lost, he ended it on a high, honoured by the senate and overwhelmed by the power and opportunity thrust upon him.

The following day he gave Claudius a lavish funeral, sparing no expense and basing it upon that of Augustus. The funeral procession, accompanied by forty Praetorians as guard of honour, passed through the Triumphal Gate and paused by the Forum, where Nero himself gave the eulogy. He praised Claudius highly; recounting the consulships and Triumphs of the emperor and his ancestors and giving particular praise to his literary accomplishments. When he attempted to speak of Claudius' foresight and wisdom he was prevented by the laughter of his audience and was forced to stop, but he concluded his eulogy by deifying him.

The emperor's body was then shouldered by a party of senators and carried to a pyre on the Campus Martius, where his ashes were later gathered by leading knights, who took them to the family mausoleum.

After the funeral, Nero attended the senate and acknowledged its support, as well as the backing of the army. He praised the memory of his late father Gnaeus Ahenobarbus and bestowed upon Agrippina every honour that she didn't yet hold. Finally, he spoke of his advisors and declared,

'I bring with me no feud, no resentment or vindictiveness. No civil war, no family quarrels, clouded my early years.'

He then outlined his future policy and renounced everything that had proven unpopular in recent years.

'I will not judge every kind of case myself,' he concluded, 'and give too free rein to the influence of a few individuals by hearing prosecutors and defendants behind my closed doors. From my house, bribery and favouritism will be excluded. I will keep personal and state affairs separate. The senate is to preserve its ancient functions. By applying to the consuls, people from Italy and the senatorial provinces may have access to its tribunals. I myself will look after the armies under my control.'

He soaked up the standing ovation and looked around him at the crowded house. Where once he had longed for no more than to be an actor or charioteer, he now felt that he had achieved his one ambition in life. This was his one true role, his destiny. He raised his head, choking back the sudden overwhelming emotion, and smiled broadly at his audience, his blue eyes glistening. He was Nero Caesar - emperor of Rome.

Chapter Twelve

NOVEMBER A.D. 54

Nero strode purposefully down the great loggia, head raised, arms swinging; still acting out with enjoyable exaggeration his role as emperor. He espied Octavia at the far end of the loggia, walking Britannicus back from his classes and his self-mocking exuberance vanished. She eyed him warily, managing to contain her own loathing which was so apparent on the face of her brother.

Nero stopped as they approached and smiled genially. His fabricated warmth was greeted by undisguised hostility.

'How caring of you to escort your charming little brother to his room,' Nero remarked, 'do you keep watch over him continuously?'

Octavia's jaw tensed. 'If necessary.'

Nero's gaze fell on the key clutched in the young boy's hand. 'No need to cling so tightly,' he said casually, 'for I have plenty more should you lose it. This is my Palace now and one of my rooms in which you sleep at night. Or not; as the case may be.' He directed his words at Britannicus, but kept his eyes on Octavia, smiling at her with irritating smugness. Britannicus' eyes widened in horror at the implication, but Octavia's expression remained blank.

'You are the emperor,' she said coldly, 'you have no one to appease but your own conscience.'

Nero grinned and stepped to one side, letting them pass with a sweeping gesture of his arm.

'Sweet dreams, my little one,' he called after them, his eyes twinkling with fun.

Once within his own room his high spirits died away. His workload was immense and there was little time for frivolity. The sight of Pallas reclining on his bed rid him of any remaining good humour.

'I expected you back sooner,' Pallas said, as though issuing a severe reprimand.

'It takes time to persuade the senate to accept new policies,' Nero pointed out stiffly. 'Today I succeeded in forbidding advocates to receive fees or gifts, so that justice may prevail rather than wealth.'

Pallas snorted mockingly. 'Well done, my Lord. So your morning has not been wasted, after all.'

The heavy sarcasm annoyed Nero. 'Let me remind you of the purpose of such an edict,' he said with the same stiffness. ' "what uses are laws where money is king, where poverty's helpless and can't win a thing?" '

'So your policies are based on the rhymes of Petronius? How admirable. No wonder that Narcissus will not return to your service. He favours the policies of a boy who lacks your classical education.'

'Have you had word from him?' Nero asked keenly.

'Not *from* him, no. But I have news *on* him.'

'Your petty jealousies do not interest me.'

'Oh, but they do, my Lord. I have had to go through his papers, in order to cover for him. They make for disturbing reading, my Lord. Narcissus is a traitor. He remains in Sinuessa not for the good of his health, but for his reluctance to serve you.' He clicked his fingers to summon the attention of a slave and pointed to the jug of water by his side, taking care not to look at the slave serving him.

'If it's no trouble, Helos,' Nero asked the slave, 'perhaps you might put the jug closer to Pallas, so that he need not exert himself further. It has been a long time since his own days as a slave; he forgets that you may not have time for such trivialities.'

Pallas glared at Nero in fury, but the young emperor ignored him and pretended to study a document.

'I have here documents intended to benefit Britannicus,' Pallas continued, his voice heavy with menace, 'information gathered for the boy, at his request, from private files. If, when he comes of age, he intends to take your place, this information - so well presented by Narcissus - will be his means.'

'And had our positions been reversed,' Nero pointed out, 'you would now be condemning Narcissus to Britannicus for attempting to aid me in a similar fashion. He has done as much work for me during Claudius' reign as he has done for Britannicus. You waste my time with your unfounded allegations. Helos, if you please, be so good as to show my visitor out.'

'I will show myself out!' Pallas snapped, furious at this final insult.

Nero grinned at Helos. 'A pity he couldn't have bought manners as well as his freedom!' he remarked as Pallas pulled the door shut behind him; knowing that he could still be heard by the freedman. ' "Even cynics who sneer are rarely averse to selling their scruples to fill up their purse"!' he called out loudly, continuing his earlier recital of Petronius' poem. 'We need not wonder how Pallas amassed his vast wealth, eh, Helos?!'

Outside, Pallas froze in his tracks, seething with fury. He looked down at the bundle of papers in his hand and only just resisted the urge to hurl them to the ground. He returned to Agrippina's room and gave vent to his feelings in her hearing.

'Oh let him ignore the charges,' she said without concern, 'Narcissus is a weak and over-anxious man; he doesn't need to be charged by Nero. The possibility alone is enough to destroy him.' She lay down on the bed and began to write a brief letter. 'We will send him the papers and the damaging conclusions drawn from them and we will point out that they are now in the hands of the emperor, who is deliberating upon which course of action to take. On the strength of the evidence there is only one action to take. Narcissus, if brought to trial, would be condemned, and he knows it. He does not need to know that Nero has disregarded the evidence and that there will be no trial.'

'And if he decides to take his chances in the courtroom?'

'Of course he won't! Would you? Condemned to death, dishonour brought to your name, the best part of your estate confiscated and your will rendered worthless?! What price would you pay for your honour, Pallas?'

He didn't reply, accepting the truth in her argument.

She sealed her letter and a variety of papers with it, handing them to Pallas.

'Have these dispatched to Narcissus immediately. It will prove every bit as affective as a death warrant from Nero's own hand, I assure you.' She smiled with satisfaction.

Burrus and Seneca made their way through the Palace, to spend the afternoon with Nero. Their conversation was hushed and hurried for they had no wish to continue it in his presence. It concerned the sudden death of Marcus Silanus, whose brother had once been prosecuted and condemned by Agrippina as a favour to Vitellius.

'Silanus must have done something to alert Agrippina to the threat of revenge,' Seneca speculated.

'Whatever his words or actions, he did not deserve death.'

'It is the openness of his murder that so disturbs me,' Seneca continued, 'the complete lack of secrecy. Poisoned at his own dinner table by a knight and one of his own freedmen, without any fear of retribution. It is known that Agrippina arranged his murder; and patently clear that she also arranged for their protection from justice. It is enough that her own lack of conscience and shame place us all in grave danger. Now she has snatched away any legal protection we could hope for. She behaves as though she is above the law.'

'Unfortunately, she is.'

They knocked at Nero's door and were welcomed by one of his slaves. Nero himself reclined on the bed with Otho, while Petronius and Senecio lay on a couch facing them.

'What have you done to keep her acerbic tongue so still?' Otho was saying, as Nero stretched forward to move an ivory chariot across a game board, 'Cut it out?!'

Nero laughed. 'Nothing so outrageous! I simply hinted that Britannicus might not have reason to sleep so well at night; and I accompanied the suggestion with looks and gestures that would have done the great Mnester proud! She lives in constant fear for his innocence! As does the boy himself, which is a happy bonus!'

'Huh! Where did you learn such tricks?!' Petronius exclaimed.

'Octavia is a master tutor in such tactics,' Otho told him, 'my friend here has learned from the very best!'

'Then I wish she was more often in our company,' said Petronius, 'she would enliven it no end!'

'I fear you mock the dignity of a great lady,' Seneca interrupted them reprovingly, 'you confuse refinement with acidity.'

'You clearly do not keep company with her,' Nero corrected him. He left the ivory chariots immobile on their board and gave the new arrivals his full attention. 'You are here on business, I take it?'

Burrus nodded. 'There is no need to break up the party. It is nothing confidential.'

'I represent the populace,' Nero pointed out, 'my business should never be confidential.'

'True, but neither should it be lampooned over a dinner party!' Otho remarked, directing his comment at Petronius.

'Were I not renowned for my after dinner speeches I should starve!' Petronius protested.

'Yes, well you'll find no subject matter here,' Seneca informed him, 'at least, not that you would dare to use in a satirical manner.'

'I presume you refer to my mother?' Nero said wearily. 'Has she made any new move to block my latest decree?'

'She seems resigned to it. Her main objection, of course, is that it is a reversal of Claudius' legislation.

'Claudius lived for gladiatorial displays; he would have made it obligatory for all citizens to hold such shows, given the chance!' Nero complained lightly, 'But the cost of them is unreasonable and I cannot see why anyone should be compelled to host such a show, least of all those in the lower ranks just setting out on a senatorial career. Financial impositions of this sort serve only to heighten the elitism of office. With or without my mother's approval, I shall decree that quaestors-designate be excused the obligation to hold gladiatorial displays, and I will see that it is passed.'

'She does not intend to fight you,' Seneca assured him, 'but I have arranged for her attendance at the meeting, on the Palatine. A door has been built on at the rear to enable her to listen to proceedings, unseen, from behind a curtain. Our failure to allow for this provision would have tempted her into a breaking of protocol, which you could not afford to risk so early in your reign. When you are firmly established in the hearts of the public, Agrippina will be excused any liberty she may care to take.'

'You need not justify your actions to me, Seneca; you have my full approval. It goes hand in hand with my trust.'

'Thank you, my Lord.'

Nero looked up at him and gave a wry smile. '*My Lord*? My knuckles still smart from the repeated raps I received for talking too much in class! It is still me, Seneca!'

Petronius smiled. 'Allow him the friendship of an emperor, my Lord, not of an upstart ex-pupil! One can take a pride in the former, but not in the latter!'

'So my friendship is worthless compared to that of an emperor?' Nero protested.

'In a nutshell, yes!' agreed Petronius, amid the laughter of his companions.

'And if I abdicated, you would desert me?'

'Not at all!' Petronius objected, 'We would love you just as dearly. But we would not boast about it!'

' "Friendship's a word and friends know its value -
 The counters slide merrily all through the game -
 Your friends broadly smiling, while fortune was by you:
 Their backs even broader when trouble came." '
recited Nero.

Petronius winced. 'You honour me with your memory, but do us all an injustice with your choice of my work.

'You are not the fair-weather friends of the poem,' Nero assured them all, 'but those you strive to impress. Boast of me if you so wish, but friendships gained by such a method will be false.'

'Who mentioned friendship?' Petronius asked in surprise, 'we seek only to gain favours!'

'You are all incorrigible frauds!'

'But wealthy frauds!'

'And noisy ones!' Burrus interrupted, 'You all seem to forget that Seneca and I came here to discuss business!'

'Forgive my disreputable hangers-on,' Nero apologised with a grin, 'and tell me your news.'

'Seneca has already spoken of the meeting on the Palatine to excuse quaestors-designate the burden of hosting gladiatorial shows,' Burrus reminded himself, 'and I assume you have your oration already prepared.

'There are, of course, the usual number of minor cases to come before you, but you need no prior notice on any of them. But an Armenian delegation seeks an audience with you and has a case to plead against the Parthians. There is considerable trouble across their borders and a strong likelihood that these minor disputes could escalate. I think the situation warrants careful discussion before you hear the delegation.'

'Would tomorrow morning be too soon for you?' Nero asked.

'It would be ideal. I have the reports to hand already.'

'Good. Then we'll deal with it first thing in the morning. Is there threat of war?'

'Too soon to say,' Burrus said non-committaly, 'my own reports suggest that war is a distinct possibility, but we must first hear what the Armenians have to say.'

'Could you leave the reports with me, this evening?' Nero asked.

'Certainly. It would be better for you to peruse them at your leisure, so that we might discuss the situation in greater depth tomorrow.'

Nero regarded him thoughtfully. Burrus had not offered the reports freely, but had arranged a meeting seemingly to explain his own decisions. Nero was conscious of his own youth and lack of experience alongside so competent a commander, but was set on proving himself able for his position. He asked Burrus to fetch the reports immediately and dismissed his friends; determined to make the trust and respect he felt for Burrus a mutual feeling.

DECEMBER A.D. 54

As the New Year fast approached, news arrived that the Parthians had broken out and were plundering Armenia. In Rome there was great concern that an emperor of only just seventeen, in power for less than three months, would not be able to cope with the situation.

The Armenian delegation was heard, but not without the murmurings of scandal. As they pleaded their case before Nero, Agrippina - her vanity soaring to new heights - walked across to the emperor's dais, with the clear intent of mounting it and sitting beside him. Everyone present was stupefied and only the quick reaction of Seneca averted scandal. He told Nero to advance and meet his mother, which Nero did. But the actions of Agrippina made it plain where the true power lay, and the lack of confidence in Rome's leadership increased.

As Burrus met with Nero to finalise stratagem in the Parthanian conflict, he did not share those doubts. Having expected the full burden of command to fall on his shoulders, he had been proved pleasantly wrong. His own advice had been unnecessary and the input from Nero every bit as valid as his own.

Burrus found Nero in the company only of Epaphroditus, his secretary, and welcomed the unusual privacy.

'What is the situation?' Nero asked immediately, as Burrus took a seat.

'Unchanged. King Radamistus has once more lost his power in Armenia, and King Vologeses of Parthia has taken control. The Armenians are as much our dependants as the Parthians and must be given our full protection.'

'Vologeses has the advantage,' Nero remarked thoughtfully. 'Radamistus has seized control of Armenia on numerous occasions, only to be ejected just as convincingly. He is unreliable and clearly unwanted by the Armenians.'

'But the Parthians cannot be allowed to plunder our dependent nations at will. And certainly not at the expense of Armenian citizens, of whom Parthia now holds vast numbers captive.'

'Corbulo and Quadratus are our commanders there. How do you rate their ability?'

'Corbulo is a strict disciplinarian; excessively so. His legions are solid and we may depend fully upon them. Quadratus is unproven in combat, but seems confident. He too can rely on the loyalty of his troops.'

'But their numbers are insufficient, particularly as I detect a note of doubt in your voice as you speak of Quadratus. I want the eastern divisions brought up to full strength by drafts from the neighbouring provinces, and they must proceed towards Armenia immediately.' Nero paused and looked down at the maps laid out before him. 'Instruct King Agrippa and King Epiphanes, of Commagene, to prepare an army and invade Parthia. And to protect the borders here,' he tapped the map as he considered his options, 'give Lesser Armenia and Sophene to Aristobulus and Sohaemus respectively, with royal status. They will be only too willing to fight with us to protect their kingdoms. In addition, it is imperative that the Euphrates be bridged.'

'These do seem to be our best options,' Burrus agreed, 'I shall see that your orders are carried out immediately.' He stood up to leave. 'By the way,' he added with sincere regret, 'I was very sorry to hear about Narcissus.'

Nero nodded numbly.

'I just don't know what to say,' Burrus said helplessly, feeling that he should add more, 'it was such a shock.'

'He was under a far greater strain than any of us imagined,' Nero said sadly, 'that he preferred to take his own life than return to the pressures of Rome is testimony. He is greatly missed, Burrus.'

The commander nodded silently.

In Parthia, the absence of the army provided an opportune moment for revolt. A son of King Vardanes, long ago overthrown by Vologeses, attempted to seize control and the Parthians evacuated Armenia, just as the Roman forces revealed their full power. Vologeses had the full intention of resuming hostilities just as soon as his domestic affairs had been put in order, but neither Corbulo nor Quadratus were aware of the internal disputes and quickly drew the wrong conclusions. Messages were sent back to the senate that the Parthian forces had withdrawn, while the two Roman commanders sent messengers to Vologeses advising him to choose peace, not war, and to demonstrate his respect for Rome by giving hostages. This presented Vologeses with the perfect opportunity to eliminate suspected rivals and, under the guise of hostages, he duly handed over leading Parthian royalties.

Celebrations to mark the successful conclusion of the war lasted until well into the New Year. As though to mask its initial doubt, the senate proposed exaggerated tributes to the young emperor. In a day of thanksgiving, Nero donned the Triumphal robe and entered the city in ovation. His statue was erected in the Temple of Mars The Avenger, matching in size that of the God himself. Nero requested the senate to authorise statues of his late father Gnaeus Ahenobarbus, but declined the offer to erect gold and silver statues of himself. He also vetoed, with some amusement, the senatorial decree that all future years were to begin in December, to honour the month of his birth; thereby retaining the old religious custom of beginning the new year on 1st January.

Serving his first consulship at the unprecedented age of seventeen, Nero exempted his fellow consul, Lucius Vetus, from swearing allegiance to the emperor's acts and, in so doing, earned the exaggerated praise and admiration of the senate, who saw a ruler willing to work with them rather than a tyrant wishing only to exert his own power.

And so ended an eventful year. Nero looked back on it with feelings that bordered on bewilderment, but looked to the new year with an enthusiasm that flooded the Palace and filled his friends with an infectious zeal.

Chapter Thirteen

FEBRUARY A.D. 55

The great banqueting hall at the home of Calenus had been newly adorned with statues and paintings; the couches, richly encrusted with precious stones, were clearly new for the occasion. The full body of household slaves had been called in to serve their master's illustrious guest; among these slaves was Acte, a slight, dark girl, in her mid-twenties, whose tasks normally confined her to the bed chambers, where she waited on female visitors and assisted the great ladies with their dressing and toilet. Like many of her colleagues, she was over-awed by the occasion and grateful that she was required only to remove empty plates from those guests seated in her designated area. If nervousness overcame her, she could do less damage with empty vessels than full ones. Calenus himself had been careful to keep his usual dining staff in the areas he intended to assign to his more important guests. Chambermaids such as Acte would be waiting on the lesser entourage of the emperor.

That, at least, had been the plan. But as Calenus proudly led Nero into the hall, it was not the exquisite furnishings and the vast display of wealth in the shape of objets d'art that caught the emperor's eye.

'Ah, you have a portrait of Lupus displayed!' Nero exclaimed with obvious approval. He all-but bounded across to the painting and examined it more closely. 'I support the Green team myself, but Lupus is the best charioteer of our time, I have to acknowledge. But I must remain loyal to the Greens and admire the skills of Lupus with the wariness of a partisan. They have such fine horses in the Green stable, you see.'

As he sank down onto a couch directly below the portrait he appeared to be expecting a reply of some sort, but Calenus was too flustered to think of a suitable response. Nero had seated himself in the most inappropriate of places and Calenus could think of no polite way of moving him. To add to the embarrassment of their host, the emperor's companions - his close friends and freedmen - were already settling down on the surrounding couches, arranged horseshoe fashion around that chosen by Nero.

Nero gazed up at Calenus with blue, unblinking eyes. The enthusiasm in his conversation and the earnestness in his expression were those of a teenage boy; not an emperor. Calenus found it disconcerting. His visions of the emperor had been only of stiffness and propriety. They had not included a seventeen-year-old boy. He had hoped, moreover, for an emperor easily impressed by wealth and fine entertainment. This boy appeared to be blind to his costly efforts.

'I confess, my Lord, to having little knowledge of horses,' Calenus admitted at last, finding his tongue, 'but one does not need to be an expert to recognise Lupus as a genius.'

'You would be surprised,' Nero told him, 'there are many so-called experts who have their homes decorated with the portraits of his rivals. Not all so easily recognise genius when they see it. A great many display my friend Vitellius. Do you not think that he was the best of our amateur horsemen?'

Calenus was again momentarily lost for words. Most homes displayed portraits of great charioteers, whether they followed the sport or not. For his part, Calenus did not follow the sport and displayed Lupus only because he appeared to be the most fashionable.

'Oh, without a doubt,' Calenus agreed enthusiastically, after a moment's pause. 'May I offer you some mead?' He barely awaited a reply and summoned the jug bearers hastily, then slipped away under the pretext of calling for hors d'oeuvres.

'This is all new, of course,' Pallas remarked disdainfully as he helped himself to a succulent dormouse. Nero and Otho were deep in conversation and ignored him. 'All very luxurious, of course,' Pallas continued, directing his remarks to Seneca, 'but if it isn't all returned by next week he'll bankrupt himself paying for it.'

'He may be the first to bankrupt himself in an effort to entertain the new emperor, but he certainly won't be the last,' Seneca pointed out. 'Instead of sneering at his efforts, be grateful that he considers you worth the sacrifice.'

'What? Calenus near to bankruptcy?' Nero remarked, over-hearing Seneca. 'He appears to live well, in spite of it.'

'Because of it,' Pallas pointed out stiffly. 'When one has had to work hard in order to amass one's fortune, as I have done, one learns to respect it and not squander it recklessly.'

'Wealth was made to be squandered,' Nero argued, 'what other use does money have if not to be spent? There is no pleasure in a coin, Pallas - only in what it can buy.'

Pallas snorted contemptuously and didn't deem to reply. Instead he waved his empty plate in the general direction of the slaves.

Acte stepped forward hesitantly. As she took the plate, Pallas pointed to the remaining hors d'oeuvres, in the centre, and, without actually looking at her, gestured that he would like more. It was clear that she was expected to serve them, something for which she was totally unprepared. She glanced around for a serving spoon, her hand hovering above the pastry-coated peafowl eggs.

'Here, let me help you,' someone offered, and she half turned, smiling in gratitude as she expected to see another of the slaves at her side. Instead she found herself confronted by the pretty features of her emperor, smiling at her engagingly.

'I think he would prefer one of these dormice,' Nero said amiably, picking one up himself and putting it on Pallas' plate. 'You needn't mind Pallas, he is an insufferable snob. He will not lower himself into conversing with slaves, even though he himself only bought his freedom a few years ago! I believe he succeeded in knocking my father Claudius down by more than half the agreed sum, such is his meanness!'

Otho, over-hearing, stifled a laugh.

'Let me introduce you to my dearest friend, Marcus Otho,' Nero said, taking her by the arm and turning her to face Otho. Completely over-awed by events, Acte simply bowed her head demurely. 'But you have the advantage,' Nero continued, 'for you already know us, by reputation, but I do not know you! Please introduce yourself.'

'I must wait upon your friend, my Lord,' Acte protested nervously, almost in a whisper, but made no move to go. Despite her fear she found the young emperor entrancing.

'Leave the poor girl alone,' Seneca scolded Nero, taking the plate from Acte and passing it to a disapproving Pallas.

'You have a right to be nervous, girl,' Otho teased, 'for you are surrounded by eccentrics! An ex-slave who refuses to speak to you and an emperor who embarrasses you with his intimacy!'

'Please, I meant you no embarrassment,' Nero apologised, 'sit down for a moment and calm yourself. Here, have my couch; your master appears to have put all the double couches elsewhere in the room.'

He stood back and allowed her to be seated. She glanced across the room and saw Calenus hurrying towards the group, which only increased her anxiety. And yet the emperor himself did not instil fear. There was something reassuring in his manner; a lack of mockery that made his intimacy seem genuine and natural.

'Is there a problem with this girl?' Calenus enquired, sweeping in to the centre of the group as though over-charged with nervous energy.

'On the contrary, she is charming company,' Nero declared cheerfully, adding a quiet aside to Acte, 'if only she would tell me her name.'

She met his grin and returned it. 'Acte.'

'Sit down and relax with us, my friend,' Nero continued, 'the entertainment already does you credit and has barely yet started.' He leaned across and asked Calenus the names of the two slaves standing nearby, then called out to them genially and requested them to fetch another couch, Acte having commandeered his own.

While Nero's blatant disregard for rank clearly disturbed Calenus, Acte found it amusing and respected him all the more for his unusual familiarity. She was made to feel at ease by both the emperor and his friends; Otho and Nero treating her as an equal, Seneca - aware that she might have been feeling a little out of place - treating her with a marked kindness without being patronising. Only Pallas ignored her; and he, it was clear, did not number among Nero's friends.

In contrast to Acte, Calenus was singularly unimpressed with Nero's familiarity and, by the end of the evening, was heartily relieved to see the back of him. He cared little for young men at the best of times, but they were a great deal more offensive when they were of a vastly superior rank. To make matters very much worse, Nero appeared to have a total lack of decorum. If there was anything more distasteful to Calenus than having to show respect to a teenager, then it was being shown undue respect by no less a person than the emperor.

Calenus felt certain that it was some form of arrogant sarcasm on Nero's part, but could have accepted it had there been any likelihood of winning Nero's favour. As it was, the evening appeared to have been a complete waste of time and expense, Nero repelling his every attempt to gain influence at Court; even to the point of throwing an expensive gift back in his face. When he had offered Acte to the emperor he had not expected him to refuse the girl, let alone insist that she should be given her freedom instead. He had not only lost a useful chambermaid, but had now to give patronage to a freedwoman, which he could ill afford.

As they journeyed home in their litter, Seneca admonished Nero for much the same thing.

'Had you not been such a gifted student, to the extent of being held up as an example to all of Rome as the Prince of Youth, I would guess that you were a complete fool! You surely cannot be so ignorant that you do not see the blunders you have made this evening?'

'What blunders? Our host was a boring old fool and I could so easily have had a great deal of fun at his expense. But I did not. I remained courteous and respectful throughout the evening.'

'Exactly! You are the emperor, Nero. You command respect - you do not give it!'

'I have the title emperor. What I am is a boy. Calenus is my elder and I respect that fact. In the name of the gods, Seneca, I am no better man for being hailed emperor! I only take orders from you and the rest of my ministers and pass them on to the public as my own!'

'I wish that you did!' Seneca snorted with mock disgust. 'You have a greater hand in politics than Augustus himself ever had! The lives of your ministers would be made very much easier if you were the puppet that you seem to think you are!'

'I have to interfere and overthrow their decisions,' Nero teased, 'for they have served for too long under my father and have antiquated views.'

'They are values that have stood the test of time,' Seneca argued.

'Under a regime of old men. With the slight exception of my late uncle, who was hardly of sound mind, I am the first emperor to come to power as a young man. I am not burdened with over-powering wives or the staid ideals of one approaching retirement. It is my duty to bring fresh ideas and innovations to the state. It is high time we experienced change and there is a majority out there for whom things can only improve. My predecessors never ventured from their elite little social circles and governed only for that minority. It is time to take a broader view and I, for one, relish the prospect.'

Seneca smiled ruefully at Nero's enthusiasm, sensing that it could lead to the young man's downfall. Privately he agreed with Nero's ideals, but he could not advice him to cross swords with the senate. Claudius had quietly harboured republican views, but had been a realist who knew better than to risk his own position for ideals that would have had no benefit on his own lifestyle. Given Nero's intelligence, it seemed illogical to assume he was unaware of those risks; yet he displayed an almost naive disregard for them. Seneca instinctively wanted to encourage him. But common sense told him that it was a dangerous attitude. Advisors were more easily replaced than emperors, and his own life could well be jeopardised by Nero's infectious desire for reform.

Chapter Fourteen

On the morning following the dinner party held by Calenus, Nero turned his back on his official duties and slipped quietly out of the Palace. Pulling a cloak around him and covering his head, he walked, unnoticed, through the ever-crowded streets and arrived in due course at the rear of Calenus' villa. There he approached a freedman and enquired after Acte, and was directed to her room across the courtyard. He entered without knocking and found her sorting bed linen for the laundry.

She gave him only a cursory glance and continued to attend to her task.

'If you are new, you need to see Afrus.'

'I believe it was Afrus who directed me here.'

This time she stopped what she was doing and studied him more closely, recognising the tones of a nobleman even if she didn't recognise the voice itself. Her long black hair - arranged in small braids and piled high on her head the previous evening - was now held in a single broad plait which hung to the left of her face. The dark narrow eyes stared piercingly at the intruder for a moment, before widening and sparkling with sudden recognition. Her small, thin-lipped mouth opened in amazement, then a smile lit her face and brought a glow to her cheeks that could not be confused with a blush.

'My Lord!' she exclaimed, 'what brings you here? Does my master know of this visit? Where is your entourage?' She stepped forward hurriedly and took his cloak, laying it across the single stool in her room.

'No one knows that I am here, with the exception of Afrus who is unaware of my identity and believes that I bring only a note for you. And to prove that I am no liar - here.' He handed her a note and she read it through. It was a short verse, extolling her virtues and beauty; and this time the colour in her cheeks was unmistakably red.

'I wrote it last night, when I retired to my chamber.' Nero glanced around the small room, furnished only with a bed, a stool, a chest of drawers and a mirror. 'I could think of nothing else all night.'

'So you have come here today, determined to take me as your mistress.' There was a trace of bitterness in her tone that wounded Nero.

'No!' he protested, 'Of course I would like to enter your bed, but who wouldn't? Do you not know your own beauty? But if I am to gain your intimacy, then it will be on your terms. I am here to gain only your friendship; your trust. I can only hope that it might lead to a deeper intimacy.'

Acte smiled at his frankness.

'My beauty has, until now, gone unnoticed. You, my Lord, are my first suitor. Forgive me, therefore, if I don't behave as I should.' Despite her words to the contrary, her ease had returned and she sat down on the bed. 'I'm afraid that I can't offer you a drink, unless you'll accept water from the pitcher there. It is fresh.'

'Am I reputed to be such a drunkard that I cannot stomach mere water?!' Nero teased, sitting down on the stool, having first pushed his cloak to the floor.

'You are reputed to be married, but I have heard no rumours concerning your drinking habits.'

'Ah. My being married does affect us, doesn't it?' He seemed to be truly apologetic, although Acte had only intended a teasing rebuff. 'I am sorry to put you in such a position, Acte. For my own part, I have so little involvement with Octavia that I tend to ignore our marriage; shut my eyes to its very existence. But I cannot expect any true lady to do the same. Perhaps I should leave now, before more than one of us should be caused hurt.'

'It would truly cause you hurt if I turned you away?'

'If your beauty alone had not been enough to win my heart, then our conversation last night would have been sufficient. We spoke at such great length I had hoped that my feelings for you were mutual.'

Acte regarded him sympathetically.

'Oh Nero, you can't address me in this manner. I'm a newly freed slave girl and you are the emperor. Under different circumstances we could have been friends; I could so willingly have been your lover. You're young and still new to your reign. Perhaps you're unaware of your improprieties. But you will change - you will be changed - and then we should both be hurt even deeper.'

'I would gladly abdicate for you,' Nero insisted earnestly.

'You could have used your position and ordered me into your bed,' Acte pointed out.

'Then I will use my position and marry you.'

Acte could see that this was no mere adolescent infatuation.

'Your marriage was arranged for a reason,' she told him gently. 'Your ministers would never allow you to throw it away - and certainly not for the likes of me! And neither would the public react kindly to your keeping a slave as your mistress. You would be cheating on the daughter of Claudius, and you know how greatly she is admired by the people. Perhaps that is why you were originally betrothed to her. None of these facts can be denied. I am a danger to you as a mistress, and marriage is an impossibility.'

Nero was surprised and impressed by her astuteness. He himself had never taken the time to consider reasons and implications, and certainly not in this instance. He had met Acte; thought of nothing more than possessing her during their one night apart, and had flown to her side at the first opportunity. He already knew that she found him physically attractive - that much had been obvious during their evening together. He had expected to meet with little or no resistance; a few brief lines of love paving the way to her bed. Beyond that, simply love eternal. Apart from a keen awareness of the political future, he lived only for the present. And, if it suited him, a repetition of the present until such time as it no longer amused him.

'Acte,' he said after a pause, 'last night I fell in love for the first time in my life. There can be no obstacles; none that I cannot overcome. I had come to believe that these feelings could never happen to me; and that they have brings as much joy as the feelings themselves. I don't want a mistress, to visit when the need is great. I want a lover and a companion; I want to share my life with you. I will do that secretly, if need be. Or I will divorce Octavia and marry you - abdicate if necessary. I will do whatever it takes. I care for nothing but to be with you. You cannot - you cannot - send me away.'

Acte's own heart emphasised the truth in those words. She could no more send him away than stop him from now sitting beside her and embracing her. Once in his arms she was as lost as he appeared to be. She grasped him tightly, hoping never to let go, for the moment never to pass. She had always prided herself on her good sense, her level-headedness. But there could be no reason in the face of such passion. This was something beyond her control: beyond his control. She held no belief in any of the gods, yet now she wondered if some great power was manipulating them both. The thoughts came and went as though time stood still, while she clung tightly to Nero and absorbed the warmth of his body, the scent of his skin, the softness of his flesh.

Nero allowed the embrace to be frozen in time simply because he was afraid to move forward; afraid to take the next inevitable step. The fears of the past few months were so close to being banished forever, and yet could still so easily prove to be well founded. He couldn't bear such a thought and kissed Acte's neck with a sudden urgency that bordered on viciousness. He wanted her now as he had never wanted anyone and pushed her down onto the bed, struggling to un-knot the belt of her tunic. They spent several precious minutes hugging and kissing and fighting in vain with too many layers of clothing, before parting company momentarily to each sit up and undress.

Nero took his time; pausing, more often than not, to watch Acte as she removed her tunic, her under-tunic and then the final layers of linen below. Her embarrassment was acute, but Nero could not avert his gaze. The entire experience was as new to him as it was to Acte; it was as though his encounters with Octavia and Otho had never taken place.

They lay back down once more, but without the earlier aggressive passion. Acte was not so relaxed with their nakedness and Nero was content simply to look, and to savour his pleasure in so doing. Tentatively they began to kiss once more, and with the fresh embrace Acte's confidence returned.

For a while they did no more than explore each other's bodies with lips and fingertips. Nero bestowed a trail of kisses across Acte's shoulder and twisted round to continue down her back. For the first time he saw the wheals across the back of her shoulders.

'Calenus?' he asked, his voice heavy with barely contained fury.

She shook her head. 'When I'm attending the lady guests I occasionally come in for a beating. If I hurt them while fixing their hair it is only natural that they should wish to lash out.'

'There is nothing more unnatural.'

'But it is a part of life. Even you must be used to such things. Have you never hit out at a slave, or received a beating yourself as a child?'

'I was flogged only once, and it is a nightmare that will live with me forever. Which makes your scars all the harder for me to bear. If anyone ever hurts you again I swear I will kill them.'

He gently kissed the scars, as though his lips could heal the wounds, then lay his cheek against her, feeling the tremors of pleasure run through her body. He was reluctant to spoil the moment, to defile her purity, but the urges became too strong and he began to make love to Acte; slowly and gently at first as they accustomed themselves to the new sensations, trying to learn what each craved and what each could give.

Nero already had enough experience to have left behind the clumsiness and lack of control of youth, and - perhaps for the first time - he was not driven by a desire for self-gratification. Her enjoyment was all the pleasure he needed; and it was like nothing he had yet experienced. There had been pleasure enough with Otho - so much so that he had anxiously wondered whether it was possible for him to find such enjoyment with a woman. Such worries had been at their strongest during his infrequent liaisons with Octavia, until he had grown to fear the very thought of her. That fear had blossomed uncomfortably into repulsion and strengthened his doubts. Now he savoured his new found security; closing his eyes with a wild relief as he watched innocence die.

After the passion had faded, the softly spoken endearments had been exhausted, and the kisses of gratitude exchanged, they settled back to consider their future. It was clear, even to Nero, that discretion was imperative, if only to avoid the wrath of his mother.

'I do not wish this to be a furtive relationship, but it would seem that we have no choice in the matter,' Nero admitted regretfully. 'As long as you do not think it to be so, Acte? I am not merely using you, you know that, don't you?'

'Of course I do! You mustn't bring this out into the open simply to reassure me! I would never forgive myself if I were to be held responsible for the destruction of your reputation. We must keep our relationship secret.'

Nero nodded, then grinned broadly, reciting:
' "People would rather swallow a lighted candle
Than keep a secret that smacks in the least of scandal.
The quietest whisper in the royal hall
Is out in a flash buttonholing passers-by against a wall;
And it's not enough that it's broadcast to the nation -
Everyone gets it with improvement and elaboration." '

Acte laughed. 'Another of your verses?'

'Not mine, alas; I lack such talent. Petronius. He is witty and cynical, one couldn't ask for two greater virtues in a friend. I could recite a hundred more off the top of my head, and perhaps double that figure with prompting. Not all by Petronius, of course! Do you like poetry?'

'I've never really had the opportunity to do much reading. What little we did at school, I must confess, I had no taste for. Perhaps now that I have more leisure time you will recommend one or two books to me.'

He kissed her shoulder. 'I had rather hoped you would put your leisure time to better use.'

'And I, as a humble freedwoman, rather hoped that I would have more free time at my disposal than the emperor of Rome! You surely don't expect to fill all of my hours?!'

'Then I will send you some books as solace!' He glanced around at the meagre surroundings. 'Do you intend to remain here?'

'My circumstances have improved a little; I'm now in charge of the chamber staff and will receive a higher salary than as a slave. Which, of course, I owe entirely to you. But I think that a local apartment would be a little out of my reach at the moment.' She glanced down at the cloak on the floor. 'Now it's your turn to accuse me of using you. But it would be more discreet if I had my own apartment. Too much risk is involved in your coming here on a regular basis.' Nero smiled. 'Consider it done. Pack your belongings and be ready to move within the week!'

Acte leaned back on the bed. 'This all seems so natural. The most natural thing in the world. Tomorrow, no doubt, I'll think it all a mere dream.' She looked at Nero assessingly. 'Are you really in love? And for the first time?'

He smiled and nodded. 'Deliriously so. And you?'

'I believe so.' She continued to study him, wondering.

He gave her a wry look. 'There has only ever been Octavia...' he hesitated, 'and you, of course.'

'For want of trying?'

'Until now. Too much else was going on in my life. I'm only just beginning to settle down.'

'Is it very difficult?'

'Ruling the empire? Inspiring! I have so many plans and such limitless resources. I can do anything.' He glanced at her ruefully. 'Well, almost anything. The only difficulty is in stopping my mind from constantly racing - I have so much to do, you see. So much needs changing.'

'But?'

'There are no buts. In private, perhaps. My mother is a little domineering and is deeply opposed to my plans. I...' he smiled somewhat sheepishly, 'I confess to being a little in awe of her. I would find it hard - I do find it hard - to cross her. Impossible, in fact.' He brightened up. 'But Seneca and Burrus are my allies. They take much of the weight off my shoulders. I have already succeeded in pushing through edicts against the wishes of my mother and the senate, without having to do a thing myself! So really, no, there are no buts.' He paused, but then continued, glad for the opportunity to have such a talk. 'More than once I have wanted to run away from it all, lead a more normal life, away from Rome. I don't think that it's something I really want. It's just a reaction, sometimes, to the pressure. To my mother's bullying. I use it as a threat. I like to think that abdication is my only weapon against her, but she doesn't even pretend to believe me.'

'Should she?'

'Oh yes. Very definitely.'

Chapter Fifteen

'And just where have you been?'

Pallas' sharp demand caught Nero off guard as he attempted to return to the Palace unobserved.

' "My Lord",' Nero reminded him curtly. 'Have you forgotten, in my absence, how to address me correctly? Or do you presume upon a non-existent friendship?'

Pallas clenched his jaw. 'Forgive me, my Lord. But we had not anticipated your absence and were uncertain as to when you would be returning. There is much work to deal with. Burrus has a number of charge sheets for you to sign and is waiting for you in your room.'

Nero stared at him icily, silently prompting with malevolent eyes.

'My Lord,' Pallas added, grudgingly.

'I will attend to Burrus immediately. You may leave your business in my room, and I will deal with it at my leisure. That will be all.'

Pallas bowed his head, silently seething, and followed behind Nero to his chamber.

'Sorry to have run out on you, Burrus,' Nero apologised breezily as he entered his room. 'What have you for me?'

'Several charge sheets and a dozen death warrants, I'm afraid.'

Nero took the collection of papers and thumbed through them to the death warrants. 'Ah, how I wish that I had never learned to write,' he sighed, as he stretched out on his bed and began to sign his name. 'Are these all completely necessary?'

'Unfortunately so, yes.' Burrus glanced across to where Pallas now hovered beside the desk, and Nero followed his gaze.

'That will be all,' Nero said firmly, giving Pallas no opportunity to argue. He waited for Pallas to leave the room, then returned to his paperwork.

'Could we not find useful employment for these people, instead of condemning them?' Nero asked Burrus, his reluctance to sign his name increasing with each warrant.

'Work parties of petty criminals often work alongside the troops, digging canals or constructing bridges,' Burrus told him, 'but there is little necessity for this and sending condemned criminals on such parties would mean endangering the public.'

'Perhaps the troops should be allowed more leisure time,' Nero suggested, 'and should supervise prisoners, rather than participating in the work themselves. The prisoners would constitute no danger with an armed guard of soldiers present.'

'It's a consideration,' Burrus agreed thoughtfully.

'It is, isn't it?' Nero's countenance brightened momentarily, then quickly clouded once more as he put his pen to the final warrant. 'It doesn't help these poor creatures though, does it?'

'Perhaps you would do better to spare your sympathy for the bereaved families of their victims,' Burrus suggested.

'My heart goes out to them, too, Burrus. But the death of a murderer will not bring back the victim. By killing for spite, are we not murderers too?'

'Perhaps. But in so doing you are saving countless numbers of other possible victims. One life to spare many.'

'And what of repentance? Of regret and reform? Our laws make no allowance for mistakes made in the heat of a moment; or change of heart.'

'If you feel so strongly on this matter, perhaps I could draw up a few proposals?' Burrus offered, 'and you could broach the subject with the senate.'

'Surely it would fall on deaf ears?'

'Not necessarily so. Given strong enough arguments and a set plan to work to, you could well win them over. You sound as though you consider it worth the fight.'

Nero smiled. 'Yes, it is, Burrus; it is. And you will back me in this?'

'You have my unreserved backing in all that you do.'

'I'll look in to it, then; draw up some plans of my own. Thank you! Thank you.'

Burrus smiled and picked up the papers. 'That completes my work. It was hardly pressing, but Pallas insisted that I should wait!'

'I could not actually afford this leisure time,' Nero confessed with a grin, 'Pallas has actually left me a great deal of pressing and legitimate business to attend to. But I will not give him the satisfaction of knowing that!'

'I trust you spent your time profitably, anyway?'

Nero's grin broadened. 'Very well, Burrus! Very well indeed!'

'Then it is worth the price to be paid, is it not?' Burrus smiled and took his leave.

Nero looked across at the pile of work left by Pallas, then stood up and turned his back on it, choosing to go instead to Otho's room.

'Where have you been?' Otho enquired idly as he entered, 'Pallas and Seneca have been chasing around after you all day.'

Nero grasped him by the shoulders, his obvious excitement raising a grin from Otho.

'What?! What is it?!'

'I spent the day with Acte! We have declared our love for each other!'

Otho hugged him. 'She gave you pleasure, then?!'

Nero flung himself down on the bed. 'More than pleasure! She cast off every inhibition that had stifled me.' He rested his hands behind his head and sighed deeply with contentment. 'I feel... alive!'

'It's what living is for,' Otho agreed, 'There is no better pastime - haven't I always told you as much?'

'Only now do I fully believe you, my friend.' Nero rolled over onto his side and hugged the pillow loosely to him, gazing across at Otho in appreciation. 'I have to confess something, Otho. I was never really comfortable with you. I held back quite a bit; I was afraid to acknowledge what I truly felt with you... I was terrified that I might end up like Spintria, with no interest in women at all!'

'So, when at last I might reap the benefits of your sudden lack of inhibition, I am to be discarded for a woman!'

Nero smiled. 'Not at all. Quite the contrary, in fact. I have much to make amends for. There is so much to be sampled and no pervading doubts to spoil my pleasure.' His eyes shone invitingly.

Otho needed no second bidding.

Otho and Senecio joined Nero later on in his room, as he completed his backlog of work in readiness for dinner.

'Otho told me about Acte,' Senecio said, picking up some of the papers beside Nero and perusing them with interest. 'These projections are hopelessly over-optimistic, surely? You lack the necessary manpower.'

Nero glanced up to see what he was looking at. 'I propose to assign most of the construction work to condemned criminals.'

'And who do you propose to assign to the amphitheatre in their place?'

'I have already cut down on the number of bloodbaths in the arena. These victims will not be missed. They will be better appreciated elsewhere.'

Senecio returned the papers to their place and thumbed through those beneath. 'How do you propose to keep your affair secret from your mother?'

'Only with much help and support from my friends.'

'You may depend on us,' Otho assured him, 'but there is no guarantee that that will be enough.'

'You must confide in Seneca,' Senecio suggested, 'for neither of us could put our names to this affair. Otho's father would disinherit him and mine would not look any more favourably upon a serious liaison between a slave girl and me, despite the fact that he was once an imperial slave himself!'

'But he would not take a rod to your back for sleeping with a slave,' Otho complained lightly.

'He would take a different view if I confessed my love for such a girl,' Senecio pointed out.

'I am reluctant to confide in anyone,' Nero said with obvious apprehension, 'for my mother has informants in every circle.'

'We can do little on our own,' Otho told him. 'You will wish to send her gifts, but you dare not use your own name and neither may you use ours. She will need an apartment; you cannot visit her in secret at the home of Calenus. The trysts must be arranged, and your absence covered. Seneca must be involved; you have no option.'

'You didn't mention that an aedile's post had become vacant,' Senecio remarked, replacing the documents he had been studying.

'What? Oh; that. It was of no consequence. I already have someone in mind for the position. Otho, didn't you say this afternoon that you had an apartment available? Does your offer still stand?'

'Of course! It isn't much, but it's not far from Calenus' villa. I'll take care of the furnishings for you.'

'We'll arrange all your meetings for you, won't we, Otho?' Senecio volunteered. 'Seneca will cover for you and arrange the gifts. There is no reason why your mother should suspect a thing.'

Both Otho and Nero shot him a withering glance.

'Well, I've heard rumours around the Palace that Agrippina seems to have no knowledge of,' Senecio said defensively, a slight trace of spite in his tone that seemed to be directed at them personally. It was enough to alert Otho to his possible conjecture.

'There are always rumours,' he said lightly, 'and Agrippina has heard enough of them to learn which to ignore. Rest assured that nothing actually happens in this Palace that she does not know of.'

Senecio seemed satisfied with his response. 'Well then, we can but try,' he declared, 'and at worst she must find out later rather than sooner.'

'I fear that is the best we can hope for,' Nero agreed.

He reclined on a couch with Seneca during dinner, taking the opportunity to discuss the use of convicted felons in building projects. Agrippina paid them no heed and reclined with Pallas, out of earshot.

'You will remember Acte, who works at the home of Calenus?' Nero said as they tucked in to the main course.

'How can I forget her?!' Seneca declared. 'I have rarely been so embarrassed for you, my boy! Your conduct last night left much to be desired.'

Nero grinned. 'I visited her today. We are lovers.'

Seneca choked on a piece of meat, waving away the jug bearers irritably as they hastened to offer him water. The sudden inability to speak saved Nero from a verbal whiplash, and when Seneca was able to voice his thoughts once more he said only, 'so that's where you were today.'

'We need your help, my friend,' Nero pleaded.

'Without a doubt,' Seneca agreed.

'Otho and Senecio will arrange our trysts.'

'Which leaves me only to invent your appointments to coincide with these meetings, I presume?'

Nero's eyes shone.

'Well, if you are serious, my boy - which, indeed, you appear to be - you may count on my aid and discretion. There is no point in my telling you of the great mistake you are making?'

Nero smiled and shook his head. 'Nothing has ever felt so right, Seneca.'

'Umm. Well it could be much worse, I suppose.'

He continued with his meal in silence for a while.

'I have a young friend by the name of Serenus,' Seneca said, as he pushed away his empty plate. 'He is single and well known for his eye for young ladies. If your Acte receives a multitude of gifts from him, no one will give it a second thought.'

Nero resisted the urge to hug him, knowing that it would attract unwanted attention. But his eyes conveyed his feelings.

'Thank you, my friend; I will not forget this.'

Seneca smiled warmly. 'You will be the death of me, young man. The death of me!'

Chapter Sixteen
MARCH A.D. 55

Nero lay back on the bed with Acte; one arm wrapped protectively round her shoulders, the other tucked behind his head, as he gazed up at the ceiling in thoughtful silence.

'Things are going badly for you, aren't they?' Acte asked, concerned by his unusual quiescence.

He hugged her to his chest, as much for his own reassurance as hers.

'Not at all!' he said breezily, though the lightness of his tone did not reflect his true feelings. 'It was a particularly hard day in court, and so far my attempts to civilise proceedings and speed them up somewhat have come to nothing. I was happy as an advocate and could willingly have argued all day in defence of my client. But I now see that it is not quite so enjoyable when one is forced to be the listener rather than the speaker!'

'I'm sorry, Nero; I have no understanding of courts or legal matters. What were the attempts you made to improve the system? I have heard only complaints that cases drag on unnecessarily.'

'My complaint also, but it seems an impossible one to cure. In my father's day barristers were overjoyed by a lengthy case! I should have thought that my introduction of fixed fees would have taught them to be more concise, but I had not bargained for their passionate love of hearing their own voices! They still continue to ramble on, but now with added hostility towards me because of the wealth they feel they are losing! As to civilising them, my good intentions have backfired. Before my ruling to the contrary they could interrupt one another at will, arguing and digressing as the fancy took them. Therefore I made it a rule that, rather than present a case as a whole, each relevant charge should be presented separately by first one side, then the other. In theory we should have a much clearer insight into what is being put forward and can form our own judgements accordingly.'

'In theory, you say?'

Nero returned her mocking grin, relaxing visibly after the tensions of the day. 'Yes, in theory. But, of course, in practise it is a licence for barristers to drone on interminably without interruption!'

Acte grinned. 'As I have said, I know nothing of the law, but I was aware of those 'interminable' cases, and that you were the sole cause!'

'So that is the word on the street, is it?!'

'I repeat only what I hear! But I imagine that I must hear far more complaints than you or your friends! Anyone in your circle would be much more guarded and polite, I expect!'

Nero snorted scornfully. 'Don't you believe it! Seneca and Burrus are quick enough to tear me off a strip if I step one foot out of place! And Mother has never tiptoed round my feelings or been inclined to humour me. She criticises my every move. Whatever is said on the streets cannot fail to be kinder than anything heard within the Palace!'

He laughed lightly, but Acte could see that it bothered him. 'They say you take far too long to pass judgement in court,' she prompted him. Despite his complaints, it was clear that he had enjoyed the topic.

'They forget the importance of my judgement,' Nero complained. 'Were they the defendant appearing before me they would welcome my lengthy deliberations. Generally, I defer my judgement to the following day, then give it in writing. Not only is it beneficial to sleep on a problem, and mull over the grievances at leisure, but also by setting it down in writing one can often see the most glaringly obvious points that might otherwise have escaped attention. That is why I insist that my judicial advisors write their opinions for me, individually, whenever I withdraw to consider a problem of the law. I can then mull over their documents in private, rather than hear them as a body. Mother believes me to be far too fussy, but she never witnessed my father's judgements. Many is the time that he would be woken from an illicit nap in order to pass judgement; and his lack of consideration to sentences and laws led to a great number of injustices. None of which ever bothered him, I might add. But I'm afraid I lack his detachment and would suffer greatly from any mistake I might make.' He loosened his embrace on Acte and made himself comfortable, lying flat on his back with his arms behind his head once more. 'I have a wonderful scheme which I shall shortly be introducing,' he continued enthusiastically, 'whereby condemned criminals shall be set to work on public projects, such as digging and building work. The beauty of it is that no edict need be passed; it's a simple matter of setting them to work on specific tasks. Burrus felt that I should exercise some power for a change, rather than enter into what is often a fruitless debate with the senate. I must confess that I am becoming a little disheartened at such a prospect. It would seem that in most cases my views differ greatly from those of the House. And, powerful though its members might be, there is one who presents even greater headaches when it comes to the passing of new legislation.'

'Your mother, I take it?'

Nero sighed wearily in reply. 'She no longer doubts the seriousness of my threats to abdicate. I have warned that I shall retire to Rhodes if the pressure on me becomes any greater. And she has certainly relaxed her grip on me, in response. Yet I feel all the more threatened by her; as though she is formulating some greater hold over me. I thought it was hard to bear the over-critical eye she kept on me. But her sudden distance is even more unnerving.'

Acte looked at him in concern, her expression mirroring his own inner feelings.

He smiled brightly. 'I complain too much! Don't take it to heart, Acte. Otho knows me well and he merely laughs at my complaints. He says I am a fool. The emperor should fear no one - least of all his own mother!'

'Otho takes few things seriously - neither you, nor your fears. You should obey your own instincts, Nero.'

Nero raised himself into a more upright position and hugged her gratefully.

'I wish you could live at the Palace,' he said, after a while.

'You are surrounded by friends; I would slip by unnoticed,' Acte teased. 'Be grateful instead for the excuse to escape every once in a while.'

'I'm thinking of taking singing lessons, did I tell you?' Nero said, at length.

'You said you'd like to be more accomplished on the lyre.'

'That too. But the lyre can be a dull instrument without an accompanying voice! Paris, my aunt's ballet dancer, says that I have a very weak voice that will take a great deal of work to strengthen and train. But if I am ever able to find the time then I shall certainly rise to the challenge.'

'I often get the impression you would prefer a life on the stage to your present position!'

'Otho is convinced of it! He describes me as an exhibitionist!'

'And what are Otho's interests?'

'Fine clothes, a good - no, perfect! - appearance and the avoidance of work!'

Acte smiled. 'It seems he has no goals left! He must be as content as you are restless. You say that your threats to abdicate are serious, but retirement sounds more like Otho's dream than your own. Could you really be happy in Rhodes?'

Nero's face clouded once more. 'There is no denying that I enjoy the challenge of my life here in Rome,' he admitted, 'but I could find enough to fill my days and tax my intellect wherever I was. The problem is that in Rome I have my Mother constantly watching over me. And that is what I find hard to cope with. It is from her, and not Rome or my position, that I would gladly run.'

Later on, as he slipped back into the Palace, Agrippina was waiting for him in the loggia alongside his room.

'Why so furtive, Nero?' she enquired acidly, 'was Seneca mistaken when he said you had been detained at court?'

'I had other business to attend to, and no wish to disturb anyone upon my return. In fact I'm surprised that you are still up, Mother.'

'Candles still burn in Otho's room, too. Perhaps he is waiting up for you, as I am. You are fortunate indeed to have such friends and family, who care enough about your well-being to see you safely in on late nights such as these.'

Nero said nothing, regarding her suspiciously.

'In fact, had you not been so late back, I would have liked to speak to you about Otho.'

'What about Otho?' Nero snapped instantly, then at once regretted his own unthinking betrayal of guilt.

Agrippina eyed him speculatively. 'He is a wild young man who causes his parents much heartache. He is rarely out of brothels and never out of trouble. He drinks heavily and you appear to make a fair effort at keeping up with him. But I am concerned that you may be attempting to keep up with him in other spheres too.' Her glare intensified. 'I warn you, Nero. If you try to follow his example the Guards will come down on you as bloodily as they did on Caligula. You dare not set one foot out of place.'

Nero flushed visibly. 'I thank you for your concern, Mother. But I can assure you, until now, such thoughts had never entered my head. I bid you good night.' He paused, to watch her walk back to her own room, but she simply stood, expecting him to do the same.

'Yes, good night, my dear. I have already kept you for too long with my silly maternal anxieties. When you have children of your own you will understand my concern. Now go, your poor wife has missed your company for long enough.'

Nero returned her sudden warm smile and reluctantly withdrew to his own room. Octavia was still awake in bed and regarded him coolly as he undressed and joined her.

'Your legal advisors have not suffered unduly from your payment restrictions,' she remarked sarcastically, 'judging by the smell of you they can afford better perfumes than the emperor's own wife! Though I must say, you keep unusually close company with them - and such late nights, too. People will begin to question your diligence if you are not more careful, my love.'

'They will question nothing if you remember to curb your acerbic tongue.'

'I heard the conversation outside the door and you need not lay the blame with me. I keep your secrets not for your sake, but for my own sense of integrity and virtue. You arouse your mother's suspicions simply by your behaviour. That you smell of a brothel rather than a court house is your own doing, and needs no gossip on my part.'

'Take care that is always the case,' Nero warned maliciously, 'for if ever I trace a careless remark back to you I shall see to it that my behaviour is such that neither you nor your brother would wish to hear it gossiped of.'

Octavia's eyes flashed with equal malice. 'And you take care, dear husband, that neither Britannicus nor I are past caring. When gossip is the least of his fears it will prove to be your downfall.'

'A chance I'm willing to take. Are you?'

Octavia sighed wearily. 'If it came to it, yes. But this is no more than a sick game to you. You have no intention of carrying out your threats and I certainly have no intention of betraying any of your intimate secrets. You may do as you wish as far as I am concerned, if it means that you leave me alone. And we may both sleep easy at night.'

Nero turned his back on her, but belied her last words. He could not sleep without the comfort of a warm embrace; the security of friendship that was normally to be found with Otho. He lay awake fretfully, his thoughts with Acte.

Without heed to caution, he finally rose and slipped on a robe and cloak, intent on being with Acte, with or without the prearranged protection of Seneca. Slipping quietly out of his room, he stole down the passageway and out into the deserted courtyard, satisfied that he had avoided detection.

Agrippina sat in her room for a long while after their confrontation, considering Nero's subtle reluctance to return to his own bedchamber. It was clear to her that he had been intending to go straight to Otho's room, and she felt equally certain that he would attempt to do so again before the night wore on much further.

As she watched him slip out of his room some time later, her patience rewarded, she wondered momentarily about his purpose. It was too late to be gaming; besides which he was a fearless gambler who made no secret of his recklessness. It seemed most probable that there were the sordid events of the evening to divulge; details of brothels and conquests, and comparisons. She could well imagine the two friends swapping stories as they grew steadily more drunk. Yet there was also a third, more distasteful, possibility that had been niggling at the back of her mind for some time now.

But any such suspicions were banished by Nero's unexpected departure, which in itself threw up fresh possibilities. Such a desperate liaison had to be intended for someone very special indeed; not merely a favoured brothel. Agrippina's eyes narrowed with annoyance as she walked briskly back to her bedchamber, her mind already racing through the implications.

As Nero slept blissfully, secure within the arms of Acte, so Agrippina slept more fitfully, her mind preoccupied by thoughts of the unavoidable challenge to come. Outside influences were already posing a threat to her power, but a lover represented the deadliest rival of all.

Chapter Seventeen

APRIL A.D. 55

The sun was just rising as Nero gave his first audience of the day. He dressed, as always, in a casual manner, preferring comfort to protocol. Robes were passed over in favour of an unbelted silk dressing gown and slippers, with an elegant silk scarf to disguise the bull-neck of which he was so conscious.

A succession of clientele looked to him for advice and assistance; as they did on each of the emperor's free mornings. Palace staff then sought orders and presented documents. The morning ebbed away in the usual current of imperial duties.

As the last of those seeking audience was ushered out, so Agrippina stormed in, scowling so fiercely at the emperor's slaves that they bid a hasty retreat.

'You could at least have allowed me to give them instruction before frightening them away, Mother!' Nero protested lightly; though himself unnerved by her demeanour.

'You dare to criticise my actions after brazenly lying about your own?!' Agrippina stood tall before him, over-powering and frightening. 'After your assurances to the contrary I find that you are no better than Otho! Worse, in fact! That a son of mine was frequenting brothels would be distasteful enough, but your amoral instincts don't stop there!'

She raised a hand, as though to strike him, and he instinctively flinched. He dared not say a word in his defence for fear of betraying a guilt she did not yet suspect.

She threw up her other hand, as though to express her despair; her point made. 'You sit there indignantly, under the belief that I know none of your secrets and that you are wrongly accused. Well, let me assure you that I know all! All, Nero! I know, for example, of your dalliance with a slave girl. Or ex-slave, should I say, by the name of Acte and under the patronage of Calenus. Oh, that you - emperor of Rome! - could stoop so low!' She sank down onto the couch, seemingly exhausted by her own anger.

'Acte's rank is of no consequence!' Nero protested, deeply offended, 'she is as good a person as any noblewoman.'

'Her lack of rank is of every consequence!' Agrippina argued fiercely, 'Messing around with one's own slaves is one thing, but striking up a serious relationship with such a girl is quite another!'

Nero's resentment intensified his courage. 'Would you not regard your relationship with Pallas as serious? Perhaps, instead of tolerating him for your sake, I should be chastising you!'

Agrippina gave a desultory laugh. 'I most certainly would not regard our affair as serious! My favours are bestowed only where they might reap the most benefit. Of what benefit is this girl to you? Does she provide you with a valued insight into the affairs of Calenus? Does she report to you on the dissidents within the commons? Or does she merely make a mockery of you, devaluing you in the eyes of the people?'

'She is neither spy nor leech! We love each other and we need no more justification than that.'

Agrippina rose once more and stared at him menacingly. 'I am sorry to hear that you are in love with her. A broken heart left the emperor Tiberius a bitter and twisted man, and I should not like to see you similarly affected. But you are young and will quickly recover. Give me your word now that you will see no more of this girl and I shall not raise the subject again.'

Nero swallowed, his mouth dry. 'No, Mother; I cannot give you my word. I intend to be with Acte as much as I can.'

Agrippina was momentarily stunned by his unexpected refusal. Time and again she had pushed him to extremes, finding him always reluctantly compliant. In fury she slapped him smartly across the face, but the determination in his expression only intensified.

'I will be discreet,' he said, his voice trembling, 'but I can promise you no more than that.'

'You'll stop seeing her - or you'll live to regret it.'

Agrippina did not wait for a response, but turned swiftly and swept out of the room, as forcefully as she had entered. Nero stared after her with unseeing eyes, before visibly regaining his composure. Taking a deep breath, he closed his eyes and steadied his nerves; then welcomed back his slaves as though nothing had occurred.

'Epaphroditus,' he enquired of his secretary, catching sight of him as he passed by the open door, 'if I were to disappear for an hour or two before lunch, what would be the most pressing business neglected?'

Epaphroditus leaned against the doorframe, considering.

'There is really nothing that could not wait until after lunch. And no more than one or two items that cannot be put off until tomorrow, for that matter. But you could not afford to take any breaks tomorrow, should you choose to defer today's business.'

'I will be absent for an hour, no more. But don't tell anyone that. Let them think that I shall be gone for the day, if that is what they care to assume. And find something particularly irritating and tedious to deposit on Pallas - tell him it is urgent and cannot wait for my return. I wish my absence to cause as much inconvenience as possible.'

'Easily arranged, Nero. And can I explain your absence, or is it to remain a mystery?'

'Explain away, my dear friend! Tell anyone who may ask that I am visiting my lover, Acte. An ex-slave. In fact, you needn't even wait to be asked! Particularly where Mother and Pallas are concerned!'

Epaphroditus grinned. 'You have a lover?! This is all very sudden - or is she merely an invention, designed to annoy the fair Augusta?!'

'Oh, she is real, my friend; very much so. I had hoped to keep our affair secret, but my dear mother, your fair Augusta, is not content with discretion. And so we must acquaint her with the alternatives.'

'Well well well, you are a dark horse; do I know this Acte? Is she on the household staff?'

'She was a household slave, but not mine; nor even a friend's. There is little likelihood that you know her. But you will meet her in good time, have no fear.'

'I look forward to it, Nero. And now, if you will excuse me, I shall go and upset Pallas!'

Nero followed him out and went along to Otho's room. Otho had not yet risen and peered at him through heavy eyes.

'Are we too early for a brothel, do you think, my friend?' Nero enquired casually, throwing open the shutters to let in the light.

Otho groaned and drew the counterpane up over his head.

'Too early?!' he complained, 'You mean too late! I have only just returned from one myself!'

'I have an hour to spare and Mother has given me one or two ideas on how best to fill my time.'

'Then let her accompany you!' Otho threw off the counterpane and slowly pulled on his tunic. 'I must say, your mother's advice on pastimes has certainly altered my opinion of her. I should be interested to hear the other ideas she has given you!'

'Well I know for a fact that we are too early for a tavern; and Acte, unfortunately, is working. You once promised me an introduction to the professional ladies of your acquaintance - well, here I am to take you up on the offer.'

'I remember no such promise. And I did have a more reasonable hour in mind.'

'My hour is fast dwindling, Otho.'

'As is my stamina. We shall share a bed between us, Nero. You may make full use of it; I shall sleep in it.'

'We'll try not to disturb you.'

'Thank you for your consideration, belated though it is. I'm sure your mother, as fun-loving as she now seems, would have allowed me to sleep on in peace.'

'My mother knows about Acte.'

Otho looked up sharply. 'Your face is marked.'

'She stormed in and ordered me to end it. I told her that I would not.'

'So I see.'

'I told Epaphroditus that I would be with Acte this morning, and if anyone should ask to tell them so. He has gone off with great delight to inform Pallas. And I am left to await the consequences; whatever they may be.' He shivered slightly. 'She accused me of loose living. Held you up as an example of iniquity. Ordered me - as is her habit - to cease such pastimes.'

'You play a dangerous game, my friend.'

'I am free of her, Otho; she does not frighten me.'

Otho privately doubted his words, but slapped him heartily across the shoulders. 'Good for you, Nero! Good for you!' He glanced at the disarray of garments on the floor beside his bed, then spotted his cloak and snatched it up, swinging it about him in a single deft movement.

Nero was taken aback. 'Ready so soon? Is this a record for you, Otho?'

'In this condition I left their embrace barely two hours ago; it will do no harm, for once, to return like it!'

Nero smiled in grateful appreciation. He knew well Otho's morning routine, and his excessive fastidiousness about appearance. It was a rare occurrence for him to forego his daily epilating poultice of bread and to emerge from his room with any trace of beard; or, indeed, any body hair whatsoever.

'Your time ebbs away,' Otho remarked briskly, 'so let us now make haste. I know of a house where two most enchanting - not to mention imaginative! - young ladies will be more than willing to accept us as a pair into their ample bed. I for one can think of no better way of passing a free hour.'

'So Mother implied.'

'Then she knows me well, my friend; she knows me well!'

When Nero resumed his work, later that afternoon following lunch, he found himself unable to concentrate and wished that he had taken his secretary's unsolicited advice and deferred the entire day's business. The excitement of the morning preoccupied him and he longed for the moment when he could steal off to see Acte and relate his experiences to her. But also filling his mind were thoughts of his mother and the possible repercussions of his open defiance.

Otho remained with him, together with several slaves, and they amused themselves quietly with a board game while Nero worked. They were gathered, as they were all aware, for the emperor's protection; though no one cared to admit it. But Agrippina did not appear; her absence proving to be as unnerving as her tempestuous presence.

'Let us go to dinner early,' Nero announced suddenly, pushing the remainder of his work to one side, 'I have seen little of Senecio recently and we can renew our friendship before the food is brought in. I have a need for conversation and comradeship this evening.'

'There can be no avoiding the confrontation you have so deliberately set up,' Otho pointed out.

'I'm aware of that,' Nero agreed quietly, 'but, whatever his motives, Senecio is a good friend and with you both beside me I can face anything.'

'You know, then, that he curries favour in the hope of promotion?'

'Of course. But it is a common weakness, and he will soon realise that he has to earn his promotion in the same way as anyone else. It would be foolish to fall out over so trivial a matter, after all that he has done to aid my affair with Acte.'

'I think it is better that he remains in hope of public office,' Otho remarked lightly, 'for precious little else would tempt one into siding with you in an open confrontation with Agrippina!'

'Otho, you have told me many a time that I am emperor. She may be the Augusta and hold all in her palm. But she does not hold me.' He grinned. 'Should I tempt you into battle with a consulship?!'

'It is enough that I am willing to risk my neck for you at all, never mind risk it further in a political career! She may well hold us all in her palm; but the senate she imprisons in her fist!'

They laughed, taking courage from mocking her, and made their way jovially to the dining hall, where they joined Senecio. In his company the jokes increased, until they felt that they had little to fear from the object of their derision.

From his couch to one side of them, Pallas regarded them disdainfully. Nero caught his glance and bristled with hatred.

'She claims to sleep with him only for the leverage he gives her,' the young emperor said, as though to himself.

'I don't doubt that for a moment,' Otho agreed, staring frostily at Pallas, 'why else should anyone wish to allow that creature into their bed?!'

'Depose him from his position of power, Nero, and you will also deprive him of his sleeping arrangements!' Senecio suggested.

'I have always tolerated him, for her sake. Yet she will not do me the honour of tolerating Acte.'

'You are the emperor, Nero,' Senecio continued, 'but it seems to be the Augusta who does the hiring and firing.'

'You claim to be free of her,' Otho agreed, 'why not allow his head to be the first to roll?'

Nero could give the matter no further thought, for Agrippina herself chose that moment to enter. Ignoring all present, she strode across to the top couch and stood over its occupants menacingly.

'You are no more than a foolish child, unfit to be emperor!' she exploded venomously. 'You defer official duties in order to sleep with slave girls! You joke with your friends while your wife has to sit through dinner in the company of her brother! You have no respect for your ministers, your position, and certainly not for me! Britannicus behaves with more decorum - as well he should. Your position was once his birthright. What you took, he was born to. Little wonder that you so lack competence in comparison!'

Nero sat up stiffly and met her hostile stare. 'There is only one minister who fails to earn my respect. While I had the option of working with Narcissus, I could tolerate Pallas in moderation. But I cannot work with him alone. Nor am I prepared to continue my tolerance merely for your sake. If my disrespect injures you, Mother, then allow me to end it here and now. You may inform Pallas that his position is terminated, with immediate affect.

'As to my wife; I will not share my bed with her, and certainly not my couch. From hereon in she may sleep as she dines - elsewhere. Let her choose any room in the Palace and vacate my own.

'And you may groom Britannicus for the role which is his by right. I will be only too happy to stand down for him, now that he is of age. I trust he proves a better puppet for you, Mother.'

The dining hall was silent.

'You will pay dearly for this,' Agrippina muttered, for Nero's ears alone.

Nero remained seemingly unaffected by her threat. They continued to face each other in menacing silence, until Agrippina turned abruptly and went to her couch. Then dinner continued as before, those present talking now in hushed voices; only their tones betraying their excitement.

Chapter Eighteen

JUNE A.D. 55

It was to Vitellius that Agrippina took her tale of woe. Though a close friend of Nero, Vitellius was ever open to additional sources of power and had always regarded Agrippina as such.

'You should have fought him over Pallas,' Vitellius now told her, as they sat sipping wine in her room. 'I can do very little on my own. Pallas was a key minister and totally under your thumb. Without him, your power has diminished quite noticeably.'

'Oh shut up, Spintria. You know nothing of the facts.'

'Then acquaint me with them.' He eased himself upright on the bed, rubbing his hip that grieved him more earnestly as the years progressed.

'They are no business of yours. Suffice it to say that if Nero still had the aid of Narcissus, he would have made fewer objections to Pallas. And on the subject of Narcissus, the least said the better. I prefer to lose Pallas than give Nero cause for suspicion.'

'Then there were grounds for suspicion?'

Agrippina smiled ruthlessly. 'Pressure of work drove him to suicide, as you well know.' Her eyes narrowed. 'Just as it could drive any man.'

Vitellius nodded his comprehension, without concern. He already knew better than to cross her.

'Meanwhile, my son grows more defiant with each passing day,' Agrippina said, after a pause. 'What is to be done with him, Spintria?'

'Were we not all rebellious at his age? A stronger hand is all that is required. He tests you, that is all. He has pushed back and believes he has won. It is up to you to show him otherwise, Agrippina.'

Agrippina fidgeted crossly, her frustration plain. 'I can show him no stronger hand, short of flogging him. And I dare not resort to the whip; not yet. It is the one thing I still hold over him, the one fear he cannot evade. He used to flinch when I raised my hand. Now he looks me calmly in the eye. I cannot allow him to throw off every childhood fear. I must keep one back; out of his mind... waiting.' She savoured her drink momentarily. 'What of Otho? Surely there is some weakness in Nero's defences?'

Vitellius shrugged it off. 'I have no doubts as to Nero's leanings in that direction. But Otho is a womaniser. They meet only to game and to swap lewd tales, of that I can assure you. Nero hides no secret, for there is no secret to hide.'

'A pity. For only a secret can hurt him.'

'I have heard it rumoured that he abuses Britannicus. Pure conjecture, of course. But enough to start gossip.'

'True or false, it is of no concern to me. Nero is quite brazen about it, boasting openly of his conquest. It is Britannicus who keeps silent on the matter. No; there is no point in opening a wound that has already been laid bare.'

'Is it true, do you think?'

Agrippina took another mouthful of wine. 'Between you and me, Spintria, the rumours were started by Nero himself. They are no more true than his liaisons with Otho, but he does not wish Octavia to know that. He torments her with such threats to her beloved brother's innocence, and I for one have no desire to set her mind at rest. Let her fret at night for fear of what is happening to Britannicus; and let Britannicus fret at night for fear of what might happen. May the accursed brats of my idiot late husband get what they deserve!'

Vitellius laughed, and drained his glass. 'You surprise me, actually. I had never regarded Nero as malicious.'

'You are naive, Spintria. He is bred to be cruel.'

'That's right! I can still remember well what your poor late Gnaeus once said to me, when the boy was still a babe in arms. That any child born to you both was sure to be detestable and to become a public danger! A strange statement for a new father to make!'

'And what a let down Nero would have been for him. It was the fault of Lepida, of course. Mollycoddling and pampering. But as you so rightly point out, the malice still shines through, given the right provocation. There is hope for the boy yet.'

There came a knock at the door and Vitellius rose slowly. 'My cue to leave, my Lady. You have other business to attend to and I fear I have been of little help to you.'

'Good day to you, Vitellius. Send whoever it is straight in.'

She watched him go, then sighed with genuine weariness at the sight of his successor.

'Annaeus Seneca, this is a rare occurrence. To what do I owe this honour?'

'Forgive my intrusion, my Lady. I seek your audience on a personal matter.'

Agrippina moved to allow space on the bed, but Seneca remained standing.

'I wish to discuss Nero. He grows quite unmanageable and you, my Lady, hold the only key.'

'My dear Seneca, I find him just as unmanageable, so don't come here looking for guidance from me. You were once his tutor, so I should expect to be able to call upon you for advice and not vice versa.'

'With respect, my Lady, that is exactly why I am here. I must urge you to turn a blind eye to his affair with this slave girl. Your stern disapproval is only serving as encouragement. He is discovering new desires, and he is of an age when rebellion seems natural. He may well be using Acte only as a means to disobey you and exert his independence.'

Agrippina's patience reached its limit. She stood up forcefully and glowered at Seneca.

'Never will I turn a blind eye; and neither will he disobey me! I simply will not tolerate this behaviour. The affair will end, if I have to break a rod across his back to stop it! Let him sleep with his wife, if celibacy does not suit him!'

'They cannot bear the sight of each other. And your threats are worthless, they encourage only further deceit. The more pressure from you, the more brazen he becomes. Very soon the affair will become public knowledge, a source of gossip and scandal.' He swallowed, uncertain how to word his next argument. He was aware of Agrippina's menacing disapproval, and of his pledge to a beseeching Nero to sway her. 'Please indulge him in this, my Lady,' he pleaded, 'Acte is a slave girl, far beneath his own class and intellect. If allowed to run its course, the infatuation will quickly fade and pass. But I fear it grows only stronger in the face of your disapproval. Nero is a young man, with a young man's needs. If he cannot turn to Acte then he will almost certainly look elsewhere. Perhaps to a noblewoman. Someone else's wife. The scandal could be far, far worse than at present.'

Agrippina regarded him thoughtfully. 'Perhaps you speak some sense after all, Seneca. He is certainly a most lustful young man and I cannot imagine anyone of his stature tolerating a mere slave girl for any length of time. Perhaps, as you say, the affair will soon fizzle out of its own accord.'

Seneca nodded. 'Without a doubt, my Lady. Although we should not be in too much of a hurry to see the back of this girl. By late evening, when drink has overtaken them, Nero and Otho do not always conduct themselves with decency. If he is not allowed to let off steam with slaves, who knows where his desires might lead? A married noblewoman could well be the least of the scandals facing your house.'

'Vitellius suggested as much himself. With this slave girl he is, at least, discreet. And more to the point, Seneca, he retains his respect. After the indignities of Caligula, the public will not stand for any slip in morals. I cannot allow his position to come under threat - not without a ready replacement to hand.'

Seneca raised his eyebrows, but said nothing.

'You may take the rest of the day off, Seneca. You have done more than enough good work this morning; don't think this talk goes unappreciated. Besides which, I require the company of my son for the remainder of today. He is still to be found in his room, I trust?'

'Indeed, my Lady. He is occupied with warrants from Burrus.'

'Very good.' Agrippina made it plain that her guest was to take his leave immediately, then hurried along to Nero's room, not bothering to knock. His door, as always, was open.

'My dear boy,' she declared cheerfully, 'it is as well Octavia has elected to sleep elsewhere, for you have little privacy here.'

'There is nothing you can say or do to make me change my mind. I will not take her back into my bed.'

'And nor do I expect you to,' Agrippina assured him, sitting beside him on the bed, 'in fact, I have just been speaking with Seneca and he has made me realise how poorly I have treated you. How can I begin to voice my sorrow?' She embraced him and kissed him tenderly on the cheek.

Nero relaxed somewhat and looked at her enquiringly.

'I'm afraid I have grossly over-reacted,' Agrippina admitted gently. 'You forget that I grew up with Caligula, and I am overly protective towards you. One day you are fooling with slaves, the next not even noblewomen are safe! And don't forget that within four years of such outrageous behaviour your poor uncle was hacked to death. What I took to be a casual dalliance frightened me more than you can imagine. But now I can see that your feelings for Acte are serious. Forgive me Nero, for all the distress I have caused you both.'

Nero smiled warmly, welcoming the reconciliation.

'It is already past and forgotten,' he assured her.

'But you will of course allow me to make amends?'

Nero hugged her warmly once more. 'There is no need; and besides, Mother, your blessing is enough. We ask no more of you than that.'

'Yet surely you must long to fetch her to your Palace? Most certainly not here, with slaves and ministers in and out all day without announcement. But a room offering suitable privacy for a young couple in love.'

'I dare not fetch her here. I am sorry I teased you so, Mother, but in truth I wish to keep my affair with Acte secret and avoid any hint of scandal. I have no wish to bring our affair into the open; and the Palace is as good as a Public forum!'

'My own room is not. Allow me to offer you its full use. I spend my days with friends and my evenings at late social functions. I ask only that I might return to it to sleep on nights when I cannot go to my villa or mansion here in Rome. Please, Nero; put my room at your disposal. No one dares disturb my privacy and Acte may come and go with discretion. I feel I have a debt to pay and will not rest easy until I have done so.'

She looked pleadingly into Nero's sparkling eyes, but he had already been swayed. He kissed her joyfully and pushed the warrants into an untidy pile against his pillow.

'Mother! You cannot dangle so tempting a treat under my nose then expect me to wait! Please say that I can send for her now? This very minute?'

Agrippina smiled indulgently. 'Ahh, what it is to be young! Send for her, go on! I will dismiss Burrus for the afternoon and deter any other visitors you may have. Now away with you, before I change my mind!'

Nero grasped both her hands firmly in his, then turned swiftly and hurried off to secure a messenger. Agrippina stared after him, her smile fading as soon as he was out of sight.

The novelty of the surroundings and the excitement they induced brought Acte and Nero's passion to a swift climax. They basked in their own pleasure for a while, lying back in silence and gazing up at the filigree panel of ivory above the bed.

The one in the dining hall revolves and rains down scents and petals,' Nero murmured casually, breaking the silence.

'Could this one?'

'Quite likely, knowing my mother.'

Acte smiled, savouring the vision in her mind.

'Something to look forward to,' Nero suggested, meeting her eyes and causing her to blush slightly.

'I'd like to see Otho again,' Acte said suddenly, sitting up, 'is he here?'

'He is here and at your disposal, my Lady,' Nero told her, sitting up and bowing in an exaggerated movement. Acte laughed and began to dress.

'I feel like the Queen of all Rome.'

'You are just Acte; and that is enough to make any woman jealous.' Nero pulled on his tunic and tied his scarf round his neck. 'I would offer to take you on a tour of the Palace, but unfortunately the Palace is not really my own and we must remain confined here, like fugitives. There is little to see anyway but extravagant finery.'

'Oh come! You do nothing but talk of the art and sculpture housed within these walls!'

'I have all the beauty I need in this room.'

Acte ignored his flattery. 'You like to believe that this means nothing to you; yet you can't deny the pleasure your position brings you. Your leisure time may be limited, but you can spend it as you please. You're not hindered by lack of wealth; you're not banned from entry to any place you choose to visit. The world is at your feet, Nero - why punish yourself with this constant guilt?'

'I don't! I truly enjoy my life. Yet I feel resentful that I have so much while others have so little. Not guilty; just angry, perhaps. I love what I have, but a great deal of it is unneeded and unnecessary. And I do feel guilt - or embarrassment, if you like - for the way my own class behave. So pompous and conceited. They confuse intelligence with education, and respect with stature. I find it annoying, Acte; particularly when my own clear-sightedness brings me only chastisement and criticism. And here we are, reduced to secrecy because our love gives cause for insult! I cannot abide this intrusion into my private life of standards that are not my own.'

'You will change them, Nero; I am convinced of it.'

'I appreciate your faith, but you have yet to meet the senate!'

'At the moment I will settle for meeting Otho!'

'Of course! I forgot!' Nero walked across and opened the door, summoning a slave. 'Fetch Marcus Otho for me, would you please, Alcides? He should be in his room, but if not try the stables.'

They sat on the bed and awaited his arrival, passing the time with a passionate session of kissing, which was interrupted by a surprised but unembarrassed Otho.

'Acte! What on earth are you doing here?! Do you have one of those for me?'

Acte blushed and turned a cheek to meet his lips.

'Have you lost your mind?!' Otho continued, turning on Nero, 'Rebellion is fine in moderation, but this is pure suicide.'

'It is neither,' Nero corrected him. 'We are here with my mother's full consent and blessing. Seneca spoke to her and made her see sense. She realises this is no mere passing infatuation and has responded accordingly.'

Otho frowned. 'One word from Seneca and these past weeks of bitter feuding are brought to a sudden end?'

'Perhaps it is due to those weeks themselves. Does it matter? What counts is the reconciliation between us - and the availability of this room!'

Otho was not to be reassured. 'Are you certain you can trust her? Can you be sure this is not merely some trick?'

'Relax, Otho! A sudden change it may be, but it is not without reason.'

'I came here expecting to find you beaten senseless. You cannot tell me this sudden change of heart is reasonable.'

Nero detected the anxiety in his voice and looked at him in surprise.

'Well, what did you expect me to think?' Otho said in response, 'a slave arrives and tells me I am required by the emperor, in the Augusta's room. Why else do you think I was so prompt?' He grinned, in an attempt to diffuse the situation. 'She might kill you yet. I am not so easily convinced as you by her sudden goodwill!'

He sat down beside Acte and poured himself a glass of wine, from the jug beside the bed. 'Have you met her yet, Acte?'

'No; and nor am I in any hurry to! The mere thought of her terrifies me!'

'Oh don't worry, she has that affect on everyone!'

'I'm afraid that's true,' Nero agreed, 'but you need never have cause to fear her.'

'So, how often are these visits to occur?' Otho asked. 'Are you to become a fixture here, Acte?'

'You must ask Nero.'

'I don't need to, my dear - his feelings are quite clear!' He passed his glass to Nero. 'You must meet Senecio when next you come,' he grinned at Nero, 'or visit, should I say! He can be quite tiresome at times, but together we make a formidable team. And Serenus! You must meet Serenus! Indeed, so must I for that matter; I know of him only by name!'

'I must thank him for all the gifts that he sent me!' Acte laughed, 'For a man I have never met he was most generous!'

'There are a great many thanks owed,' Nero pointed out, 'but first and foremost I must thank my mother.'

He met Otho's glance.

'To your mother!' Otho proposed, taking back his glass and raising it in a toast. But Nero could see that his doubts remained.

Chapter Nineteen

JULY A.D. 55

Agrippina lay in bed, staring broodingly at a fabulous jewelled dress hanging at the front of her own robes, which now paled in comparison. It did not strike her as a fair exchange for the use of her rooms.

'A nice garment,' Rubellius Plautus commented, following her gaze, 'very, very expensive. How did you come by it?'

She jerked out of his embrace and sat up.

'A gift from Nero.'

'And that annoys you?!'

Agrippina fixed her eyes on him, considering. He was new to her intimate acquaintance and, as yet, untested as an ally. Pallas would have seen her scheme before she had even mentioned it and, for no more than that, she missed him. But he was no longer of any service to her, while Plautus...

'If I choose to allow it to do so,' she said, matter-of-factly.

'I am interested to learn how a gift might annoy you, particularly one so impressive, lest I might make the same mistake.'

'My dear Plautus. Like Nero, you are a great great grandson of Augustus; but you do not share the same family cunning! With your pedigree, and your loyalty towards me, you are never likely to err as Nero has now done.' She smiled. 'Were you ever to obtain his throne - and were I ever then of a mind to depose you - I could use such a gift to publicly destroy you.'

Plautus sat up, with interest.

'I am keen to hear more; go on.'

Agrippina feigned anger once more. 'I am the Augusta! Yet he gives only a small fraction of what he owes and keeps all else from me! The great wardrobe of past wives and mothers of emperors, all now withheld; while he tosses this meagre offering in my face and expects in return my public gratitude!'

Plautus clapped. 'I am impressed, Agrippina. But at whom will this performance be aimed?'

'At all who will listen. And, of course, all who will support you.'

Plautus let out a breath. 'Oh no, Agrippina! No, no, no! I want no part of this. You are in a secure position for such dangerous games; I am not.'

'You have no part,' she rebuked him sharply. 'Only when Nero is gone will we look for a new leader. Only then will I put forward your name and noble ancestry. Until then, you are to say and do nothing.' Her tone mellowed. 'It is my destiny to scheme,' she said, stroking her fingers across his chest, 'and yours to keep me amused. So amuse me, Plautus.'

Plautus, with little genuine interest in politics, was happy to resume his former role once more.

Agrippina's careful comments on the dress, which she now wore regularly, were well aired. Though she said little on the subject herself during the days that followed its arrival, it became the favoured topic of all dinner parties at which it appeared; leading to discussions of the emperor's many other failings, which Agrippina was happy to fuel.

'It is little wonder he treats me so shabbily,' she declared breezily, one evening at a party given by Junia Silana, 'for he shows no respect for anyone. He mockingly speaks to slaves as though they were his peers; and he buys friendship so freely that he now thinks nothing of buying that of his own mother, too!'

'I heard last week that he bought the lyre player, Terpnus, a villa at Neapolis,' Junia commented.

'Oh, a mere drop in the ocean! You know, of course, of that cheap little slave from Asia Minor who now takes his fancy? Well, she expressed a delight in some objects we have in the Palace and now owns the pottery in Sardinia from whence they came, no less! And young Marcus Otho...'

'Ahh; young Marcus Otho!' Junia said wistfully.

'Well you may strike that one from your list if you have no wish to be beggared!' Agrippina advised. 'He currently has debts of some two hundred million sesterces, would you believe! That we should even see two million in our lifetime would be a miracle! And who bails him out without a second thought? Nero, of course. He willingly throws away millions in order to keep men of such importance bound to him.'

'That slave you mentioned, Acte? Is she not his mistress?'

'He makes no secret of the fact, Junia. Octavia has been removed to another part of the Palace altogether. I would sympathise with the poor child if there were not the consolation that it spares her his company. But, then, what are we to expect, given his family history?'

'Little need be said on that subject!' Junia agreed.

'Ha! You don't know the half of it, not the half, darling! I can freely list our crimes, my own included, for none match my greatest sin - giving birth to that monster!'

'Really, Agrippina! That's our emperor of whom you speak!'

'Our emperor?!' Agrippina scoffed. 'A common usurper! He stole the throne from Britannicus, as well you know - and then only because he had me poison Claudius when the boy was too young to succeed him!'

'Poison Claudius?!

'Indeed. The eunuch who now serves Nero sprinkled poison on some mushrooms. Have you never heard Nero refer to them as "the food of the gods!"? His own private sick joke, not meant to refer to their taste, I assure you. And there was an end to Claudius, just as my own brother had put an early end to his predecessor. And my father, too! Driven to his death before he could succeed Tiberius and restore the Republic!'

'*No*! Not Germanicus!'

'It is no secret that witchcraft or poison took him.'

'But it was Tiberius' doing, surely?'

'Caligula's, darling. But even he balked at the cruelty of Nero's own father. Gnaeus was a sick man, believe me; but a priest in comparison to his own father!'

'I've heard tales about him. Did he not once poke out a senator's eyes?'

'Apparently the senator took his favourite seat at the circus, or made an unfortunate remark about his robe, or some other such trivial insult. So you see, Junia - Nero's paternal ascendants compliment those on his maternal side perfectly. We are, I'm afraid, an evil brood.'

'Oh, but Agrippina, the boy is an absolute charmer!'

'As was Caligula, need I remind you. And they both had incestuous designs on me! Caligula I could not dare refuse; but Nero, as yet, does not threaten my life. He dallies only with that slave because he cannot have me.'

Junia was shocked. 'But in all our years of friendship you have never once hinted at such atrocities!'

'How could I? Have you no comprehension of shame or pride? Yet this is what he has now brought me to. His own actions are such that my family's previous record no longer brings shame.' She sighed wearily. 'But that I could have contrived the succession of Britannicus, rather than Nero.'

Junia nodded in sad agreement.

'Tell me again, Agrippina - how much is it that young Otho owes?'

Otho, at that moment lying exhausted in the arms of his benefactor, was not concerned with debts or their absolution. His interest in money did not extend beyond the unlimited spending of it; a tendency with which he had infected Nero, who now slept beside him.

Yet Otho could not sleep. He was aware of Agrippina's vacant bedchamber; and Acte's imminent arrival.

He slipped carefully out of Nero's loose embrace and donned a clean robe from the emperor's own collection, before deserting his companion for the rooms of Agrippina. There he reclined thoughtfully on the bed and awaited the arrival of Acte; who had earlier been sent word that the Augusta intended to spend the night at the villa of Junia Silana.

'Otho! Don't tell me he has appointed a deputy!' Acte said in surprise, on entering the room.

Otho sat up slowly. 'Have no such fear. He merely rests before your arrival; I'll fetch him in a moment. But tell me first, Acte - are you happy with this situation?'

'You know that I can never be his official consort. More than this I can't hope for. Yes; I am happy.'

'I don't mean your relationship in general. I mean here; this room. This sudden generosity and tolerance. Does it not concern you?'

Acte sat down beside him. 'It concerns you, doesn't it? You were against this from the start. But who could know Agrippina better than Nero? He trusts her in this; and that is enough for me.' She eyed Otho speculatively. 'You don't seem so convinced of his safety?'

'I lack his trust.'

'Should I?'

'Agrippina should never be trusted. She does nothing unless it suits her own interests. And I cannot see why these trysts, which so obviously anger her, now suit those interests. I am frankly fearful, Acte; and nothing I can do or say will convince Nero of this unknown danger.'

Acte considered his warning. 'No one holds more sway with him than you. And he has never underestimated his mother. I've seen him in mortal fear of her. Yet now he is relaxed. He becomes more pliable again. Don't you think that alone is her object?'

'His pliability is not enough. Fear is the only way she can force his hand; and I don't therefore trust this new found alliance between them.'

'But you yourself have never seemed afraid of her?'

'I personally have no cause to fear her. I have never influenced Nero against her wishes or posed a threat to either her own or his position. My status is such that my death is not worth the risk it would cause. And only my own father could order me a flogging, which is by far the strongest hold she has over Nero.'

Acte smiled. 'Your father's strong hand seems to worry Nero more than you. Is there nothing you fear, Otho?'

'Well certainly not the whip. It is an old adversary and can only break the flesh, not the spirit within. For Nero, that invokes terror enough! He cannot abide the mere mention of the word blood! He has always been a wretched coward. His horsemanship is only outstanding because the ground beneath him looks so hard; and his sword-play is exceptional only because the blade of his opponent is so sharp!'

They laughed, amiably.

'So, what does terrify you?' Acte asked.

Otho smiled, with no small degree of embarrassment.

'You would think it foolish and laugh.'

'You don't know me at all, Otho.'

He shrugged. 'It is no secret, to be honest. I was found out long ago, during history lessons. Reduced to a quivering wreck at the mere mention of Brutus or Cassius!' He shivered. 'I told you it was foolish.'

'Not to you. Why do they scare you so?'

'It isn't really them, as such, but what they stand for. Civil war. The very thought of it chills my blood.' A visible tremor ran down his spine and he blushed slightly. 'I have as healthy a fear of death as any man. But, for the most part, it can be seen coming and so avoided, if at all possible.

'But civil war is an unseen enemy. Friend pitted against friend; brother against brother. A situation where, instead of looking out for one's friends, one can only look out for oneself. Self-preservation at all costs. I could trust you, for example, no more than you could trust me. An unpleasant thought, wouldn't you agree?'

Acte nodded, sombre. 'But it can't happen in our lifetime. Nero is young, and a reformer. The populace grows more content by the day. We, at least, are safe from such fears.'

Otho looked at her. 'Those very reforms which cause the populace such contentment are already giving rise to much ill-content within the senate. We are never safe, Acte.'

'Ah, but you don't mix with my people! He is loved and worshipped - and there are more of us than of your sort!'

Otho kissed her affectionately on the forehead.

'Dear Acte. Sheer numbers mean nothing. It takes only a handful of soldiers to keep the masses in order. And it takes only one man to control those soldiers.'

He drew back from her and allowed himself a rueful smile.

'Or one woman,' Acte said, as though reading his mind.

They sat in contemplative silence for a while.

'I had better fetch Nero,' Otho said, rising slowly and stretching.

'No need,' Acte pointed out happily, 'I recognise his step.'

Someone was indeed already at the door and Nero entered jauntily, casting a glance at Otho as he pushed the door shut behind him. He raised a hand theatrically to his brow and turned away from the pair.

'Oh! Betrayed by my closest friend! How did I not see it coming?'

'A minute sooner and you might have done!' Otho joked crudely. 'And now I am off to seek out my much-needed bed. Next time do not leave us so long, Nero - I am not as young as I used to be!' He bowed, long and low, and blew a parting kiss to Acte as he left.

'Have you waited long?' Nero asked apologetically, when they were alone once more.

'No; actually your timing was perfect. We had quite a chat, Otho and I. He fears for you greatly, you know that, don't you?'

'He never allows the subject to drop! I preferred the old, uncaring Otho to this tiresome worrier!'

'That was only because he had nothing to worry about. Are you certain - really certain - this isn't a trick?'

'Mother and I have never been on better terms, I assure you. She says it is because she knows I am happy with you; but the truth is, it does not please her at all. Seneca convinced her that, given time and indulgence, this affair will end. So, you see, it is a trick - but double-sided, and to our own advantage.'

Acte relaxed at this, and they entered into the gentle passion that would carry them without sleep through the night. As they finally lay back and watched the sun glint through the gilded shutters, Nero smiled sleepily at the thought of his defeat of his mother's trickery, leading to this newfound security.

He was an adult; and emperor. And now truly free of her.

Chapter Twenty

SEPTEMBER A.D. 55

Nero had just returned from a day spent in court when Agrippina swept into his chamber.

'You look tired,' she remarked, sitting down beside him. 'Did you condemn Julius Densus?'

Nero shook his head. 'No; I refused to allow the prosecution.'

Agrippina fought visibly to remain composed. Nero watched her, warily.

'But my dear,' she said gently, 'he was accused of favouring Britannicus. Can you afford to be so dismissive?'

'I have no wish to see a return to the treason trials of old. Cases such as his are a result of petty rivalries and jealousy; and I have made it clear that I will not be a party to them.'

'But in this instance can you be certain that it is no more than that?' Agrippina suggested. 'For it is on just such a subject that I wish to talk to you. Britannicus is now an adult and there are many who regard him as the true heir to his father's throne.' She paused. 'I have no wish to alarm you unduly, my sweet, but I know of a number of plots - still in their infancy at this stage - to depose you in favour of Britannicus.'

She saw in his eyes that she had, indeed, alarmed him, and continued.

'I have it on good authority that Britannicus himself plans to murder you before the year is out. Rumours are rife about your misconduct and poor family history, though the gods know it is no worse than his! Public sympathy is with him, and growing daily. I can see nothing to prevent him from immediate action. Of course, no evidence exists. One cannot hope to bring him to trial.'

Nero reached for her hand in agitation.

'Then what can be done?'

Agrippina hesitated. 'He plans to poison you, so I am told. You! Who have never had a day's illness in your life! How he will raise suspicion! Whereas he, on the other hand, is a sickly boy and always has been. If you were to poison him, his death would be put down to yet another attack of epilepsy.'

Nero's agitation turned to horror as he slowly digested her words.

'You cannot be suggesting that I murder him!'

'If not for your own sake then for mine. Without you, my love, I am a dead woman.'

'But I can't... I can't murder him... it isn't possible... I can't believe you have even suggested it!'

He rose from the couch and paced fretfully.

Agrippina fell to the floor before him and wept bitterly.

'Nor I, my love, nor I! But it is a mother's instinct; a blind need to protect her child, her only loved one. Oh I beg you, Nero; I beg you with all my heart - poison him, before he puts an end to you!'

'No!' he cried out in consternation, 'you cannot make me do this! I refuse to listen to you!'

The tears turned instantly to fury. Agrippina rose up at once and grabbed him by the arms, gripping him so tightly that he bruised. He struggled to pull free of her.

'You will listen, and you will listen well!' she snarled. 'This is not advice, nor yet a plea. I order you to kill Britannicus, and the gods will not be able to help you if you fail me!'

'Slaves! SLAVES!'

Two of Nero's own slaves appeared instantly.

'You will hold the emperor securely while I have him flogged,' Agrippina ordered fiercely, 'for he has grossly insulted the Augusta!'

'Yes, my Lady,' the two terrified slaves said in unison, and stepped forward to replace Agrippina's strong grip with their own. Nero writhed in terror and succeeded in pulling free.

Agrippina sneered at him in satisfaction.

'You are dismissed,' she told the slaves, who retreated gratefully at a run; then to Nero she continued, 'you see, my boy, that even your slaves are not your own. You treat them as your friends, but they serve fear more readily than love. If Britannicus is still alive by the end of the week, then you will be his victim; no matter how ready you might think yourself for him. And I will be his second victim, of that you may be certain. You may have no regard for your own safety, but I value mine. For my own protection I will see that you obey me. And you now know what you can expect from me if you fail.' She smiled cruelly. 'You will be a sitting target for your stepbrother if you are bedridden for a week. Think on, Nero.'

She calmly left the room, but paused just outside the door. Nero sat weakly on the bed, his arms hugged tightly around himself.

'There is a woman in the gaol by the name of Locusta,' Agrippina told him, 'she was convicted for brewing poisons. Britannicus was enquiring of her whereabouts only yesterday.'

Nero listened to her departure, then smacked a fist down onto the bed in frustration, as he fought to hold back his tears. A searing maelstrom of anger, fear and shame churned within him and he stood up sharply, striding to the door and slamming it shut violently.

For a moment he stood with his back pressed firmly against the door, against the outside world; his head raised towards the ceiling as he gulped back tears of relief at this all too brief security.

As the tears flowed freely once more, he lowered his head and closed his eyes, and slid slowly down the door, onto his haunches. Then the misery and degradation of his situation flooded through him and he wept bitterly; huddled in a ball against the door.

After a while he recovered his composure and called for a messenger.

'Summon the Colonel of the Guard, Julius Pollio,' he ordered, 'I must see him immediately. Immediately, do you understand?'

The slave nodded and turned to leave, but Nero was beside him in an instant and stopped him.

'No, wait, Tubero. It would be better if I went myself. See to it that I am undisturbed for the remainder of the day, would you? I will see no one, Tubero; no one.'

Without waiting for a response, Nero strode purposefully away and out into the courtyard, untying one of the horses tethered by a Guard and riding hastily out of the Palace grounds. He headed, at a canter, to the city gaol and, once there, quickly located Julius Pollio.

'You have a woman by the name of Locusta in your custody,' he told the colonel, with uncustomary shortness, 'I demand her immediate release.'

'May I ask on what grounds, my Lord?'

'No, you may not. Fetch her; and quickly.'

Pollio did as he was asked and disappeared into the gaol, returning within a short space of time with a female prisoner, her wrists tightly bound. Her lank, dark hair was tangled and filthy, her general appearance undernourished and dishevelled.

'Will you be requiring an escort?' Pollio enquired.

Nero grabbed Locusta roughly by the arm and pulled her hurriedly to the horse.

'Thank you, but that won't be necessary,' Nero informed him. 'Mount up,' he ordered Locusta, then climbed astride behind her and kicked the horse into an immediate canter.

Locusta struggled to keep her balance, while Nero fought with the horse to keep it going at an unreasonable pace, with an unreasonable load. Both riders were too breathless for speech and it wasn't until Locusta had been bundled unceremoniously into Nero's bedchamber that they spoke.

'I gather, Caesar, by the urgency, that you require some form of antidote?' Locusta said calmly, surveying her surroundings.

'Nero will suffice. And I require a poison. A small amount, no taste, instant death.'

'Ahh.' She nodded.

Nero watched her closely, surprised by her dignity and lack of awe at her surroundings. It occurred to him that this was not new to her and he began to wonder just how his mother had come to hear of her.

'Has Britannicus approached you?' he asked.

She looked at him warily. 'No. Why should he?'

She seemed too much on the defensive. The distrust aroused within Nero a new fear.

'I require the poison immediately. For tonight. Can you do it?'

Locusta nodded, her inner relief well hidden. For a moment she had feared that the emperor and his stepbrother knew of her role in their father's death.

'I can try my best, Sir, but I can't promise it. The poison will need to be tested before I can guarantee its strength.'

Nero's suspicion intensified at this apparent play for time, but he knew too little about the subject to argue.

'You will begin immediately and waste not a single moment. What do you require?'

'My hands freed, for a start. And a drink and some food.'

'You will get nothing until I have the potion!' Nero said furiously; but cut her wrists free roughly with a dagger. 'Now, what do you require to make your potion?'

Locusta rubbed her wrists and carefully recited a list. Nero wrote each item down on a wax tablet and sent Tubero on the errand of procuring the ingredients and implements. He eyed Locusta suspiciously as they awaited the return of the slave.

She was looking round the room with renewed interest, but, to Nero, seemed to betray an unpleasant familiarity with certain items of furniture. Her eyes certainly lingered on Claudius' desk and he felt the hair rise on the back of his neck.

'The Augusta, Agrippina, told me of you,' he remarked.

Locusta showed no surprise, but said nothing.

'In fact, this is all at her insistence,' he continued, surprising himself at his attempt to justify to her his actions. 'I must eliminate a threat.' He thought of Acte and longed to be with her; lying beside her, his head on her breast, telling her of these events as though they were still mere suggestions.

Tubero returned, together with two companions. When the various plants and jars had been laid out before Locusta the slaves were dismissed, and Nero turned to the paperwork on his desk. He signed a succession of documents without reading them, allowing Locusta to work at her own pace without interference, but unable to concentrate on his own tasks.

The late afternoon had passed into evening when Locusta finally announced that the potion was ready. Nero led her out to the courtyard and watched as she tried it on a goat, brought out from the kitchens, but the mixture proved to be little more than a strong laxative.

The tension of the afternoon erupted with the failure of the poison and Nero directed the full maelstrom of his confused emotions at the unfortunate Locusta. Dragging her back to his room, he picked up the unused whip; until now never retrieved from where it had once fallen, behind the desk. Self-contempt and hatred for Agrippina fused and found an easy target in Locusta. The intensity of his emotions exploded with the first stroke of the whip and he flogged her violently; until a vision of blood clouded his mind. He dropped the whip and fought to subdue the sudden nausea.

For all his fury, he had done little damage to Locusta, who took the beating in her stride. Her clothes, though no more than filthy rags, had afforded some protection and she had escaped with little more than heavy bruising. She caught her breath and returned to her brew.

'Forgive me, Locusta; I have behaved shamefully.'

She glanced up at him. 'It is not my place to forgive you.'

'My life depends upon this mixture.'

'Mine too, I believe.'

Nero closed his eyes. 'No, I won't be brought to this,' he said, as though to himself.

Locusta continued to stir her brew.

'Your life does not depend upon your success or failure,' Nero assured her, after a short silence.

'Am I to return to the prison when you have done with me?'

Nero felt an overwhelming need to cry, but steadied his nerves and shook his head.

'No; you may go home, or where ever. Do you have a home?'

'I did, until convicted. Now I have neither home nor money.'

'Your problems, at least, are easily rectified. When you leave you shall have both. I only hope that you can solve my own so simply.'

Locusta looked at him. 'Who is this meant for?'

Nero smiled. 'I really don't know, Locusta. There is one I could kill without sorrow; but I have no need for his death. But another I could not kill; and she poses me the greatest threat.'

'It is for her, then.'

Nero looked into her face. 'You know her, don't you?'

'You have to ask?'

'Am I the only one ignorant of her crimes? Tell me, Locusta; how do you know her?'

Locusta regarded him carefully. 'I am no longer a young woman. I have served the Augusta well, but for no better reward than imprisonment. What do you offer me, Caesar?'

'My name is Nero; and I have already made my offer. You have an apartment at your disposal in any Quarter you choose and a purse of twenty thousand sesterces to take with you. For whom did you brew your last potion?'

'For Agrippina, obviously. But you would like to know who she intended it for, I take it?' She considered. 'I have brewed more than one for her and the results have never come to my ears. But there was one in particular, made from the poison of mushrooms. Shortly after I supplied it, Emperor Claudius passed away.'

Nero swallowed and closed his eyes once more.

'You really didn't have any idea, did you?' Locusta said.

'Did it require a large dose?' Nero asked numbly.

'Only enough to sprinkle on a meal without detection; much like this one.'

'How could it have got past his food taster?'

Locusta shrugged. 'All I did was supply it. I can only assume that it didn't.'

Nero pulled back the hair from his face. 'Are you done yet, do you think?'

'I need to test it, to be certain.'

'Don't bother, Locusta. If you think it is ready then just go. Just go.' He wrote a hasty note and sealed it with his ring. 'Take this to Seneca; Tubero will escort you. Seneca will give you all you need.' He didn't watch her go, but lay back on the couch and stared hopelessly up at the ceiling.

Tubero returned, to inform Nero of Locusta's satisfied departure. He was immediately sent in search of Burrus, who arrived promptly, quite clearly dragged from his dining table.

'What on earth's going on?' Burrus demanded. 'You look awful, Nero. Have you eaten this evening?'

Nero shook his head, not bothering to rise from the couch where he still reclined miserably. Burrus sat down beside him.

'What has gone on? The slave tells me you have been entertaining the poisoner Locusta since your return from court.'

Nero could not answer.

'Your conduct in court this afternoon has aroused nothing but admiration,' Burrus said, fishing for a reaction and receiving none. 'Over there, in the pot - is that one of Locusta's potions?'

Nero sat up sharply and embraced Burrus, burying his face against the commander's neck.

'All is lost!' he wept bitterly. 'All is lost.'

Chapter Twenty-One

Burrus, Seneca and Epaphroditus sat solemnly on the couch facing the bed, where Nero leaned weakly against Otho.

'The threat from Britannicus is non-existent,' Burrus reiterated, as his companions nodded, 'but what of the threat from Agrippina?'

'Non-specific, as yet,' Epaphroditus insisted.

'She is keeping all her options open,' Seneca agreed.

'But it is all within our control,' Epaphroditus said confidently. 'The situation as far as we can ascertain is that she has whipped up public feeling against Nero and left the path clear to deposing him, should she so wish. But she has shown no signs, as yet, of wishing to do that. In fact, this attempt on Britannicus' life is a clear indication that she intends to keep Nero in her power for a good deal longer. It was no more than a ploy to get him back in harness. Fear, guilt, blackmail - her age-old weapons.'

'Yes, but the ploy has failed,' Seneca pointed out. 'If Nero does not poison Britannicus, what, then, will be her next course of action?'

'Look, it's quite simple,' Otho said impatiently, 'Agrippina wants a puppet and Nero will not be that puppet. If this attempt to regain control over him fails, then she will look elsewhere. Why concern ourselves with the ifs and buts? He lacks the courage to murder Britannicus and keep her sweet, so it is up to us to deal with her.'

'In what way, Otho? She has yet to do anything wrong,' Burrus reminded him.

'We can only sit this out,' Seneca agreed.

'And, in the meantime, Nero is perfectly safe,' Burrus assured them all. 'Agrippina can do nothing without a replacement and the forming of a new party cannot go undetected. When the opportunity arises, I shall be ready to prosecute - and condemn.'

Nero shuddered and pressed tighter against Otho.

'Throw that stuff away,' Otho said, gesturing to the pot that still stood, ignored, on the dead charcoal fire, 'and let us forget this nonsense ever occurred.' He drew back gently from Nero and looked him in the eye. 'She has no wish to harm you, understand that, Nero. She simply requires more power than you allow her. Burrus can deal with her string of candidates; she herself can remain safely outside of the law; and you may continue, unharmed. Now, let us go about our lives as before. Yes?'

Nero raised a smile and nodded resignedly.

'Will I send for Acte?' Otho suggested; but it was met with a weary shake of the head.

'We must retire for the night,' Burrus said, appreciating Nero's exhaustion; and his companions rose with him and said their good nights. Otho followed in their wake, but Nero reached for his arm.

'Stay,' he requested quietly; finding his voice for the first time since confiding in Burrus earlier that evening. 'I can't sleep alone. And I just need to sleep.'

It was during breakfast the following morning that Nero first met with Halotus since speaking to Locusta. He drew him to one side, where their conversation could not be overheard.

'How much did you accept for the murder of Claudius?' he asked bluntly, 'And how much will it take to ensure my safety?'

Halotus looked horrified. 'I would give my life for you, Nero! I killed him only for you; and no amount of money would induce me to have any hand in your death.'

'What do you mean *for me*? I knew nothing of it!'

'Your mother and I... well, she arranged it. I just helped her. But we did it for your sake. That is... she said he would hurt you. She wept for you.'

Nero sighed and gave him a friendly hug.

'Nothing has changed, Halotus. There is no one I would rather trust with my life. But I didn't quite understand; and I grew frightened.'

He returned to his couch and finished his breakfast.

'You seem well this morning,' Burrus remarked with some surprise, joining him. 'You had us all quite worried yesterday night.'

'I worried myself, Burrus. It was all too inescapable, too frightening. It came as such a shock, you see. I had thought, at last, that I had the better of her; that I had control.' He smiled wryly. 'That is never to be so, is it?'

'I'm afraid it is unlikely.'

'I thought I had her friendship, at long last. It's all I have ever wanted. And it was worth having, too; even for that short space of time. We got on quite well together, Burrus. Do you think it was simply pretence on her part?'

'No, of course not! She can't help but be fond of you. But fondness has no place in Agrippina's heart. She never allows it to hold sway. She needs to control; it's in her nature.'

Nero nodded to himself, with resigned acceptance.

'I miss Aunt Lepida; and Narcissus.' His tone betrayed the doubts he struggled to dispel. 'I'm going to remove her from the Palace.'

Burrus was taken aback.

'We can remain friends, providing we both know where we stand,' Nero continued, unemotionally. 'Is my great-grandmother's house still available? The mansion of Antonia would be most suitable, do you not think?'

'It would indeed.'

'It would flatter her to receive it?'

'I could think of no better gift.'

'And it would cushion the blow of my withdrawal of her military bodyguard and the German Guardsmen?'

Burrus swallowed. 'You mean to take no half-measures.'

'None whatsoever. I will not be threatened.'

Burrus studied him, disliking this new harshness in his tone. 'Nero, how close did you actually come to poisoning Britannicus?' he asked gently.

For a moment Nero stared blankly at him; then the blue eyes shone with all their usual intensity.

'As close as I ever wish to come,' he admitted regretfully. 'But for Locusta, Britannicus would now be dead.'

'Might I suggest, then, that her bodyguard be added to my own staff here; and that the German Guardsmen now serve you? Their loyalty is unquestionable - they will still be laying down their lives for you long after the regular Guards have fled in defeat!'

'Then let it be so, Burrus. Have the German commander report to me at his earliest convenience; and inform my mother of these decisions.'

'Will I tell her of Antonia's mansion?'

Nero considered it. 'Yes,' he agreed, 'let this be official, not personal. She severed all personal ties with me when she threatened me.'

'It is for the best, Nero.'

Agrippina accepted her dismissal from Court as inevitable and found reconciliation in the grand residence of her late grandmother; recalling with affection the many childhood days spent within the exquisite walls. Antonia had been very much of the old school and the refined classical decoration reflected the great woman's strength of character; broken only, in the end, by the discovery that her grandchildren had destroyed her beloved son Germanicus.

'Of course, this was not her original house and furnishings,' Agrippina told Junia Silana, one evening shortly after moving in. 'Caligula burnt it to the ground as a prank, when he was just a small child. What a boy he was! I remember her outrage at catching him and Drusilla in bed together, when they were no more than twelve and thirteen at the time!' Agrippina laughed, as she looked back on those times.

Of all her former friends, Junia alone remained loyal; the others recognising the Augusta as an enemy of the state and deserting her as a matter of prudence. Nero himself had so far paid her only fleeting visits; and then only with an armed escort in attendance.

'Grandmother was furious!' Agrippina continued. 'Claudius was called back to Rome; not that the old buffoon had any greater control over us all than she did! Ah! such an uproar!'

Junia stifled a bored yawn. 'Just as well none of your other brothers survived, for such incest would really have offended the old woman's sensibility!'

'Nero exhibits the same tendencies, of course. His lust, I am sure, knows no bounds.'

'Unlike my own, Agrippina. Since your exile from the Palace I have been kept a virtual prisoner here in your company, away from all suitors!'

'Utter rot and you know it!' Agrippina laughed scornfully. 'No one summons you each day and, besides, I see no eligible gentlemen banging at your abandoned door!'

'There is one who is keen enough,' Junia retorted. 'For a while he preferred my company to the brothels, until you laid down your greater claim on my time.'

'I suppose you come here only out of pity?'

Junia was offended by her derisive tone. 'Who could not feel pity for you, banished like a common criminal from your own Palace!'

Agrippina remained unaffected. 'So, who is this old nobleman who finds you cheaper than a whore?'

'I am far from cheap, Agrippina, and he is far from old. I may soon be in better acquaintanceship with your son than you! Marcus Otho has always had an eye for me and loves no sport better than seduction.'

Agrippina only just succeeded in controlling her features, so that Junia saw nothing of her outrage at this news.

'Marcus Otho?!' Agrippina laughed neutrally. 'What would he want with a woman twice his age?! He is hardly out of the taverns and brothels long enough to pay court to you!'

Junia adopted the same sneering tone. 'No doubt he simply wants my wealth, which is fine by me when I can have his body in return.'

'You know of his debts, of course?'

'Whores, horses and dice. All part of the attraction of a young man. Of course, you have always been obliged to court the more senior of the nobility, haven't you, Agrippina?'

'If young men are your fancy, why not pay court to Julius Vestinus. He keeps a household of handsome hand-picked young slaves who could no doubt keep you both satisfied.'

'So does Lucius Secundus. They wouldn't per chance be two of your disillusioned old cast-offs?!'

Agrippina laughed heartily at her friend's acidic wit. 'Go on! Go to your young lover! Do you think I can stand your company for a moment longer than is necessary?'

Junia stood up, grateful for the opportunity to escape. 'Don't worry,' she said breezily, 'I shall see that he puts in a good word for you with Nero; if only for the fact that I miss your parties at the Palace!'

Agrippina watched a slave show Junia out, then called for her cloak and had her sedan chair made ready.

'Send a runner to the Palace and find out where Marcus Otho is,' she told a slave.

He hesitated. 'My Lady, the lady Junia Silana already sent a messenger. I believe, my Lady, that Marcus Otho will be at the Palace all evening.'

Agrippina cursed. 'Then send the chair for Rubellius Plautus and have him come immediately.'

'My Lady, he is here already. I saw his horse tethered when I sent the messenger.'

'Well thank the gods that something is going right for me! Now get out.'

Plautus was shown in as the slave backed out.

'You took your time,' Agrippina remarked.

'I could find no one to water my mare.'

'And is she watered now?'

'I sent one of your kitchen maids out to her. Why the concern?'

'Because you now need to borrow one of my own animals,' Agrippina cursed, as though it were due directly to his own stupidity. 'You must ride out to the Palace immediately for me.'

Plautus sighed wearily. 'I had expected dinner and sex.'

'You can expect neither until you have spoken with Marcus Otho.'

'What would I wish to speak to Otho about?! He's nothing but a lazy, self-centred reprobate!' Plautus flopped down onto a couch, with clearly no intention of moving.

'He is exactly as you say,' declared Agrippina in exasperation, 'and he is also a terrible influence on Nero. The two of them are as thick as thieves; forever giving the impression that they have the advantage over me. It is nothing, I know; yet their delight at my supposed ignorance is an added insult.

'And now, not content with squandering a vast fortune and living off Nero's charity, he intends to strip bare the purse of my good friend Junia. Well, I will not stand for it, Plautus, do you understand me? I will not stand for it.'

'What will you have me say to him?!' Plautus protested. 'I barely know the man!'

'Mock him, Plautus. Let it be known that he will be open to ridicule if he marries a woman so old and immoral as Junia. She is well past her prime and her conduct has never been that of a lady. Otho is a vain young man; and easily deterred.'

'I fail to see the urgency,' Plautus yawned. 'I will speak with him, if it makes you happy. But it can wait until tomorrow, when I shall no doubt see him at the races.'

'Then make yourself comfortable there, Plautus,' Agrippina said angrily, 'for I meant what I said. I am going through to my dinner now and then I shall be retiring. Good night.'

'But Agrippina!'

'*Good night.*'

Plautus spoke with Otho the following day, at the circus. Otho listened to the disparagement of his latest mistress without apparent interest, but he made a point of bumping in to Plautus a little later in the afternoon.

'Any luck, Plautus?'

'Not bad at all, Otho. I've been following the Reds all day and I've done very nicely out of it, too.'

'And which lucky lady benefits from your good fortune?! Are you still seeing Agrippina?'

'Indeed I am. A fine woman, Otho! And I hope to be seeing her for a good deal longer yet. And you? You surely can't really be serious about Junia?'

Otho shrugged. 'She knows a trick or two!' He grinned. 'But if she's getting too keen on me then it's time to call it a day, don't you think?'

'You're well rid of her, if you ask me.'

Plautus continued to gaze nonchalantly at the activity on the track; and Otho watched him assessingly. The casual aspersions on Junia, he knew, were in fact orders, and came from a higher source. He also knew better than to disregard them. Junia, for all her enjoyable quirks, was already a bedmate of the past.

It remained only to tell her.

Chapter Twenty-Two

OCTOBER A.D. 55

'I would like to read for you now a piece from my latest work 'On Clemency',' Seneca announced proudly, 'which was inspired by, and is therefore dedicated to, our beloved emperor, Nero.'

The dining hall resounded with polite applause, as the emperor and his guests reclined on their couches, enjoying the usual evening's entertainment of music and recitals. Since Agrippina's expulsion from Court, Nero had taken great pleasure in surrounding himself with friends and professionals, in an attempt to dispel the worries of recent weeks.

'I'll wager the chosen piece isn't equal in length to its introduction!' whispered Petronius, sharing a couch with Nero, as Seneca recalled in great detail Nero's unwillingness to sign death warrants.

'I hope you are right!' agreed Nero, under his breath. 'Remind me to have Burrus exiled for telling such tales in the first place!' He glanced about the large room expectantly. 'Do you see Paris anywhere?'

'No, I don't believe I do.'

'Most unlike him to be late...' his voice trailed away as he became aware of Seneca's disapproving eye fixed upon him.

'Always the schoolmaster!' Petronius muttered into his fist, masking his indiscreet chatter with a false cough.

Seneca paused and awaited their full attention, before continuing.

'Happiness is vouchsafing safety to many, calling back to life from the brink of death, deserving a civic crown for clemency...'

'He would exhibit greater clemency himself by sparing us this recitation!' complained Petronius.

'...No decoration is fairer or worthier a prince's eminence than this crown awarded for saving the lives of fellow citizens - not trophies torn from the vanquished, not chariots blooded with barbarian gore, not spoils in war...'

'It is little wonder Otho deserts us!' groaned Petronius.

'Not even Seneca at his talented best could hold Otho's attention. He devotes his evenings to far more pleasurable pursuits than these.'

'And is his pleasure still to be found with that Silana woman?'

'From the fuss that she has been making, I fear not. She has taken his desertion very much to heart and her messengers are becoming quite a nuisance, in fact.'

Petronius stole a wary glance at Seneca, but Seneca was now too intent upon the conclusion of his speech to notice any lack of attention among his audience.

'So he now seeks solace in the arms of a prostitute?'

'They are far more willing to see the back of him!' Nero laughed.

'He has never deserted them long enough to put it to the test!'

'Well, if he ever does break their hearts, at least they could not afford so many messengers!'

'You jest, Nero! After years of his custom there is nothing those ladies can't afford!'

Nero glanced around anxiously as Seneca bowed to his audience and sat down. 'Paris is still not to be seen. Could he have already arrived, unnoticed?'

'It is totally beyond Paris to arrive unnoticed! Perhaps your Aunt Domitia has greater need of his services tonight than you.'

'Aunt Domitia is far too old and frail for ballet lessons - nor any other lessons, for that matter! And I doubt Paris would have such inclinations, even were she not so elderly!'

'Then I recommend you read some of your own work, Nero, before Seneca makes use of this hiatus and gives us another burst of his latest nonsense!'

'He is a writer of quality, Petronius, which you are not,' Nero pointed out lightly, 'for that, at least, you should show some tolerance. Ah! There! It is Paris, at last!'

Domitia's freedman hurried across to the emperor in a state of extreme agitation and made no apology for his lateness.

'Nero,' he said at once, 'I have come away from all manner of scenes at your aunt's house. Another of her freedmen, Atimetus, returned with alarming news as I prepared to leave. He would have come directly to you, but Domitia would not let him do so without first knowing every detail herself - and then she felt it best to send me.'

'What details? What news?'

'News of the worst possible sort, Nero. Treachery and conspiracy. Atimetus met with two friends of Junia Silana. Perhaps you know them? Iturius and Calvisius? They have evidence of a conspiracy, Nero, and intend to prosecute the Augusta.'

'Prosecute my mother?!'

'Atimetus swears it is true. Silana has been much in the Augusta's company of late and has seen more than enough to bring the case to trial. Iturius and Calvisius are to prosecute her for inciting Rubellius Plautus to revolution. She plans to marry Plautus and see him win your throne!'

'Calm down, my good fellow,' Petronius insisted of Paris forcefully, in an attempt to quell Nero's intense alarm, 'you are far too excited and speak nothing but nonsense. We are well into our cups at this stage and require a slower, more detailed account, if you please.'

'What more is there to tell?!' Paris retorted. 'Agrippina is to be charged with inciting her lover to revolt!'

'I must go to Burrus at once!' Nero burst out, rising from the couch in panic.

'Be still, Nero,' Petronius insisted impatiently, 'this whole story smacks of over-excitability. We are relying upon the hearsay of Atimetus alone. And, if it is true, are we to trust the motives of Silana? You said yourself the woman is quite insensible with heartache at the moment. Agrippina has Plautus, while all Silana has is the expensive memory of our own dear Otho.'

'But Burrus saw this coming!' Nero argued. 'Otho warned that she would seek another candidate and Burrus swore he would deal with it. I must tell him immediately.'

He pushed past Paris and headed off at a run, for the rooms of Burrus.

'You confounded fool!' Petronius cursed Paris, as they watched the emperor depart. 'Why come at this late hour? Could it not have waited till the morning? You were the boy's tutor when he was but an infant - surely you, above anyone, would know how easily frightened he is?!'

'We are dealing with his mother,' Paris pointed out. 'Domitia knew well enough that at any hour other than this he would refuse to listen to such allegations. If he is not frightened into action, he will side with Agrippina every time. And the woman is a menace, as well you know.'

'All I know,' said Petronius threateningly, 'is that the boy has been living on his nerves these past few weeks and was all but insensible when last she posed a threat. You may tell Domitia that if this is no more than a tantrum of jealousy, then Burrus will secure her own death warrant - and those of Silana and her prosecutors, too.'

Such a view was also being taken elsewhere in the Palace, as Nero poured out the limited facts to Burrus.

'I cannot see how any of this can be substantiated,' Burrus said doubtfully. 'We have all been watching her so closely; yet this has seemingly escaped us. If it is her intention to put Plautus on the throne, then it can only be a long-term objective. She hasn't yet made any attempt to lay the foundations for such a venture.'

'She has already whipped up public feeling against me!'

'It is a vague start; but not enough. We need evidence of meetings, of co-conspirators - of a firm plot. To jump in too soon, with too little evidence, would be a grave mistake.'

'Is it better to wait and charge her with my murder?!'

'I would do nothing to endanger your life, and you know it. So try to relax and see this in its proper perspective. Think of the animosity between Domitia and your mother; and of Junia Silana, too. Neither would be sorry to see her condemned. And neither can they claim to be acting unselfishly for your good alone.' He gestured for Nero to sit beside him. 'Do you see that this can wait until morning, and that you may sleep easy tonight?'

'I cannot even think of sleep.'

'Then go to Acte. If you cannot sleep then she will lay awake with you. In the morning, take her to the stables to see those new horses of yours, freshly up from the south. Or go to the amphitheatre and choose her one of the wildcats of which you are so fond. You say they can be tamed, with patience. Who better to save the poor creature from the arena than Acte?'

'I hate to see them, hungry and terrified, in those pits.'

'Then I will not tell you of their fate, when released into the ring.'

Nero shuddered. 'I know it well enough. I was forced to watch the so-called spectacle by Claudius. Even the great striped tigers retreat in fear when let loose against their tormentor. They run, not attack. What spectacle is that?' He looked at Burrus, helplessly. 'Why are we so cruel? Why must there be this torment?'

'Tomorrow morning you may end the torment for one, at least.'

'And in the meantime, Burrus, I am no better than those pitiful, persecuted creatures.'

Burrus smiled compassionately. 'All will be resolved before you have even returned to the Palace, I give you my word.' He patted Nero firmly on the shoulder. 'Paris is a sensationalist. It makes him a wonderful ballet dancer - but a hopeless messenger.'

Nero nodded. 'He frightened me unduly, I confess. But I trust you implicitly, my friend.'

'Then go to Acte. Will you be needing an escort?'

'I have never yet!'

'Very well, then. Enjoy yourselves - and don't rush back!'

The following morning Burrus roused Seneca and informed him of the situation, then gathered together the more trustworthy of Nero's staff. In the company of Phaon, the Greek freedman who had replaced Pallas as Minister of Finance, and Epaphroditus and Seneca, Burrus duly set off for the home of Agrippina.

'Now remember,' Burrus warned grimly, 'you are here only as witnesses and must say nothing. I intend to throw my weight about, for I have precious little else to throw at her.'

When the door was opened to them, they pushed past the astonished slave and went directly to Agrippina's bedchamber, without announcement.

'What is the meaning of this?!' Agrippina demanded in fury, dismissing at once the slaves who were arranging her hair and make-up. 'How dare you barge in on me in this vulgar fashion!'

'The following charges have been brought against you by Iturius and Calvisius,' Burrus told her, his tone and manner menacing, 'we have come here to note your answer to them.'

He read the charges formally and she laughed scornfully.

'Iturius and Calvisius, you say? Then I know from whence the charges come! I suppose you are aware that as well as falling out with Nero, I have also managed to upset Junia Silana? Did it never occur to you to check the facts before so foolishly laying them at my feet?!'

'The facts of the case are inescapable,' Burrus retorted, unshaken, 'so their origin is of no consequence. The charges themselves will hold sway at the trial, not the interests of the accusers.'

'The charges that I am to murder my own son?!' Agrippina laughed derisively. 'You know as well as I that these charges are fabricated. I am out of favour with Nero; it is no more than that, and no reason to scheme for his life! That I damn him to the Furies and call for his blood does not mean that I would happily see him dead! Have you never threatened a loved one, Commander? Have you never cursed Nero?!'

She faced her accusers without fear and laughed venomously, saying, 'Junia Silana has never had a child so I am not surprised she does not understand a mother's feelings! For mothers change their sons less easily than loose women change their lovers. If Silana's dependants Iturius and Calvisius, after exhausting their means, can only repay the hag's favours by becoming accusers, is that reason for darkening my name with my son's murder, or loading the emperor's conscience with mine?'

She stared at Burrus with undisguised scorn. 'As for Domitia, I should welcome her hostility if she were competing with me in kindness to my Nero - instead of concocting melodramas with her lover Atimetus and the dancer Paris. While I was planning Nero's adoption and promotion to consular status and designation to the consulship, and all the other preparations for his accession, she was beautifying her fishponds at her beloved Baiae.

'I defy anyone to convict me of tampering with city police or provincial loyalty, or of inciting slaves and ex-slaves to crimes. If Rubellius Plautus or another gained the throne and became my judge, there would be no lack of accusers! For then I should be charged, not with occasional indiscretions - outbursts of uncontrollable love - but with crimes which no one can pardon except a son!'

She thrust her wrists at Burrus and demanded defiantly, 'Bind me and take me at once to the emperor. Let him hear the charges against me.'

'He has been told of them already. I am here by his order.'

'You cannot deny me the right to see him.'

'He is not at the Palace.'

'Then I shall await his return in your custody.' She sneered at Burrus. 'What is it, Commander? You surely cannot fear a prisoner in your own custody? Perhaps you doubt your ability to protect the emperor?'

'Against you, Augusta, there is no protection.'

She smiled in satisfaction.

When Nero returned to the Palace later that morning, he was disconcerted to find that his mother was awaiting an audience with him.

'She waits for you in her former rooms,' Seneca informed him with reluctance, 'Burrus is with her and will not dismiss the guards or slaves present, no matter how much she demands a private audience.'

'What was her response to the charges?'

'She laughed them off. Epaphroditus has her reply fully noted.'

'Then I will see him first.'

Epaphroditus was summoned and solemnly read through Agrippina's response. Nero listened without comment.

'She speaks the truth,' he said at last, as Epaphroditus came to a close.

'Burrus believes he can build a case against her,' Seneca assured him.

'Yesterday evening Burrus believed there was no case to be answered.'

'It has all come about too soon, and in unfortunate circumstances; yet we must make the best of it.'

Nero met his eye. 'She too will make the best of it.'

He looked vacantly to Epaphroditus. 'Send Narcissus to my room, would you... I have something there.'

'Narcissus?' Epaphroditus glanced disconcertedly at Seneca.

Nero caught the surprise in his voice. 'Did I say Narcissus? I'm sorry; it doesn't matter, anyway.' He said no more and took with him an escort to Agrippina's room.

She sat benignly on the bed, calm and composed; belying the need for the number of guards present.

'You must despise me,' she said simply, as he nodded a curt greeting, 'I have publicly denounced you for all manner of crimes which were not of your own doing; yet now I bring the greatest shame of all to our tarnished family name. I will stand trial as a traitor - and I can offer no defence.'

'Since I would judge you in court, I may judge you now,' Nero said coldly, 'I can at least spare us both that indignity.'

Agrippina regarded him carefully. 'There is nothing to judge,' she said regretfully, her voice quivering. 'I was banished from your circle, I was sour and vengeful. And through my bitterness I incited a good number of eminent people to speak out against you. It was never my intention, but the result of my vindictive words is there for all to see. I cannot retract them; and so I must accept my guilt.'

'And Plautus? Was he to take my place?'

'Were anything to happen to you I would always protect my own interests - it is my nature, Nero. I am a survivor and I have no room for conscience, of that you can be certain. But we are mother and son. There is no love stronger, though we may loathe the very sight of one another. Plautus is in love with me now, but who can predict the future? How can I pin my survival on the fickle wiles of love?' She threw up her arms in despair. 'You know that my very survival depends wholly upon your own. Only you can forgive, where others condemn.' She allowed herself a rueful smile. 'What bitter irony. For all my unpunished crimes, in this I am innocent.'

Nero had wept silently throughout her discourse and could say nothing now. He turned in confusion and anguish to Burrus, but the commander could offer no comfort. He merely shook his head in defeat, acknowledging the futility of a trial rather than the Augusta's innocence.

Agrippina took note of their silent exchange, but gave nothing away in her countenance.

'I accept my own guilt,' she said now, 'but I ask one thing only of you, my dearest son. The friends who have stood by me will now fear greatly for their lives. Please remember that they played no part in any conspiracy and deserve no punishment. Rewards may go to my accusers, but I beg you to spare my supporters.'

Nero looked again to Burrus, in sudden desperation; but needed no advice.

'I will not reward your accusers,' he assured her, 'but I will see to it that those who have stood by you receive handsome reward. I can see by your own innocence the absurdity of these charges against you, which owe more to jealousy than fact. If this is a trial, Mother, then you are acquitted.'

Agrippina at once fell weeping at his feet in gratitude, then calmed herself and stood up to embrace him. Her smile faded as he shrank from her touch.

'But you fear me? My own son, in fear of me! I wish now that you had condemned me, for I deserve death for striking such fear in so pure a heart.' She turned away, then swept round once more and cursed viciously. 'No! It is not I who provoked such fear, but my accusers. It is they who deserve death. Let it now be my turn to bring charges. Condemn them, Nero, for this hurt they have caused us. Condemn them, I say.'

Nero trembled visibly. 'On what grounds?'

'Why, the fabrication of charges, of course! You are quick to dismiss cases against others when brought about by jealousy and rivalry. Here is just such a case on your very doorstep and yet you do nothing to punish the guilty.'

'There is no reason for execution!'

'No; there is not. Because privately you side with them and believe me guilty.'

'That is nonsense!'

'Perhaps so. More likely that you know me to be innocent, yet still plot with them to destroy me.'

Agrippina was crying in earnest now and Nero held her to him in comfort.

'I have acquitted you, Mother. I have confirmed your innocence and protected your good name. What more can I do to convince you of my love for you?'

'Execute my enemies! Spare me the pain of seeing them daily.'

Nero gently stroked her hair. 'They will be exiled. You will not see them in Rome again.' He looked across at Burrus. 'See to it, would you, Commander? And escort the Augusta back to her mansion.'

Burrus nodded; while Agrippina smiled in obvious satisfaction at his inability to thwart her.

Nero did not watch them depart.

Chapter Twenty-Three

NOVEMBER A.D. 55

Nero lay on his bed, allowing a pair of Rottweiler puppies to chew his fingers.

'You have no flocks of sheep to be herded and protected,' Burrus observed, upon entering, 'your two new friends there will lead a leisurely existence in your ownership.' He sat down on the bed and gently fondled the ears of one of the pups.

'They were not destined for their usual farm work,' Nero remarked quietly, his mind clearly elsewhere, 'I found them at the amphitheatre, thrown in with a litter of Mastiffs.' He pulled a hand away from the puppy and rubbed the sore fingers without thought. 'Did I do the right thing, Burrus?'

'I suppose one could argue that Mastiffs are bred with the arena in mind, but these fellows certainly had no place there.'

Nero looked at him sharply. 'I didn't mean the dogs, Burrus.'

The commander smiled and shook his head. 'No; I know. And what are they to be called, Nero?'

'This is Mysticus - you may remember the dancer of that name who was so beautiful that no less than two knights died during the very act of making love to him!'

Burrus laughed. 'Who can forget him! And this chap?'

'Palamedes, unjustly sacrificed by the Greeks in the Trojan War - as written by Euripides, of course. Perhaps that was only fiction, but the fate awaiting my little Palamedes was real enough. Did I escape mine, Burrus?'

'She will always be a threat to you, Nero, I can't tell you otherwise. But I hope we frightened her today. Made her more aware of her vulnerability.'

'Made her more wary.'

'Yes, that too. But then, so are we.'

'Speaking of which, I would like to appoint Xenophon Minister of Greek Affairs.'

'He is very well respected, I agree. But as your doctor, can he be replaced?'

'I have letters from two quite brilliant young doctors from Greece, both by the name of Andromachus and both highly recommended by Xenophon himself. I think he will be the first to understand why I would prefer to see this change.'

'I suspect the reasoning behind it myself. I imagine you learned more than you care to divulge during Locusta's visit here?'

'What is there to hide from you, Burrus? My mother poisoned Claudius. And neither Halotus nor Xenophon is innocent in his death. Halotus I trust. But Xenophon... I prefer to take no chances.' He gazed, distractedly, at the two puppies. 'I continue to learn from Locusta. She can neither read nor write, but she sent word via Tubero - a slave she saw in my service and knew to trust - that she has been brewing ante-dotes for my mother.'

'Ante-dotes?! Why ever didn't you say something?!'

'To what purpose? Who are these ante-dotes for? Herself? Britannicus? Does she intend to poison me? Or my stepbrother? Or does she safeguard herself against such an event? Does she believe that I would poison her? Or should we both fear Britannicus?' He swept the puppies up into his arms and cradled them to his chest.

'Would Locusta brew a poison without telling you?'

'She owes me no loyalty.'

'But she warned you of the ante-dotes.'

'This time. And next time, Mother may offer a better reward. I know only that there is threat all around me - but I do not know from where.'

Burrus could not conceal his concern, yet knew that he dare not allow Nero to brood on such troubles. 'Well, we have dealt with her for the moment,' he said lightly, 'and can expect to have as much notice again when next she threatens you. In the meantime, there are plenty of state matters to occupy us. I think we should concern ourselves with current affairs and forget any private troubles, don't you?'

Nero looked at him. 'Are they not one and the same?'

'Not always, Nero. For example, the no small matter of public disturbances at games and displays, whether here or in the country. The situation has become quite intolerable. Any decision you make would be welcomed by all.' Burrus smiled. 'The senate would back you and no one would rally against you in protest. A pity to ignore so rare an opportunity to please all!'

'A pity indeed. And how exactly do I please them? I could ban pantomime actors altogether; but how many would I then offend?'

'It may not come to that, Nero. I can't actually suggest any solution, but I have no doubt you'll think of something yourself.'

'Short of a full ban, I can't.'

Burrus turned to leave. 'Have a think about it, that's all.'

He left the room, without further comment. Nero curled himself up around the now drowsy puppies, but did not join them in their sleep.

Acte's villa at Baiae provided a welcome respite from Rome over the next few weeks, and it was there that Nero was to be found; relaxed and revitalised, in the company of Acte and his dogs.

Yet he knew that such seclusion could not continue, and welcomed the inevitable call to duty when at last it came, in early December.

'Burrus! You are here for an edict on the public disturbances, I take it?' Nero greeted his commander, as Burrus joined him by the pool outside, where the young emperor sat looking out over the bay.

'You are looking well, Nero. The rest has done you good.'

'It has made me edgy and eager to return to work. What have you for me, Burrus?'

Burrus grimaced and was slow to reply.

'Come now, you're not nearly anxious enough to be bringing me bad news!'

'Well, no; the news is not bad. But Pallas and I have been charged with conspiracy, Nero.'

'This is a joke, of course?!'

Burrus could not help but smile. 'It is no joke, Nero - but I grant you, it is as good as.'

'That you and Pallas have worked together to conspire against... me, I presume?' Nero laughed heartily.

'That Pallas and I have ever worked together at all is joke enough! But, yes, we are accused of plotting against our emperor.'

'By whom?'

'Paetus.'

'Ah.' Nero saw the light. 'Does anyone back him in this?'

Sitting down beside the emperor, Burrus laughed scornfully. 'Does anyone back him? Most certainly not! Why should our greedy friend share his profits from the confiscated properties of guilty parties! He brings charges alone - and fills his purse alone. Such are his methods.'

'Well, he made his fortune from confiscated properties during the last reign, so I shouldn't show surprise that he now attempts to build on it further. Nevertheless, I am surprised, and no little offended. Not only should he be taught that this distasteful practise must cease, but his example held up for all. I will not tolerate such things and I wish it to be known.'

'There is one final embarrassment to add to all this, Nero. I myself am due to sit on the tribunal when the case comes up.'

'Then sit you shall, Burrus. It is no more embarrassing and ludicrous than his case against you. If he chooses to make a mockery of our legal system, then let us follow his lead. That one of the accused is also the acquitter - as you surely must be -

is hardly likely to deteriorate matters any further. And you must be a severe judge, my friend. This case is to serve as a warning to all.

'You will sit on the tribunal, Burrus, and you will pronounce acquittal. Furthermore, you will banish Paetus and see that all his records on forgotten debts are unearthed and destroyed. There will be an end to this distasteful habit, once and for all.'

'Very good, my Lord.' Burrus leaned back and gazed out over the bay; contemplating not the view, but Nero's bitterness. Not for the first time, he wondered at the young emperor's ability to cope with the stresses of his position.

'Of course, Nero, you have not yet heard the most distasteful part of all,' Burrus said, after a short silence.

'There is more?'

The commander laughed. 'Only Pallas being Pallas! When I told him of the charges he was naturally horrified. But only, it seems, because Paetus claims they were substantiated by Pallas' slaves. He was most indignant at the mere suggestion that any of his household would know of his private affairs! "I do not converse with slaves or freedmen," he insisted!'

'He *is* a freedman!' Nero scoffed.

'But above all others, it would seem! I asked how he managed to get anything done if he never spoke to his staff. "With notes and signals of the hand, Commander; with notes and signals of the hand."! The man is a pompous ass!'

'The man has always been a pompous ass, Burrus. Could you not contrive to acquit yourself and condemn him?!'

'He must live with himself, Nero - is that not condemnation enough?'

They laughed heartily and continued to watch the boats in the bay.

'What of your edict to curb public disturbances?' Burrus enquired casually. 'Had you given it any thought?'

'Plenty, Burrus; plenty. My dogs are inside somewhere with Acte. You would be amazed at how much they have grown, in just these few days, it seems. They have more freedom here than they had in the Palace and yet they are so much better disciplined. The more freedom we give them, the more respect we gain from them in return.'

'Then they are a far cry from your horses!' Burrus laughed.

'Horses clearly lack our intelligence. Without strict discipline, they become insecure and troublesome. The dogs seem brighter altogether. They resent too much control. Rather like ourselves, don't you think?'

'Young men have always been inclined to rebellious phases, I cannot deny.'

'So it seemed to me. And so I considered these disturbances, and the fact that they have grown steadily worse despite our stepping up security. Or because of, perhaps?'

'I miss your point?'

'Perhaps the more we restrict the people, the more they rebel.'

Burrus considered it. 'A possibility, I grant you.'

'No, no; much more than a possibility, Burrus. The troops are resented - their very presence antagonises and incites. My solution is to withdraw them altogether.'

The commander took a mental step backwards. 'We're not discussing a couple of puppies here, Nero.'

'We never were.' Nero smiled reassuringly. 'Believe me, Burrus, I have given this matter a great deal of thought. And I am convinced that the withdrawal of all troops at public games will put an end to disputes.' He grinned at Burrus' obvious misgivings. 'Times are changing, Burrus and I want it to be known. This case with Paetus, for example. Condoned and even encouraged in the past. Troops everywhere. Spies. Treason. Fear.

'That was the past. This is my time, with my rules. I want the public to see the difference, to recognise the change. Not only will I withdraw the troops from the games, but I will withdraw them from the streets. No honest citizen of Rome will have cause to see a soldier during a normal day. Have you any idea of the sense of freedom this will create? Not to mention the removal of your men from the temptations of public displays, which can only improve discipline.' He patted Burrus' leg firmly. 'This will be a good thing, Burrus; a very good thing.'

The commander remained unconvinced. 'If I cannot convince you otherwise, Nero, then I can only do as you ask. But you understand that I am not in agreement with this decision?'

'We cannot always be in agreement, but that doesn't mean I value your advice any less. Remind me now - what was your advice in this matter?'

Burrus laughed. 'You know very well I had none to offer, so who am I to argue with you! But in the meantime, what am I to do with my troops?'

'Yours is the only profession that has yet to comprehend the concept of leisure time. I suggest you train them in such matters.'

Nero rose and stretched.

'If my stomach does not deceive me, it is time for an early dinner. You'll join us, of course? There is no business in Rome that cannot await your return. Besides which, the Saturnalia fast approaches and I have so many arrangements to make - outside of Palace ears! Tell me, Burrus, what gift would you most like, were money no object?'

'Money will very soon be of great object to you if you are so careless with it at this early stage. A gold goblet will suit me well, and no more.'

'A gold goblet indeed! The very gift I already have selected for Pallas - and a thousand other menials! I was thinking more in terms of a set of finest glass... or a horse, from Spain... or a fine hunting dog, for your newfound leisure time! What do you say, Burrus?'

'I say you are incorrigible, and I hope to the gods you entrust your shopping to Acte - or we will all be answering to Britannicus come the next Saturnalia!'

'Saturnalia?' It was Acte, who had approached them, unheard.

She was followed, almost instantly, by the two young dogs, who leapt upon Nero vociferously. She attempted to drag them away, before emperor and dogs ended up in the pool.

'I took you to be discussing important business, not the festivities!' Acte complained. 'They are weeks away! And you, my Lord, are the same man who mocks all religious ceremonies and claims to have no belief in the gods!'

'As indeed I have not. But I like to buy gifts for my friends and get as drunk as the next man!'

Acte snorted in mock disgust. 'So what makes the Saturnalia any different?!'

'His reputation is such that they have already named a drink after him,' Burrus laughed, 'your favourite drink, Nero, is now known commonly as 'a Neronian'. But I wouldn't touch it myself - it is no more than iced water!'

'Boiled iced water,' Nero corrected him, 'and neither Otho nor Senecio will touch it either, so I wonder at the necessity to give it a common name!'

'But it is the favoured drink of the Emperor!' Burrus argued. 'It is drunk in all the fashionable homes.'

'I suppose Pallas drinks nothing else,' Acte ventured, which brought forth a greater chorus of laughs than she would have expected.

'I wonder what hand signal he uses when requesting one?!' Burrus pondered.

'Don't worry, my dear,' Nero explained to Acte, 'it is a private joke and I will tell you all over dinner.'

He bent down and pressed the dogs into reluctant acquiescence. Burrus followed suit and together they walked back to the villa.

'I suppose, Commander, that you are here to summon Nero back to Rome?' Acte suggested, with obvious regret.

'You know that I go willingly,' Nero protested.

'Yes; yes, I do.'

'You will not be returning, Acte?' Burrus asked, surprised.

'I'm uncomfortable in the city. I'm still just a slave and a mistress, and my presence can do Nero no good.'

Burrus could not argue the point. Nero, it was clear, had already tried and failed.

'It's a wonder, then, that you bother to return yourself,' Burrus said to Nero.

The emperor smiled ruefully. 'If I had ever seriously intended to abdicate I would have done so by now. My bed is made, Burrus; for good or bad.'

The weeks leading up to the Saturnalia saw several disturbances in Rome. Despite his inclination to pooh-pooh such supposed portents, Nero was called upon to conduct a purification of the city. The Temples of Minerva and Jupiter were struck by lightning and damaged by fire, necessitating their re-dedication by the emperor. Only Nero failed to see any significance in these events.

'The whole of Rome speaks of portents and ill omens,' Agrippina declared, as she stood with Nero at one such ceremony. She seemed to Nero to be strangely ill at ease.

'You pay no heed to such gossip?' he gently mocked.

'I pay heed to all gossip. My life depends upon it.'

'Upon careless fires and bolts of lightning?'

'Upon the talk of the people, Nero. These events signify something, you mark my words. The last such portents foretold your accession.'

Nero eyed her warily.

'Come, Nero, I do not threaten you. Here, with your guards to each side of me? I speak not of mortal danger. I have no need to speak of Fate - for she speaks for herself. Only you disregard her.'

'And the people? What do they say?'

'They say that your name is black, truly. That Britannicus is the true heir. That the gods will not rest until justice is seen. And if that does not frighten you, Nero, then you are stronger than I. For if they speak the truth, then neither of us will survive into the New Year.'

Nero looked her steadily in the eye. 'Fate had no hand in my accession. I may have no fear of acts of nature, but I know well how to guard my back.'

'You wrong me, Nero. And you will regret it for the remainder of your days. But at least know that I forgive you.' She turned away, in the full knowledge that she had struck a raw nerve.

Burrus laid a hand on Nero's shoulder. 'It's embarrassing enough to surround you with guards whenever you're in her company. She is, after all, the Augusta, and I cannot simply ask her to leave,' he said, in apology.

Nero shook his head. 'It's of no consequence, Burrus.' But it was plain from his features that it was.

'I have had all I can stomach of these religious ceremonies,' he said lightly, 'have some wise man declare them successful and allow me to retire to the Palace for the duration of the Saturnalia.'

Burrus could not fully mask his disapproval.

Nero grinned. 'Look about you, Burrus. Do they really care if we've appeased the gods or not? Do any of them truly believe in the gods, or do they simply believe in the ceremonies - and the public holidays?!'

'Nero...'

'Who are these festivities for - ourselves? Or the gods?' Nero teased. 'Don't answer me, Burrus, for to do so honestly would bruise your morality.' He turned away from Burrus, without waiting for a response, and walked across to his sedan chair.

'Is this the end, then, for this year?' Burrus called across to him.

'I rely on you to make it so!' Nero called back cheerfully; and departed.

Once back at the Palace, he was quick to throw himself into the pleasures of dinner. Making certain that Otho, Petronius and Senecio obeyed the call to his couch, he endeavoured to shake off the memory of his mother's words.

'You're in fine spirits, Nero,' Senecio remarked, 'I take it the purifications have been successful and all is well with Rome again?'

'Your guess is as good as mine,' Nero corrected him, 'and I feel worse now than if I'd never retired to the country at all. So you must all get me thoroughly drunk and away from this accursed city, if only in spirit!'

'Away from it at this time of year?' Otho laughed. 'Are you mad?!'

'What good is the season if I have no one with whom to share it?' Nero complained.

'Acte refuses to come?'

'Steadfastly. And it is all the fault of you, my so-called 'friends'. But for your cowardice, we would by now be married.'

Both his tone and manner were too light to be taken seriously and his companions merely laughed at his woes.

'Saturn shines bright in the sky,' Otho said, 'the season is too well underway to air complaints and grievances.'

'I have yet to see it,' Senecio queried.

'You must be outside to see the great star!' Petronius teased.

'This is true,' laughed Otho, 'it can rarely be seen from inside a tavern!'

'On that we may safely take his word,' Nero verified, 'for there is no greater expert on the interior of taverns than our Otho here!'

'It is a shame to break up so warm a party,' Petronius remarked, after several more pitchers of mead had been emptied. 'Could we not keep this going through to the day after tomorrow and begin the festivities early?!'

'I would be well able for it, Petronius,' Otho said heartily, 'were it not for the fact that I must pay court to my patron on the morning itself. I am, as usual, short on funds and in dire need of a particularly extravagant gift.' He leant closer to Petronius, under the pretence of excluding Nero from the conversation. 'I've heard it rumoured that our new patron was labelled miserly last Saturnalia, so he may push the boat out this year to redeem himself.'

'What do you want of me?' Nero demanded, feigning offence, 'A villa each? Be grateful for your patron, however miserly his gifts - for he, poor soul, has no patron to cheer his sad year. There is only one man in the empire under patronage to no other - and that luckless being is myself. Is that not bad enough, without burdening me with friends such as you?! You're all down for a set of silverware each and I'll hear no more said of it!'

'Had I known I would have ordered five hundred and one sets of silverware - and held one back for myself when handing them all out to my slaves!' Otho complained, with bitter tuts, 'And thereby saved myself the chore of calling on my patron on the morning!'

'You might mock,' Petronius rebuked them all, 'but it is a sad indictment of our times that the traditional gifts are no more imaginative now than in the time of the kings.'

'Were it not for the 'unimaginative' togas handed out each year, my clients would have no formal attire,' Senecio objected, 'I would go so far as to say they depend upon it. A fine crystal goblet is of little use to the average working man.'

'And I suppose a lifetime's supply of silverware is of every use to the average slave?' Petronius retorted.

'What, then, do you give to your household?'

'A poem or a short story, to suit their tastes,' Petronius lied; winking to allow the lie be known.

'Which, of course, they can sell as readily as silver, in order to buy their freedom,' Otho volunteered.

'My stories and poems sell for more than the average price of silver! Depending, of course, upon the names I use!'

True to the wishes of Petronius, the party continued well into the early hours, and the Saturnalia itself was not long in arriving. On the morning of the shortest day of the year, Nero, as all patrons, saw each of his clients and household in turn; thanking them for their service during the year and presenting them with thoughtfully chosen gifts.

'No others fret so anxiously over their gifts,' Acte had gently scolded him, during one of their numerous shopping trips together the previous month. But now he took pleasure in reaping the full benefit of such cares, in witnessing the genuine delight of each recipient. The less thoughtful, and probably depended upon, gift of a toga was given to each client as an additional token.

Although it was not expected, each of Nero's slaves presented him with a gift, which totally overwhelmed and delighted him. It was therefore in the best of spirits with which he rejoined his friends for dinner that evening and the party that followed.

As custom dictated, dice were thrown to choose a King for the Day.

'Your lives are going to be sheer misery!' Otho threatened, sitting back smugly after his throw of three fives.

'You haven't won yet,' Petronius warned him confidently; but promptly failed to match him.

Others followed; and lost.

'Sit back and watch me rest the crown from the Etruscan Royal House itself!' Nero declared, and threw his dice carelessly, without any true thoughts of winning.

His audience watched, in stunned silence, as each of the three dice came to a halt on six. A moment later, cries of congratulations and loud applause rang out.

'It's a fix!' complained Otho.

'What does he want to be King for a Day for?' agreed Senecio. 'He's King all year round!'

'He should have been barred from throwing,' added Lucilius, the noted Greek poet recently introduced at Court by Nero.

'There are others still to throw,' Nero pointed out, 'stave off your complaints until I have actually won.'

The remaining guests took their unsuccessful turns, then everyone sat down in a large circle, as the amusements began in earnest.

The 'King' set about ordering each of his 'servants' in turn to perform some amusing task, designed to enliven the drunken revelry. To spare blushes - and the irritating protestations - Nero was careful to cause no embarrassment and each victim threw themselves whole-heartedly into the entertainment.

'Paris! You must perform one act of a ballet, taking every part!' Nero ordered of the famed dancer. But drink had by now taken its toll, and Paris could not rise from the floor.

'Lucilius, then! A poem, if you please.'

Lucilius rose slowly and entered the centre of the ring. 'An ode to a great lady,' he announced, 'much loved and respected by us all, I am sure.' He burped loudly and had then to wait patiently for a round of applause to die down. 'This is the ode,' he pointed out, stiffly.

'Nicylla dyes her locks, 'tis said,
But 'tis a poor aspersion.
She buys them black, they therefore need
No subsequent emersion.'

He bowed and accepted the cheers with customary dignity. 'Thank you.'

Nero applauded heartily and requested a song from the lyre player Terpnus; then Petronius rose for a second time, un-requested, and burst into verse.

'I should love my wife like my income:
But I must confess to my shame
That I wouldn't love my income
If I thought it would stay the same.'

By this stage of affairs the entire party was drunk and overly intimate. It was suggested that the younger guests, seated on couches some distance from the adult party, should be invited to join in. The junior members of Court were unused to such drunken behaviour and their embarrassment was acute.

'Let them back to their couches,' Nero pleaded in their defence, embracing Otho passionately as though no one else shared the room.

'Put him down! You don't know where he's been!' Petronius protested; and Otho pushed the young emperor away disdainfully, grateful that at least one friend among them cared something for their reputation.

Nero was aware of the intervention and resented it. He glanced at the retreating young noblemen and hailed Britannicus.

'You can stay,' he told the boy, 'no one has a right to send away a young prince.'

Britannicus took his place reluctantly, beside Seneca. Yet he could not avoid Nero's malicious gaze.

'Who shall be my next victim?' Nero mused, his eye fixed steadily on Britannicus. 'The newcomer, perhaps?'

There were general cries of protest, for Britannicus' discomfort was plain for all to see. But Nero paid no heed.

'Into the centre,' he ordered, 'and amuse us in any manner you wish.'

No one present fully expected the boy to obey, but Britannicus did as he was instructed and faced them all with surprising composure. With barely any hesitation, he began to sing an ancient tragic song, the subject of which was a boy's displacement from his father's throne.

The courage he had shown had already won him respect and approval; and now his audience were quick to air their sympathies with him, seeming to identify his plight with the characters in his song. Even Petronius made space beside him and invited the boy to fill it, congratulating him fondly on his performance. For a moment, the host was forgotten.

Nero looked round at his guests, all of whom were too drunk to conceal their true feelings, so it seemed. He met Britannicus' eye; and this time it was he who shrank from the callous stare. Without saying a word, he rose awkwardly to his feet and stumbled out of the great dining room; Otho following.

'You pushed me away,' Nero rebuked him bitterly, 'why follow me now?'

'Four legs are better than two,' Otho said simply, taking the emperor's weight on his shoulders, 'though my own two are no steadier than yours.'

'I would rather crawl,' Nero said, cursing, and tried to pull free.

'You would think that, having no useful position in life, I would have no concept of personal honour,' Otho told him, ignoring his weak efforts.

'Your concept of honour differs vastly from mine.'

'Yet it exists, my very much loved young friend.' He kissed Nero firmly and met with no resistance. 'You may not mind being the talk of all Rome - but I do.'

'They are against me, in there, to a man.'

'No one is against you. But neither is anyone against Britannicus. He is entitled to his sympathisers.'

'And do they include the public? And the Guards?'

'To the Furies with him, Nero! You will have a sore enough head come the morning, without bringing it on yourself now! Forget the boy!'

But Nero could not forget the boy.

Chapter Twenty-Four

DECEMBER A.D. 55

'What does he think he looks like?' Agrippina complained, as she sat down to dinner with Seneca and his wife, Paulina.

Nero, reclining on one of the main couches, was dressed in a brightly coloured Greek robe, tolerated in Roman circles only during the casual atmosphere of the recent festivities. Nero, having developed a fondness for the fabric, could see no reason why such garments should be locked away for the rest of the year, and had had several other robes made up.

'He's a young man,' Seneca reminded her, 'he breathes fresh air into our stuffy lives.'

'He brings disgrace to our family,' said Agrippina bluntly.

She had been invited to the Palace by Paulina and was aware that her presence was an embarrassment to her son; yet she appeared insensible to the heavy guard present and treated the dining hall as her own - a fact which did not escape Nero.

'She has contrived to gain invite every evening since the festivities,' he complained to Burrus, 'Why does she insist upon spying on me in this fashion?'

'You must make it clear to your own guests that your invitation does not extend to their friends,' Burrus suggested.

'Who am I to dictate their friendships? If I welcome them, then I must also welcome their friends. But my mother has never before been among them. She seems suddenly to be acquainted with every sister, mother and wife of my circle - and they know full well that she has been as good as banished from the Palace.'

'It's probably just a passing thing,' Burrus reassured him, 'she means to get her own way, having been snubbed over the Saturnalia. And there are plenty to take pity on her, because of the goodwill of the season. A few more days and the New Year will probably see an end to it all.'

'And until such time, my dining room is to be filled with Guards,' Nero complained further.

'It is a wise precaution, my Lord.'

'But not very conducive for entertaining, you'll agree?'

Burrus smiled.

Although Nero returned the wry smile, it was clear that he found the Augusta's presence increasingly more disturbing. Burrus resolved to see that she would secure no further invites; with or without the emperor's knowledge.

The remains of the first main course were being cleared away when a minor disturbance seemed to break out at one of the other tables. It was that reserved for the children at Court, but only the children themselves seemed in any way excited by the events.

'What occurs?' Nero queried, paying scant regard himself. A slave was despatched to investigate and returned hastily.

'My Lord!' he said urgently, in a hushed voice, 'It is Britannicus! They say he is poisoned!'

Burrus started visibly, but Nero showed no concern.

'He has collapsed, my Lord - they believe him dead.'

'Tell them to ignore him. It is one of his fits and will pass.' Nero glanced down towards the couch in question.

'Perhaps you should go and see the boy,' Burrus suggested.

'He's an epileptic,' Nero pointed out, 'why should anyone suspect poison, in a room full of Guards and with a full staff of personal food-tasters to hand?'

'Nevertheless, they appear to be convinced the boy is dead and he is certainly showing none of the usual convulsions which accompany his fits,' Burrus urged.

'Then go and see him yourself, Commander. I have no interest in him, alive or dead.'

Annoyed, Burrus followed the slave to where Britannicus lay. It was immediately obvious that the unfortunate boy was dead, but Burrus checked for all signs of life before having him covered and arranging for his removal.

'It was the water, Sir,' a young boy by the name of Domitian informed him, 'his drink was too hot, Sir, so he added water from the pitcher that was there. But it had only been put down just then, and look - it has already been removed, Sir!'

'Nonsense, child, his drinks are tasted, as is his food. How was he, before his collapse?'

'His drink was tasted, Sir, but it was too hot,' the boy insisted. 'No one tasted the water - I saw a slave put it down myself, and take it away just as quickly!'

'Which slave?'

'None of these.'

'Would you know him again if you saw him?'

The boy frowned in concentration. 'No, Sir,' he said, at last.

'You foolish boy!' Burrus snapped, though privately alarmed by his tale, 'tell your tutor to keep you away from sensationalist fiction and read a few classics, instead!'

He instructed the slaves summoned to remove the boy's body to his chamber and then returned to Nero. As he passed by Agrippina's couch he paused to relay the news.

'*Dead*?!' she repeated incredulously, struggling to keep her voice down. Her astonishment and horror seemed to Burrus to be frighteningly genuine. 'But how?'

'He took one of his fits.'

'He hasn't had a fit in years!' She looked across to Nero and stared at him fixedly. He was laughing with Otho and eating the next course, which had already been brought out to him. 'Does he know?' she demanded.

'He does not care, Augusta,' Burrus replied.

The slaves were already fetching out the next courses, as though nothing had happened, but Agrippina could not bring herself to eat. Her agitation confused Burrus.

'He really is dead, then?' Nero asked, as Burrus rejoined him.

'Yes, he is, Nero - and you are hardly exhibiting the necessary decorum.'

'Britannicus and Octavia have told me frequently enough that I have no decorum, owing to my common background. I would not now dream of dishonouring the dead and proving him to be a liar.'

'Nero! Pull yourself together! What do you mean to do?'

'I mean to do nothing, Burrus. How did he die?'

'He was poisoned.'

'Impossible!'

'He was deliberately handed a hot drink and a slave was ready with a pitcher of cold water, which had slipped by his tasters.'

'Which slave?'

'It isn't known. He collapsed as soon as the drink passed his lips. There's no avoiding the conclusion, Nero.'

'The conclusion is that I poisoned him. After the events of the Saturnalia, who would argue any other case? Have his pyre erected now and his body gone, tonight. I want no doctors near him and no questions asked.'

'Nero! You cannot do this! There is no precedent...'

'There is every precedent and I am fully able to handle the situation.' He looked across to Agrippina, who still sat steadfastly watching him. 'She is to know that she cannot get the better of me. See her fear? It is because I have none, Commander.'

Burrus looked to Otho. 'Tell him this is no joke - the son of Claudius, his own step-brother and brother-in-law, is *dead*.'

Nero reached out swiftly and held both the commander's hands in his own. 'Trust me, Burrus,' he said softly, 'I know now that it is no joke, but it comes too late. When everyone else showed interest and concern, I showed none. And coming so soon as it does to the fiasco of the other night, that is damning. I am already damned, Burrus. Nothing I can do now will change that. So let me go on with my act and at least win one battle.' He sank back into his couch and dipped a finger casually into a lemon syllabub.

Agrippina, still watching, could stomach no more. She rose and sought out Octavia, who had been taken by nursemaids to her chamber.

'My poor, poor child,' Agrippina said gently, entering the room uninvited and dismissing the maids immediately.

'They will not even allow me to say goodbye!' Octavia sobbed. 'He is already on his pyre!'

'But my darling, that's not possible.'

'Step outside and see for yourself!' Octavia all but screamed. 'I believe it was ready for him before he even sat down to dinner!'

'Now now, my love; I know you are distressed, but...'

'How else do you explain the pyre? I am telling you, that monster, my husband, had it built and waiting for him!' She collapsed, sobbing, into her pillow.

'You suspect Nero?'

'My brother has no other enemies. All sympathised in his plight - as was made perfectly clear only last week.' Octavia's distress turned to bitterness as she rounded on her mother-in-law. 'You can scheme and plot in his defence all you wish, but it will count for nothing against the facts. He is a murderer! He killed our father and now he has killed my brother! He is a monster, and all shall soon know it! The kindest thing he ever did was to finally end my brother's suffering - for death must have been a blessing compared to the abuse he endured at the hands of that fiend!'

Agrippina listened to her tirade with interest, but made no attempt to offer comfort. When it was clear that Octavia had nothing else to impart, she slipped back out of the room and rejoined her hosts in the dining room.

'What is going on?' Paulina asked, 'Seneca has gone off with Burrus and everyone is whispering of murder; yet Nero is behaving as though nothing has happened!'

'Nero is the only one unaffected by shock,' Agrippina said darkly. 'I can find out nothing further myself, but it would certainly appear that the poor boy was poisoned. Draw what conclusions you will.'

Paulina looked across at the emperor, currently enjoying the lyre playing of Terpnus.

'When is the funeral to be? Any word?'

Agrippina laughed at her naivety. 'Funeral! The boy is already on his pyre! Octavia is much distressed by this final callousness by Nero. Although she takes comfort in the fact that death has at least released the poor child from the horrors of Nero's nocturnal visits.'

'Agrippina! Surely not...'

'What can I say? That Octavia wrongs him? I have been for so long excluded from his company that I have no idea to what she eludes. She is his wife; perhaps she knows him better than I.' Agrippina shook her head sadly. 'I no longer know what to believe of him. Only the other evening he declared that mushrooms were the food of the gods! An innocent remark or a sick reference to my poor Claudius?'

'Seneca will hear no wrong said of him,' Paulina said defensively.

'I say nothing, one way or the other. I'm the boy's mother and will always remain biased in his favour.' Agrippina took a sip of wine to steady her nerves.

'What do you make of Nero's behaviour?' Seneca inquired of Burrus, alone in the commander's room.

'Disturbing, to say the least.'

'*Disturbing*?! I see it as tantamount to suicide! The boy's openly throwing the gauntlet to that woman, as though he welcomes ruin!'

'By poisoning Britannicus, you think?'

Seneca laughed at such a suggestion. 'She poisoned Britannicus, as a warning to Nero. And, no doubt, because it suited her plans. She may no longer back Nero, but she would welcome Britannicus as emperor even less. Two birds with one stone - except that she threw wide of one mark.'

'If he was attempting to show Agrippina that he was unafraid of this threat, his acting was convincing. Agrippina seemed more shaken than Nero.'

'Come, Burrus; how can you doubt him so?'

'The pyre, for one. One cannot build a pyre in advance of an 'accidental' death.'

'And if the pyre was not for my brother?'

Burrus and Seneca swung round at the first sound of Nero's voice and flushed guiltily.

'We thought you were still listening to Terpnus,' Seneca apologised.

'Mother left, so there was no point in continuing the pretence.' He looked at Burrus earnestly. 'It is pretence, Burrus. I'm as frightened as you. But the pyre was in the yard already. It had been built for the child of one of the kitchen slaves, but the mother apparently disposed of it in the marshes, against the father's wishes. Abandoned, in the hope of being picked up by one of the poor childless scavengers, or dead already, I cannot say. It is said that if you seek a child, you may take your pick of newborn babies there. But I am not disposed to pry into the private lives of my household, unless they choose to seek me out as confidante. The point is, I gave instruction for Britannicus to be removed as quickly as possible. I was hardly expecting it to be immediate, but so be it.'

'I'm sorry, Nero, but I hardly suspect Agrippina of this crime. If you had seen her shock...'

'Oh, I've seen her shock on many occasions,' Nero interrupted unemotionally, 'from whom did I inherit my own acting skills? But as to suspecting her, I remain unconvinced myself. Otho would be happy to believe anything of her. He speaks of her as some kind of mythical monster. Were I not so fond of him I would find it insufferably hurtful. But in this instance we have argued all evening. Claudius was old and infirm and disgusting to as young and attractive a woman as my mother. I could almost condone the manner in which she hastened his death. But I cannot believe her capable of cold-blooded murder.' He entered the room fully now and sat down on Burrus' bed. 'I don't honestly believe Britannicus was murdered at all. He probably took a drink over the Saturnalia, which triggered his epilepsy. He rarely took fits and seemed to have outgrown it, but I know little about such complaints and believe it more reasonable to suppose that a fit killed him than poison. If Mother killed him, then I have proved to her that her efforts were in vain. If a fit took him, as I believe, then I hope I have led her to suppose that I, too, am capable of cold-blooded murder. Perhaps now she might fear me.' He smiled. 'Either way, I'm afraid, I can only look upon his death as a blessing. It would be sheer hypocrisy to say that I ever liked the boy, as all of Rome knows.'

Burrus' concern could not be allayed. 'You are no more than a boy yourself,' he retorted, 'and you play too dangerous a game. It is my job to deal with matters such as these and if Seneca and I have ever agreed in anything, it is that you are thrusting your tender neck into the noose! Leave well alone, Nero, I urge you.'

'And supposing, Commander, that he was murdered - and not by my mother? That someone else saw him as a threat to me and removed him? If I leave too well alone, in whom do I place all my trust?'

'Nero!'

The emperor smiled. 'Of course I trust you, Burrus; implicitly. But I have to look out for myself. I am not the boy you think me and I cannot remain forever in your care. Let me at least try to take care of myself!'

They all relaxed somewhat and Seneca called for some wine.

'If it was poison, we must tighten our defences,' he remarked, as he passed round the pitcher.

'I eat and drink nothing that has not passed Halotus first,' Nero assured him. 'Pythagoras is not only my cupbearer, but he is the most noteworthy of Rome - and considers himself to be the most noteworthy ever to handle a cup! He cares nothing for my meagre life, but he would rather die than sully his reputation by carrying poison!'

They laughed.

'The public will be expecting a full state funeral when they hear of the death,' Burrus said, introducing the sombre note once more.

'What? And encourage them to mourn and weep the loss of their Prince - and regret the accession of the Usurper?' Nero shook his head. 'If you thought I never paid attention during lessons, Seneca, then think again. Am I not mistaken in saying that there is an old tradition of withdrawing untimely deaths from the public gaze?'

'Yes... but... '

'Then I shall publish an edict to that effect. I am, after all, too distressed by my brother's death to face my public and glorify his death with pomp and ceremony; none of which will bring him back.' He grinned at his two advisors. 'Will that do?'

'My Lord,' Burrus said with feigned grimness, 'you inherit more than mere acting skills from the Augusta.'

They drained the pitcher and retired belatedly to their chambers; Nero finding his already occupied, by more than just his dogs. However furiously he may have argued with him earlier that night, the emperor was relieved to see out the remainder within the security of Otho's undemanding arms.

The New Year brought with it no protests at the demise of Britannicus. Though rumours were rife within the Palace, Nero's popularity with the commons remained unaffected. It was with renewed fervour and confidence that he settled down to his second full year in office.

'I have here a list of appointments,' he told Epaphroditus, as the secretary presented him with the usual morning's work, 'take a run through it with everyone if you so wish, but I can foresee no problems. Bar one, perhaps.'

Epaphroditus scanned the list of names and noted, with no little satisfaction, that Nero's ministers consisted exclusively of his own Greek freedmen. 'Anyone interesting among them?' he inquired.

'Phaon has secured his official post as Minister of Finance.'

The secretary smiled. 'Anyone would be better than Pallas, but Phaon could not be more deserving.'

Nero grinned and confided, 'I personally would regard my new Foreign Minister as by far the most interesting of them all. Perhaps when you see him you will understand my sentiments!'

'Good grief, not Doryphorus! I have yet to meet him, but there isn't a female slave who does not whisper his name in the halls! Something of a ladies man, is he?'

'I rather hope not, but we shall see.'

Epaphroditus laughed, then took the list away for further approval. Nero had barely settled in to the work left by the secretary before Seneca appeared and returned the list, in no uncertain manner.

'Aha, that didn't take long,' Nero remarked, without looking up.

'Beryllus,' Seneca said simply. 'An able Greek tutor he may have been, but you owe him no favours.'

'I give him no favour. He is the most suitable candidate for the post. What exactly are your objections, Seneca?'

'The man is corrupt! Completely bribable. You can't make him head of Greek Correspondence - whatever his virtues, they are far outweighed by his greed.'

'Have no fear, Seneca, I was aware of his weaknesses from the moment he first stood before me in the class room. Where you would expect a hundred lines, he would settle for a few sesterces! But his virtues are such that I am prepared to overlook such faults. He must answer directly to me; and I must countersign and pass everything he handles.'

'And he is aware of this?'

'Absolutely. Without my seal, any document he issues will be invalid.' Nero looked up and smiled. 'Of course, he is also under the impression that this is the case with all my ministers. I had no wish to insult the man to his face.'

'Yes; well. Other than Beryllus, I can see no problems. They would all seem likely to mix well; and are certainly qualified for their posts.'

'Mix well, Seneca - there you have it. I want no backstabbing and jealousy in my offices. We can at least be open and frank with one another. I believe that counts for more than mere qualifications.'

'So I hope it may prove, Nero. And now I had better announce that I have pushed ahead of Phaon, who awaits an audience.'

'Oh good, send him in, would you?'

A tall Greek duly entered and sat down without ceremony on the couch.

'Good to see you, Phaon,' Nero welcomed him, 'How are you finding it here?'

'Comfortable, as is only to be expected. I only moved in yesterday.'

'I wasn't actually expecting you so soon. I was quite surprised when I saw your mare in the stables this morning.'

'You recognised her, then?'

'She is one of Tigellinus' finest! I'd know her anywhere. If a man on your previous income could secure himself an animal of that quality from the Spanish stud of Tigellinus, then that is the man I want in charge of my finances!'

Phaon laughed. 'So I owe her my office!'

'What can I do for you, anyway? I presume you didn't drop by to discuss horses?'

'Just a social call, Nero. I have a few ideas for changes within the Treasury this year. Limits on private expenditure; securer methods of drafting wills; the allowance for free seats in court - more or less all the points you raised when last we met and the means to put them into practise.'

'Excellent! I shall call Epaphroditus and we'll discuss these things at once.'

Nero sent a slave to fetch his secretary and they were soon arguing the finer points of law and drafting edicts.

'You've taken up rooms in the Palace, then?' Epaphroditus asked Phaon, as they ended official business and settled back to enjoy a pitcher of mead.

'My own villa is too far on the edge of town,' Phaon explained.

'I'm on site myself,' Epaphroditus told him, 'we must arrange to meet up in the evenings.'

'What of your social life?' Phaon inquired of Nero, 'I haven't noticed Acte anywhere around?'

'She stays occasionally; but she dislikes it here. We have the villas at Baiae and Neapolis, which suit us both far better.'

'So you're free to join us in our social pursuits when in Rome, then?!'

Nero grinned. 'Very much so. I shall look forward to it.' He tidied away his wax tablets in a neat pile and rolled up paper documents in his drawer. 'Would you like to join me at the baths before lunch?'

His suggestion was readily accepted and they made a convivial party as they left the emperor's rooms.

The death of Britannicus and the threats of the previous year were already no more than a dim and distant past.

Chapter Twenty-Five

FEBRUARY A.D. 56

Nero was lying flat on the floor, with a large slab of lead on his chest, when Burrus entered his room. The commander stepped carefully around him and sat down at his desk.

'I presume this is another of Terpnus' absurd ideas?'

Nero struggled to find his voice. 'Hardly absurd, Burrus. It's a proven exercise to strengthen the voice,' he pointed out, breathlessly.

'So be it. But we cannot conduct business in this ridiculous fashion.' He leant forward and removed the lead from Nero. 'This is surely more harmful than the diet he has put you on. The man is only a lyre player, Nero - you could at least check his theories with one of your Doctors' Andromachus before putting them into practise.'

'I did. They both agree that fresh fruit is harmful to the vocal chords and that Terpnus is correct in recommending dried fruit and onions.' Nero sat up and endeavoured to catch his breath. 'I might also point out that he isn't 'only a lyre player'! He is the best musician and singer to have graced a stage and I am proud to accept his tutelage.'

'The Palace is filled with actors and artists and they would all have you believe that they are the greatest discovery known to Rome!' Burrus complained. 'And if only their followers were not so easily fooled I would have no cause to disturb you now.'

'The fighting in the theatres has got worse?'

'Very much so. Discipline within the ranks has deteriorated with the increase of leave; the troops are causing nearly as much trouble as the public; and the various factions in the theatres are intent upon slaughtering one another!'

Nero sighed. 'I did my best for them, but failed. Publish the following edict. All ballet dancers and their hangers-on are to be expelled from Italy. The troops are to be stationed once more within the theatres. And there is an end to it, sorry though I am to have my hand forced in such a manner.'

'I'm sorry, too, Nero; I know you wished to avoid this. But the checks on forgery have been a great success.'

'At least one of my edicts has been worthwhile!'

'Come, now! The senate is perfectly in favour of its increased prerogatives - it is only in practise that the house murmurs complaint. No one enjoys an added workload, however much they may privately welcome it.'

'All I have asked is that Treasury suits come before a board of arbitration. Matters of State cannot be entrusted to a solitary judge. And all legal appeals are to be addressed to the senate, too. It is not unreasonable, and hardly an increase in workload. Why then do they berate me so?'

'Such power is new to them. And you are also a novelty. They'll push you as a child might push its nurse; you need hardly take it personally, Nero.'

Nero smiled. 'It is hard not to.'

'Well, then, if the matter of the ballet dancers is now finalised, I have no further need of your time. Would you like me to replace the lead?'

'Thank you, Burrus, but I have work to attend to now. Phaon is due in an hour or so and I have barely looked at the tablets he left in to me last week.'

'Oh, I gave some maps to Doryphorus.' Burrus remembered. 'Trouble with the Armenian borders again. I felt he should familiarise himself with the disputed areas.' He caught something in Nero's reaction and looked at him questioningly. 'Was that alright?'

'Yes, of course; why shouldn't it be?'

'You needn't worry, the skirmishes are only minor and of no significance.'

'I'm not worrying, Burrus. But Phaon will bring in so much work with him, I can hardly spare anyone else a moment. The maps will wait, won't they?'

'I can see no reason why Doryphorus would even trouble you with them. I mentioned it only in passing.' Burrus smiled privately to himself and shook his head. 'I shall be away for the remainder of the morning, by the way. I have an appointment with Thressalus; my throat still troubles me and I'm hoping he'll prescribe something useful. As long as it isn't a lead weight and a diet of dried onions and garlic!'

Nero laughed and reclaimed his seat at the desk. 'The best of luck, Burrus. If Thressalus fails you, then you may avail of one of my own doctors.'

Burrus pushed the lead slab with his toe. 'Something to look forward to, I'm sure!'

When Burrus had left and Phaon had made his brief visit, Nero summoned Patrobius, the Minister of Leisure, to tell him of the expulsion of dancers. Patrobius was hardly surprised.

'Were you not involved in some violent incident yourself at the theatre?' the minister inquired.

Nero blushed. 'It was some years ago, Patrobius, and a very unfortunate accident. But I can at least claim to understand the passions that incite these disturbances. I presume Marcus Otho made some mention of the fact?'

'Claudius Senecio, actually. We travelled together to look at some new horses for the Blues. Beautiful beasts, from Persia.'

'I saw them. We must arrange an outing together when next an acquisition is made. And meantime, would you look at these plans I have for a new gymnasium on the Field of Mars. Phaon has them, too. Perhaps you could work together and see how feasible they are?'

Nero handed over the scrolls and allowed his attention to wander momentarily.

'Are the new Persians still stabled on the Esquiline Hill?'

'Pardon?'

'The new team for the Blues. Are they still in the overflow stables?'

'Oh; no, they're at the Circus Maximus.'

'Shall we take a ride out to see them?'

'Certainly, Nero. When?'

'Now!'

'But I understood your day to be spoken for. I was surprised to be summoned at all!'

Nero sighed. 'I suppose it is impractical. Not that I'm busy. But I need to be available for my staff. They were good-looking animals, though, were they not?'

'Not a patch on the Greens, Nero!'

When Patrobius had left, Nero returned to his work, but it was a mere half-hearted effort. He knew that Patrobius was a gossip and that his staff would soon know that he had excess time on his hands. The thought of their intrusion - and the intrusion of one, in particular - distracted him mercilessly. It seemed that he had been unable to concentrate on even the simplest of tasks since the appointment of his new Foreign Minister.

The inevitable call came shortly after lunch. Like most of Doryphorus' visits it was hardly necessary; but Nero had been listening for his step as though in expectance of something urgent.

'Commander Burrus left me some papers to look at,' Doryphorus explained. 'I thought it best to leave them with you, now that I have studied them. I have added a few notes of my own that might be of interest to you.'

He leant across Nero and set the pile of tablets and scrolls down in front of him.

'Anything wrong, my Lord?'

'Nero, please,' the emperor insisted, 'and no, nothing at all.'

Doryphorus raised his eyebrows. 'Only...?'

'No, really, there is nothing wrong.' Nero flushed a little and gestured for him to go.

Doryphorus smiled and quietly made to leave. He hesitated as he reached the door.

'Perhaps I might go over some of those maps with you?'

Nero studied the papers before him, afraid to look round. He needed no help with the maps; and was certain Doryphorus knew that. Yet the certainty failed him.

'I... I think I shall find them straightforward enough. But thank you, all the same...' He stopped short; unable to speak his name. He was aware that Doryphorus continued to linger in the doorway, although he resolutely kept his attention on the papers before him. Only when he heard the minister depart did he trust himself to turn round.

'Slaves! Slaves!'

The two dogs leapt up from their sleeping place beneath his bed and added their barks to his calls. He scolded them impatiently, as two slaves hurried to his aid.

'Calm yourselves, there is no panic; though these two brutes would have you believe there was murder! Where is Tubero?'

'Umm, around, my Lord, I expect...'

'No matter. Perhaps you could take a message for me, please, Aurin? And Tudrus, are you free to prepare a horse for me?'

The slave shuffled awkwardly.

'Forgive me, I didn't quite mean that literally. Could you go to the stables and have them prepare me a horse?'

The two slaves readily gave their consent and Nero hastily scratched into a wax tablet.

'Give this to Marcus Otho please, Aurin. I have absolutely no idea where you might find him - although you would be wise to try his tailor first... but that is only a guess, of course... Palamedes! Lie down!' Nero pushed the young dog away from him and ushered the two slaves out before they could be subjected to any similar show of affection.

'Tudrus! Wait one moment! I may as well walk with you,' Nero called, after a moment's hesitation, and hurried to catch up with him. 'Mysticus! Palamedes!' He fell in step with the slave, while the two dogs bounded ahead. 'I hope you don't mind them, Tudrus; they're a terrible nuisance, but too full of affection to scold. No price is too high to pay for such love, wouldn't you agree?'

Tudrus said nothing.

'I believe I've only seen you once or twice before,' Nero continued affably, 'would you not normally work in the Palace?'

'I carry out repairs and maintenance, my Lord. Just now I was fixing a shutter in one of the rooms.'

'Oh dear; and I suppose now I am delaying you. You go back, Tudrus - I am well able to summon my own horse.' Nero hesitated and watched, with regret, as the slave turned back.

'No, wait, Tudrus. You are not the only one with more pressing chores to attend. Let me walk with you again; I can afford this free time no more than you.' He called the dogs back and rejoined the slave. 'I had a sudden urge to go for a ride. I hoped Marcus Otho might have joined me. And it is a perfect morning for a ride, wouldn't you agree?'

'It's bitterly cold out, my Lord.'

'But dry and bright. Ah well; it is not to be.' He slowly pushed open the door to his chamber and returned to his desk.

Though the maps for which Doryphorus had offered his assistance were simple enough, Nero could not concentrate on them; his mind preoccupied by the offer itself. He didn't bother to reprimand the dogs when they fought over a pillow stolen from his bed; and he was still staring unseeingly at the provincial borders when Otho at last arrived.

'I had expected to find you riding in the grounds,' he remarked, stepping through the damp remnants of duck down. 'You preferred to stay in and pluck some unfortunate bird, I gather.'

Nero turned round and glanced at the mess, seeing it for the first time. The two dogs thumped their tails happily as he half-heartedly cursed them.

'They belong in the stables,' he complained to Otho, 'as do I. But I had no real wish to go riding, any more than I have a wish to remain here. I don't really know what I want.' He looked at Otho. 'That's the problem, you see. I don't know what I want.'

Otho merely grinned. 'I think you do. And if your ignorance is genuine, then any member of your household could readily supply you with the answer! You have been alternately listless and exuberant since the appointment of your new Foreign Minister. If there is any other reason for your lovelorn behaviour, then forgive me!'

'Is it so obvious to him, do you suppose?'

Otho sat down on the bed and stretched himself out. 'Credit the man with intelligence, Nero - he is your minister, after all.'

'But is it right, Otho?'

'Right? You tell me.' Otho considered the question lazily. 'Is it right that young male slaves be made to keep their hair long, for the sake of beauty; while all good men of Rome should cut their locks immediately upon assuming adulthood? What do you read into that, my friend - and is there really any need to question right and wrong?'

'Given my position, there is every need.'

'Not where there exists privacy and discretion.'

Nero sighed and joined Otho on the bed.

'It is so senseless and unjust,' he complained. 'Octavia despises me, yet we have free rein to express our love as we wish. And you and I must cover our trail to avoid shame and humiliation that we don't even feel. It isn't my shame, Otho! I would proudly tell every stranger in the street if I could. My shame is that I can't.

'And Acte. I have no comprehension at all of why I should feel shame at taking her as my mistress. How can they tell me she is not good enough for me to marry? When Octavia was! What is birthright but a matter of chance?

'And I - I had the luckiest throw of all the dice. My right of birth is to command all Rome. Yet here am I, bowing to the commands of all of Rome.'

'In my experience - which, incidentally, is vast,' said Otho, 'you have only to tell the man your feelings and your troubles will be over. At worst, it will be he who is left to listen to them, instead of me.'

'How can I tell him?'

'Then wait for him to make a move; and continue to suffer as you do now until he does.'

'Do you like him, Otho?'

'I have yet to actually meet him. If he is as attractive as he looks, then I can say nothing against him.'

Nero sighed. 'He distracts me so.'

'So might Acte, had you not had the common sense to press your suit immediately.'

'You are determined I should make a public fool of myself?'

'I can think of no better advice. Let's go and drag Senecio from his office and make a nuisance of ourselves in a tavern until dinner!'

Nero sat up. 'Now, that is good advice. And if I can get drunk enough, I might act upon the remainder of your advice during dinner.'

'An event neither Senecio nor I would miss for the world!'

Nero laughed and slipped an arm around Otho's shoulder. 'Where would I be without you, my friend?'

'Sexually frustrated. Don't bring love into it, you have others for that. Love is one disease I intend to avoid for as long as possible. I've seen the havoc it wreaks on others!'

Those chosen to sit at the emperor's circle were limited that evening. Doryphorus was neither surprised nor uncomfortable to find himself sharing Nero's couch; though he betrayed nothing in his demeanour.

'The maps proved straightforward,' Nero said casually, as they ate; though he avoided his companion's glances.

'Is it Baiae that you retreat to?' Doryphorus asked, after a lengthy break in conversation.

'Otho has a villa there. And Acte has a villa at Puteoli, which isn't far. I stayed there for some time before the Saturnalia. We have another near Neapolis, at Velitrae - that is, Acte does. Have you ever been to Neapolis?'

'I have had the pleasure on many occasions. A truly beautiful area.'

Nero toyed with the food on his plate. The invitation on his lips could get no further.

'You know of Acte, of course?' he asked, instead.

'I have heard her spoken of.'

'I love her deeply.'

He continued to stir the remains of the food on his plate.

'When I met Acte - even before I first spoke to her - I was captivated. Her looks, her mannerisms - everything about her. And when we spoke, I knew that I wanted her. Before we ever declared our love or shared our passion I already knew that I wanted her with me for the rest of my life. If anything were to happen to her, I'd end my life. And I knew that then just as surely as I do now. Do you believe me?'

Doryphorus said nothing, but nodded with complete understanding.

Nero swallowed, afraid of the reaction he might invoke. 'Then will you believe me,' he asked carefully, 'when I say now that I love you?'

'I believe you,' Doryphorus said simply, betraying nothing in his face.

'Because I am your patron, Emperor of Rome, and you can do nothing but?'

'Because I have been attracted to you from day one. I knew the feeling was mutual and did all in my power to draw you out; yet you steadfastly ignored me.'

'I was so afraid you would laugh in my face.'

'Nero, no one could ever laugh in your face.' Doryphorus placed a gentle hand on his shoulder. 'And it has nothing to do with your being emperor.' He smiled, aware of the suffering he had so instantly alleviated.

Nero, too, smiled; then quietly began to laugh, the relief of his emotions intense. Still somewhat disbelieving, he raised a hand to Doryphorus' face and hesitantly stroked the near-white skin.

'Oh, Doryphorus; you don't know just how much I have longed to do that.' He laughed again and hugged Doryphorus tightly to him. 'Just to say your name! I hadn't even been able to trust myself to say your name!' He released him from his elated grasp and leaned back on the couch momentarily, to recover himself. 'I'll dismiss Terpnus and Paris and we will retire immediately.'

'Why dismiss them, Nero? They are both worldly men, I am sure. I personally find an audience enjoyable - and what better accompaniment could we have for our first expression of love?'

Nero was momentarily nonplussed. 'Not here, surely?'

Doryphorus grinned. 'Of course not! Though you were ready to consent, weren't you?!'

'My feelings at present are beyond my control! If you wish Terpnus and Paris to join us, I will not refuse you. Yet experience has always taught me to be discreet.'

'Believe me, Nero, the experience is far more pleasurable without it!'

Knowing the singer and dancer to be trustworthy, for their livelihoods and newfound wealth depended upon it, Nero had no misgivings in consenting to Doryphorus' request.

'I had not realised inhibitions could be so stifling,' Nero declared the following morning, as he lay alongside Doryphorus in the darkness, waiting for the first of the slaves to enter and light the candles.

'You are a natural actor, Nero - and all actors require an audience. Besides,' Doryphorus pressed, 'none of this was new to you.'

'It's always new, Doryphorus.'

'And do you always grant freedom to the nearest slave?!'

Nero sat up sharply. 'Oh, the gods! I'd quite forgotten Paris!' The vague recollection of declaring, in the euphoria of spent passion, Paris to be free born now came flooding back. 'My aunt will be furious! He was the favourite of her freedmen and now I have deprived her of all patronage!'

'Paris will continue to keep the old lady happy now that he is a free born citizen of Rome.'

'You clearly know neither party. His dearest wish was always to be free of her and only my love for her prevented me granting it. I fear that love may from hereon go unrequited.'

Doryphorus laughed and made to get to dressed. Nero stretched out a lazy arm to prevent him from doing so.

'I am tired of secrecy, Doryphorus. Stay with me and let the opinions of the slaves go to the Furies.'

'I care nothing for gossip, Nero. But I have work to attend to and early appointments to keep. For their sake and not yours I must hasten my departure.' Doryphorus continued to grope in the darkness for his robes.

Reluctantly, Nero pulled on his own robe and lit a spill from a torch out in the corridor.

'The slaves will get a surprise this morning, one way or another,' he joked, flooding the room with candlelight. 'I rarely stir before Epaphroditus fetches me in my work for the day.'

'Yes, well, he is one of my early appointments, so I must certainly stir.'

They dressed and parted; Nero settling down for an early start to the business of the day, while his slaves took the two dogs for their morning's exercise.

'Good night?' Epaphroditus inquired, when at last he appeared.

'Very! Now all I want to do is see Acte. Can you arrange the time for me?'

'Not this week, Nero - the senate is bubbling away furiously. They have all manner of proposals to set before you. The weekend, perhaps.'

'Not soon enough, I want her with me. I can't bear this separation.'

'Send for her, Nero! The Augusta's rooms are at her disposal and you can both travel to Baiae at the weekend. She hasn't been in Rome for months, she'll no doubt welcome the visit.'

'Do you think so?' Nero asked uncertainly; knowing her better. 'She is always so uncomfortable here; and now...'

'Nero, she must be missing you just as much as you are her. A brief stay in the Palace is but a small price to pay, don't you think?'

Nero brightened visibly. 'You're right, of course, Epaphroditus. Could we defer this morning's business while I make the necessary arrangements? I shall work all the better when once we can settle down without distraction.'

'You have an hour to make your arrangements,' the secretary told him firmly, 'and not a moment more!'

Chapter Twenty-Six

Acte lay on the bed; gently stroking the two dogs sprawled across her legs, as she watched Nero working at his desk.

'It's a good thing, isn't it, that they came to you first?' she asked, not speaking of the dogs. 'It shows that they understand your views, I would have thought.'

Nero shook his head. 'The senate was afraid to put this through behind my back because it knows full well that my entire administrative staff are my own ex-slaves. It has nothing to do with respecting my views.'

'But at least now you have the chance to make your views publicly known,' Acte insisted.

Their weekend in Baiae had already been sacrificed to official duties and much of their time at the Palace had been given over to the subject of the senate's current pressure. It had been demanded that patrons be empowered to re-enslave any undeserving ex-slave, and the proposal had considerable public support. But the consuls had refused to put the motion through without first consulting Nero.

'If I rule against this,' he complained to Acte, 'I shall be made personally responsible for every crime committed by freedmen. And yet how can I endanger the rights of the innocent, just for the guilty few?' He raised his pen once more. 'I must rule against this. But the current laws need to be redefined and clarified.'

He finished his letter and sat back. 'There! I have written to the senate requesting that it gives separate consideration to every charge brought by a patron and that it must not diminish the rights of ex-slaves in general. But I really need to spend some time with the consuls to address this whole matter.' He smiled at Acte. 'Not, however, now. It can wait.'

He bade the dogs lie down under the bed and took their place across Acte's lap. She stroked his hair soothingly.

'Why won't you stay here?' he asked her again.

'How many more reasons must I give?' she protested, combing his locks with her fingers and feeling the contentment flood through him. 'I'm sorry, Nero, but I couldn't fill my day here without you. You have your daily business to attend to, your musicians and poets in the evening, your lovers as and when you want. You know that I can't play a part in any of those things. For how long could I drift around the gardens throwing sticks for the dogs?'

'You would soon grow to enjoy the after dinner entertainment,' Nero insisted, 'and I would have little need for lovers with you permanently beside me.'

Acte laughed. 'Of course you need them! You love them, Nero! And as to your poets, given time they would become even more tedious than they are now! And your office? How am I to assist you each day when even now I understand less than half of what you say?! All this business of praetors and tribunes which Epaphroditus has been hounding you with since my arrival - I don't even know what it is that they do and why one should have more power than another!'

Nero hugged her tightly and buried his face against her breast. 'You and Otho are the only sensible people in Rome - that's why I need you here. You're my only grip on reality.'

'Reality? I thought your grip was on something else entirely!'

They laughed, and kissed; and drifted gently into the lovemaking that had interlaced Nero's official duties since Acte's arrival. When at last they lay back in contentment, neither felt like sleep.

'Tell me about the things you were discussing with Phaon and Epaphroditus,' Acte prompted, knowing that it weighed heavily on him.

'Petty squabbles and demonstrations of power.'

'They're as common in the street as in the senate,' Acte pointed out. 'The freedman issues orders to the slaves beneath him as though he owns them; and I had to answer to senior slaves - and bully the juniors. We all like to hold a particular position, Nero.'

'Quaestors hold the lowest rank in office and yet are responsible for Treasury and public accounts,' Nero told her slowly. 'There are twenty in all, and for the most part they serve as assistants to the higher ranks. Twenty bitter and ambitious men, resenting the higher ranks and too keen to be among them themselves. Would you put them in charge of accounts?'

Acte laughed.

'A tribune accused a quaestor of over-zealousness in relation to the compulsory sales of poor men's property. It was probably only a small incident in a sea of many, and so I have transferred the Treasury and public accounts to a new board of commissioners, who are all skilled and qualified former praetors. My ambitious quaestors will still scheme their way to the top, but at least they'll no longer trample victims along the way.

'Aediles are the next step up the ladder. They want to move on, but know better how to win promotion. Hard work and dedication is now their key to success. They are responsible for the general care of the city and thanks to them it is faultless.

'And then we have our twelve appointed praetors. Second only to consuls and worthy of their rank. Trusted and proven. The senate has only just forbidden tribunes to encroach on the authority of praetors; so now they are the very law itself. In fact, at the same time, several of the tribunes' powers were curtailed, as were those of aediles. The lower ranks always strive for the higher, and generally abuse their own powers in so doing. Hopefully, we have curbed such practises.

'Phaon and I have agreed that fines imposed by tribunes should not be entered into Treasury records for the space of four months, to allow time for appeal, which can be lodged for adjudication by the consuls.' Nero yawned. 'Lots of little discussions, leading one to the other, and all for the purposes of putting an end to these insufferable squabbles and jealousies and general back-stabbing.' He curled up against Acte and closed his eyes. 'Everyone is encaged by restrictions, be it for good or bad. And I am no exception.'

The restrictions imposed upon Nero by office were eased somewhat over the coming months by Doryphorus, whose imaginative sexual innovations were reflected in Nero's daily business. The emperor increasingly exerted his independence and self-confidence; and resented all the more the intrusions of office in his private life.

'Am I the only young man at Rome who has never roamed the streets tossing vagabonds in blankets?!' Nero asked Otho one evening, as they sat with Senecio and Doryphorus, listening to a poetry recital by Lucilius.

'You are the only young man at Rome who rules the empire,' Otho pointed out, 'it disqualifies you from all else, I'm afraid.'

'But it's a recognised coming-of-age ritual!' Nero complained. 'Why would you not take me with you when I asked?'

'You were a mere child. How could I have kept face with my friends, with you in tow?!'

'Take me out now, then!'

Otho laughed. 'Now? I'm an old man of twenty-four, Nero! I couldn't outrun a one-legged beggar, never mind a healthy one!'

'In just a couple of months I shall be nineteen and too old for such activities myself. Everyone from my senators to my slaves can look back on their wild youth - while I have done nothing more rebellious than stand up to my mother or indulge in indecent role-playing with Doryphorus!'

'Then you already have more to boast of than the rest of us!'

'Don't mock me, Otho; I'm in earnest.'

'Then what is stopping you? Attire yourself as a common slave, don a cloak for added secrecy, and make mischief with your friends.'

'I'll go with you,' Senecio offered, 'I have no reputation to protect, after all.'

'Count me out,' Doryphorus said quickly, 'I can share Otho's excuse; although, of course, I look so much younger!'

They laughed; and earned a rebuke from Lucilius for their indiscretion.

'I can't tolerate this,' Otho complained, rising, 'it is enough to suffer his poetry, without his added effrontery. Good night, gentlemen. Don't be in a hurry in the morning to call for that delightful young chambermaid of yours, Senecio!' He winked and strode purposefully away, across Lucilius' designated stage area.

'Who shall go with us, Nero?' Senecio asked.

'Tubero and Aurin.'

'Who?'

'Two of my slaves.'

Senecio pulled a face. 'It is enough to dress as a slave, without keeping company with them, too. My cousins Aemilius and Ateius will make admirable companions, and they have a wide circle of intimates who would be only too happy to join us. It should be quite an escapade, Nero!'

'One of many, Senecio! Tomorrow night?'

'Why not?'

They drank to their future engagement and indulged Lucilius with hearty applause.

The following evening they assembled immediately after dinner; Nero accompanied by Aurin, much to Senecio's contempt.

'Is he one of the emperor's boys?' Aemilius inquired privately of his cousin.

'His slave only, to fetch and carry for him and do any dirty work.'

'But he speaks with him!'

'Our emperor likes to keep us in our place,' Senecio sneered. 'He may be younger than us, but he is quick to remind us that in his eyes we are no better than members of his household. Why else do I rot in my father's business while Greek freedmen fill the emperor's cabinet? Were I to become one of his boys myself, it would not earn me office!'

'Well, my Lord,' Aemilius declared, as they were introduced, 'you look every bit as good as your model here! I do declare that I wouldn't give a gold piece for you if you were led before me in the market!'

'Then you had better get used to calling me Lucius, before your remarks become treasonable!' Nero joked.

'Lucius! That takes me back,' Senecio said fondly. 'Our favourite haunt then was the market. And the shop where they made the expensive sweetmeats!'

Nero threw an arm around his shoulder. 'Then let that be our first port of call! And this time our disreputable band needs no sesterces!'

When they returned to the Palace late that night they were excessively drunk and heavily laden with purloined goods. Nero succeeded in limiting his business the following day and the young men met up once more immediately after lunch.

'I can't remember half of these things,' Senecio said doubtfully.

'I can't imagine why we ever wanted any of it!' Ateius laughed. 'Have your slave there take them away, Nero.'

'There's enough here to fill a shop!' Aemilius joked. 'By the end of the week we'll be able to set up in business!'

'Then that is exactly what we shall do!' Nero declared. 'We'll turn the Palace gardens into our very own market place!'

'Complete with brothel?' Aemilius asked hopefully.

'Why not?! Doryphorus and I could run it ourselves!'

They all laughed uproariously at such a thought, and began to lock away their hoard.

'Have you much to occupy you this afternoon?' Aemilius asked Nero.

'Enough to prevent us from meeting again until after dinner.'

'And where shall we start the festivities this evening - a tavern or a brothel?'

'Surely we can allow time for both!' Nero insisted.

'Then we'll meet at Plancina's house. Is that agreed?'

The others readily consented and the group broke up.

If the conversation in the brothels and taverns was not enough to alert the populace to Nero's clandestine activities, then the thriving 'market' by the Palace lake gave further hint. Nero's was not the only gang roaming the streets at night, but it was the only gang to give genuine cause for alarm. Most teenagers could be seen off with a few threats and the occasional punch; but when the first rumours of Nero's involvement began to circulate, no victim could dare to retaliate.

Burrus was the first to confront Nero and attempt to put an end to the escalating violence.

'I can appreciate the opportunity to escape the pressures of office,' Burrus told him at dinner, one evening early in winter, 'but it is now time to call a halt to this nonsense. You are endangering both yourself and the public and I can no longer condone these actions.'

'Come, Burrus, you are too serious by far,' Nero protested, 'I have endangered no one! We rob stalls and snatch purses; we taunt noblemen and torment beggars. But we cannot be accused of violence. However rowdy we become, I would not permit such extreme behaviour.'

'Nero, you molested the wife of one of my officers only last week! You cannot deny it, for the man knows you well enough and is an uncle of one of your companions! At what point do you consider your behaviour to be extreme?!'

Nero blushed. 'It was mere high spirits. I meant no real harm; and no one was hurt.'

'Whether it be directly or otherwise, you are personally responsible for an unprecedented increase in murders and attacks, Nero. Decent people insist upon being home by nightfall; so afraid are they of walking the streets at the present time.'

'But, Burrus, that has nothing to do...'

Burrus would allow no interruption. 'It is entirely due to you, because you alone have put an end to retaliation. No one dares fight back, for fear of striking the emperor. And now every street gang in the city adopts your disguise in the hope of being mistaken for the emperor and avoiding retribution. Pseudo gangs are dropping bodies down the sewers nightly and I refuse to differentiate between them and you, Nero.'

Nero was horrified. 'We are just having fun, Burrus. No more than any other young men have done. How can I be held responsible for the actions of others? Let the people retaliate if they wish - it would do me no personal harm, and, if it did, it would be no more than I deserved. Otho regularly sported black eyes! It's all part of the excitement!'

Burrus shook his head in exasperation. 'Nero, when will you understand that your own views mean nothing? It isn't enough for you to gratefully accept a beating. No one will dare give it. You've given every cut-throat in Rome a free licence to kill!'

'It is unfair to blame me!' Nero snapped angrily. 'For the very first time in my life I am doing normal things with normal people of my own age. I am allowed to be Lucius Ahenobarbus instead of the Emperor Nero. You can't take that from me. None of them can. And I refuse to be swayed by emotional blackmail.'

'Nero, please...'

'Leave me alone! You have no say in my private life; none at all.' He rose up angrily and pushed past the slaves who were still serving the main courses.

Resentment increased Nero's thirst that evening; and wine increased his lust. Plancina and her willing ladies were scarcely enough to satisfy him and he was dragged unwillingly from their beds by his impatient companions.

'Come on, Lucius; we've had our fill,' Senecio urged, 'Let's join up with those new boys in from Antioch. If we hurry, we'll catch them at the tavern on the corner.'

'We used to share them,' Nero complained, 'I don't know why he lets me down now. This is just... nothing.'

'You're drunk,' Senecio laughed, wrongly interpreting his words, 'come on lads, help me drag him out. He must be too drunk to get it up, we'll be here all night if we wait for him to relieve himself!'

Aemilius kicked a used sheaf beside the bed. 'He has relieved himself already, he's just too drunk to know it! A few more goblets of mead will soon sober him!'

They finally persuaded him to leave and set off for the nearby tavern, but there was no sign of their newfound friends. Nero quickly grew impatient to be out on the street again and they reluctantly drank up and left.

'I enjoy the freedom,' Nero told Aemilius emphatically as they left, 'not the drink itself. And the freedom to wander into taverns is not the only pleasure open to me. You might complain, but I am anxious to savour everything, not merely linger over one aspect alone.'

'A commendable attitude, Lucius!'

'What is commendable?' Senecio demanded, joining them. 'Is the emperor to give office to a Roman citizen at long last?!'

'Now that is commendable!' Ateius cried in approval, pointing to a woman approaching them, in company with her husband.

'That's Helvia and the senator Montanus,' Nero told his friends, eyeing the couple resentfully, 'You see before you a man who will let me do nothing. If I tried to put through a motion to give him a hundred extra gold pieces a week he would veto it!'

'I'd give a hundred gold pieces for his wife!' Ateius said, to general whoops of approval.

'I'll take her for nothing,' Nero retorted, 'and let him veto that!'

He ran forward and blocked the path of the couple, who had already grown wary of the approaching group and were now attempting to cross the busy road. Nero stepped blithely between them and linked his arm with Helvia.

She pulled free of him in disgust.

'Let go of me, you filthy creature!'

'Unhand her!' Montanus snapped, pushing Nero viciously into the road.

Nero narrowly avoided a merchant's cart and resumed his position at Helvia's side, slipping a hand inside her robe and instantly giving rise to her horrified screams. Montanus at once set upon Nero, and the other young boys were quick to join in the melee. Nero himself struggled free and pushed Helvia against a cart, pulling roughly at her knotted belt in an attempt to disrobe her.

Her frantic cries soon attracted the attention of several onlookers, albeit reluctant to involve themselves, and the boys decided to make a judicious escape.

Montanus had faired well in the skirmish and had no wish to be deprived of revenge now. He set off in instant pursuit, with his wife following dazedly in his wake.

The boys raced for the narrow street ahead, knowing that another leading immediately off it would soon lose them within the tangled maze of unlit lanes. But, as the wildly roaring group swept into the sanctuary, Nero stumbled and lost momentum.

Seeing a boy within his grasp, Montanus lunged forward and caught at the cloak flapping out behind his fleeing assailant. He caught only the hem, which was instantly snatched back from his fingertips; but it was enough to throw the boy off balance once more and cost him a vital step.

It was enough for Montanus. Nero called out urgently to his companions, but his cry was lost among their triumphant whoops of victory. He felt the cloak tighten suddenly about his throat and he was wrenched violently back, as the rest of the gang vanished into the night. Again, his ankle twisted and collapsed beneath him; but this time he went straight down.

And Montanus was upon him.

'You murderous little cut-throat!' spat the senator, kneeling hard upon his stomach and holding cloak and tunic alike so tightly at his throat that he could neither turn his head nor catch his breath.

A solid fist hit him squarely on the nose and a second punch had landed before the pain of the first had even registered.

Nero had known nothing like it. The pain drove a breathless scream to his lips, choked and muffled by the blood filling his mouth. He gagged on the vile substance, fighting for breath; his eyes blinded by the stinging tears that seemed to fill his entire head.

He was aware of a woman's screams and another blow to his face. He struggled to writhe free from the relentless grip of his attacker, no longer able to gauge his own strength or position. He was conscious only of those awful, frantic cries, and the fluid blinding his eyes and his senses. A myriad of colours, made with tears; his pain.

Helvia was screaming for *him*; not for Montanus. It seemed to come to Nero from within, not any sound or word he picked up in her cries. Montanus was killing him, and there was nothing she could do to assuage his blind fury. Nero struggled all the more desperately, kicking and writhing in sheer terror for his life.

'Otho! You bastard!' he cried aloud, not knowing if his words reached his lips, 'You bastard! You didn't warn me!' He fought furiously in his panic, no longer seeing the senator above him. 'You didn't say I could get hurt! You said it would be fun! You didn't tell me this could happen! Otho! You've killed me! And I hate you!'

He sobbed in rage and terror, cursing Otho again and again. It occurred to him, in a brief moment of sanity when the colours seemed to darken, that his dying words would be the very next curse; and the pain of betrayal engulfed him.

'Don't let me die hating you, Otho. Otho!'

He cried out for help, not knowing who he called or why; or even if the words existed outside of the colours at all. But the pressure on his chest lessened, and he felt his head being raised from the damp pathway. He knew the moisture matting his hair was his own blood; and the colours filled his mind with confusion.

He was being shaken violently.

'Talk to me! Talk to me, you filthy little vagabond!'

He couldn't open his eyes. But he knew the voice of Montanus, cutting through him like a knife. He began to sob once more; desperate for the release of Death that was too slow in coming.

'Who did you call, damn you?! The name - *tell me the name*!'

He was shaken again. Unbearable; yet in full consciousness borne. He tried to speak; felt only the thick warm blood bubbling on his lips, making a nonsense of his words.

But Montanus heard something, and the words had a chilling affect.

Nero's head fell back on the ground. The weight was gone from his body. Blood and colours and still Montanus' voice.

'You called for Otho. Marcus Otho?'

Montanus sounded hollow. Defeated. The voices echoed around Nero's head, as though floating above him.

'You can't leave him now!' Helvia was protesting, 'You have to finish him!' She was hysterical; terrified.

'A moment ago you were pleading for his life!'

'And you wouldn't listen to me! And now you've gone too far and he'll die - and he'll name you first!' She broke down pathetically, adding weakly, 'If you walk away now, you'll bring the soldiers to our door.'

'They'll come anyway,' said Montanus wearily.

'You think that band of cut-throats would come forward?!'

Montanus ignored her and raised Nero's head once more, by way of the knot of garments at his throat, still held in a fist.

'Tell me the name! It is all that will save you now.'

Nero struggled to form the words. He hoped that he said Marcus; but no longer had the strength to care.

'Then I am truly done for,' Montanus said softly, letting his victim's head gently down. 'There are many gangs claiming to be led by Nero; but none can claim the acquaintance of Marcus Otho. No common thief would even know his name.'

Helvia's voice rose in panic once more.

'What do you mean? What are you saying, Montanus?!'

'I am saying that everything we have heard is true. The pseudo-gangs really do imitate an original. Before you lies the emperor, Helvia - and I have met my own death this night.'

'No!' sobbed Helvia, 'It cannot be! It cannot be!'

'Come!' said Montanus, with sudden urgency. 'We waste too much time. His friends must surely have missed him by now and will soon be here. I set out to protect you and if we don't run now then I will have failed.'

It sounded to Nero as though they were both sobbing, but their tears were soon beyond his hearing. Instead, he lay alone, crying with pain and fear; with disbelief that Death could pass him by for such misery; that the comfort of unconsciousness would not take him. He cried for his own ignorance; that he had brought this on himself without realisation. If he could only have known; if the time was his to turn back.

And Otho had always painted it as such fun. And now he would die hating him. He sobbed bitterly.

'I don't want to hate you... I don't want my last words to be against you...

'I don't want to die.'

Chapter Twenty-Seven

DECEMBER A.D. 56

'I don't want to die...'

'And nor will you, my love; nor will you.'

Ecloge gently sponged Nero's face and smiled at him warmly as he opened his eyes.

'Otho!'

'Otho is away from Rome,' Ecloge told him patiently, 'and cannot be summoned. But Acte and Doryphorus are here, and both eager to see you.'

Nero began to speak once more, but neither Ecloge nor Alexandria, tending him, could make sense of his words.

'Should I call Andromachus?' Alexandria asked.

'Not yet. He's awake, but barely conscious. You may tell Acte and Doryphorus that there's still little improvement; and send another messenger to find Marcus Otho.' Ecloge shook her head disgustedly. 'I'm eager to see him myself - I have a few choice words of my own to say to that young man!'

Alexandria tutted in assent. 'He's very nearly been the death of our poor boy, make no mistake.'

'Well at least this will put a stop to this stupid gang nonsense, once and for all.'

Alexandria went about her errands and returned a short while later, to let Ecloge off for a break.

'He'd be as well to stay unconscious for a good while yet,' she told Ecloge, as she checked her patient, 'they've found Otho at long last, but the Augusta is here now; and Commander Burrus is waiting to tear him off a strip - as well he deserves, frightening us all like this!'

Nero stirred once more and Ecloge bent to kiss his brow before leaving. His eyes flickered briefly, then focused on her face.

'Ecloge?'

'Yes! Yes, my love! Your Ecloge!'

Commotion immediately ensued; slaves were summoned, Andromachus called, and the sudden press of visitors kept firmly at bay. Only when the doctor deemed fit were the visitors admitted, one at a time. The threats and recriminations, so well rehearsed in the antechamber, were now abandoned, as each in turn merely wished the emperor well and quietly departed once more. It was clear that, though conscious, he was still far from recovery.

'How could you allow this to happen?!' Agrippina demanded of Burrus, as soon as they were in the antechamber once more. 'He was beaten to within an inch of his life! Where was the Guard?'

'Acting upon his own instructions, Augusta. But he will never again be allowed to leave the Palace without them, I assure you.'

'And I shall never again be banished from his company,' Agrippina insisted, 'for threat that I am, I pose less of a danger than his staff!' She looked across at Acte. 'You may make alternative arrangements. My slaves will fetch over my things immediately and I will not be leaving the Palace until Nero is well enough to order me out. I trust you will be allowed to make use of the household slaves to remove your things? I shall be retiring to my rooms immediately and have no wish to be disturbed by you.'

'Acte has her own slaves and I shall set them to work at once,' Otho volunteered, swiftly rescuing the unfortunate Acte. 'You may wait with me,' he told her kindly, 'while a guest room is made ready.'

Agrippina smiled at his gallantry. 'Still sharing, Otho? I thought your tastes were finer than Nero's.' She nodded curtly to Burrus and left the room.

Acte had never before felt so small. She looked round at the room filled with polite strangers and saw in her mind only the bruised and swollen face of Nero, as far removed from her now as the villas she craved for escape. She longed simply to run, but instead lowered her head miserably and wept.

Otho embraced her and offered what little comfort he could.

'No one pays heed to what she says,' he assured her, 'the woman is pure poison to us all.'

Acte gently shook her head. 'It's just that I'm so lost. I'm nothing, without him.'

'He'll be fine. I've survived worse hidings a dozen times over.'

'Are you not Acte, that wealthy young freedwoman who owns potteries in Sardinia and villas on the coast?' Burrus reminded her.

She smiled at him. 'No; I'm the slave Nero took as a mistress. And that's all I will ever be.'

The group slowly dispersed and Burrus walked with Otho and Acte.

'I believe you may have saved his life, Otho.'

'That's not what Ecloge would have me believe! You could be forgiven for thinking I talked him into getting himself beaten by some madman!'

'It wasn't some madman,' Burrus said grimly. 'It was Montanus.'

'What? The senator?'

'According to Senecio and the others in the group. The problem now being that Montanus has committed suicide. Very sudden and no explicable reason.'

'But that's dreadful!' Acte exclaimed.

'There's a connection, of course,' Otho guessed.

'Helvia is distraught, naturally. But it would seem that Nero mentioned you, Otho. When Montanus heard your name, he knew at once with whom he was dealing. I presume he expected the Guards to be sent after him and has at least spared Helvia some disgrace. Yet the question remains, do we tell Nero?'

'It would stop these nocturnal outings,' Otho agreed.

'It would destroy him!' Acte protested.

'My dear girl, had Montanus not recognised Otho's name, Nero would now be dead.'

'Beggars fight back just as strongly as senators,' Otho told her.

'I am far more concerned at the news of Montanus' suicide,' Burrus said. 'Had he retaliated and lived, the pseudo gangs may have weakened. But this will only strengthen them.'

'Then allow the news to go no further,' Otho suggested simply.

He helped Acte settle into her new room, watching as she carefully checked through her cases of perfumes and bath oils and make-up. She glanced up at him, aware of his gaze, and smiled guiltily.

'I take too much pride in them, I know. The other ladies are so matter-of-fact about such things,' she admitted. 'But I always dreamed of having such wonderful cases - and I never for a moment imagined that I ever would. I still can't quite accept it, even now.' She fingered the bottles of scents. 'As soon as backs were turned, I'd play with the bottles fetched by the great ladies who were guests of my master. And look, Otho - now it's without guilt; and the bottles are mine!'

He smiled. 'And that little box, there?'

'You nearly said shabby, didn't you?' she rebuked him playfully. 'That little box is the most treasured and precious of all. That is *my* box. All the scents and make-up and hair braids that are mine, and have always been mine. These others; they're mine, too - but that still isn't the real me yet. I don't think it ever will be.' She blushed, suddenly. 'I can't imagine talking to Doryphorus in such a way. In fact, I haven't spoken a word to him.'

'Perfectly excusable, you haven't even been formally introduced.'

'What's he like?'

Otho sighed. 'Pleasant enough, I suppose. A little too full of himself, perhaps.'

'You don't like him.' She made it a statement, not a question.

'When did I say that? And, besides, does my opinion matter?'

She looked up at him, and saw her own feelings reflected in his face; just as she had seen them in the face of Doryphorus. A sense of something shared seemed to make her relationship with Otho more comfortable. Yet that same sense seemed also to turn her instinctively against Doryphorus. She puzzled on this now, as she had earlier, in the anteroom of Nero's chamber.

'Perhaps he is too self-confidant, too secure. Too... threatening?' Otho suggested, as though reading her thoughts.

Acte laughed. 'Or we are too insecure! Love is something indestructible. It can't be broken or escaped. Only those who don't really have it can feel cause for jealousy. We are fools to even think that might apply to us!'

'There speaks a woman of wisdom! Our friend Doryphorus certainly never suffers from jealousy. He has put it to me on more than one occasion to join them both; though I would find nothing less appealing! He didn't sit in the sick room looking at us with fear and envy.'

'Oh, but he did,' Acte corrected him. 'He's no less human than we are.' She ran a finger over the tops of her bottles to see that they were all in place and closed the lid. 'But I still can't like him!'

Otho laughed and put the case on the dressing table for her.

'He will be alright, won't he?'

'He'll be up and about before his birthday!' Otho assured her.

But in that, he was mistaken. Nero celebrated his nineteenth birthday, firmly ensconced within his sick bed, and was not fully recovered until well into the New Year.

FEBRUARY A.D. 57

'I wish you wouldn't go out with those friends of yours,' Acte said as she sat, embraced in Nero's arms at the Circus, watching the horses warming up for the final race of the day.

Nero held her tighter and kissed her cheek. 'But of course not! It's your last night in Rome - how could I even think of doing such a thing!'

'Not tonight, Nero; I mean when I'm away. I worry about you so much as it is.'

'There is nothing to be worried about,' Nero insisted, smiling at her concern. 'I can no longer step foot outside the Palace without the Guards accompanying me. The only compromise I was able to reach was that they follow at a good distance, and only intervene if I look to be in trouble. But surely that's enough to set your mind at rest? Heaven knows, it's more than enough to spoil my own fun.'

'How can you call it fun?!' Acte protested.

'Acte, how would you describe your feelings now, after all those years of oppression? Do you think I don't feel it too? Just to be normal; to run and jeer and fight and do the things my friends are doing, without thought. What does it really feel like to you - never having to answer to someone?'

'You fight a good case, but you do have someone to answer to! You can't inflict such worry on the people you love.'

'I'm deeply sorry for what I did, and now I have the protection of an escort. Let that be enough, Acte. The horses are already lining up and I have no wish to spend our last hours in argument.'

Otho and Senecio joined them just as the race went off.

'You nearly missed it!' Nero complained. 'What are you on?'

'Anything but the Blues. No one will hear of them losing, so we harvested a few private wagers!'

'The Blues!' Nero laughed scornfully. 'When they see the new stallion on our team they'll forget there is such a colour! Look at the way he handles the turns... and the strength of him! He's carrying the entire team as well as the chariot!'

'I'm having my mare covered by him,' Senecio announced.

'Not this season!' Nero and Otho objected in unison.

'It would hardly blunt him.'

'Look at him! He's flying! An oat short in his rations would blunt him!'

They continued to discuss his progress, as though there were no other horse in the race. And when the Green team finished ahead by a very clear margin there were no cheers. Most of the crowd had lost their money on the Blues; and Nero and his companions had never for a moment considered any other result. Senecio and Otho immediately scurried off in search of their newly acquired debtors.

Acte leaned softly against Nero and he put an arm around her once more. 'My old apartment stands empty not far from here,' she reminded him.

'You don't want to go back to the Palace.'

She smiled and nestled in tighter against him.

'Your apartment it is, then. Is it still furnished?'

'Does it matter?'

Nero drew his cloak around her. 'I suppose not.' He noticed how cold she had become. 'Come; we don't have to wait for the others.'

He turned to the ever-present Guard. 'You may see us to a sedan, and then you are dismissed. I will back any excuse you choose to give Burrus,' he added, seeing their reluctance to obey, 'but I will condemn you to the arena just as quickly if you defy me now.'

'But where can we say you are?'

'Marcus Otho will tell you. See them safely back to the Palace and you will have no need of your excuses until the morning - if, indeed, I am missed at all!'

The emperor pulled his hood up securely and leaned drunkenly against Acte, so that they looked like any other race-goer as they stepped into the sedan. Acte gave the address and they were borne away in the anonymity that Nero so loved.

'You don't mind, do you?' Acte whispered, as they kissed in the sedan.

'Why would I?'

'There isn't even a bed, you know.'

'My cloak is soft.'

They stepped down at the apartment and searched for a way in. Once inside, Acte gathered together some charcoal scraps and lit a fire, while Nero laid out the cloak above their discarded clothes to form an adequate mattress. They were soon swaddled tightly within the warm woollen fabric.

'We have nothing but a fire; yet the only things I miss are my dogs.'

'I wish it could always be like this,' Acte sighed.

'It can be any way we want it.' But then he sighed too. 'But not whenever we want it. But is that not so for everyone?'

They lost themselves in passion, for a while, then lay back and watched the shallow flicker of the flames.

'It will die away soon and I have no more fuel,' Acte said.

'It matters not; we will soon be asleep. Let's just enjoy their dancing while we can.'

'Do you watch the flames like this... at the Palace?'

'Never. Is that important to you?'

'Yes...yes, I think it is.'

She was content; though there was so much more she would have liked to ask, had she the courage. But ultimately, she knew, she did not want to ask, courage or not.

They awoke early, the pre-dawn chill of the room seeping under the cloak and ending their fitful sleep. They shivered and clung to each other; laughing as they struggled into their clothes while trying desperately not to lose the small comfort of the cloak.

'We're early enough for a carriage,' Acte said, 'I can travel straight from here and simply have my things sent on.'

'I could come with you,' Nero volunteered, 'and see you settled in.'

Acte shook her head. 'You know you can't spare the time.' She smiled at his disappointment. 'The days fly by, Nero. We have only two weeks to suffer, which will make those following days all the sweeter.'

Perhaps she betrayed something in her expression, for Nero turned away from her and said quietly, 'I too suffer during those weeks apart.'

She put a finger to his lips. 'Let's think only of those days we can spend together.'

'Please, Acte; please come back to the Palace with me. We can gather your things together...' He could see that there was no fighting her decision, yet he protested, for his own sake. 'I can't go back on my own; any more than I can remain on my own while we're apart.'

But it was useless, they both knew. They left the silent apartment and wandered along the dimly lit street, already busy with street vendors and clients hurrying for early appointments; wagons filling the road as the final deliveries were made, while their owners blocked the walkways as they unloaded their goods. First light would once more see a ban on the larger wheeled vehicles, though the streets would be congested enough with handcarts and sedan chairs, riders and pedestrians.

They began to hurry now, as the first of the street lamplighters appeared, to extinguish any which still burned. Nero still cherished the vain hope that they would even yet be too late for a carriage; but several empty ones passed by, on their way out of the city, and Acte hailed one with relief. The journey to Baiae would be made more tolerable by the speed and comfort of a carriage; though Nero was too preoccupied with the pain of separation to give any thought to such practical matters.

'Know only that I miss you!' he called after her, as the horses stepped out.

He watched them until they were no more than a blur, lost in distance and traffic, before hailing his own sedan and returning, reluctantly, to the Palace.

There he found his room occupied by Otho, who had already sent slaves to fetch breakfast for them both.

'What time did you get back?' Nero asked, hastily changing his clothes and attending to his toilet.

'The Palace was asleep. We passed no one and both you and your escort have avoided the embarrassment of a lecture from Burrus. You're not seriously going to wear that, are you?'

'Did Phaon leave in anything yet?'

'No one has been in. I called the slaves myself. I have a hunger and thirst that have only abated with the sight of your tunic! We did nothing but drink and share whores from the time you left us, it is a wonder I am not wasted to a skeleton!'

'Never mind food, Thalamus is a more urgent requirement,' Nero complained, eyeing his tangled locks in the mirror and calling loudly for his barber.

Thalamus promptly arrived, together with the slaves bearing breakfast, and Nero picked at pieces of bread while enduring the daily torture of having his hair styled.

'What do you think of the idea of bestowing pensions on good racehorses?' he asked his companions.

'Only one step short of elevating them to the senate!' Otho laughed. 'What were you doing? Looking through some of Caligula's policies?!'

'I've seen a good many horses worthy of the senate,' Thalamus agreed, 'which is more than I can say of the senators I've seen!'

'Joking apart, do you not think they deserve an honourable retirement?' Nero argued. 'Why should that stallion we saw yesterday end up in the market when his pace has gone - to be sold as meat or for cart work?'

'And who would stable him and feed him, for no more than the memory of a few special victories?' Otho asked.

'Ah, but who would do the same in exchange for full expenses and a weekly fee?' Nero returned.

'I would!' Thalamus jumped in.

'You and any property-owner in the country,' Nero agreed. 'Which is why I wish to bestow pensions on racehorses.'

'And who is to keep me in my old age?' Otho inquired.

'Bed down with the horses,' Thalamus advised, 'they owe you that much, the money they've stolen from you over the years!'

Phaon entered, catching only the last part of the barber's sentence. 'Ah, provincial governors again!' he remarked, sitting down on the edge of the bed and raising an eyebrow at its crisp condition.

'No, racehorses, actually,' Otho explained, 'which is why the bed wasn't slept in. We haven't actually retired yet!'

'I didn't know race meetings went on till dawn.'

'If they did, I might still have some money left in my purse!'

'On the subject of money and racehorses, Phaon...' Nero began, but Phaon raised a hand and interrupted him.

'Whatever it is, you may end the thought right there! You gave the city population a New Year bonus of four hundred sesterces a head and paid forty million sesterces into the Treasury - you are not a poor man, Nero, but you have over-stretched yourself to the point where it is wiser not to mention racehorses at all!'

'My dear Phaon, I have no intention of spending any more of my own money!'

'Then that sounds even more ominous!'

'If you are going to argue over money, then I shall leave,' Otho said, 'I make it a point of conscience not to know how much in debt I am forcing my creditors each time I borrow money from them!'

'Do you need any, my friend?' Nero asked.

'No, no,' Otho generously waived his offer, 'your horses need it more than I.' He nodded to Thalamus. 'You have worked magic on him, Thalamus. He could easily be mistaken for a cheap charioteer! If you have a moment to spare, I could profit from some similar magic myself.'

The pair departed, leaving Nero to more serious conversation with Phaon.

'As Consul this year, my income must be more than sufficient to cover expenses?' he verified.

'Indeed, you have little to concern you financially - within reason, of course.'

'The whole idea of money is to spend it! Finances are never going to be of concern to me, Phaon! What is of concern is in what way it is to be spent. And, incidentally, I do wish to include racehorses in the State budget.'

Phaon sat back, a willing recipient of new ideas. 'Go ahead,' he said mildly.

'You understand that the idea of a pension is to provide the recipient with the means to live out a long and comfortable retirement?'

'Go on.'

'So you will not, therefore, laugh when I ask that horses of eminence be granted a State pension?'

'I'm not laughing, Nero.'

'Is it within our means?'

'How many animals would we be talking about, in any given year?'

'One good horse a year; possibly, sometimes, two... for somewhere in the region of fifteen years from the Circus to the grave.'

'Food and stabling? No more than that?'

Nero nodded.

'Then it hardly requires figure work, Nero. I can tell you now that the dent in the Treasury will be negligible. But be careful how you phrase it when allowing it to reach the ears of others. I'm sure Caligula was once full of good intent... '

Nero smiled. 'Otho was already kind enough to remind me of such extremes. Now; the rest of my public. There is precious little public money around, would you not say? Homes tend to be inherited or rented. So what is the next biggest expense for most Romans?'

Phaon considered the question, though Nero had clearly meant it to be rhetorical.

'Slaves,' Nero told him. 'The current purchase tax is a mere four per cent. Surely, we can afford to waive such a tax? It can mean little enough to the State budget, but a great deal to a small personal budget.'

'Have you even considered the figures, Nero? Do you know the thousands - millions - spent each year in the slave market?'

'You mean we depend upon the four per cent?'

'Very heavily, Nero.'

The emperor considered it. It was really such a minimal amount and would make only a minor difference to the average family budget; yet it was clearly a necessity to the Treasury. To decrease it would be of no benefit whatsoever.

'It must be transferred to the dealers,' Nero decided. 'Waive purchase tax and take it, instead, from those who can afford it. The public in general will be marginally better off - and your books will remain unaffected. Is it agreed, Phaon?'

'I see no case against it, Nero.'

'Good! Then let it be so.' He regarded Phaon thoughtfully for a moment. 'The Treasury benefits a great deal from a tax as low as four per cent?'

'It would benefit a great deal from one per cent taxes, if the expenditure was high enough.'

'And are we still running at as great an annual profit as in previous years?'

'Equal, if not higher. There are certainly no problems as regards budget. The plans for your amphitheatre, for example, are well within our means.'

Nero sat forward. 'Then we could also well afford to run at far less of a profit margin - particularly as projects such as the amphitheatre are not annual affairs.'

'Don't simply spend it because it's there,' Phaon cautioned.

Nero smiled. 'I would prefer it if it wasn't there at all. What use is it, when the State already has all that it requires, while most of the population goes short? Why leave funds rotting in the Treasury - and people rotting in the streets.'

'That's a little extreme, Nero!'

'Extreme? I walk among the poor. I find sport in tormenting old beggars and drunks. Heartless I may be, but blind and stupid I am not. My victims exist and there is no point in trying to tell me otherwise, Phaon.' He sat back again. 'Now then; what are we to do about it?'

Phaon looked perplexed.

'Come, Phaon; you are quite happy to bestow pensions on horses. You don't even have to bother with figure-work in order to do so. And yet you balk at the idea of alleviating the misery of the poor!'

'Nero, that is grossly unfair!' Phaon protested.

Nero grinned. 'Indeed it is. I should at least give you a proposal, before I accuse you of shooting it down!' He poured himself some water. 'A proposal, then. Abolish all of the higher taxes.'

'Just that? All of the higher taxes? No request for figures?'

'Just that, my friend. What need have I of figures? If the purchase tax on slaves is low, because the expenditure on slaves allows it to be so, then the higher taxes must be derived from fairly intermittent means. I put it to you, Phaon, that we profit so marginally from them that we can actually survive without them.'

'This needs to be examined more deeply, Nero. I could not possibly agree to any decision here and now.'

'That I accept. But look into it, Phaon. Without actually impoverishing the State, lower considerably, where you cannot altogether abolish, every tax you can. You will probably find that only the richer men of Rome benefit directly from the changes; but what benefits the wealthy must ultimately benefit the poor. A safe and sanitary well-lit street is inhabited by as many slaves and peasants as noblemen, is it not? And who profits from increased trade and turnover of shops and taverns, other than the merchants themselves?'

'I don't need convincing, Nero, I'm behind you all the way. I'll do my best, I promise you.'

Nero nodded. 'Thank you.' He began to grin once more.

Phaon eyed him with suspicion. 'Yes?'

'Public seats in court - could they be provided, free of charge, by the Treasury?'

'Yes, Nero! Let your poor of Rome fill every seat! It will make little more dent in the budget than your racehorses!' Phaon stood up and bowed sweepingly. 'Good day to you, my Lord - I shall make my hasty exit while I still have funds!'

Nero laughed and lay back on the bed, patting it idly and at once summoning the two eager dogs to his side. He didn't bother to sit up when the Minister of Leisure made his entrance.

'Ah, Patrobius, I'm glad you are here!'

Patrobius, wary of the dogs, refrained from sitting down.

'I have the details of the building work on the Field of Mars for you,' he told the emperor, 'and the chief engineer wishes to make an appointment to see you.'

'Tell him I shall be at the site myself tomorrow and will speak with him then.'

'Then that will be all, Nero?'

Nero sat up lazily. 'Not quite. I wish to publish the following edicts. It is to be forbidden for provincial officials to hold shows. And it is to be forbidden for any person to be killed during shows, whether that person is a criminal or gladiator. Is that understood?'

Patrobius stared at him.

'Would you prefer it in writing?'

'No, no... it's just... '

'It's just an end to oppression and extortion,' Nero said simply. 'That will be all, thank you.'

He watched the disconcerted minister depart and smiled softly to himself.

'A fine morning's work, my boys, wouldn't you agree?'

He stretched out beside the dogs and absently rubbed their ears.

'A fine morning's work... and a lifetime ahead.'

Chapter Twenty-Eight

JANUARY A.D. 58

Burrus, Doryphorus and Nero sat throwing dice with Senecio and Otho, trying to relax and kill time before embarking on the serious business of the evening. Yet tension was high and the dice proved no cure.

'We should have spent the day at the Games,' Otho said, throwing badly.

'I have no taste for the Games,' Nero pointed out.

'And neither do I, thanks to your interference,' Senecio complained. 'Without the threat of death, the combats are no better than fencing matches! I haven't bothered to attend for nearly a year, now.'

Nero ignored him and won the throw.

'Don't you think it unfair to subject the populace to your own particular whims?' Senecio continued; then stopped, aware suddenly of what he had said.

Nero merely smiled. 'Most of my subjects are happy to accept my policies without question.'

'We are supposed to be enjoying ourselves,' Burrus reminded them, taking his turn.

'And is this all the enjoyment we are allowed?' Senecio protested. 'No proper Games; no provincial Games whatsoever! Why, they used to be the most spectacular!'

'My dear Senecio, you are a gentleman of leisure, with no interest in public office, so I would not expect you to understand...'

Senecio sat back in horror. 'But I am striving for office! Do you think me a man of leisure through choice?'

'I'm sorry, Senecio; I had no idea,' Nero apologised, only Otho recognising the joke in his voice and smiling in anticipation. 'It's just that you are always with Otho and me - at the Circus, the gymnasium, the baths. I took you to be as ambitious as Otho!'

'My father is a mere ex-slave. I can no more depend upon his support for expensive leisure than I can look to him to buy me office. I must find a post by my own powers.'

'I understand your point fully, my friend,' Nero told him sincerely. 'Obtaining office is a very elitist thing. The best positions have a tendency to go to those who can afford them, not to those best qualified for the post. And yet, when I do my best to stamp out such practises, you are the first to complain.'

'Throw the dice,' Burrus ordered irritably, 'I came here to have fun, not to endure your petty squabbles.'

'You object against the abolishment of the provincial Games?' Nero asked Senecio, ignoring the commander. 'Such Games being the most spectacular, as each official strove to outdo another, and host better Games than his rivals. And for what, Senecio? For office! How quick the public are to vote for a man who gives them a better day's sport than another. And how slow they are to realise that it is they who pay for such splendour! Those Games were a massive public financial burden - as oppressive as extortion. And State-funded Games are still held; the citizens of the provinces have not lost out.'

'Games, Nero? Fencing displays!' Senecio snorted in disgust.

Nero picked up the dice and sat back, as though holding them to ransom.

'Is there anyone else here who objects to the lack of bloodshed in the arena? Anyone else who would prefer to have seen ten thousand men lose their lives?'

'Yes, all of us!' Burrus said in frustration, 'Now hand over those dice and let us get on!'

'The senate was ready to deify you,' Doryphorus said seriously, 'when first you were consul and you exempted your fellow consul from swearing allegiance to the throne. This is now your third consulship, and your third fellow consul exempted from swearing allegiance. No less a grand gesture, but no longer recognised as such. The little popularity you ever won with them has been frittered away a hundred times, Nero! The war may make you a popular man once more. But your grand gestures only serve to increase the antagonism of the senate. No one appreciates the thought behind your policies - least of all those who most benefit! They are too ignorant to recognise their salvation and are as aggrieved as the rest of us at the price to be paid!'

Otho grinned. 'A reply, please, Nero! You must have one for him?'

'My reply is that I do not act for recognition or appreciation. Your words are accurate, Doryphorus - but wasted!' He made as if to throw the dice, then stopped. 'The interest is fast dwindling from this game. What say you to an increase of stake? Say, four thousand gold pieces for each pip of the winning throw?'

The others laughed and nodded their assent, Otho clearing the pool.

'Well, that's it,' he declared, 'Senecio and I are now amply set up for the evening, so don't look to win it back or delay us further with more arguments!'

Burrus threw up his hands in disgust. 'Corbulo's man will be here at any moment; you may as well go now.'

The pair needed no second bidding and made their exit immediately.

'The messenger is insufferably late,' Doryphorus complained, 'Could we not simply begin without him?'

Nero shook his head. 'Without Corbulo, there would be no war. I am happy to bend to the wishes of Vologeses and Tiridates; but if a Roman Commander cannot count on the support of his own emperor then it is time for both commander and emperor to stand down.'

'How can you talk of compromise, when the might of Rome is at issue!' Doryphorus objected.

'When has the might of Rome ever been questioned?' Nero laughed. 'I would much prefer to see the situation resolved amicably. After all, both sides are chasing the same end - only the means are disputed.'

A slave announced the overdue arrival of Sentius, just arrived from Armenia as representative of Commander Corbulo. He was accompanied by Epaphroditus, who had been instructed to wait for him and debrief him. Drinks were sent for and the war council commenced.

'What exactly is Corbulo's problem?' Nero inquired.

'King Vologeses of Parthia has given the throne of Armenia to his brother Tiridates as a gift,' Sentius explained, 'but the throne is not his to give. Rome had granted the kingdom to him following the overthrow of Radamistus...'

'Precisely because King Tiridates was popular with the Armenians, Parthians and Rome,' Nero reminded him, 'so why are we now all citing war over the choice?'

'His popularity is beside the point, my Lord. The throne is in the gift of Rome, not Parthia. The commander believes most strongly that we should recover Armenia, for it is a territory once conquered by the mighty Pompey himself.'

'Pompey loses none of his glory in the mistakes of subsequent generations,' Nero pointed out.

'Our actions reflect upon his glory, my Lord.'

Nero smiled. 'Go on.'

'Commander Corbulo is insistent that Tiridates accept the crown from Rome; and Tiridates himself is happy enough to do so. But Vologeses will not allow him to hold the throne as a gift of a foreign power and has rallied his troops against us. Parthia now means to win Armenia for itself and that, my Lord, is definitely a slight against not only Pompey - but Rome herself!'

'So we must win Armenia and force Tiridates to accept the throne,' Nero verified.

'No, my Lord. His loyalty is questionable. Corbulo means to crown Tigranes King of Armenia, to punish Vologeses and Tiridates for such effrontery.'

Nero smiled.

'Nero, if I might clarify the situation,' Doryphorus stepped in. 'We sponsored Tiridates purely as a means of pacifying the situation. But his pacific role has obviously failed. He is up in arms against Rome himself! However derisible you may find the circumstances, they still need to be dealt with.'

'I'm sorry; I had no wish to mock national pride. I understand fully the seriousness of the situation and the need for it to be resolved fully in our favour. But when the problem first arose I was determined to secure a pacific conclusion - and I reiterate that wish now. The Parthians are a great race, as deserving of their pride as Rome. This must be settled accordingly. Which means an end to talk of insult. Both sides are too great for so petty a fight.'

'We cannot march against Tiridates, only to grant him the Kingdom,' Burrus said. 'We have no choice but to sponsor Tigranes.'

'I understand that,' Nero agreed. 'We will sponsor Tigranes and subdue Parthia. But hopefully victory will be swift; whereupon, in honour of Parthia, we shall offer the throne to Tiridates. This whole war is a gesture, Burrus. But that doesn't make it less of a war.'

'Corbulo also seeks permission to discharge the weak and the elderly and replace them with recruits from Galatia and Cappadocia,' Sentius requested.

'Of course, he may consider it done,' Nero consented, 'you may remind him that he need not seek permission on the general operation of his troops. Recruitment and discipline is entirely down to him.'

Sentius nodded.

'Have you eaten?' Nero asked him, when they had finished discussing the directives to be taken back to Corbulo.

'Not yet, my Lord.'

'Is this your first stop since entering Italy?'

'More or less, my Lord.'

'Why ever did you not speak up for yourself sooner!'

Nero called for his slaves and sent Sentius away with Tubero, to be fed and bathed and given a luxurious room for the night.

'You may take any horse from my stables, too - but not the small chestnut mare, I am extremely fond of her and she suits Acte particularly well,' Nero called to Sentius as he departed.

Sentius thanked him profusely, then was gone, together with Burrus.

'Are you deserting me, too?' Nero asked, as Doryphorus gathered up his things and made to leave.

'It is late, Nero.'

'So it is, Doryphorus. Too late for you to go now.'

Nero watched him as he reluctantly set his things back down on the desk.

'Why are you so unwilling to share my bed?' he asked softly.

Doryphorus stiffened, but did not turn round.

'We can cavort freely in our brothel by the lake,' Nero said mildly, 'and play at wild animals and savages in the gardens. You will even make love to me here, in my room, with Petronius looking on and Terpnus setting our moans to music. But you won't hold me, Doryphorus. You won't keep me in your arms until morning.'

'You must have noticed,' Doryphorus muttered, apologetic; embarrassed. 'You are insatiable. Any man would struggle to keep up with you. But I... I find it always a struggle. Without the excitement, the role-playing... even with... at least that way you don't notice my... my lack of response.'

'And do you think that matters?'

'Does it *matter*? Nero, it is the most important thing in the world, to me! I thought it the very end of my world when first it happened.' He turned to face Nero. 'It isn't something one simply learns to live with. I will never learn to live with it. And I can never comfortably lay with you, dreading the moment when you might ask of me that which I cannot give.'

'I'm asking it of you now, Doryphorus. Lay with me. That is all I ask.'

Doryphorus remained hesitant, but Nero reached out and pulled him firmly towards the bed.

'I ask only to be held,' he insisted, 'it is all I have ever asked.'

And when, at last, they were lying naked together in the bed, Doryphorus knew him to be telling the truth.

'I think, perhaps, Ecloge or Alexandria may have nursed me as a child when I was sick or hurt,' Nero said quietly in the dark, 'but I have no recollection of ever being sick or hurt. Aunt Lepida would sometimes take me up on her lap; but I didn't want her embrace. I wanted my Mother's; but she wouldn't give it. She flogged me once; and I bore it because I thought, in the end, she would have to take me up in her arms. But it was Otho who held me. Otho who soothed me and nursed me. And I quickly learned to fake tears and fear and all the other childish ploys that would force me back into his arms again. And really; this is all I ever wanted... '

FEBRUARY A.D. 58

That winter was a severe one. Corbulo's troops were kept under canvas and reports of their suffering were received in Rome with depressing regularity. Ice had to be removed and the ground dug before tents could be pitched. Frostbite caused the loss of many limbs; sentries froze to death. It was told how the hands of one soldier, carrying firewood, became so frozen that they snapped off cleanly, still fastened to his load.

Such harsh conditions induced many deserters. Corbulo, who moved among his men at work and on the march, made no allowances. Deserters were immediately captured and executed. In other armies, the first and second offences were always excused.

Nero read these reports with sorrow, drawing no solace from the battles won.

'I don't want this,' he confided to Doryphorus, 'but I know that I have no arguments against it. I have always longed to withdraw our troops from Britain; yet I refrain from making the order because it would reflect upon the glory won by Claudius. How, then, can I expect my people to ignore the effrontery of Parthia, when the glory of Rome itself is at stake?'

'I hope you won't air such doubts in the senate,' Doryphorus warned.

Nero smiled ruefully. 'No; I will be the shining patriot and draw strength from the courage of my troops, to enable me to fight my own battle.'

With this in mind, Nero made his way to the Curia of Julius Caesar in a better frame of mind than might otherwise be expected, arriving in time for the opening of business at the first hour of the day. The fact that business was unlikely to be concluded before nightfall did little to deter him; although, as usual, there were fewer than two hundred present, of the nine hundred members of the senate. Few senators could stomach the unmercifully long sittings, even though the two or three day sessions were convened just twice a month, with an annual closure during September and October.

Nero viewed the dismal turnout with no small amount of bitterness.

'They are willing to lie and cheat and murder for a seat in the House,' he complained to Seneca, 'yet loathe to take up that seat when once it is theirs. How long are their hours, when taken over the entire period of their year?'

'A good deal shorter than your own, Nero - but I defy you to convince them of that fact.'

Nero declined the challenge and instead stood before the House to bring his own case to judgement.

'You will forgive me, gentlemen, if I defer the scheduled business of today, but I have a far more pressing case to bring before you on behalf of my public.'

The senators shuffled uneasily in their seats and Seneca started visibly.

'I have no idea to what you refer,' he whispered aggrievedly, 'you should have discussed this with me beforehand.'

'One battle is enough,' Nero insisted, in a private aside, 'and even if you were to side with me in this, I can manage equally well alone.'

He waited for order to return to his audience, then continued.

'I have received persistent complaints from members of the public against the so-called 'farming' of taxes...'

'Private individuals have no right to approach you with such trivialities,' the senator Thrasea complained, 'do they not suppose you have more important business to deal with?'

Nero regarded him steadily.

'There is no more important business than public 'trivialities', Thrasea. It is Thrasea, isn't it?'

'It is, my Lord, and I do not deny their importance. But there are proper channels and...'

'Find me a common man who knows of proper channels and I shall insist that he follows them,' Nero said impatiently, 'in the meantime, I shall continue to hear any one who takes the trouble to approach me. And let me tell you now, Thrasea and gentlemen, that more than one person has approached me on this subject - and over a long period of time. I cannot afford to wait for 'proper channels', gentlemen, and I hope that you will therefore bear with me in this.

'It has been brought to my attention, shall I say, that groups of knights have farmed the indirect taxes in certain provinces for their own gain. The accusations are such that the charges cannot be denied; yet the practise is a difficult one to stamp out. I have decided that the only definite way of putting an end to such extortion is to abolish every indirect tax.'

The murmur of objection ran through the Curia.

'In the name of the gods, boy, this should have been discussed!' Seneca complained. 'How could you be so foolish...'

'Don't make me fight two battles,' Nero insisted.

To the senate, he said, 'For years this practise has been condoned - a perk of office, to which we willingly turn a blind eye. How many perks of office do you possess? Expected to sit in the House for twelve hours at a time, for as much as a week in every month? And what worthy service do the provincial knights provide, other than lining their own pockets?

'If we continue to condone such abuse, we will find ourselves faced with rebellion! That so many complaints have been made to me proves that the public lacks our apathetic tolerance. They demand justice and our posts demand that we give it. I trust that you are all behind me in this?'

The senators rose from their seats with a resounding, 'Hear, hear!'

'Then you will honour my intention?'

'To the very best of our ability,' declared Thrasea.

'That sounds ominous,' Nero muttered to Seneca.

'They are behind you to a man!' Seneca said encouragingly.

'Really? Let us see what progress they have made when next we convene.'

'Come, Nero - this enmity between you will soon be of your own making. What greater ovation do you need?'

'I need this bill passed, Seneca. And, until then, I will not trust their ovations.'

He settled back to listen to the regular business of the day and ended it by once again offending Seneca and conferring substantial annuities upon three impoverished senators.

'You will live out your years in the poverty you have just saved them from,' Seneca complained, 'if you continue to listen to every hard-luck story brought before you. Granius, it is true, has lost his money through no fault of his own. But the other pair squandered their inheritance with excessive extravagance!'

'Why make distinctions, Seneca? All three are now poverty-stricken. All three are now in need of assistance.'

'They are undeserving and should be taught a lesson!'

'What lesson?' Nero asked with amusement. 'True gentlemen always throw their money about.'

'So you have said on numerous occasions.'

'That is the very purpose of money! Fortunes are made to be spent. It seems to me that anyone who can account for every penny spent must be a stingy miser!'

'Within reason, Nero! Within reason!'

'It is their money and their choice, Seneca. If they need it, they may have it. I am not about to reward the sorriest story that can be concocted, anymore than I intend to impose conditions upon how annuities are to be spent. It is neither my business nor yours, my friend.'

Seneca threw up his hands in despair.

The next lot of news to arrive from Armenia was a good deal more favourable. Corbulo's forces had won a succession of battles, successfully storming three forts in a single day. They suffered few Roman losses and, in the capture of one fort, killed every adult male without a single Roman loss. The non-combatant population was sold into slavery.

But at home, Nero found the news as disappointing as his own setbacks.

'These are honourable people,' he told Epaphroditus and Seneca as they travelled together to the Curia of Julius Caesar. 'They are fighting for the glory of Parthia, just as we fight for Rome. Losses on either side I could bear. But the Armenians? Their national pride is such that they are happy to ally themselves to Rome or Parthia as demand dictates. We are killing our former allies because on this occasion they have joined the wrong side. Surely Vologeses must find this as distasteful as I now do? I should never have given Corbulo so free a hand.'

Seneca said nothing in response, privately satisfied that the emperor had more to worry about than the forthcoming proceedings. Though the senate had publicly applauded Nero's intention of abolishing indirect taxation, it had actually done all in its power to prevent it from being put into operation. At the last sitting, the senators had finally insisted that the empire could not survive without such revenues. Seneca feared retaliation from the emperor, though Nero had given no hint of what was to come.   Arriving early enough to witness the sacrifice and prayers, the three companions duly took their places in the House. This time, Nero allowed the day's business to run to schedule, before standing up to address the House at the close of what had appeared to be a fairly short day.

'Gentlemen,' he began, 'I have given due consideration to your claims that Rome would collapse with the loss of any further revenue and I can only concur. However, in considering this matter, I happened upon a very simple solution - so simple, in fact, that it requires no legislation and no passing. I need only tell you how it is to be - and you need only give your assent.

'By order of the emperor, all regulations governing every tax are to be published. They are to be made easily accessible to all members of the public.'

'But such matters of State are private!' Vestinus Atticus protested, 'They have always been confidential and, in my view, should always remain so.'

'We cannot simply give our assent,' Thrasea argued, sarcastically mimicking Nero's tone, 'This is a proposal requiring detailed discussion and nor do I see anything in its favour to suggest that it would be passed, even after such discussion.'

'Then you are as blind as you are rude!' Nero told him angrily. 'I have already given my order and it is to be no more than obeyed! Private matters may remain private. Public affairs must be made public. Of what, exactly, are you afraid? Do you have more to hide than the knights of the provinces?'

No one dared voice their objection, though the discord rippled throughout the tiers just as loudly.

'Furthermore,' Nero continued, 'claims for arrears are to lapse after a period of one year. Praetors at Rome, and governors in the provinces, are to give special priority to cases against tax collectors.

'From this day forward, soldiers are to be exempt from paying tax, except on what they sell. Merchant ships are also to be exempted from assessment and property tax.

'I have already made all necessary calculations myself, with the able assistance of my Minister of Finance, Phaon, and so I need not trouble you for an opinion. The matter is therefore brought to a close and it remains only for me to thank you for your attention and bid you all a good evening.'

Nero stepped down immediately and made his exit, much to the confoundment of his audience. Seneca and Epaphroditus hurried after him.

'Oh, well done! Well done!' the secretary declared joyously, slapping Nero heartily across the back. 'I will be repeating this story to my great-grandchildren! To see Thrasea put in his place! Even his mother-in-law bows down to him!'

'You spoke of enmity when first you raised this issue,' Seneca said more sombrely, 'I trust that you are aware you have well and truly ignited the bridge?'

'You warned that it was of my own doing,' Nero reminded him, 'and now I trust that you can see it is not.'

'One throw of six and another of two threes!' Epaphroditus pointed out, 'What does it matter anyway? What matters is the outcome - and my Lord, here, is the victor! Both morally and effectually!'

'I feel only a knot of anger that it has come to this,' Nero said, 'there is no satisfaction in your so-called victory.'

'Then imagine the knot from which they now suffer,' Seneca soothed.

Nero allowed himself a smile.

Chapter Twenty-Nine

MAY A.D.58

The Basilica Iulia was, as always, packed. The rows of seats provided free by the treasury, at the behest of Nero, were occupied by three times their intended number. And the main attraction itself owed no little to Nero. For Suillius Rufus, the perpetrator of the vast majority of Claudius' brutalities, had been charged with fleecing the provincials as governor of Asia and embezzling public funds.

Earlier that month, Nero had granted the prosecution a year for investigation. The current business, therefore, was centred upon charges relating to Rome, for which witnesses were readily available. Suillius was accused of forcing the former consul Quintus Secundus into civil war by his savage indictments; of driving two noted noblewomen to their deaths; of striking down three ex-consuls; and of wrongly convicting countless knights.

'My Lord,' Suillius pleaded, when it was finally clear that the defence had done little to sway the judges, 'I cannot deny these crimes, but I acted only on the emperor's orders.'

'My step-father never insisted on any prosecutions,' Nero told him, 'as his papers prove.'

'But the orders did not come directly from the emperor himself,' Suillius cried in panic, 'I acted on instructions from Messalina. How was I to know that she had not first consulted her husband? I am but a servant, my Lord.'

'It matters not from whence the orders came,' Nero said grimly, 'it is the instrument of these atrocities, the man who was paid to commit such crimes only to blame them on others, who must be punished.'

Cowardice alone had prevented Suillius from opening his veins and avoiding the trial, yet still the outcome came as a shock. He fell to the floor in abject terror, as the Guards closed in on him to prevent any attempt at escape.

Nero waited for the pitiful display for mercy to peter out.

'Publius Suillius Rufus, I hereby give sentence. For your crimes against Rome it is my decree that you are to be banished from her shores. Your estates are to be confiscated and you are to live out the remainder of your days in the Balearic Islands. I understand that you have children?'

'A son and daughter, my Lord.'

'Then they may retain half your estate.' Nero signalled to the Guards. 'Get him out of my sight.'

Two ex-governors of Africa were next to stand trial, on various petty charges, but were acquitted by Nero. It was clear, by the end of proceedings, that the large crowd gathered had had something of a disappointing few days.

'None of your usual dwelling over verdicts,' Seneca remarked, as they made their way out to the sedan, 'I suspect you had already reached your decision long before the accused were brought before you.'

'Indeed, Seneca. Vile though I find him, Suillius is, after all, a mere servant. It came down to their lives or his. Would you kill for me, Seneca?'

'Indeed I would not! I am a man of honour.'

'Never mind honour. You have the courage to take your own life in preference. That Suillius even stood trial is proof enough that he lacks such courage. Why punish him for being human? If cowardice is to be a crime, then let me be the first to admit my guilt.' Nero gave Seneca a sideways glance. 'Anyway, you say that you would not kill for me?'

'I would fight for you; defend you, if need be. I would not commit the atrocities ordered by Messalina.'

'Would Burrus?'

'Burrus is a soldier. And a gentleman.'

'So you are uncertain?'

'Nero! You delight in twisting all that I say!'

'I had no intention of teasing. It's just that... it's just that I still wonder, sometimes, about Britannicus...'

Seneca made a disparaging grunting noise in response; afraid to admit that both he and Burrus had suffered from similar doubts themselves.

'Epilepsy, weak heart... we shall never know the truth. And it's too far in the past to concern us now,' he conceded.

They climbed into the sedan and Seneca hesitated in giving instruction.

'There is to be a party tonight at the home of Vestinus. Would you prefer to go straight there?'

Nero shook his head. 'I am in no mood for parties. And certainly not those of Vestinus. I cannot abide the man.'

'Otho, Senecio and Petronius are attending.'

'Then they will not miss my company, will they? Straight home, if you please.'

Seneca gave the order, with some surprise.

'I assumed that's why you had finished so quickly,' he queried, as they set off for the Palace.

'In actual fact, it is far more exhausting to deal so swiftly with the cases than to take my usual length of deliberation,' Nero admitted, 'but for which I would have been happy to attend any party - even that of Vestinus! As it is, I can concentrate on my own music lessons without the distraction of my non-appreciative friends!'

'Well I hope you don't include me among them! I happen to think you are making excellent progress.'

'Thank you, Seneca. There are times when I have my doubts! Though I'm particularly pleased with my lyre playing.'

'And so you should be, my boy; so you should be.'

At the mansion of Vestinus, dinner was still being served. The courses were many and extravagant, and Otho and his companions were not the only guests who were beginning to feel bored.

'These affairs are so tedious,' the lady Poppaea yawned, 'not even the slaves offer diversion.'

'Oh, but they are so very attractive!' Camilla pointed out.

Poppaea raised her eyebrows. 'Attractive to look upon. And that alone. Have you not noticed, my dear, that they never look upon you?'

'You mean it is not simply down to good manners?'

Poppaea laughed at her naivety. 'Why else do you imagine that he keeps such a well-chosen household?! I'm afraid that when the gentlemen are invited to enjoy some after dinner entertainment, the ladies will be invited to leave!'

'Then I may as well leave now!' Camilla complained, 'I had already made my selections! These tiresome dishes were but a prelude to the main course! We may leave together, Poppaea.'

'Leave? Do you not think it makes an interesting spectator sport? Far more diverting than the Games.'

Camilla shuddered. 'Not at all to my taste, Poppaea.'

Her friend smiled. 'Very much to mine, my dear. Though the fact that I cannot first manhandle them rather takes the shine off the evening. If I had at home something akin to a man to whom to return, I might not mind so much.'

'Poppaea! Poor Rufrius! It is most unseemly for the wife of a knight to mock him so in public!'

'Were he by my side I would not have the opportunity. The man is a bore, both socially and sexually.'

'My dear, you go through husbands at a faster rate than we go through barbers!'

Poppaea yawned once more. 'If you seriously intend to leave, then I suggest you do so now, while there is a break in the courses. I might stretch my legs and see if I can't find something to divert me. That gentleman over there, for example. Do you know him?'

'The one so well dressed?'

'The gods, no! The younger one, beside him.'

'Claudius Senecio. His father is a freedman, a merchant.'

'Then not worth my attention.' She rose with Camilla and kissed her lightly on the cheek. 'Safe journey home, my dear - though if Rufrius is to ask, we both left together, of course!'

She watched her friend go, then mingled with the other guests who were attempting to walk off the previous courses.

Otho, who had been waiting for just such an opportunity, now threaded his way to her side. She attempted to avoid him, without success.

'Poppaea, isn't it?'

She eyed him disdainfully without reply.

'Allow me to introduce myself - Marcus Salvius Otho.'

She nodded, without disguising her lack of interest; but her eyes quickly sharpened as she recognised the significance of his name.

'Ah yes! Otho - the emperor's right-hand man, so I believe?' She raised her eyebrows and smiled suggestively, so that there could be no mistaking the double entendre.

Otho was at once both shocked and excited. He stared at her; temporarily at a loss for words as her eyes moved across him assessingly.

'Your husband?' he ventured, breaking the moment's silence, 'Does he never accompany you to parties?'

'He takes no interest in such things. We have a great many differences between us, which only divorce will resolve.' She smiled to herself and stroked the back of her hand across Otho's chest, down to his waist. 'I am sure that your lovers are not plagued by the problems that have spoilt my marriage?'

'If you would allow me to be your escort for the remainder of the evening, you could discover the answer to that question yourself.'

'Too much of the evening still remains,' Poppaea complained lightly. 'I look forward to discovering the truth, when the moment presents itself, but until then I will be more than content to rely on your own opinion. Surely, you are not hindered by false modesty?'

'Not at all. And yet you can hardly expect me to discuss such things over the dining table?'

'Then we must share a couch, my dear escort, and you may whisper privately in my ear. I am sure that you have learned a great many things from Nero; and discretion in particular.'

Never before had Otho encountered such open seduction. He followed Poppaea to a double couch and stood back to allow her to be seated first.

'My dear Otho,' she protested with feigned surprise, 'you would have to be very discreet indeed if you intend to take the outside edge!'

Otho sat down and reclined on the couch, Poppaea positioning herself elegantly in front of him and immediately picking at the morsels laid out before them. She engaged their neighbours in conversation and didn't bother to dismiss the slaves who hovered close by. Otho found it almost impossible to touch and caress her, though the urge to do so had never been so strong. She kept her body pressed firmly against his and the slightest of movements aroused him. At times he longed for nothing better than to get up and walk away from this temptress who so tormented him. Yet it was physically impossible; and that in itself was pleasurable.

He whispered to her seductively, kissing the back of her neck and playing with the long tresses of her pale auburn hair. Occasionally she returned his whispers, taking pleasure in shocking him; but always she rejoined the general conversation, as though no intimacies were taking place at all. Otho's frustrated energies were re-channelled into drinking wine and watching the great water clock, positioned at one end of the room.

At last, when he thought that the party was never going to end, Poppaea rose without warning, the shock of which enabled Otho to do so without embarrassment. They thanked their host and declined his insistence that they stay for further entertainments, walking out to the sedan chairs in the street.

Otho helped Poppaea with her cloak, superbly decorated with a peacock sewn in silk threads, and she made no obvious objection to the caresses he was quick to bestow in the process. But as he attempted to step up into the chair with her, she refused him.

'My husband is a knight!' she protested, 'I could not possibly be seen in open adultery. I will speak to him about divorce, but until then we must choose our moments together carefully.'

'But you just can't leave me like this!' Otho protested in return, 'No one need know that we travelled home together. You must offer me some relief, Poppaea!'

Poppaea leaned forward and kissed him. Despite all her teasing, it was the first physical move she had made towards him, but it was all too brief.

'Go back to the Palace tonight,' she told him, drawing away from his embrace. 'Perhaps the emperor will offer you the relief you need. I will send you a note in the morning and we will meet tomorrow. And then you must tell me all that passed between you, so that I may imagine that it was I who lay with you and pleasured you so, and that this parting never took place. It must be special, Otho - and you must spare me no detail tomorrow when we meet.'

She blew him a kiss and withdrew behind the curtain of the chair, leaving him flushed and burning and all too eager to fulfil her request. He succeeded in summoning a chair, though he felt blinded by drink and lust, and could not gain the sanctuary of Nero's chamber quickly enough.

'Oh, thank the gods you are alone!' he cried out in relief, sinking down beside the emperor on the welcoming bed.

The two dogs emerged noisily from beneath it and greeted him fervently.

'Why the commotion?!' Nero complained, 'I had only just fallen asleep! I thought you had better things to do with your time than pursue me.'

'Nero, who knows of our intimacy? Who knows of our secret?'

'You're drunk!'

'When am I sober!' Otho stretched out beside him and embraced one of the dogs. 'I'll tell you who knows and who alone. The girls at the brothel. The girls who have seen us share and would tell no one but each other. And tonight I met a noblewoman. A noblewoman who shares in their secrets - and no doubt in their work, too!'

'A noblewoman and a prostitute! Too good to be true! Surely, they would permit me to marry *her*!' Nero joked.

'My friend, I would have lied in court if I thought I would have been believed and sworn on my life that Acte was of noble birth. But I would sooner strike you down dead than see you marry this beauty!' He sat up and began to undress. 'But that's not to say that I won't allow you to share her!'

'Generous to a fault. Who is she?'

'Poppaea, the wife of Rufrius Crispinus. Soon to be ex-wife!'

'And she's a prostitute?!'

'I greatly doubt it. But I have no doubt whatsoever that she is as valued a client with our ladies as we are. And Nero, I have never in my life met anyone quite like her!'

Nero grinned sleepily. 'So it seems. So; tell me a little more.'

'I wasn't joking, Nero. She knows that I'm your lover. It seemed to excite her! The woman was positively indecent! And beautiful. So beautiful. Hair the colour of palest amber. Skin like silk. So very soft; silky...'

Nero tired of the drunken ranting. 'Tall? Short? Thin? Fat? Old? Young? So far we have a foul-mouthed woman of silk with hair I can't begin to imagine!'

'Amber, Nero. Like the jewels women wear. And my height; and perfectly, perfectly thin. A complexion that would put even Doryphorus to shame - though far more ruddy.'

Nero laughed. 'A corpse has more hue than my Doryphorus! Go on.'

'What more is there to tell? The woman is perfect! And mine!'

'Yours? In an evening?'

'She already speaks of divorce.'

'Then it is true love! And you had always vowed to avoid it!'

'You speak of love, Nero. I speak of lust! Insatiable lust!'

Nero smiled. 'Then permit me to offer a remedy, my friend.'

The summons arrived from the Lady Poppaea almost immediately after sunrise, and led Otho to the library beside the Forum. He had only to wait a few minutes before a sedan chair stopped beside him and the elegant, bejewelled hand of a lady beckoned to him from within the curtain.

He climbed in eagerly beside her and began immediately to kiss and caress her. This time she made no attempt to curb his passion and he pulled the tunic away from her shoulder, to reveal a firm, well-rounded breast. She wore none of the usual layers that normally hampered his progress and he groaned in delight at such a discovery.

They made love orally in the sedan chair, before finally alighting at Otho's apartment, where they spent the day in passionate and repeated lovemaking.

'Oh, I am not able for this!' Otho groaned at one point; though Poppaea was able to prove him wrong.

'Is your lord the emperor able to test your stamina?' she teased.

'He could test even your own! I know my own failings, my love, and am happy to admit to them.'

'You have no failings; none that matter to me. Don't ever be envious of Nero, for I am sure he must have many.'

'I am not envious; and no, he has none! Too inventive for my tastes, though I am sure you would not consider that a failing!'

'How inventive? Would you like to demonstrate?' Poppaea coaxed. 'I am always receptive to new ideas!'

They lost themselves in passion once more, but then rose and dressed for refreshment.

'Does that slave-girl he's reputed to keep arouse him as you do?' Poppaea enquired casually, as they drank wine.

'Freedwoman,' Otho corrected her, 'Acte; and I'm sure she does. He tried to bribe us into swearing she was of noble birth so that they could marry! As if any of us would be believed! I so love his innocence!'

Poppaea laughed.

They returned, soon enough, to the sumptuous bed, where Poppaea continued to enquire from time to time about Nero's sexual appetites, without once allowing Otho to feel that that was, in fact, her only interest. She begged him to treat her as he treated Nero; and as she fulfilled the desires of Otho, so too she learned about those of the emperor.

By the time a chair arrived to take her back home for the evening, they had discussed her imminent divorce and their immediate marriage to follow. Otho watched her depart, then sank back on a couch; utterly exhausted, but happier than he had ever been in his life.

Chapter Thirty

AUGUST A.D. 58

The crowds reassembled at the Basilica Iulia when the next case of major scandal came up before Nero. But the emperor had more on his mind than the pettiness of politics, and again disappointed them.

Relying solely on the unpopularity of Suillius and the lenient punishment dealt out to him, accusers attempted to bring charges against his son for extortion. Suspecting that the charges had only been brought against him for vengeance, Nero vetoed the proceedings.

Senecio was among those so grossly offended by the decision.

'This is ridiculous, Nero!' he complained the following morning, when they travelled together for a fitting of clothes in preparation for the wedding of Otho and Poppaea. 'I wonder you don't abolish the courts of law altogether, when you obviously have no interest in maintaining justice.'

'I have absolutely no idea what you're talking about!'

'Any number of crimes are brought before you - and all are acquitted! Even murderers escape with their lives!'

'Life imprisonment; hardly a life,' Nero objected. 'Would you regard it as a let-off were you to be so sentenced - or a punishment?'

Senecio conceded defeat, although he had plenty left still to say on the matter, as the other clients at the tailor's soon found.

'It's a crying shame that the family can be left unpunished for such atrocities,' Aemilius agreed with his cousin, as they waited for Nero to emerge from his fitting.

'Exile!' Senecio snorted in disgust, 'He thinks so little of us that the crimes of Suillius against our families are worth nothing more. And why exile? So that Suillius might live in gratitude, to be called upon once more, at any time, to thin the ranks of the nobility!

'Every emperor feels the need to rid the empire of possible threats. Anyone bred for the throne has cause to fear for his life! But Nero talks to peasants in the street as though they are knights! He grants office to Greek freedmen! He is a far greater threat than any emperor our families have known.'

'What threat is a man who won't even condemn the likes of Suillius?' Aemilius asked mildly. 'He was great sport on the streets with us. He treated me as an equal, not with contempt.'

'Wake up, Aemilius! It's all one big joke to him - on us! He treated that slave boy of his as an equal, too. If putting you on a par with that boy is not contempt, then you must be a hard man to insult!'

Aemilius merely laughed.

'Well, my Lord,' he said, as Nero stepped out before them, 'there will be no finer bride than yourself at the Greek wedding - but shouldn't you now model for us the clothes you are here to collect?!'

'That is precisely why I prefer to come out for fittings, rather than bring tailors to the Palace!' Nero laughed. 'It is much more fun to dress up with one's friends; even if they are men who lack taste!'

'You stand before me in that garb, and have the audacity to say it is I who am tasteless?!'

'Otho is renowned for his fastidiousness in appearance. I cannot be shown up for a beggar beside him, now, can I?'

'Well, Nero, you need have no fear of that! Not even the poorest of beggars would accept that tunic as a handout!' Senecio quipped.

Nero grinned. 'You have yet to see the cloak I have chosen to go with it! As a complete outfit, they look stunning.'

'Stunned is just the reaction I would predict!' Aemilius agreed.

'Not suitable for a wedding?' Nero conceded at last.

'It is hard to think of an occasion when such a tunic would be suitable,' Senecio agreed, 'but Otho's wedding is completely out of the running.'

'I shall have it anyway,' Nero said cheerfully, 'I'm rather fond of these poppies sewn round the edges. They make a fair substitute for the real thing. The gardeners insist on ripping them up from the Palace grounds as weeds.'

He opted, instead, for a short, fringed tunic and elaborate gold cloak, which seemed almost commonplace in the wake of his other acquisition. Senecio chose a far more formal and sombre tunic; while Aemilius, who had no wedding invitation, had come only to collect several casual tunics for home use.

The three friends left the tailor and retreated to Senecio's apartment for a midday meal.

'Do you know Poppaea?' Senecio asked Aemilius.

'I know of her, certainly; though we have never met.'

'I feel I know her!' Nero laughed. 'I've seen very little of Otho since they met, but when we do meet his conversation is of Poppaea and Poppaea alone!'

'Why do you not come out with us anymore, Nero?' Aemilius asked.

'I haven't the time, Aemilius. I'm no longer a teenager. And, if I need any other excuse but those, Acte objects!'

'Acte objects! There lies the crunch!' Senecio scoffed. 'And now Otho is next among us to enslave himself to the vagaries of a woman!'

'He was enslaved long before she ever agreed to don the saffron veil!' Nero laughed, 'But it is the same for all of us and we wouldn't wish it otherwise.'

'He's at the Temple of Isis today, performing some ancient rite to bless the union,' Senecio said.

'He follows the cult of Isis?' Aemilius asked, surprised.

'Fervently. He publicly celebrates the Rites, though I find it distasteful myself.'

'I know nothing of it,' Aemilius said, 'except that I've seen them dressed up in their linen smocks - and the worshippers all appear to be female! I don't profess to know Otho well, but what I do know of him leads me to conclude that he does not worship Isis for religious reasons!'

Nero laughed heartily.

'I hear they drench themselves in blood,' Aemilius said with a shudder.

'They drink the blood of Isis to ensure an afterlife,' Senecio told them.

'They've been drinking her blood for two thousand years or more!' Nero mocked. 'Have they not drained her yet?!'

'I'm not sure that they drink it, they may bathe in it,' Senecio explained, 'it's symbolic.'

' "Eat my flesh and drink my blood and I shall grant you life eternal",' Nero quoted. 'I wonder what the good goddess meant when she asked them to sample her flesh?!'

'Well, it won our Otho over, anyway!' Senecio laughed.

'I have an aversion to cults,' Nero said. 'They are a little too fervent in their beliefs for my liking. Our own gods are kept alive only for the sake of custom. We have only to go through the motions of worship, without being expected to truly believe. Such beliefs are a little antiquated in this modern age, don't you feel? Besides, I can't really object to the Roman gods, who ask of us only that we party!'

'We sacrifice to them,' Senecio pointed out.

'But they don't ask it of us! We choose to make offerings. I haven't yet heard a god demand it of us!'

'You made Claudius a god,' Aemilius remarked neutrally.

'Because he is worthy of the status,' Nero told him. 'In our concept of the gods, he has every right to sit among them.' He smiled ruefully. 'Although, with hindsight, I begin to question that right. It is possible that I made an error in judgement. But I am only mortal, so can I really decide who is to be deified?'

'Poppaea, Otho says, is a Jew. The Jews believe that portents will predict the coming of their god,' Senecio said doubtfully. 'To believe in a god moving among us as a mortal is too far-fetched to be credible!'

'Caligula should have been a Jew!' Aemilius laughed.

'They call their god the Messiah,' Nero said. 'Claudius once had a great friend, a real character; he used to tell me a wealth of stories about him! He apparently satisfied every portent and was therefore convinced he was this Messiah. His name - King Herod. He was the king of the Jews! But still there are countless others who claim to fulfil the prophecies. If they cannot even accept their own king, who are they to accept?!'

'That has something to do with those Christians,' Aemilius said. 'They must be a faction of some sort. We were going to attend one of their underground meetings one night, after falling out of Plancina's! Have you ever been to a secret meeting of one of these underground cults?'

Senecio nodded with fond memories; while Nero shook his head.

'Great fun!' Aemilius continued, to the agreement of Senecio, 'absolutely anything goes! They make it up as they go along, according to the warmth and willingness of those present. Sometimes it's a drinking session, with plenty of drinking games; sometimes an orgy; sometimes no more than a gaming session. But we wouldn't go in to the Christian one. Every lowlife and cut-throat of Rome could be seen signing up.'

'That's the problem with these new cults,' Senecio agreed, 'they have gained an unsavoury reputation and attract the wrong crowd altogether. None of them last. They're either shunned from polite society - or massacre one another!'

'But Isis is hardly a new cult, and look how unsavoury it had become in Augustus' day,' Nero reminded them. 'An established and ancient religion in Egypt; and only a cult because we adopted it as such. The Roman worshippers probably know nothing of the true ways of worship. All religions become corrupted and confused when brought to Rome by new priests who know too little of their traditions. There are Romans today who call themselves Jews, but I wonder if their foreign counterparts would recognise them! No, I think the ever-growing number of underground sects is a dangerous thing and this idea of meeting up just for the sport of it should be stamped out.'

Senecio pulled a face. 'Then what are we to do for sport, Nero? We have no Games, no sects...!'

Nero grinned. 'A slight slip of the tongue and you might have answered your own question! What more do you want in life?!'

'There won't be enough of it in Otho's life, from now on in!' Senecio laughed.

'I wouldn't say that,' Nero corrected him, 'Poppaea is apparently most active; and neither seems she the sort to object to his continued presence at Plancina's.'

'Then he is fortunate indeed in his choice of wife!'

'Is she so fortunate in her choice of husband?!' Aemilius joked.

They continued their meal in high spirits and joked crudely of the forthcoming marriage; Nero recalling his own nuptials with no lack of detail. It was therefore nearer to late evening than the designated late morning before he finally returned to the Palace.

'Where the gods have you been!' Epaphroditus rounded on him, the moment he entered his chamber, 'You were supposed to meet with the Frisian delegation before lunch!'

Nero shrugged an apology. 'I have no excuse; I completely forgot and lunched with Senecio and his cousin. Who was I to see?'

'Verritus and Malorix. Doryphorus entertained them for the afternoon and they are now taking dinner with Octavia.'

'Let me change and I'll make my peace with them. Was Doryphorus successful in his quest to keep them happy?'

'Perfectly; indeed, they entertained him! A delightful pair, by all accounts!'

'Oh?'

Epaphroditus smiled. 'He took them to Pompey's Theatre. They were greatly impressed and particularly fascinated by our customs. He had to explain to them about the seating arrangements and the distinctions made between Orders. No sooner had he done so - and in quite elaborate detail, too! - than they spotted men who were quite obviously in foreign dress, seated among the senators!

'Poor Doryphorus had to explain that these men were delegates of a nation noted for its courage and friendship with Rome, and they had therefore been granted this compliment.

' "But no race on earth is braver or more loyal than the Germans!" Verritus declared; and they at once moved down and sat among the senators! Doryphorus nearly flushed when he told me! But it seems the spectators were delighted and gave them an ovation; and the senators were wholly won over by our brazen pair.'

Nero smiled. 'I'm glad to hear they were treated with the respect they deserved. I think I might like these new friends of ours.' He gestured towards the bed, where a slave had laid out one of his new tunics. 'What do you think, Epaphroditus? Will it be suitable for our meeting, or offensive?'

'I'll keep my own opinions to myself, Nero; but I think the Frisians will prefer something a little more formal. They've been so impressed by the grandeur of

Rome that to see the emperor in anything less than his most elaborate toga would be a disappointment.'

'A toga!' Nero raised his eyes heavenward. 'I could dress myself and be seated with them in a matter of moments! But, if you feel that it's grandeur they deserve, then it's grandeur they shall get!'

He called his slaves and they helped him dress; arranging the complicated folds of the toga while Thalamus set his hair. Slaves and barber hampered one another relentlessly; the barber coming out best only in the battle of spoken rebukes. Nero finally dismissed him, though his task was far from complete, and made his way to the dining hall.

Octavia, on seeing him enter, made her apologies and took her leave, and he sat in her place, on the couch shared by the two Germans.

'My dear Verritus, Malorix,' he said warmly, grasping them by the shoulders before settling down beside them, 'I hear that Doryphorus has kept you suitably entertained and therefore I'll make no attempt to bore you with my fruitless excuses. I trust you will forgive me and allow me to discuss your claims over dinner?'

The two rulers of the Frisians nodded their acceptance and immediately launched into their appeals.

'Germany has been at peace with Rome for longer than our own lifetimes,' Malorix pointed out. 'The old governor, Paulinus, set his troops to completing the dam across the Rhine. There was never a question that they might be needed in renewed hostilities.'

'We moved our people from swamp and woodland to the lands Paulinus had reserved for his troops,' Verritus broke in, 'we've built houses, tilled the land and sown fields. Never once did a Roman come forward to claim this land. It is only your new governor, Avitus, who now threatens us with 'The Power Of Rome', as he puts it, to return to our old lands.'

'Our old lands were too poor to support us,' Malorix pleaded, 'and we had worked this land ourselves - which must give us the right to retain it!'

Nero took a drink from his goblet and said carefully, 'I have heard it rumoured among the Germans that our troops have been for so long inactive that they have, in fact, been forbidden to enter into hostilities. Perhaps your people believed such rumours and therefore decided to acquire land which was apparently freely available?'

Malorix smiled. 'Does the reasoning behind our actions really matter? The outcome remains the same. We have settled a wilderness.'

'Our troops are kept busy, but the dam will soon be complete,' Nero pointed out impartially. 'It is then that they will look to farm their piece of land, in retirement, as a reward for their long service. A long service of protecting your people. And they will continue to protect your people - for it is now their land, too.

'When I first learned of your intrusion, I immediately granted you new lands close by. I did not, for one moment, consider sending you back to swamp and woodland. I understand that Avitus offered you these new lands?'

'What good are they to us, un-worked and unsettled?' Malorix protested.

'Today you impressed an audience with your sense of national pride,' Nero told them. 'For that, I would like to reward you. I therefore grant you both Roman citizenship.' Before they could offer their stunned thanks, Nero continued. 'I grant this so readily because your pride is something to be respected. And you showed that we have just such a sense, which is why you were so warmly received among us. National pride may or may not be a virtue - it can cause injustice. In this instance, I believe it will; but you must remember the reasoning behind my decision and respect it.

'I must uphold the decision of Avitus and order you to evacuate the land. You may return either to the lands I granted you, or your old lands. But you have dared to question the might of Rome and I must, therefore, show my hand. Avitus will be under instruction to send in the cavalry to remove any who disobey my order.'

The two Frisians studied him intently, while trying to phrase their protest. He smiled warmly, reluctant to destroy the congenial mood.

'Gentlemen,' he said affably, 'would you allow us to take your land, uninvited?'

He took a dish from one of the slaves and offered the contents to his guests, who accepted his offering as readily as they accepted his words. The evening continued pleasantly, despite the unsatisfactory outcome for the Frisians.

'Tell me, have you ever attended a Roman wedding?' Nero asked them, as they made ready to retire at the end of the evening.

They shook their heads.

'Then you must allow me to extend an invitation to you both, on behalf of Marcus Otho, who will be most honoured to have you as guests at his wedding to Poppaea Sabina.'

The invitation was gratefully received and the evening successfully concluded.

Verritus and Malorix were predictably enchanted by the wedding ceremony, which took place the following week. They particularly enjoyed the procession to the groom's home and participated heartily in the licentious singing, even though they had little comprehension of the words.

Among the three small boys accompanying the bride was Poppaea's eight-year-old son Crispinus, who immediately latched on to Nero. When his ceremonial duties were fulfilled and Otho and Poppaea had been left to make use of their privacy, Crispinus accompanied the emperor and his party back to the Palace.

He courteously shared the nuts that had been thrown to him during the procession; and talked incessantly, much to the amusement of his older companions.

'Do you have many fish ponds at the Palace?' he asked Nero. 'My father taught me to fish, but then he spent his time away and I've hardly got to go out since. Do you have lakes to fish in Germany? My tutor says there's nothing but trees and swamps in the accursed country. I think he was there once, but he didn't much care for it.'

'If you'd refrain from insulting them, I'm sure my two friends here would be happy to tell you a little more about their country than your tutor appears to know,' Nero told him with a grin, 'and as for my fish ponds, I have a wife who would see you thrown into the Tiber should you ever attempt to hook one of her fish!'

'You have tame carp?! Everyone claims to have tame carp, but I've never actually seen any. I was at the fish market once and the ponds were teeming with fish, but only because they were so over-crowded. I think they would have swum away quick enough if they could. My mother took me to the new market last year and we watched you open it and you said something, but I've forgotten what it was now, and Mother said you were quite a catch, which was funny, because it was a fish market!'

Nero laughed. 'Did she indeed? And what of your new stepfather? Do you think he'll take you fishing?'

'I've not met him. They never seem to meet when I'm there and Mother never mentions him at all. She speaks of you all the time, she said I should take extra care to be polite and to impress you and not to get on your nerves. Would your wife mind if I put the fish back again afterwards?'

'I'll tell you what, Crispinus - I won't tell her if you don't.'

'Well, it will have to be another day, because I haven't my fishing rod with me and I don't think I'm allowed to go back home for it. But Mother says we'll be spending all our time at the Palace from now on, so I can fish any time I want.'

'And what else does your mother say?' Nero prompted.

'Oh, all sorts. Mainly about the Palace and showing off to her friends. And she called Marcus Otho something funny, only I've forgotten what it was now, and my tutor rapped my knuckles when I told him. Do you know, he once beat me nearly to death because I'd forgotten some of my Greek verbs.'

'That's very hard, you should get a new tutor. Did you need a doctor?'

'Oh, no, I was all right afterwards, but he's always doing it, especially if I don't learn my poetry. I hate poetry, don't you? My friend's tutor is much worse and nearly kills him... Wow! I say! Are those your dogs?'

The small boy was immediately bowled over by the two large Rottweilers as they entered the gardens and Nero left him to play with them, grateful for the lapse in conversation.

'You clearly have a skill with children,' Verritus remarked, 'you enjoy them. It is at such times that I miss my own family. I have two girls and a boy.'

'Then you are a rich man indeed. Acte and I have been trying for a child for some time now... I suppose these things are in the lap of the gods.'

'Can your wife not bear you children?' Verritus asked in surprise.

Nero at once regretted his injudicious remark. 'Not at the moment, it would seem,' he said, diplomatically.

'Do many noble people reside at the Palace?' Malorix enquired, with reference to the intentions, hinted at by Crispinus, of Poppaea and Otho.

'Very few!' Nero joked. 'There are always rooms available for my friends and guests and Otho has always been one of the more permanent residents! I imagine he wooed his good lady purely on that point alone!'

The wedding guests finally congregated in the dining hall, where Nero provided lavish entertainment. By the time of their departure, the Frisians had much to relate on the splendour of Rome.

And Marcus Otho had returned to the Palace, a married man.

Chapter Thirty-One

'No work this morning, Nero?'

The emperor raised his eyebrows.

Otho grinned and sat down beside Nero and his young companion. 'I know what you're thinking, but my wife does occasionally sleep.' He glanced at the young boy seated alongside them beside the fishpond. 'Don't I know you?'

'I should say so, Sir! You're my new stepfather! Do you fish?'

Nero shook his head violently to advise Otho of an answer.

'I throw dice, drink heavily, spend money on horses and entertain ladies of ill-repute,' Otho declared seriously, 'but, alas, I do not fish.'

'So, how was your first night of wedded bliss?!' Nero asked him quietly.

'Blissful, as were all my pre-wedded nights!'

'Is that a real word?' Crispinus enquired. 'It's a jolly good one, if it is, although I bet you my tutor would beat me senseless if I tried to use it.'

'Do people often beat you senseless?' Otho asked.

'Actually, never,' Crispinus confessed.

'Really? You surprise me.'

'Look, there's Palamedes,' Nero said, spotting his dog as it sought shade against a far wall, 'he seems at a loss. Take him off and find Mysticus, would you?'

Crispinus needed no second bidding and raced off after the unfortunate animal.

'So that's Crispinus, is it?' Otho said, watching him go. 'Tiresome?'

'Lively. Like his mother?'

'You could so describe her!' He was suddenly distracted. 'Is he safe with those dogs?'

'He gives as good as he gets! If you were to ask how safe my dogs were, I would be more hesitant with an answer!' Nero laughed. 'I did attempt to warn him against such rough play, but he is both fearless and deaf!'

'Then he is indeed the son of his mother!'

'Rough play?'

Otho winced theatrically.

'And when do I meet this mysterious beauty of yours?'

'You met her yesterday!'

'One of a multitude wishing the bride well!' Nero protested. 'It's as though you don't trust me!'

'It's Poppaea I don't trust!' Otho laughed. 'Now that she is securely mine, I will introduce you! Tonight, at dinner.'

'I'm to be your first dinner guest?'

'The gods, no! I've scarcely a denarii to my name at present. We are to be *your* guests. Look out, the boy is on his way back.'

'Come with us, down to the stables,' Nero suggested to Otho, 'I promised him I'd show him the horses; now is as good a time as any.'

'I'll meet up with you later,' Otho said, declining his offer, 'at the moment there is only one member of his family whose company I seek!'

He made his escape before Crispinus could rejoin them. The young boy bounced across to Nero and sat beside him on the wall once more.

'I'll have one of my slaves take you fishing on the lake, if you like,' Nero suggested to him, conscious that he should make some attempt to return to his normal duties.

'Great! Can Palamedes and Mysticus come, too?'

'Definitely not; they'll have the boat over.'

'They'd keep still, I'm sure. They'll be fine. Come on, boys!' He whistled to the dogs and raced off to find boat and slave, not waiting for Nero's assistance in the matter. The emperor shook his head and made his way back in to the Palace to find Epaphroditus.

His reluctance to settle at his desk, he knew, was greatly due to the previous day's wedding ceremony. It had engendered no fond memories of his own; only rekindling the sharp longing to make Acte his wife. And his bitterness had been intensified by her enforced absence from the wedding party. No amount of pleas and threats had swayed Seneca or his ministers. Otho's wedding was a state affair; and Nero's consort could be only his wife.

Acte herself had offered some small protest, fond enough of Otho to bravely raise an argument; but to no avail. Her embroidered silk gown, bought specifically for the occasion by Otho himself, remained with her in Baiae; while all of Rome stepped out to see Otho and his new bride.

Nero found himself distracted, too, by the nuptial bed so close to his own. He knew well what it meant to share a bed with Otho; and Acte's absence only inflamed him further.

It was without interest or care that he finally went through his paperwork; wishing now that he had used Crispinus as an excuse to spend time at the stables.

'Have you seen Otho this morning?' Doryphorus enquired, stopping in to hand over the latest despatches from Armenia.

'He is well, and eager to introduce his new wife at Court.'

Doryphorus grunted.

'First impressions, Doryphorus?'

'First impressions are usually the most accurate - and I cared very little for the lady,' Doryphorus confessed.

'That much is obvious! But why?'

'I couldn't tell you, Nero. But I don't like her.'

'She's incredibly beautiful. Probably the most desirable woman I've ever set eyes on.'

'I once saw a cheetah in the arena. That was a beautiful creature. But it tore a man to shreds.'

Nero laughed. 'You should be on the stage, Doryphorus! Besides, I would imagine there'd be no shortage of men willing to be torn asunder by Poppaea! I myself would be first in the queue!' He looked at Doryphorus teasingly. 'You're not simply jealous, are you?'

'Why must I suffer such questioning!' Doryphorus protested. 'I merely professed a dislike for the woman. I have met her once; and would prefer not to meet her a second time. A gut feeling and no more.'

'Hmm. And what news of the war?'

'A rout, basically. It can go on for little longer, if the reports are true.'

'Good; then I'll read Corbulo's reports. I haven't the stomach for bad tidings just now.'

'No; and neither has Seneca,' Doryphorus said pointedly.

'Is he still smarting over my outburst?'

'His neurosis has never been more painful. I left him this morning contemplating suicide.'

'My heart bleeds for him,' Nero retorted, with deliberate spite. 'It is an unpleasant task indeed to tell a man that his chosen consort is unfit to be seen in public.'

'Come, Nero - you know well it was not personal.'

'Yes, of course! And does Seneca not know the same? Of course I'm going to attack him, in the defence of Acte! But there is no need for him to sink into depression! If Acte and I have not slit our wrists, then his own must surely be safe!'

'Then tell him! He feels very bad about it.'

'I've known him far longer than you have,' Nero told him, 'and I was always going to visit him today. But I would prefer to let him wallow in self pity for just a bit longer!'

Doryphorus grinned. 'Nero, you are cruel!'

'And so were his words,' the emperor said, but without rancour. 'Still, I suppose it would be better to see him sooner rather than later. Can you spare me?'

'I'm done. Epaphroditus, however, is a different matter.'

'Epaphroditus isn't here. And neither, my friend, shall I be, when he does appear!'

Nero swept the desk clear and left with Doryphorus; nevertheless checking carefully lest he should meet his secretary en route. Having successfully evaded his duties, he had no intention of returning to them and spent the remainder of the day in Seneca's amiable company. Together they prepared for dinner and eventually walked through to greet the emperor's guests.

'She seems a most personable young woman,' Seneca remarked as they awaited the arrival of Otho and Poppaea. 'We had quite a chat at the wedding party and I was most impressed by her level of education.'

'To be frank, I found her a tease,' Nero told him. 'She barely allowed me two words and kept quite a deliberate distance.'

'Oh, no, I found quite the opposite. The good lady went out of her way to entertain me. She knew my work inside out.'

'Aha! So that's why you were so smitten!'

'Not at all!'

'And what does it take to 'know' your work inside out? An ability to quote the odd passage during a brief conversation?'

Seneca shook his head in despair, but could offer no retaliation before the lady in question herself made her entrance. Leaving Otho in her wake, she made an immediate b-line for Nero. The emperor stood up to greet her.

'My Lady Poppaea Sabina, I am at your service,' he announced, with a sweeping bow.

She merely laughed and took her place on his couch.

'I am very pleased to hear it, my Lord. There is nothing quite so convenient as having an emperor at one's command!'

She patted the space beside her; an affable, casual gesture. Yet, for a moment, Nero was reminded of his mother and the explicit orders in her similar gestures.

Before he could accept her offer, however, Otho had slipped in and taken his place.

'Sit down, Nero! You hardly need a formal introduction!'

'Oh, we've already had one,' Poppaea declared with an air of boredom, 'and now this boy is at my service. Yet I do not see food or drinks at our disposal. One wonders what benefit it is to have an emperor at one's beck and call.'

'Forgive me, my Lady,' Nero apologised; and called for slaves.

Otho conveniently moved to one side of his wife and allowed Nero to take the spot originally offered.

'So, this is the grandeur of Palace life,' Poppaea said approvingly; casting a glance at her surroundings. 'If this is to be a regular occurrence I shall require a complete new wardrobe.'

'Then you should have married someone with money!' Otho joked. 'You may wait till the Saturnalia, when our patron here might just present you with a gown.'

'This! From a man who cannot pass a tailor with his purse intact! My husband here could safely discard every garment worn, rather than wash it, without ever having fear of running out!'

'And quite rightly so,' Otho protested. 'Women, however, need no clothes in order to look their best!'

Nero smiled. 'I imagine that to be the truest remark he has ever made. But you, my Lady, would compliment even the most humblest of gowns.'

She leaned towards him intimately. 'If you would only drop the formality, you would have no need to leave so much to the imagination.'

'And you, my dear,' Otho breathed into her ear, as he leaned over her neck to hear her words, 'would have no need for such subtle enticements were you to only sit back and get to know the man. Frankness is by far a quicker medium.'

Nero grinned. 'Subtlety? The pair of you are as open as a book! While you, Poppaea, have set your son to endearing himself to me as my own - and you have blatantly won over my friends in order to win me - your husband has been selling your charms as a Spaniard might sell his best racehorse! So don't think that any invitation proffered to your bed comes as any shock to me!'

'Well, really! Were I any sort of lady I would leave immediately. But fortunately for you I am the wrong sort - and so I shall remain!'

'And if we genuinely intended such an invitation?' Otho asked carefully.

Nero regarded Poppaea.

'Then I might genuinely be interested,' he answered. 'But you don't; do you?'

Poppaea laughed. 'It is such a delightful game. And yet games can become boring if the rules remain unchanged.' She studied Nero's face. 'What do you say, my Lord? Shall we extend the boundaries?'

Nero looked to Otho, who shrugged lazily.

'I am the lady's husband, not her guardian. And you know my will better than I.'

'Then the matter rests in your hands, Poppaea. Or do you just tease?'

She smiled. 'I do far more than that, Nero. Shall we arrange a private dinner for tomorrow evening?'

'Gladly.'

The remainder of the evening passed in general conversation that didn't hint at the words exchanged in opening. Nero surveyed his would-be lover with intrigue; fascinated more by the compulsion behind her actions than by the seduction itself.

A poetry recital followed dinner and Nero read some of his own work, which was warmly received. Before he could announce Paris - and contrive an invitation to partner him in the chosen piece - Otho spoke up loudly in opposition.

'One is duty bound to sit through recitals when it is one's emperor who recites,' he pointed out, 'but there is no law in Rome that can enforce our continued attention when once the emperor takes his seat! Accomplished though I am sure Paris is, he is no slave girl - and therefore not my idea of after dinner entertainment!'

'Forgive me,' Nero apologised to his other guests, 'but I must concede in some small degree to the wishes of my guest of honour. We will forego the talents of Paris for this evening and instead return to literature. Perhaps Marcus Otho approves of Petronius?'

'Marcus Otho most certainly does,' the man in question returned, 'providing it's none of that poetical nonsense we have already been forced to sit through!'

'Let me read my latest piece,' Lucilius called from a different table, 'it would change your view of poetry totally, Otho.'

'I fear it would only vindicate it!' Petronius retorted and rose from his couch before his invitation could be snatched by another. 'Here is a piece from my latest satire,' he continued, 'which, as you can see, I have failed to fetch with me. So I shall tell you a tale, in what might be rather a waffling manner, of what I will call 'a gentleman's private appendage' - for fear of giving offence to some of the ladies present - and it's repeated failure to spring into action when required.' He waited for the laughs to subside before continuing. 'I might also add that the unfortunate hero of this cautionary tale bears no resemblance to any person, living or dead; or any emperor of Rome, living, dead or seated on the couch beside me. In fact, I cannot stress enough that this is not based upon our good ruler here, who has never discussed such problems with me or sought advice for such an affliction.'

Again, the hall erupted with laughter, and Nero feigned embarrassment. It was, however, more genuine when he looked up once more and caught the eye of Doryphorus.

'Your friend appears acutely discomforted,' Poppaea remarked, following his gaze. 'Is there a loose tongue in our midst?'

'Perhaps, by chance, Petronius has hit a raw nerve,' Nero told her.

'You disappoint me. I always find a loose tongue to be quite an asset in a man. Don't you?'

Both Nero and Otho laughed heartily; much to the satisfaction of Petronius, who had reached a particularly humorous point in his speech.

'Shall we retire to my chamber?' Nero suggested, when Petronius had finally brought the evening to an enjoyable conclusion.

'Tomorrow we shall have a private party of our own,' Poppaea insisted firmly. 'Tonight we are guests of honour and must conduct ourselves as such.'

'You will learn, Nero, that the lady is as contrary as the donkeys she keeps,' Otho warned.

'You keep donkeys?'

'A strong herd, all homebred. Their milk makes an excellent face cream.'

'And is easily absorbed by the brain, I fancy,' Otho joked.

'Very well, then,' Nero agreed, 'until tomorrow.'

He rose from the couch and saw out his guests; Poppaea allowing no special attention to be paid her, though Nero felt the intimacy of their conversation allowed it. He watched her leave and was surprised to find that it hurt to be parted from her.

Preferring to sleep alone that night, he lay awake for several hours; thinking of Poppaea.

The following morning he sat through his audiences with unusual impatience and could concentrate even less on the ensuing administrative work. Not even the arrival of Xenophon to discuss events in Greece could arouse any interest from the emperor and it was only when the day's business had ended and preparations for the evening had begun that Nero at last relaxed.

'The entire household has been complaining about your preoccupation,' Petronius told him, as they bathed together before dinner. 'Don't tell me you are feeling left out, now that your little playmate has a new consort?!'

'He hasn't been my playmate for many a year. I barely see him, Petronius. Even now, it is his wife who presses the invitation.'

'And the wife who so distracts?'

Nero grinned. 'She is very beautiful, you will accept.'

'Masked by a saffron veil, I do indeed accept it. But I saw little of her last night and now I understand that none of you will be at dinner tonight?'

'That is indeed so, Petronius. We are having a private function, in my own room.'

'What manner of woman is this new wife of Otho's that he does not allow her to mix with the rest of us and that you must go to such inordinate trouble to impress her?!'

'A beautiful one! I told you already; what more answer do you need?!'

Petronius watched him dress, fascinated by the more elaborate than usual lengths to which Nero was going.

'Anyone would think you were intending to make advances to the lady, such is your dress and over-powering perfume!' Petronius mocked.

'Oh, but I am!'

The mocking smile fell from Petronius' face. 'Do I hear you right? You seriously intend to pay her suit?'

'You look shocked, Petronius! And it is she who has already made the advances.' He looked at his friend with amusement. 'What? Did you seriously think I would attempt to steal Otho's new bride?!'

'Well, I must admit, you had me quite fooled momentarily. Beware that those fine silks and perfumes don't fool Otho, too!'

'He would be disappointed if I made no effort. Poppaea is very special indeed and must be treated as such.'

'Yet it looks for all the world as though you intend to bed her.'

'But I do, Petronius! The act has been agreed upon. Otho has kept no secrets from her and she wishes to be part of it too.'

Petronius sat down heavily on a stool and raised a hand for silence.

'You confuse me, Nero. Are you saying that both Otho and Poppaea are in agreement that you bed her?!'

'You make it sound like a wager, Petronius! It is merely an extension of friendship. Otho has always shared my bed; and now he brings to it his wife. At her own insistence, I might add. We all see it as a perfectly natural arrangement.'

Petronius was horrified.

'There is nothing more unnatural!'

'How can you say that, when such scenarios fill your books?'

'That's fantasy, Nero, not real life!'

'Why should it not be real life? What possible harm are we doing? This is the natural climax of friendship.'

'You play a dangerous game, Nero. No friendship can withstand the jealousies of love. If you insist upon living out the plots of my books then you will already know that!'

'Any true friendship can. Those two in your latest book are not true friends - they are rivals. Why, you would never find Otho and me arguing over so beautiful a boy as your Giton! We would share him, and so afford ourselves even greater pleasure from him. It would never occur to us to do otherwise.'

'With one for whom you hold no affection besides lust, perhaps. But would you so readily share a woman? The deeper your love for Acte, the more you shield her from Court.'

'I shield Acte not for my own interests, but for hers. Poppaea is different. She has a genuine desire to be shared. It would cause her no heartache, no insult. The suggestion first came from her lips, without any prompting on Otho's part.' Nero smiled. 'You live in the world of fiction, my friend. Do not concern yourself with the false worries of reality. Why, have you ever known us to quarrel after a night at the brothel? The real pleasure is in the shared experience. Doryphorus wasn't the first to show me that. Do you suppose Otho knows nothing of what goes on between Acte and me? Otho and I are as one; you speak of us as rivals.'

'As indeed you soon will be! You speak of prostitutes and betrayal in words, but never yet of love. She is his wife, Nero! Nothing good will come of this.'

Nero merely laughed. 'Your wonderful histrionics would rival Paris on a public stage! Perhaps you know me too well to credit me with good sense; but at least acknowledge Otho to be sensible. Do you really think him capable of making so drastic a mistake?'

Petronius snorted at so weak an argument. 'Otho thinks through his penis; and you, you have no heed of consequence. I hope to goodness the lady has more sense and runs from you both!'

Nero grinned. 'She probably will, Petronius! Still, allow me to live in hope and preen myself without further protest!'

Petronius bowed to his wishes and left him to the mercy of Thalamus, the barber. It was only after the last lock had been curled expertly into place that Nero deemed himself fit to attend the private dinner.

He entered Otho's once-familiar chamber and looked around him incredulously. Poppaea's influence was already visible and her taste in expensive objets d'art faultless. Nero smiled admiringly.

'You have some exquisite possessions, Poppaea; not least your husband.'

She returned his smile. 'No doubt Acte has worked similar magic on your own apartment.'

'Acte has very much simpler tastes.'

'A pity she could not join us; we would have made quite a cosy little party.'

'She cares little for parties or, indeed, Palace life in general.'

'No? And is she aware of exactly all that Palace life entails?'

Nero blushed slightly. 'She is in Neapolis.'

Poppaea smiled, nodding. 'Oh... I see.'

'No; I don't think you do see. I wouldn't hurt her for the world.'

Poppaea studied him carefully. 'But how could you, Nero? She is in Neapolis.' She smiled at him evocatively.

They settled back on a shared couch and picked at the selection of food served by Halotus. Nero watched Poppaea in fascination, captivated by her statuesque beauty and frightening dominance. Her confidence and overt sexuality attracted him as keenly as the innocence and charm of Acte, sending the same feelings of longing coursing through him; until he could not bear to look away from her.

She tantalised him with the provocative way in which she ate - and knew it; gazing at him disarmingly as she soaked up the excitement he betrayed. He left his own food untouched.

Otho, too, merely toyed with his food, barely raising any to his lips. He was all too conscious of the fact that his wife had never yet staged such an act for him.

Eventually Halotus cleared away the un-emptied dishes and left the three friends to their privacy.

They were quick to make use of it.

Chapter Thirty-Two

SEPTEMBER A.D. 58

'I'm not comfortable with what you're asking of us,' Otho told Poppaea once more, as they dressed for dinner, 'it has nothing to do with childishness or jealousy!'

'Nero had no complaints.'

'Because Nero has no objections to your whims and fantasies. The gods know, he shares half of them!'

'I'm asking no more of you than he has. You were happy enough to tell me of your exploits - less happy, it seems, to demonstrate them.'

Otho turned round to face her. 'I'd tell you any details you wanted to hear! I'd tell you I slept with the Augusta if it got you into my bed! But I won't perform for you, like some trained animal! Nero accepts that and is content to look elsewhere; I suggest you follow his example.'

'And look elsewhere, Otho? Why, I need hardly look further than Nero to get what I want.'

'Then look no further, Poppaea. Let Doryphorus make up your party; and leave me to Plancina and her girls.'

'Oh, I would - and willingly!' Poppaea said spitefully, 'but your loyal little friend would throw me out just as speedily.'

Otho embraced her, though she remained stiff in his arms.

'Come, Poppaea, don't let's fight. You know I love it when you tease.' He weakened as she softened. 'I'll let him do as he likes, but not with you looking on. You must be a part of it, too.'

Poppaea kissed him. 'Now that you have submitted, it is enough. I'll play with him myself.'

Otho laughed. 'You're a perfect bitch, Poppaea.'

'How else could I collect so many husbands?! And don't you all love me for it.'

Otho did not need to speak in reply.

Nero lay on his bed, left unsatisfied by Doryphorus and successfully guessing at the reason behind the late arrival of his two guests. The very thought turned his stomach.

The fact that Otho shunned him in her presence hurt him. But the sight of her enjoying Otho pained him more. It wasn't jealousy; and neither could he admit to possessiveness. But he could not bear to see her with Otho; could not bear to let her out of his embrace... could not bear to let her return to her own chamber...

He sat up, angered by feelings over which he had no control.

'Doryphorus!'

Tubero arrived instead. Doryphorus, it transpired, had gone into the city with Phaon.

'That saves me the effort of calling for Phaon, then, doesn't it?' Nero remarked.

'But surely it's too late to be thinking of work, Nero, even if they were still available,' Tubero protested.

'I can think of nothing but the war, Tubero. How can I relax until it is resolved?'

'Perhaps you should go into the city yourself - with some of your friends. Try to push the war out of your mind altogether.'

Nero smiled. 'Tubero, I deliberately set my mind to the war, because it is infinitely preferable to thinking of my friends.'

Tubero risked a cheeky retort. 'You could always invite the Augusta to join you.'

'Good point, Tubero! Perhaps my friends are a welcome diversion after all!'

He dismissed the slave and busied himself with the documents left by Doryphorus; until Otho and Poppaea at last made an appearance.

'I'm sorry we are late, Nero,' Otho apologised without concern. He grinned. 'We were otherwise engaged!'

'I was about to go to dinner without you; indeed, forego dinner altogether and concentrate on dispatches from Armenia.'

'How very dedicated,' Poppaea said scornfully, 'Can we now go to dinner? I've worked up such an appetite.' She watched, with satisfaction, Nero's reaction.

Otho, too, noted it.

'I was thinking of taking Poppaea for a break to Bauli,' he told Nero, as they walked together down to the dining hall.

'Where the gods is Bauli?' Poppaea asked.

'It is the name of my mansion at Baiae. Nero will tell you - there is no finer place in the empire! A perfect residence for my beloved wife.'

'You would hardly whisk her away already, my friend,' Nero protested, 'we've barely had time to get to know each other. Besides, the weather is far from ideal at this time of year.'

'You've had nearly two months of our company,' Otho reminded him lightly, 'during which time you have come to know my wife slightly better than I! I think it's time I got to know her too, don't you?'

'I care nothing for the supposed finery of your coastal mansion,' Poppaea said, 'for it surely cannot compare with the Palace. Don't begin to suppose you can take me away from this elegance so soon.'

'Don't begin to suppose that you are loved so devotedly that you can disobey me at will,' Otho warned. 'If I say we are to retire to Baiae for the winter, then that is what we shall indeed do.'

Poppaea laughed. 'Then I wish you and Crispinus a happy time of it! Nero and I shall remain here.'

'I sometimes think, Poppaea, that you married me only to win Nero.'

'Then you are more astute than I ever gave you credit for,' Poppaea retorted.

'Oh, come on!' Nero protested, 'this is neither the time nor the place to be arguing! You are still newly weds, after all - and not even embittered old couples have the audacity to fight while in the company of their emperor!'

'If it were not for the company of our emperor we would not be fighting,' Otho snapped.

'Then perhaps it is for the best if you do both leave for Baiae,' Nero conceded, 'for I would not wish to be accused of intruding.' He pulled away from Poppaea's loose embrace and walked on ahead.

Otho took Poppaea's arm and held her back.

'Just how close was I to the truth?'

'Far too close for comfort, Otho; so don't push your luck.'

The arguments intensified as the weeks wore on. Poppaea made it clear that she preferred Nero's company to that of Otho; and Otho grew to loathe her very presence. More frequently than not she remained with Nero and often did not return to her own apartment for days at a time. Otho, for his part, avoided the Palace as much as possible; and was hardly missed.

And at last came the news from Armenia that Nero had long sought.

'I have a dispatch from Corbulo!' Doryphorus announced eagerly, waking Nero before even the slaves had been in to take out the dogs. 'It arrived during the night and the runner considered it important enough to wake me; though I felt I could leave you sleeping a little longer.'

Nero sat up immediately.

'Poppaea! Wake up! You should hear this too!' He turned on Doryphorus sharply. 'It is good news, I take it?'

'My Lord, I would wake you for nothing less!'

Nero took the scroll and scanned it. 'Artaxata has surrendered!'

Poppaea yawned. 'And Artaxata is?'

'The capital of Armenia, my darling. The war is at an end.'

He read the scroll through slowly to himself before sharing it with his companions.

'Corbulo prepared to put the city under siege, but the gates opened voluntarily,' he told them. 'The people surrendered their property and it was an altogether bloodless victory. The city has now been set alight and razed to the ground.'

'And what is the point of that?' Poppaea protested. 'What use to us is a city of ashes?'

'Of no use at all, my love. But Corbulo's army is not large enough to provide a garrison strong enough to hold a city the size of Artaxata.'

'Huh! And you call it a bloodless victory.'

'Cities can be rebuilt, Poppaea. Lost lives can never be replaced.'

'And so - more triumphal celebrations?' Doryphorus suggested.

'After last time? I think not, my friend! We were a little presumptuous then; and I hardly dare tempt fate a second time!'

'But I asked the slaves to summon Patrobius the moment he rises,' Doryphorus told him anxiously, 'I felt certain you would wish for some form of celebration.'

'My new amphitheatre and gymnasium is complete on the Field of Mars. We could hold Games in honour of its completion,' Nero suggested.

'A splendid idea!'

'Gladiatorial displays! And wild beast hunts!' Poppaea enthused.

'You and Phaon can arrange it with Patrobius,' Nero agreed, 'but remember that I will permit no one to die.'

'Not even for this?' Poppaea pressed.

'Why else would I emphasise the fact? The senate is cunning enough to allow exceptions under special circumstances - and I am no less cunning enough to be aware of that!'

'I shall go and arrange finances with Phaon and Patrobius, then,' Doryphorus said.

'And I shall organise my own celebration,' Poppaea declared, rising from the bed and going across to the wardrobe in search of some clothes. 'I shall go into the city with Camilla and Silia and we will spare no expense in honouring your great victory!'

Nero smiled. 'Think of me, won't you?'

'I'll have Silia choose you a tunic. I know of no one else who can match your outrageous tastes!'

They dressed quickly and went their separate ways, Poppaea happy to forego breakfast and meet with her friends; Nero preferring to walk off his excitement with his dogs.

Down by the lake he recognised a rider, watering his horse.

'Otho!' he called, 'Is that another new animal you have?'

Otho led the horse over to him. 'On loan from Vitellius. It is too much for him, with his disability. I am happy enough to tire the beast out for him, although he is hardly a difficult ride.' He patted the chestnut affectionately. 'And what brings you out so early?'

'Good news. Artaxata has been won. Poppaea has gone into the city for a celebrationary shopping spree!'

'Celebration? I'm surprised she even knows where Artaxata is,' Otho sneered.

'She didn't, actually!'

'Still, any excuse, Nero.' He pulled the horse round sharply as it attempted to lash out at one of the dogs. 'Vitellius obviously doesn't keep dogs.'

'I don't think that old greyhound of his has moved from his couch in the past two years!' Nero laughed.

'That's right! I'd forgotten her; one gets so used to simply stepping over her! No wonder these lads distress the poor beast!'

The two friends began to walk along, towards the stables.

'So, my beloved wife is spending your money as quickly as she spent mine,' Otho remarked, 'and now she can buy silk instead of linen.'

'Don't be bitter, Otho.'

'Bitter? I am anything but, my friend. I have learned a valuable lesson - and I hope you will avail of my advice before you learn it too.'

'Petronius begged me not to become involved with her. Never once did we think that it was you who would fall foul to jealousy.'

'He begged me too, Nero. And it took all my might to convince him that you were too generous by nature to suffer jealousy. How wrong I was.'

'You blame me?! When it has been your spite and bitterness that has destroyed us?'

'Wake up to yourself, Nero! It isn't spite, but truth. She used me and now she uses you. How can you not see that?'

'What you fail to see, Otho, is that we love each other. That she loves me more than you is a fact with which you clearly cannot cope.'

Otho laughed scornfully. 'She loves you as devotedly as your poets and dancers love you! You fill the Palace with sycophants and now they fill your bed, too! Look at what you've become - paying Paris and Terpnus and that damn fool Lucilius to spout utter rubbish, because Petronius leads you to believe it is art! And now you're fool enough to believe that bitch loves you too, when all she really loves is your title!'

Nero struck him full in the side of the face and knocked him to the ground.

Stunned only momentarily, Otho raised himself on one elbow.

'They all do, Nero.'

Agrippina sat beside Nero on his couch at dinner that night and Burrus immediately came up beside her. She sneered at him and embraced Nero lovingly.

'You are happy to stand idly by and see him drink himself senseless, yet you are quick to protect him from his own mother!'

'The drink is less dangerous, Augusta.'

She laughed at him and pressed her lips to Nero's ear.

'What is this, my love? Your favourite drink was once boiled water. Why now the need for wine in such excess?'

Nero leaned against her and rested his head on her breast. 'The battle. Have you not heard? Victory in Armenia.' His words were slurred and each sentence an effort.

'There is nothing I do not hear,' she told him gently, 'so tell your mother your problems, my loved one, for I know you cannot tell Poppaea; and Acte is not here. Neither, too, is Otho, is he?'

Nero shook silently in her arms and she rocked him gently, kissing the back of his neck and fondling his hair.

'Poppaea will be back soon,' Burrus warned.

'Poppaea and her friends are currently in a brothel, Commander! A slave fetched back her purchases and there is no one here who does not know why she is so late behind them.'

'Let him go, Augusta. He is too drunk to shun you.'

'What are you afraid of, Commander? I am a broken woman, excluded from Palace society. Britannicus is gone. What threat can I now offer? Allow me the pleasure of his company, when it is all I have left.'

Nero sat up and gestured vaguely to Burrus, her words absorbed and noted. 'Let us alone,' he requested weakly, 'let us alone.' He nestled back down into her breast.

Otho sat with Petronius and Vitellius in a tavern, not far from the Circus.

'You may have the horse,' Vitellius told Otho, 'it is the kindest thing I can do for the beast.'

'Or for me?'

Vitellius patted him on the shoulder.

'Shouldn't you be getting back to the Palace?' Otho asked him. 'Without your applause and pleas Nero feigns too much modesty to join Paris in a dance.'

'You're right, I should head back. But there'll be no dancing tonight, Otho.' He stood up to leave and his slaves ran to fetch his chair. 'I shall bid you both goodnight, then. Take care of the horse, Otho. It would be a shame to see it rot away in my stable.'

'I shall, Vitellius; thank you.'

'Less of a noble gesture than a safeguard,' Petronius remarked, when once Vitellius was out of earshot. 'One day he might need you.'

'He's no peasant himself. One day I may need him.'

'Nero will be another Augustus and outlive us all.'

'Nero is a damned silly fool and there is nothing I can say or do to convince him of her scheming, Petronius.' He looked across at Petronius. 'I beg you, Petronius, as his friend, watch over him - and watch out for her.'

'Whatever scheming she may have resorted to in order to secure her current position, you may rest easy that it was not for the sake of politics. Her only goal is the prestige and wealth of being Empress. She will never be a threat to him, Otho. On the contrary, my old friend, have you ever seen him so blissfully happy as he is with her?'

Otho started to reply, then stopped. He could lie to Petronius; but not to himself.

'You have grown up quicker than Nero and left him behind,' Petronius said, 'perhaps that is how it should be left, my friend.'

'I loved her, Petronius.'

They sat in silence, neither interested in the drinks before them.

'How can I remain in Rome?' Otho said. 'The governorship of Lusitania is available. Do one thing for me, Petronius - put it to Nero that I should be given office there.' He smiled without pleasure. 'That is, if Poppaea has not already done so.'

NOVEMBER A.D. 58

The unconditional love of Agrippina, for which Nero had always longed, had at last been offered; and gratefully accepted. Though her apartments in the Palace had been given over to Poppaea and her friends, Agrippina was a regular and much welcome guest once more, sharing Nero's couch at dinner and travelling out with him by sedan chair whenever he was called from the Palace.

This reconciliation did much to dull the pain of Otho's departure, until he was barely missed at all. But outside of the Palace grounds his absence was all too noteworthy. Court gossip was always prone to public lampoons and soon the most popular rhyme on the lips of the commons was Otho's scandalous fall from favour.

" 'Otho in exile?' 'Yes and no;
   That is, we do not call it so.'
'And may we ask the reason why?'

'They charged him with adultery.'
'But could they prove it?' 'No and yes;
It was his wife he dared caress.' "

Chapter Thirty-Three

14TH DECEMBER A.D. 58

'Happy birthday, darling.'

Acte kissed Nero tenderly and sat back to watch him open his gift. He smiled with genuine pleasure as he pulled back the straw packing from the case and glimpsed for the first time the white myrrhine goblet. He raised it carefully to his nose and basked momentarily in its delicate scent.

'It's beautiful.'

She hugged him tightly. 'Oh Nero, what a difference to your nineteenth. I couldn't even shop for a gift for you. We were so afraid for you.'

'I've survived far worse than that beating,' Nero said wryly, 'and I dare say I'll survive worse yet. None of which matters when sitting here by your side.'

After a while, Acte ventured carefully, 'Nero, there are a lot of rumours flying about. What's going on at Court?'

'If you mean that vile rhyme about Otho, what more can I tell you than you already know?'

'I'm more concerned about Agrippina. You're the only one who actually trusts her.'

'And I have good reason to, my love. Whatever has occurred in the past is now buried and forgotten. I can remember her once promising to step aside from politics, when once I was emperor, and to become a mother to me. That time has now come. There is no scheming or hidden motive - though the gods know that Poppaea is convinced Mother only vies for my wealth!' He grinned. 'She is only worried that Mother might spend it quicker than she!'

'Nero! That's an awful thing to say!'

'I love her dearly, but if a more powerful man than I presented himself I'd lose her tomorrow!'

'But still, Nero... they say...' Acte hesitated. 'They say the most vile things about the Augusta's return to the Palace. What they suggest you do together in a sedan chair does not bear repeating.'

Nero sighed. 'Questions of incest? Perhaps she is never to be forgiven for her questionable past.'

'But why such rumours now, Nero?'

'Because, for the first time, we are close. She sits with me; she hugs me; we kiss good night. Such normal, trivial things. The simple things of which I was for so long deprived. It is not her fault, Acte; but she created the brush with which she will be forever tarnished.'

'Take care, Nero.'

Nero hugged her all the tighter.

'Let us go into Neapolis together this afternoon and shop for the Saturnalia. Instead of my usual slave's attire, I'll don your own clothes and pass as your sister!'

Acte laughed. 'You had best wear a veil, then - even though it will give you more respectability than you deserve!'

Nero rose and pulled her to her feet with him. 'Come! Let's have a mad dressing up session! Poppaea has a friend named Silia who dares me into the most outrageous costumes! It is the most wicked fun - and totally private! You'll hear no vile gossip and nor will I be in any danger of a hiding!'

'Today you are twenty-one, Nero! How many more years will it take before you are grown up?!'

They spent a happy time at the market and despatched all bar one of their purchases directly to Rome. Nero carried that sole item back to Acte's villa, losing his veil in the process.

'How do you propose to hide it from Poppaea until the Saturnalia?!' Acte laughed, as the cheetah cub mewed long and loudly at its new surroundings. 'I suppose it may lodge with Senecio?'

'At the moment I am more concerned for the safety of the dogs! It may be small, but by the gods it knows how to scratch!'

'Poppaea will look like one of those grand Eastern Queens you see in the paintings, when he is big enough and well-trained enough to sit at her feet.'

'Exactly why we chose him,' Nero agreed, 'if he is a he, that is!'

'How long before we'll know?'

'I have absolutely no idea! I suppose it would be best not to name him at all! Do you remember going to the amphitheatre to choose ourselves such a cat?'

Acte smiled. 'I can't believe Palamedes and Mysticus were ever that small. We carried one each, in our arms, just like that little cub. And now they must each weigh more than the pair of us put together!'

'So it seems, when they launch themselves at me! Perhaps this little mite will be no match for them after all!'

'I'm glad we found them - they're so much more fun than some elegant looking cheetah.'

Nero held the cub at arms length. 'We'll judge that when it grows up a bit. In the mean time, it has just relieved itself on your best silk gown!'

Back at the villa, the cub received a wary introduction to the two dogs. After an initial bout of hissing and barking, which saw the dogs come off very much worse, the three animals settled down to a more agreeable truce.

'How can I separate them now,' Nero said, watching them as they slept peacefully together, 'Poppaea will have to receive him early. But, then, I shall not return to Rome until the very last moment.'

'I wish you did not have to return at all.'

'Come with me, Acte. Even if it is just for the festivities.'

'They're particularly what keep me away! I couldn't join in with the party games, or choosing a king! Whatever the king asked of me would show me up for the fool I am! And the Augusta will be there. She makes me feel like something horrible she's trodden in. And now Poppaea, who sounds so glamorous and so very proper.'

Nero laughed. 'Proper?! That is something she most definitely is not!'

'You know very well what I mean. She's a lady, and I would be beneath her.'

'Silia and Messalina would welcome you as a sister. They certainly could never be classed as snobs.'

'They alone. And how do you spend your time with them? Playing Doryphorus' bizarre games, which I would be far too embarrassed to do. No, Nero, this is my home; not Rome.'

It was an argument Nero had heard too often to dispute. Instead he enjoyed what little time he could alone with Acte, before imperial duties summoned him once more to Rome.

He spent the festivities largely in the company of Agrippina, appreciating her companionship far more than the lavish gifts with which she had showered him. They laid together on the couch, laughing drunkenly at the tasks performed by their friends according to the wishes of that year's king; Agrippina absently stroking Nero's leg as he fell asleep against her.

He awoke sharply, aroused and sweating, and conscious that it was not in bed with Poppaea that he lay. At once he was aware of Agrippina's un-maternal touch and he recoiled in horror. Agrippina merely smiled at him, unperturbed.

'A nightmare?' she enquired, leaning forward to kiss him.

He drew back still further.

'Come, Nero; don't feign disgust now, simply because a few close friends can see us. You never once complained before.' She looked to those on the adjoining couch. 'Have you ever seen him raise such objections?' she asked of them.

They laughed and shook their heads.

His head reeled with too much wine and fearful confusion. He rose shakily and sought out Poppaea, who lay with her friends, pampering her gift from Nero. He squeezed in beside them, much to their pleasure.

'The Augusta is like one of those useful little ponies they keep on stud farms,' Silia commented approvingly, 'what do they call them? Teasers? She has raised your blood most commendably!'

He pushed her hand away aggressively.

'Whatever is wrong, my love?' Poppaea asked.

'She continues to smile at me as though nothing is wrong!' Nero muttered. 'She was touching me.' He shuddered.

'She is always touching you,' Poppaea complained, 'all hugs and kisses and oh so false; trying to win back your favour and see me back out on the street.'

'No, no... she *touched* me, Poppaea. As you would.'

The three women laughed at the notion.

'It comes as no surprise to me,' Messalina said, 'she bestows her favours wherever she thinks they'll find greatest reward. You have been tempted into every other lurid pastime so far - why not incest, too?! Who can blame the woman for trying!'

'Do you believe I have encouraged her?' Nero asked.

'No!' Poppaea assured him. 'That woman needs no encouraging.'

'Acte spoke of vile rumours... I paid no attention.'

'I've heard no such rumours,' Messalina said reassuringly.

Poppaea laughed. 'You hardly mix in the same circles, darling! Who knows what the commons gossip of? Keep away from her, Nero. It is as simple as that.'

Nero looked at her accusingly. 'You were against this reconciliation from the start. Such simple advice, to see her banished once more from my company.'

Poppaea merely smiled. 'She is no rival of mine. Let her stay, if you wish. Let her continue to fondle and arouse you, if that is how little you value your title. If she has you deposed, I can, as easily, have your successor.'

Silia and Messalina laughed uproariously and even Nero allowed himself a smile.

'What do you think? Seriously?' he asked of Messalina. 'Have I misread her touch and over-reacted?'

'How can I answer? I was hardly the recipient. Perhaps you were dreaming of us, my sweet! You were asleep; and you have been drinking. By all means give her the benefit of the doubt, if you feel she deserves it.'

Nero was readily pacified and beckoned to Agrippina to join them. She settled herself on the floor, at his feet, and the festivities continued. As she gently massaged his feet, he felt shame for having thought so low of her; knowing that his alarm had largely been triggered by Acte's own distrust.

Having so easily dispelled such doubts, he relaxed once more in her close company, and allowed her more liberty than he might otherwise have done so. In the drunken revelry that filled the days leading up to the New Year, Agrippina took full advantage of his lack of guard and openly caressed him; preying shamelessly upon him during the midday meal, when wine had left him senseless.

Gallus, her latest love, was among the first to voice his objections.

'The whole of Rome whispers of your incest,' he complained. 'I have heard you bragging of it at dinner tables! Must I force you to choose between us?!'

'It is not unthinkable that I could win his love. My own little brother loved me for a while; though I was too young and foolish to take advantage. I disliked his attentions and saw myself in exile for my sensibility. But Drusilla had him in the palm of her hand! There was nothing he would not do for her! It was she who held the reigns, not he. She died an empress, while I rotted away in exile.'

'And so you hope to make amends with Nero? Then you may kiss me good bye, Agrippina.'

'I will do no such thing, my dear Gallus! I hope to bind Nero to me once more and you can choose to stay or go - I love you no less for my dalliance with Nero. Try to see it as a means to an end, Gallus. On the other hand, if I fail, then the Guards will depose him for his lack of morality - which I have well publicised! If you are my lover, dearest Gallus, I shall see that it is you who succeeds him. Of course, if you choose not to stay, I can always nominate other distant relatives with imperial blood in their veins - and a debt to the Augusta.'

'Has he yet entered your bed?'

'You need to ask?'

'I hear that he has. He sleeps with slaves and ministers alike. And yet he seems always to recoil from you, before drink renders him too insensible for anything other than sleep.'

She smiled. 'But still, you wonder... just as the Guards must. So, do you stay; or do you go, Gallus?'

He smiled. 'I stay.'

'I thought you might.'

Agrippina settled beside Nero once more that evening and trusted to the pure lust she hoped she had engendered, in the face of a lack of free-flowing wine now that the festivities were over. Despite the argument she had presented to Gallus, she could not yet be certain that the Guards could be turned against Nero, and had still to rely upon her charms. She pressed them all the more fervently now, before the fast-dwindling opportunities petered out altogether. It proved to be a costly error.

This time his senses were not too dulled to be aware of the unnaturalness of her touch. And his original abhorrence was amplified by the realisation that he had fooled himself so easily during the past few weeks.

'Get away from me!' he cried out angrily, overturning a tray of goblets in his haste to back away. Burrus arrived instantly by his side.

'Have her escorted away!' Nero insisted. 'I cannot tell you what she has just now attempted, but you will see that she is never again allowed within the Palace! Get her out, Burrus!'

Burrus nodded to his men and carried out Nero's instructions as quietly as the situation allowed. The dinner guests looked on.

'Now what is the matter?' Poppaea complained, uncomfortable under such piercing focus. 'I warned you not to tolerate her, only to be ignored. And now you have her arrested for no more than daring to sit beside you!'

'She did more than that, Poppaea.'

'And only now does it disturb you?'

Nero rose in distress. 'I trusted her.'

'Perhaps with good reason,' Burrus told him gently. 'You have heard rumours and they have unnerved you. Without such malicious suggestions filling your head, the Augusta's actions would probably seem harmless. You were not afraid of her yesterday, after all.'

'Oh, but, Burrus - my skin crawls to think...'

'Don't think, Nero. You have been so happy knowing that she loves you. Does that count for nothing? I will see to it that you are never again alone in her company. But don't punish yourself for mere rumours, Nero. Just remember what she truly means to you.'

'How can I remember beyond this? How can I ever think of anything but what she has just done?' The tears that had started to well now subsided. 'I don't know, Burrus... you say I am confused by gossip; yet I know what she did.'

'But did she?'

Nero considered his words. He desperately needed to forgive Agrippina; a fact that Burrus knew all too clearly.

'She plots and schemes, it is in her nature,' Burrus continued. 'Horses are in your blood, Nero. For her, it is domination. And you have been raised to accept a standard of life that would seem outrageous to many. Just as her behaviour strikes you as outrageous. Spare a thought to how she was raised, Nero. With Tiberius and Caligula, and Drusilla and the empress Messalina. We cannot begin to imagine the degradation of Palace life then.'

Nero raised a smile. 'Always I am wrong to trust her. And I am not.' He met Burrus' stare and returned it steadily. 'Just as I am wrong to trust you. Even now, as my friend, you are prepared to lie in order to protect me. She meant to seduce me, Burrus. A final attempt to conquer me, because that is how little I mean to her. How little I have ever meant to her. I am no more than her key to the empire and you know that; yet you are willing to excuse her simply to spare my tears. Do you not think that is all I have ever done?' He tore roughly at the gold snakeskin bangle on his arm and pulled it off. 'Would you like to know what I really feel, Burrus? Now that the constant pretence of excuse is over?' He hurled the bangle across the dining hall. 'It may remain where it falls, Burrus. I don't care if I never see it again.'

Chapter Thirty-Four

FEBRUARY A.D. 59

It was Burrus who called the meeting; summoning all of Nero's ministers, as well as Anicetus, Commander of the Fleet, and various trusted troops.

'I need the majority,' he told Seneca, as they walked along together to Nero's chamber, 'for I hardly see it likely we can convince Nero.'

Seneca laughed at the very notion.

'He is, at least, now terrified of her,' Burrus said defensively, 'which will make it easier for him to bend to the majority.'

'Easier? It will be easier simply to ask Agrippina to kill herself and have her polite assent!'

They entered Nero's chamber and sat on the couch nearest the bed. Others had been fetched in specifically for the gathering and were already fast filling up. Nero welcomed each new visitor cheerily, as though to convince himself that the debate about to take place was of no consequence.

'Well, gentlemen,' Burrus began, when the informal greetings were over and the room was hushed, 'what are we going to do about the Augusta?'

It was immediately obvious that no one was willing to speak up in Nero's presence.

'Regardless of grounds, it is impossible to prosecute,' Nero said, aware that he would have to make the first suggestions and dreading every word. 'She had a case to answer once before, but didn't get to court. And I know that I am the first to blame in that instance.'

'Even had she got to court, we would not have gained a conviction,' Burrus admitted. 'There was no lawyer in Rome willing to prosecute her; and now there is no lawyer in the empire not within her pay.'

'And do we have any charges?' Anicetus asked.

'Does it matter? But, yes, there are sufficient charges. Incitement, treason, plotting... I could go into detail and list names, but it is all irrelevant under the circumstances. If we cannot use fair means, we are compelled to adopt foul.'

'We are going beyond the fabrication of charges?' Nero asked.

'Both unnecessary and futile, Nero. We all know that.'

'Can the Guards not simply enforce her suicide?' Anicetus suggested, somewhat tactlessly.

'I am fully aware that we are meeting now to arrange such options,' Nero said, 'but I cannot send the Guards to murder her. She is the Augusta. She is my mother.'

'We are, nevertheless, proposing assassination,' Burrus reminded him. 'It is a simple case of her or you, Nero. Already the Guards would have rebelled, had they not seen for themselves your innocence in her allegations of incest. I could say or do nothing to sway them, when once their decision had been made. But the troops further afield hear only rumour. At present, they are happy to follow the example of the Guard and hold faith in your innocence. But if they are paid to march against you, then march they will. The Augusta plots to depose you and will have no hesitation in resorting to financial offers, if the blackening of your name is not enough. And she is the daughter of Germanicus. In the eyes of both the public and the provincial troops she can do no wrong. She is the Augusta. The blood that saw you so readily accepted is stronger in her veins, Nero.'

'It is only as Germanicus' brother that Claudius came to power,' Anicetus pointed out. 'Your words make a great deal of sense, Commander. The man has become something of a god in death and public sentiment is far stronger than the loyalty of troops. We are still not so very many years away from civil war, though no one here remembers it. I would therefore view assassination as a crude form of suicide. Nero may as well step down now, than await the wrath of the public.'

'She is to be murdered; but it is to appear accidental,' Nero said bluntly. 'Deal with it, Burrus. It would not be the first time, would it not?'

Burrus looked confused.

'You are a soldier, Commander - trained to kill.' Nero smiled privately; old doubts dispelled as he saw that Burrus' confusion was genuine.

'Nero, with respect, the Commander is a soldier, trained to kill in combat and totally lacking in guile,' Anicetus said. 'I, on the other hand, was once your own tutor. From a background of imperial slaves, I may not be trained in the art of killing, but I would certainly be qualified in arranging accidental deaths!'

'Then the job is now yours, Anicetus. But please involve me no further.' Nero looked around the room. 'Is there any other business to discuss, while you are all gathered?' He was met by awkward silence. 'I thought not. Then you will have no objections to my taking the remainder of the day off. Tubero, would you please summon Terpnus and Paris for me.'

The plays of Euripides proved only a short term distraction, though a welcome one as Nero threw himself whole-heartedly into his favourite roles. But at dinner he had once more to face those with whom he had conspired to plot his mother's death.

He retired to his chamber with Poppaea, but her views on the subject were hardly sympathetic.

'I am only surprised that it has taken you this long to take positive action against her,' she complained, 'I am hardly the person to tell you whether or not you are now reacting correctly. The gods know, I have suffered as much at her hands as you.'

'Well there's a statement in need of further clarification,' Nero remarked bitterly, 'what injustices has she dealt you in the past few months?'

Poppaea rounded on him in indignation. 'I gave up my husband for you! But have you even considered divorcing Octavia? No! And I shall tell you why - because you live in such fear of Agrippina. She has done me only one injustice - kept you from me.'

'This is the first I have heard of marriage; and you are quick to rush in to new vows, when the last are still warm on your lips.'

'I consider it fortunate to have met you, not unfortunate that it was ill timed. And I make no secret of the fact that I like the security of marriage. What argument do you have in protection of your own marriage?'

'I have none. It is no marriage at all.'

'Then for how long must I remain your mistress?' she demanded bitterly. 'How can Octavia be deserving of the title empress? Which of us is at your constant side? Which of us guides you through the decisions of the day and soothes you through each night? Is it that you are afraid to divorce a woman you barely recognise if, by chance, you pass her in the corridors of the Palace? Do you wish to protect the feelings of a virtual stranger at the expense of my own?'

'Of course not; you know that I would do anything you ask of me.'

'Why, then, these postponements of our marriage? I suppose my looks and victorious ancestors are not good enough. No! I think that you are afraid that, if we married, I might tell you frankly how the senate is downtrodden and the public enraged by your mother's arrogance and greed. If Agrippina can only tolerate daughters-in-law who hate her son, let me be Otho's wife again! I will go anywhere in the world where I only need hear of the emperor's humiliations rather than see them - and see you in danger, like myself!'

It had been too long a day for Nero to now retaliate. Instead he held her close and soothed her as best he could. He thought, as always, of Otho, but there were no regrets. With Poppaea at his side, as empress, how much would he regret the loss of his mother? Agrippina's repeated threats and violent behaviour never ceased to terrify him. He shivered involuntarily at the thought of her touch.

Despite the presence of Poppaea in his arms, his thoughts strayed to Acte. She, too, had urged him to rid himself of his mother, without thought of her own advancement. But Acte feared for his safety; just as strongly as Poppaea feared for her status. He thought once more of his mother's unwelcome touch.

'She is as good as dead,' he told Poppaea regretfully.

Anicetus took his plans to Burrus, when once they were formulated. In the full knowledge that Agrippina had been regularly taking ante-dotes to known poisons, he was aware that it was imperative that no suspicion be aroused. Since her most recent banishment from the Palace, the Augusta had lived in constant expectation of death. Precautions had also been taken at the Palace, where those same ante-dotes were taken by Nero, Halotus and his cupbearer Pythagoras.

Burrus read through the detailed proposal and studied the accompanying plans.

'Flawless,' he conceded, 'and yet she may still be too suspicious to accept the invitation. What then?'

'She'll accept. A supposed reconciliation with Nero will be far too tempting an opportunity; and the delights of Bauli are not readily given up. She is only human, Commander.'

Burrus grunted. 'In that, I have my doubts! But there is enough to perhaps trick her. Bauli, however, is out of the question.'

'But it can't be! The whole plot revolves around it! The anchorage it hosts, the delights it offers. Why is it to stand dormant this year, of all years?'

'Because it belongs to Marcus Otho. His family have always played host to the imperial family at each Festival of Minerva. But Otho is not one for tradition. Or for our present emperor.'

'Then you must convince him otherwise, Commander! I have heard the rumours too, you know. But I have more sense than to believe them! If Nero and Otho truly had fallen out with one another, Otho would not now be in the comfortable post of Governor of Lusitania! He would be battling the wild dogs in the arena!'

'The Governorship is Nero's equivalent of wild dogs, Anicetus. I could, perhaps, beg use of the mansion from Otho. But I cannot promise you that I can get Nero to make use of it.'

'I need use of the harbour there, Burrus. It is as simple as that.'

'I'll do my best.'

MARCH A.D. 59

The invitation was delivered by one of the emperor's slaves. It would have been more proper to have sent a freedman, but Nero never had been one for making such distinctions. Agrippina accepted the note from her own maid and read through its contents with a certain amount of distrust.

'He has invited me to Baiae, to celebrate the Festival of Minerva with him,' she told her companion, reading through the note once more with sharp assessment. 'I do believe that I am winning him back once more.'

Gallus, lying beside her on the couch, cast his eye over the note.

'Beware of a trick,' he warned, 'do they not plot against you at the Palace?'

'This is no trick,' Agrippina assured him, without concern, 'a mother knows her own son. Nero is weak and immature; he needs me. I knew with time this note would come.' Her fingers curled tightly round the note and she held it close, as though drawing in the prey itself. She remained wrapped in her own thoughts for a moment, then casually tossed the note to the ground and slid down beside Gallus once more.

'Of course, this means a change of plan,' she mused, apparently indifferent to the caresses Gallus now bestowed upon her. She played with a lock of his hair, winding it round her finger, then unwinding it, as her mind ran through the possibilities. 'We need no longer find a replacement for emperor; instead we must replace his advisors - I was mistaken in giving positions of power to Seneca and Burrus. I expected them to return the favour whenever called upon to do so, but their loyalties lay firmly with Nero and they have fought me ever since his accession. They are behind the attempts on my life. Burrus even had a strong enough case against me to see me condemned, when I planned to depose Nero in favour of Plautus. He divulged the entire plot, but I had only to weep at Nero's feet to secure forgiveness. The boy is no better than a sad puppy; no matter how I tease or hurt him, he remains forever loyal. He is of greater use to me left alive. It's Burrus and Seneca who need to be eliminated.'

Gallus half sat up, resting on one elbow and studying his mistress intently. 'Can you be certain of that? The emperor is no longer a boy. And even if you can regain your former influence, what use is he as your puppet? I hear that Burrus has only to present him with a death warrant to be signed and he is reduced to tears! If your puppet cannot even condemn a murderer to death, of what service will he be to you?'

'Burrus does not know him as his mother does. There is evil bred into him, one must only find a method of extracting it. Nero will be eager enough to spill innocent blood in order to preserve his own, of that you have my guarantee.'

She summoned her secretary and penned an immediate reply.

Nero habitually attended the Festival of Minerva, which ran from the nineteenth to the twenty-third of March, each year at Baiae. When friends and acquaintances questioned his wisdom at inviting his mother to attend, he announced simply that,

'Parents' tempers must be borne, one must humour their feelings.'

But there was still considerable surprise at his choice of guest of honour.

Nero met Agrippina at the shore as she arrived by sea from Antium. He welcomed her with outstretched hands and warm embraces. Gone was the wariness of the past few weeks, when he had met her only with an armed guard in attendance, afraid to be left alone in her company. As they embraced on the shore, one of the imperial naval captains staged what appeared to be an accidental collision with her galley, destroying it totally.

Agrippina considered the incident with suspicion, ever mindful of threats. Gallus had warned her of a possible plot and she wondered now if she would have been wise to believe him. But knowing that she would be safe at least in Nero's own company, she travelled with him to Bauli, the mansion at the bay between Cape Misenum and Baiae, and walked with him down to the shore to view the ships at anchor there.

Alongside the warships on which she was accustomed to travelling was one especially luxurious ship, anchored slightly away from the rest.

'Do you approve of my latest acquisition?' Nero enquired, his eyes sparkling.

'You can expect to travel in style and comfort from now on, certainly,' Agrippina agreed, 'if, indeed, it is intended for your own use. But no doubt you mean it as a gift for some writer or artist who has won your admiration.'

'How astute of you, Mother! It is indeed intended as a gift. But for someone who has earned far more admiration than a mere artist. The ship is intended as a compliment to you, as only an emperor's mother can be complimented. It will transport you to the feast at Baiae in the luxury that you alone deserve. I hope that it will heal all breaches between us.'

'And I thought that I could no longer be surprised by your absurd generosity!' Agrippina regarded the ship thoughtfully. 'A pity to waste its maiden voyage on a short trip to Baiae, we must save that honour for a more worthy occasion. You will not be offended if I choose instead to travel with you by sedan chair? We have not spoken intimately for so long now, there is a deal to catch up on.'

Nero, too, had been gazing out upon the ship with mixed feelings. It had been designed by Anicetus not for its obvious luxury, but for its hidden menaces. Rather than being disconcerted by his mother's reluctance to travel on the fateful ship, Nero accepted her request with genuine pleasure.

They travelled by chair to Baiae, Nero's animated conversation so full of genuine affection that Agrippina began to trust to her original instincts. Once seated alongside him at the feast in the position of honour, all her fears were allayed. They picked at the hors d'oeuvres of succulent dormice sprinkled with honey and poppy seeds, and peahen eggs encased in rich pastry, and Nero spoke to his mother intimately, telling her in private whispers of his love for Acte and Poppaea and of his grief at the rift between himself and Otho. She patted his arm reassuringly and, far from shrinking from her touch, Nero welcomed her caresses, revelling in the motherly love for the first - and last - time.

Glass goblets of mead were replaced with vintage wine as the first of the two main courses was brought in. The emperor and his guests could choose between plump fowls, richly decorated hares, sows' udders, lobsters and a variety of fish. As the guests tucked in to these delights, a false panel in the ceiling revolved to reveal an intricate panel of fretwork in ivory. A shower of sweetly-scented petals cascaded down from the pattern of holes, as well as tiny gifts of perfume for each of the ladies present. The second of the main courses consisted of an immense wild boar, roasted to a crisp golden brown. The carver slit open the stomach and the guests cried out in surprised delight as a dove, released by the carver, appeared to fly out.

Nero kept the festivities going for as long as possible, enjoying the company of his mother. But as the night wore on he could delay her departure no longer and walked with her down to the quay. He had been particularly boyish and clingy throughout the evening and Agrippina saw no reason for alarm in his over-attentiveness now. This time she accepted the offer of the new ship, to take her back to Antium, and paused to share an emotional farewell with her son. He embraced her tightly, laying his head on her breast and kissing her repeatedly, reluctant to let her go. Accompanied by Gallus and her maid, Acerronia, Agrippina boarded the ship and waved a fond farewell to her son. He wept as he waved back, knowing that he was looking upon her for the final time.

Agrippina was lying on her bunk, with Acerronia at her feet, when the deck above collapsed onto her. Gallus, watching the stars from the bow, was killed instantly, but the raised sides of the bunk saved Agrippina and her maid from serious injury, though Agrippina's shoulder was badly hurt.

General chaos ensued. The oarsmen threw their combined weight to one side in order to assist the capsizing of the ship. The bunk and its captives were immediately submerged in the moonlit water. In panic, Acerronia freed herself from the wreckage and began to splash wildly in the water, screaming,

'Help me! I am Agrippina, the emperor's mother!'

Agrippina, following in her wake, trod water quietly in the shadows, observing the reaction of the oarsmen as they immediately dashed the unfortunate maid to death with oars and any wreckage that came to hand. Suspecting nothing less, Agrippina sensibly remained silent and swam unobtrusively towards a group of fishing boats anchored only a short distance away.

It had been almost twenty years since Caligula had banished her from Rome, but suddenly it seemed like only yesterday that she had been forced to earn a living diving for pearls, until Claudius had recalled her from exile. The experience had stood her in good stead for this evening's stage-managed 'accident'. How fortunate, she reflected, that she had kept her lowly career from her son, who was clearly unaware that there was no stronger swimmer in Rome than his esteemed mother.

Reaching the boats, she was helped aboard by eager fishermen, who had witnessed the disaster and recognised the illustrious survivor. They took her swiftly to the shore, where already a large group of people had assembled, their torches lighting the beach. At the sight of her they began to cheer and rejoice at the safe arrival of the Augusta.

News of her rescue was quick to reach Bauli. Nero fell to his knees at the household shrine and wept for this sudden redemption. Burrus, however, was far too alarmed to pander to his emperor's sensibility.

'Get up, Nero,' he demanded roughly, pulling him to his feet, 'we must work quickly to salvage what we can from this disaster.'

'But she is saved, Burrus! We never should have done this thing, and now we have been given a reprieve, a second chance to begin again.'

'And a second, and a second. How many more second chances can there be, Nero? She must know that the wreck was no accident. Her only salvation now lies in our deaths. She will bring troops against us before tomorrow is out - all of Rome will know of your treachery!'

'It was never my treachery!' Nero sobbed, panic-stricken, 'I prayed for her safe deliverance, even as I let her board that ship. The gods have granted me this.'

'The gods have no hand in this! She must be dead before dawn, or we shall all perish!'

Anicetus burst in, not knowing if the news he brought had yet reached Burrus; but it was immediately apparent to him that it had.

'We could yet be saved,' he informed the commander, 'for I passed the Augusta's freedman, Agerinus, outside, awaiting an audience with the emperor. Epaphroditus is delaying him, until we have considered an action.'

'Grant him the audience,' Burrus told him, 'and we'll consider our options when once we have heard him. I want Seneca here first; have him summoned.'

'How can you discuss this so calmly?!' Nero protested. 'We have plotted a murder! Please, let it be a lesson to us that we have failed.'

'And so it will be, Nero!' Burrus snapped, 'one that we will learn in chains, as we are dragged to the Tiber. When once murder is planned, it must be seen through to the end. Accept her death, Nero.'

Seneca joined them and Agerinus was shown in, under escort.

'I have been sent by my mistress to report of her safety under the divine intervention of the gods,' he told Nero. 'She wanted you to hear as quickly as possible that she had been spared death, before news of the unfortunate accident broke your heart. She says that the ship struck a fishing boat and capsized, and she was flung into the water. The oarsmen did their best to assist her, but she was beyond their reach and feared that she would never again see you, my Lord. Then she was pulled to safety by the crew of another boat. Her first thoughts, my Lord, were of you and I was immediately dispatched with her news.'

He bowed respectfully, hoping that he had been as convincing as Agrippina had insisted. As he did so, his knife slipped from his belt and clattered harmlessly on the marble floor.

The Guards immediately seized Agerinus, and Burrus snatched up the knife.

'What was the true purpose of your visit?' Seneca demanded, seizing the opportunity the moment it was presented.

'To deliver my mistress' message,' Agerinus insisted fearfully.

'And that requires a dagger?!'

'A knife, to open seals and despatches.'

'And to assassinate emperors!' Seneca permitted him no further defence. 'Burrus, have this man held and send your Guards to arrest the Augusta. It is clear that she sent this messenger to murder our emperor.'

Agerinus fought his captors in sheer terror.

'Be still,' Burrus advised him quietly, 'you are no more than a tool and will walk free if you act sensibly and hold your tongue.'

He turned to Anicetus. 'Take my best men and arrest the Augusta. You know what to do if she attempts to resist.'

Anicetus smiled and nodded.

Agrippina sat in her bedchamber, a maid arranging her hair as a distraction to the events of the night. She could not know whether to expect the successful return of Agerinus, or the invasion of the Guards; but knew that it would be one or the other.

She sat up stiffly at the sound of the people outside and gestured to the maid to stop. They listened to the murmur of voices throughout the house, raised in anger and protest, some cries of panic. The maid backed away from her mistress fearfully.

'Soldiers!'

'Indeed. But let them be met with dignity, girl. Come, attend to my hair as you were.'

Within minutes, the door was forced open and Anicetus and the Guards entered.

'What is the meaning of this?' Agrippina demanded.

'You are under arrest for the attempted murder of the emperor,' Anicetus informed her coldly.

She laughed at him. 'Arrest me, then. I shall be happy to stand trial.'

He signalled to the Guards, who at once drew sword. Then he simply nodded.

The maid screamed as her mistress was stabbed again and again. Agrippina made no sound, but drew back her robe and clutched at her stomach.

'Stab me here,' she whispered weakly, 'from whence he came.'

And she said no more.

Chapter Thirty-Five

It was Seneca who broke the news to Nero.

'It's all over,' he told him gently, 'the Augusta resisted arrest and then stabbed herself, to spare you the shame and humiliation of her trial. In the end, Nero, she thought of you.'

Nero was predictably grief-stricken and insisted on rushing straight to her side. Neither Seneca nor Burrus could dissuade him.

Agrippina had been laid out on a dining couch, a clean mantle in place and fresh linen replacing her blood-soaked clothes. Nero fell to the floor beside her and held her hand, speaking to her soothingly as though she were merely in a fever and would even yet recover.

Then the grief became too much to bear and he pulled at her lifeless limbs, trying to wrap them around him, trying to embrace her. He stroked the cold skin of her arms and repeated feverishly how smooth and flawless her skin was, how beautiful she had once been, how cruel and undeserved was her death. The night passed as he sat on the floor, her arm pressed to his face.

Eventually Ecloge and Alexandria were summoned, and together they managed to ease him away from the body. He was insensible with grief and they had no difficulty in coaxing him away to an awaiting coach to transport him back to Bauli.

Burrus arranged a simple cremation as soon as the emperor was safely away, during which one of Agrippina's more devoted slaves stabbed himself. The commander was glad to leave the house and push aside the unpleasant memories of what he had witnessed.

'How is he?' he asked of Seneca, flopping wearily onto a couch in the main room.

'Ecloge says he is insensible with grief, far worse than she has ever seen him. Apparently he has curled himself into a ball on the bed and will neither speak nor move. He won't eat or drink, it is as though he is oblivious to their very presence.'

'I feel like doing the same,' Burrus said, 'it has been too long a night. Let us snatch a few hours while we can. Nero is in capable hands.'

'The doctors Andromachus have been sent for,' Seneca told him.

'Then he will be in even better hands when they arrive. Depriving ourselves of what little sleep is now left to us will not help him, Seneca. Do as you wish, but I am retiring. Good morning to you, my friend.'

Seneca watched him depart, but was too disturbed by the rush of events to consider sleep himself. Before long the sun had risen and the first of what proved to be a steady succession of visitors arrived at the mansion, to seek audience with Nero.

'The emperor is indisposed,' he told them all simply, and Epaphroditus took down their names and messages.

'So far I have one message and about a hundred names to go with it,' the secretary complained, as the morning wore on. 'Congratulations on your fortuitous escape.'

'Perhaps we should allow them in to see him,' Seneca suggested, 'it might bring him to his senses, hearing so much goodwill from so many people.'

'The nurses prescribe rest. Which is a rather effortless cure for a man comatosed in his bed!'

'They flutter about him as though he is still their babe in arms. We shall see what the doctors have to say on the matter.' He yawned and allowed his eyes to close. 'I think I shall take a short nap. You can deal with the well-wishers, but summon me as soon as the doctors arrive, won't you?'

In the event, only one doctor Andromachus arrived, the other being detained in Rome by Poppaea, whose son had contracted a mild fever. But Nero remained bereft of all senses and all Andromachus could recommend was his removal to his beloved Neapolis.

'The surroundings may relax him and bring him round - and the visitors must certainly be curtailed,' he advised. 'Allow his favourite musicians to entertain him; and his dogs to be with him.'

'They are still at the Palace!' Seneca complained, 'why ever did you not fetch them down yourself?'

'I left the moment I was summoned. It is hardly my place to gather up the imperial pets and allow them room in my carriage.'

'Well at least he will have Acte to nurse him,' Seneca said bitterly, annoyed at the lack of result from Andromachus.

The entire household was set into motion and the following day they had moved on to Neapolis. But the change of scene did little to alter Nero, who remained curled in his bed, refusing to acknowledge even the presence of Acte.

That night he was plagued by nightmares, tossing and turning feverishly and crying out in fear. Acte slept with him and did her best to soothe him, to no avail. At last, the unseen terror became too great and he awoke with a start, sitting upright and trying to catch his breath.

'It's alright, everything's alright,' Acte said gently, stroking back the hair from his face, 'it was just a dream.'

He turned to face her. 'It was so real, Acte. Ants, ants all over me, and fire, and Asturia...'

He began to tremble and she held him close.

'I... I don't remember you being here... I don't remember coming here...' He looked around the room, suddenly disorientated.

'You were ill, feverish,' Acte explained. 'Andromachus suggested a short rest, here in Neapolis.'

'Little Andromachus? It must surely be little Andromachus. Big Andromachus will barely excuse me for a day!'

Acte smiled. 'You're feeling much better now, anyway.'

'Could I have a drink, please? A little boiled water?'

'I have some ready for you.'

She poured him a glass and watched him sip at it.

'It was so horrible,' he said quietly. 'The Furies were chasing me with whips and burning torches. I was steering a ship, then someone tore the tiller from my hands. I couldn't see them. And Octavia was there, pulling me down into total darkness, and hordes of winged ants swarmed over me. And then we were in the Theatre of Pompey and the statues of the nations began to advance on me and hem me in, so that I couldn't escape; and Asturia, my favourite horse at the Palace, turned into an ape. Except that she kept the same head and whinnied, whinnied a tune. Then the doors of the mausoleum opened by themselves and a voice from inside called "Enter Nero".' He drank some more of the water. 'This wasn't just once, Acte. It was over and over again, the same dream, always the same.'

He put down the glass and sank back on the bed.

'I'm afraid to ever go to sleep again.'

'Sometimes dreams are like that,' Acte said soothingly, 'soon you will have forgotten it.'

'I hoped to wake up and find it was all a dream. But I know she's dead. I held her in my arms. I held her, but it wasn't her. Limp and lifeless and cold.'

'Try not to think about it, Nero. Let me get a book and read to you.'

'No, it's late, I ought to try to sleep once more.'

Acte smiled. 'Nero, you've slept for three days. Perhaps you'd prefer to get up.'

'Three days? I had no idea. But it is late, you must be tired yourself.'

'It hardly matters, Nero. We get so very few moments like this. Let me just sit here and read to you.'

'What am I to do, Acte? I murdered her. And the whole of Rome must know that.'

'She committed suicide, Nero. Some say that the accusations against her were false, others believe her guilty of attempting to kill you. But for whatever her reasons, Nero, she took her own life. You did not murder her. No one thinks that.'

'They know everything. They sing songs about Otho. They even believe I murdered Britannicus.'

'I've also heard it said that your mother had him poisoned. They know nothing of your private life. You are quite open about Poppaea and you can't hide Otho's appointment. But I have never heard a word whispered about Doryphorus or Poppaea's friends. Why should they know anything about your mother's death?'

Nero sighed. '*I* know. And I must carry that guilt forever.'

The following morning he resumed his duties and composed a letter with Seneca, to be sent to the senate. "I can hardly believe that I am safe from her now. Nor do I derive any pleasure from the fact," he wrote; otherwise leaving the composition to Seneca. They explained in detail the plot involving Agerinus and the Augusta's suicide at being exposed.

'It is only a white lie, Nero,' Seneca assured him, 'she plotted to kill you, but perhaps not at that particular time or with the help of Agerinus. But still, she plotted, nevertheless.'

'And the suicide?'

'Anicetus told us so. Do you doubt his word?'

'I heard Burrus give him the order.'

'I heard Burrus tell him to act if she tried to resist. And apparently she did. We were not there, Nero. We must trust to the judgement of our Guards - that is what they are paid for.'

'While I am addressing the senate, I have a few more points I wish to bring up,' Nero said.

'Perhaps we should wait a little,' Seneca suggested nervously.

'No, no, it's nothing shocking. I would just like to recall all the exiles she had banished, whether in my time or Claudius'. And I would like the ashes of Lollia Paulina brought home and a tomb erected for her. She was Caligula's wife and a member of our family. It is only just.'

'I can see no objections being raised on any of those counts, Nero.'

'Good. Good...' Nero seemed momentarily satisfied, then stared off at something only he could see, distracted once more by whatever haunted him.

He lingered in the cities of Campania, passing his days in the theatres of Neapolis and Pompeii, Baiae and Herculaneum; afraid to return to Rome. All around him were reminders of his crime, chalked onto walls and sung in the streets. In the market at Puteoli, as he walked in slave's garb with Acte, they passed one such joke painted across a disused shop front.

"Alcmaeon, Orestes and Nero are brothers,
Why? Because all of them murdered their mothers!"

'And no one is suggesting that I killed her?' Nero asked Acte ruefully. He looked at the graffiti regretfully and said,

'In reverence to thy age I dread to speak
What I well know must pierce thy heart with grief.
I am unholy in my mother's death,
But holy, as my father I avenged.'

Acte looked at him. 'I've heard that before, haven't I? What is it?'

He smiled. 'A passage from a play by Euripides - Orestes. Orestes himself spoke the lines. You see, his mother murdered his father and exiled him. She then sought to disgrace his sister, but Orestes put an end to her. She was as evil as any theatrical villain; but still it broke his heart to kill her. My mother poisoned Claudius.'

'I'm sorry, Nero. I had no idea. You never said.'

'No; I never said. Yet still it appears on walls in the provinces. I am unholy in my mother's death, but holy, as my father I avenged.'

SEPTEMBER A.D. 59

By the end of summer the commons had grown restless for the return of their emperor, though sheer terror kept him from them.

'You must return to Rome,' Seneca insisted, tired of the constant stream of excuses.

'I will be arrested the moment I set foot within the city!' Nero protested, convinced of the truth in his words.

'Utter nonsense, boy, and you know it!' Seneca scolded, 'Soldiers could have been sent for you at any time, do you think your very distance from Rome protects you? No, Nero, your very innocence protects you! You have done nothing for which you can be arrested and the very idea is pure fantasy! You would be nearer the truth if you admitted to yourself that you enjoy swanning around the provinces with Acte, attending one performance after another.'

'I have continued to work,' Nero protested, 'most of my ministers are here with me - Phaon and Epaphroditus plague me day and night. And much of my free time is spent in tuition with Terpnus and Paris. I think the occasional visit to the theatre is acceptable, don't you?'

'It is indeed acceptable,' Seneca conceded, 'but your continued absence from Rome is totally unacceptable and must end.'

'Look around you!' Nero demanded, pointing to the wall of the public baths, 'what does it say, there, right in front of us?'

'It informs us of the various sexual abilities of one Flavus and where he can be contacted,' Seneca said disdainfully, 'would you like me to note it down for you?'

Nero grew impatient. 'No; there, just above it! "Aeneas the Trojan hero carried off his aged father; His remote descendent Nero likewise carried off his mother: Heroes worthy of each other!" Tell me, Seneca, are my fears pure fantasy - or is my nightmare a portent?'

'It matters not to me, Nero. The decision has been made, without any assistance from poetry scrawled on public walls, and you will begin the journey to Rome tomorrow. And there is an end to the matter.'

Nero was far from happy, having long since convinced himself of his imminent arrest. Guilt had over-ridden his despair at Agrippina's death and the same terrifying nightmare had plagued him nightly. Though he pleaded desperately with Burrus and Seneca, he could not revoke their decision.

The journey back to Rome was both slow and swift. Nero noted each familiar landmark with dread, knowing that while it still signified the miles left to travel it only brought him ever closer to his fate. Acte remained with him and they were joined by Poppaea, but they could no more offer comfort than Seneca and Burrus.

It was only as they approached the city itself that Nero realised his mistake. Long before they reached the city walls they began to pass rows of people, dressed in holiday clothes, lining the way to welcome him. Within the city enormous crowds lined the streets to greet him and all along his route were tiers of seats, as though set out to celebrate a triumph. The senators wore their finest gala clothes and their wives and children lined up beside them.

Nero's relief knew no bounds. He cheered as heartily as those who had come to greet him, waving to them frenziedly and calling out to the many he recognised amid the throng. Gradually what had by now become a procession made its way to the Capitol, where Nero paid his vows.

'Your worst fears confirmed?' Acte joked quietly, as they left the shrine.

Nero smiled and hugged both his mistresses to his side.

'I deserve none of this.'

It took several days for the full strength of public feeling to sink in. And with it came the realisation of the invincible power of his position. He discussed it again and again with Acte, finally giving in to the arguments raised by Senecio so often in the past.

'He insisted that I would have absolute power, and I was equally insistent that I would be a slave,' he told Acte as he relived those arguments. 'I could enforce any rule I wished - providing it could first pass the senate. I could behave in any manner I liked - but if I offended the populace I would be overthrown. I could basically do as I wished, but if my morality slipped in any way then the Guards would assassinate me. In short, my power was worthless.

'But what Senecio knows better than I is the boundary of public acceptance. How far does my morality need to slip before I need watch for the Guards? I can sleep with my ministers and apparently commit incest with my own mother without upsetting their sensibilities. On paper I might offend my public, but in practise I can murder every member of the imperial family without giving rise to anything more serious than a sardonic poem. It is true that I remain a slave to the senate, but at what price? Outside of public office I can quite literally get away with murder! A fair wage for slavery, wouldn't you agree?'

Acte smiled. 'As always, you over react. You can't do anything by half measures, can you?!'

'I seem to have spent my whole life fighting against the restrictions imposed by my position. Only to find that there never were any restrictions!'

'You forget that you haven't actually committed any murders or incest,' Acte pointed out, 'you are the only one who believes you should be punished. So you're not actually getting away with anything. Don't think for a moment that you could really murder one of your family and escape the Guards.'

'And what of public opinion? What of rumours and jokes?'

'No more than that, Nero! They don't truly think you capable of murder. And the Guards saw for themselves the extent of your so-called incest. They were there at the death of your mother, not you. Never mind public opinion, Nero. The public knows nothing.'

Nero sighed. 'It still seems to me that I under-estimated the full extent of my authority. Whether I am free to kill at will is irrelevant, the freedom alone is all that I require. I no longer have my mother to fear. I can now begin to live, Acte. Anything I wish to do is there to be done.'

'It was always there, Nero.'

'And I was always too afraid, Acte.' He smiled; a youthful wicked grin betraying the tease. 'I intend to fulfil an old ambition,' he confided.

'You intend to push your luck for the sheer impudence of it!'

'Not at all; though that comes as an added bonus! No; I am going to drive in races, Acte. I am going to compete with my own four horse team.'

She shook her head. 'You'd best put your murder theory to the test first,' she advised, 'because it will take nothing less than murder to convince Burrus and Seneca!'

Nero intended to raise the issue immediately, but the following day was called away to the villa of his Aunt Domitia, who had been confined to bed throughout his absence and was now pronounced as dying.

'But what exactly is wrong with her?' he asked of her doctor as he waited to see her.

'It is no more than severe constipation, my Lord, but at her age there is nothing that can be done.'

'But that's ludicrous!' Nero protested. 'If that is the best you can do then you are dismissed.'

He summoned a runner and sent for one of his own doctors, with instructions to fetch a strong laxative. Then he entered the darkened sick room, without waiting for leave from the nurses.

'Ah, my little Lucius,' Domitia murmured fondly at first sight of him, 'they told me you would not come. Soon you will be all that is left of our family. When will Octavia bear you a son, my little one?'

'Son or daughter, it's all as one, Aunt,' he assured her, sitting on the edge of the bed, 'your blood will still flow through its veins and our memories will keep you alive. But there's no hurry for that yet, you will live long enough to see my children for yourself. What can I fetch you? Fruit? Wine?'

'It pains me so to eat, little Lucius. And they ply me constantly with vile concoctions. If nothing else passes my lips before I die, then I will at least die happy.'

'Let me ply you with one last mouthful, Aunt. My own doctor is on his way and he will soon have you sitting up and enjoying the best of meals once more.'

'Yet another vile concoction!'

'If I am all that remains of your family, then you are all I have left,' Nero reminded her. 'You will take whatever he prescribes, if only for my sake.'

He stayed with her until Andromachus arrived, and sat with her while the doctor gave her a laxative.

'It could well be too strong for her,' Andromachus warned him in private.

'Her own doctor was prepared simply to leave her to die,' Nero responded.

He remained with her until she drifted off to sleep, then returned to the Palace. But before he had retired to bed a messenger arrived to inform him of his aunt's death.

He sat up for the remainder of that night, his thoughts dwelling on Domitia and his much-missed Aunt Lepida. He remembered Domitia's final words and finally drifted into a fitful sleep; aware that he was the last of the Ahenobarbii. Once more the Furies hounded him. And a voice beckoned him from within the family mausoleum. This time, he was certain, it was Lepida.

Chapter Thirty-Six

SEPTEMBER A.D. 59

'Nero, there is a young Greek boy trying to gain audience with you.' Epaphroditus hesitated. 'I would have turned him away, but he is so very desperate to see you. And he bears an extraordinary resemblance to Poppaea. Uncanny, really.'

'Poppaea has a Greek brother, perhaps?!' Nero laughed. 'Has he been searched?'

'Thoroughly. The only harm it can do is to waste a few moments of your time. Shall I grant him an audience?'

'Of course grant him an audience!' Nero laughed, 'the intrigue is killing you and I have no wish to be your murderer!'

Epaphroditus grinned and went off to find the boy, returning a few moments later and introducing him as Sporus. The young boy, no more than thirteen or fourteen, certainly reflected the secretary's description of him, a fact accentuated - and deliberately, it seemed - by the arrangement of his hair, which was long and fair and set in the curls favoured by Poppaea. Though his features could not claim true family resemblance, there was enough about him to suggest an obvious likeness. Nero studied him carefully.

'You are not so naturally pale, are you, boy?' he enquired, reaching out a finger and gently brushing the boy's cheek.

He sat back in his couch and smiled, examining the residue on his finger.

'Is this now the fashion in Greece? It hardly surprises me, in a country where already the men where short floral tunics and rings on their fingers! I don't mock you, boy,' he added hastily, rising from the couch to better display his own Greek-style tunic, 'you can see that I take an interest in such things and try to keep up. But I have yet to hear of face powders!'

He sat back down.

'Now tell me, Sporus - why do you crave this audience?'

The boy glanced round nervously at Epaphroditus.

'I can't promise you privacy,' Nero assured him, 'for Epaphroditus notes everything. But I can assure you that he is trustworthy. Nothing you say or do here will go any further.'

'My Lord, I know not what to say to you. I can never remember a time when I have not longed to meet you. This is the moment I have lived for. And this alone.'

'I commend you on your eloquence. But I find it hard to imagine you have travelled so far merely to look at me!'

'My Lord, I have every coin of your reign here in my purse, which I keep with me at all times and would never dare spend. And I have a portrait of you on canvas by Famulus, kept rolled and here at my belt. I would travel anywhere to look upon you.'

Nero laughed. 'A painting by Famulus? And how did you come by that without spending your precious coins?'

'A worthy sacrifice and one quickly replaced. I keep only one of each coin, my Lord.'

Nero concealed his amusement. 'Forgive me, Sporus, I misunderstood.' He considered his guest for a moment. 'You clearly come from a good background, Sporus. Are you not missed at home?'

'I have not run away, my Lord. I told my father of my intentions and he told me that I could go, and you could take me if you so wished.'

Nero could not hide his smile. 'Did he indeed? I suspect that he meant that quite figuratively. Let the Furies take you, boy!'

'For you, my Lord, I would.'

This time it was Epaphroditus who could not contain his laughter. 'He's an earnest little fellow,' he laughed, 'what are we going to do with him? We must keep him.'

'Well, there is little point in sending him away to be bathed and dressed - whatever tailors and barbers he employs are far better than mine! Since he is not displeasing on the eye and craves only to sit in silence and look upon me, then that he may do! Sit down comfortably, Sporus, and tell me what else you require. Food or drink?'

Sporus sat down as he was asked, but refused any further offers.

'He is completely over-awed,' Epaphroditus whispered to Nero, 'but give him a day to recover and I fancy he will prove as much a pest as Crispinus. Will I send for his parents to collect him?'

'Look at him, Epaphroditus - I fancy his parents have already moved house!' He rose from the couch and took his secretary to one side. 'I wonder if he is familiar with Petronius' Satyricon? Does he not strike you as the perfect Giton - a freeborn boy of extraordinary beauty content to live off his lovers for no higher price than beauty alone? Is it as deliberately contrived as his hair and make-up, Epaphroditus?'

'A question you must put to him, Nero. But he is determined; enough to employ any trick necessary, I imagine.'

'Then at least Petronius can supply us with the answer to your question of what to do with him. He will be perfectly safe if I entrust him to the care of Doryphorus. And then Petronius' story-lines are free to develop as they will.'

Epaphroditus laughed. 'You think they might?'

'I certainly hope so, my friend! It is not often that such a gift is presented to me!'

'And you and Doryphorus will eventually end up trying to kill one another, while the boy deserts the pair of you for Vitellius!' predicted Epaphroditus, recalling the plot of the book which was currently so popular.

Nero laughed. 'Now that would be too uncanny. I might take a stronger belief in the gods were it to prove so!'

'Poor old Vitellius certainly would!'

OCTOBER A.D. 59

Nero was permitted to drive a chariot.

He had expected greater opposition from Seneca and Burrus and, in the aftermath of his aunt's death, had postponed his request until now. Burrus had been predictably horrified, but relented with little pressure.

The only condition set was that Nero was to limit his races to a private enclosure, built for him in the Vatican Valley by Burrus and Seneca. It was a condition Nero readily accepted, happy to limit his practise sessions to a private audience and convinced that he could race publicly when once he considered himself able.

However, the public soon learned that the emperor himself was racing within the enclosure and gathered in small groups outside. Nero was quick to allow them admission and took such pleasure in performing in front of a genuine race crowd that he was soon issuing invitations to circus regulars.

Neither Seneca nor Burrus could mask their strong disapproval and they were equally quick to reprimand him.

'This is deplorable behaviour!' Seneca told him in fury, 'You have taken advantage of our goodwill and shamed us in unbelievable fashion! Just as we had the enclosure erected, so we must now take responsibility.'

'You know full well why we had the enclosure built,' Burrus joined in, 'and the very least you could have done was to respect our wishes. This is probably the worst scandal to have hit the Imperial house and you have brought us down with you.'

'What scandal is there in driving a chariot?' Nero protested. 'There isn't a home in Rome that does not hang the portrait of a charioteer in pride of place. Every house has at least two or three portraits of racehorses - and probably the names of one or two of them inscribed at the family shrine. If you were on half the salary of our best charioteers you would consider it a windfall! Why this foolish snobbery? Let the lower classes have fame and fortune, but perish the thought that their skill should be elevated to a higher class! And what of gladiators, Burrus? Are they not as skilled as any of your men? Do they not command far higher salaries for their skills? And yet what would you say if your daughter fetched one home as a suitor? If either of you can explain this misplaced ranking, then I might step down from my chariot. Until that time, I am proud to drive with even the lowliest of charioteers and I defy you to stop me.'

'The senate is actually calling you depraved!' Seneca argued. 'Depraved. That's their very word.'

'Because I drive in private races?!'

'Because you are the emperor and you drive in races, yes!'

'And what if I turn actor, too? Would that make me even more depraved?'

Both Burrus and Seneca laughed nervously.

'So the senate labels me depraved,' Nero continued, 'is that supposed to frighten me into submission? The senate has detested me from the start and now I am past caring.'

'You should care,' Seneca warned.

'I care about you, so wash your hands of me. The last thing I want is to bring you both down with me. But I am going to continue driving in races - and I am going to act.'

'Oh, now come on, Nero!'

'I'm serious, Seneca. It's what I want to do.'

Once again neither Seneca nor Burrus could return with a convincing argument against his proposals.

'Let him take to the stage,' Seneca muttered to Burrus as they left the emperor's apartments, 'for he will find no one willing to join him on stage and there are precious few plays for the solitary actor.'

But Seneca had underestimated Nero.

There were more than enough noblemen willing to degrade themselves on a private stage at the Palace, in return for lavish gifts. Nero was left with no shortage of fellow actors - and, indeed, actresses - and the question of bribes and gifts was never raised beyond the walls of the senate. Those who shunned the iniquities of Nero's circle failed to appreciate the one element of more importance than rank and wealth - pure fun.

There was also a deep satisfaction of personal achievement in all those who joined with Nero in his beloved plays of Euripides. In the finest tradition of tragic drama, they accompanied themselves with lyres, though it was an instrument so much harder to master than the pipes, and the strings were made to resound like the human voice. The plays themselves were mainly lyrics, interspersed with only small lines of dialogue. Even so, it was only Nero himself who dared to take on such inappropriate female roles as Canace in Childbirth and Niobe Turned to Stone.

The dedication of the actors led to excessive rehearsals, and boredom for those not directly involved. Nero therefore set up brothels and taverns in the woods Augustus had planted around his naval lake and handed out large purses to his guests to spend freely when not required on stage. His theatre sessions became increasingly popular, until there reached a point when Nero felt secure enough to take to a public stage.

Though still fairly weak, his voice was a deep, if muffled, bass and the desperate and emotional role of Nauplius was considered an ideal debut for him by Paris and Terpnus. Seneca would have no part in such aberrations, but Burrus, only under much protest, agreed to be present in the audience. A battalion of Guards and its officers was also invited and the performance proved a resounding success. Nothing could now deter Nero from his chosen path, though Burrus and Seneca lectured at length and the senate threw up its hands in despair.

As his twenty-second birthday approached, they were saved from further ignominies by the intervention of state affairs. The first shadow of a beard had for long been threatening on Nero's boyish chin; now came the occasion of his first shave.

It was always a momentous occasion in any boy's life, but for the emperor the celebrations were even more lavish. Having shaved his chin for the first time, Nero placed the hair in a gold box studded with pearls and officially dedicated it to Capitoline Jupiter. He then invited the Vestal Virgins to watch the celebratory athletic competitions.

In addition to such traditional celebrations, he also instituted the Youth Games, a festival of drama that proved once and for all that public feeling was at odds with the sensibilities of the senate. There were no shortage of volunteers for the amateur plays and neither birth, age nor official status deterred people from acting in both Greek and Latin style. Eminent women, too, were happy to perform indecent parts, all accompanying their performances with gestures and songs. Though Nero had never thought beyond his own passion, he had successfully brought the theatre to the masses. But each step closer to the masses alienated him still further from his own class.

The period of Games over, Nero was called once more to official duties, allowing the Greek boy, Sporus, to sit in on all audiences.

'His presence is neither necessary nor beneficial,' Seneca complained, introducing a foreign delegation, 'and how exactly do I explain it?'

'He sits quietly with the dogs and interferes with no one,' Nero pointed out, 'I suggest you say nothing in explanation. They may draw their own conclusions - which I suspect will be that he is the slave employed to mind the beasts. Now allow Doryphorus to introduce my guests without further complaint.'

Nero's passion for the arguments of philosophers stood him in good stead for the ensuing audience. King Ptolemy, the last king of Cyrenaica, had recently died and had left his lands to Rome. Those who occupied the lands claimed title, but had been voted against by the adjudicator. They now brought their appeal before the emperor.

'What can I do but uphold the decision of my adjudicator?' Nero protested amid their own heated protestations, 'when he was doing no more than honour the final wishes of your late king?'

'It was never his wish!' scoffed one delegate, 'To give away his lands to a foreign power? No! He made his will purely to flatter you, as is expected of all dying noblemen!'

'But not all dying noblemen do so,' Nero argued, 'how am I to differentiate between flattery and a true desire? If it were truly so common an action I would not hesitate to rule in your favour. As it is, I hold Ptolemy in great respect and am indeed flattered to have been so honoured by him. The least I can do in return is to uphold the decision and see that his final bequeathment is gratefully accepted.'

'My Lord, we expected nothing less,' said a delegate bitterly.

'Then why bring this appeal before me? Because you expected a fair and just decision. And so I uphold the decision of my adjudicator, but I add just one proviso. Your occupation of those lands is hereby legalised. Yes, they were given to Rome. And in her gratitude she grants occupancy to those who claim title.

'Gentlemen, I understand your bitterness and so I say nothing against your outbursts. But please understand that I must always endeavour to please both parties.

It is not always possible and we must be grateful for the simplicity of this settlement. But in cases where there must be a loser, then they may take consolation in a just decision. Never, my friends, expect less from me.'

Patrobius, Minister of Leisure and therefore always under pressure, was next to burden Nero with problems.

'The city's doctors have been inundated with very seriously wounded townsfolk from Nuceria,' he reported. 'Wounded and mutilated men and women have been brought in to the capital, as Nuceria itself cannot cope with so many injured at once. A lady doctor there reports tending fifty people in a single day and some of her colleagues claim higher figures.'

'And how is this?' Nero asked, 'I have heard of no natural disaster?'

'It is only too natural,' Patrobius sighed. 'A gladiatorial display was staged in Pompeii and half of the audience came from Nuceria. There were the usual taunts; and then, apparently, stone-throwing. Then swords were drawn and chaos ensued. The Nucerians have come off by far the worst. It is an all too frequent occurrence in these country towns, but this is the most severe case yet reported.'

'And can our doctors cope?'

'It is under control at present, Nero. We have more than enough medical men and women within the city and they are simply tending whoever lands at their door. A more organised system could be implemented if the need arises, but I believe there are no more casualties to come.'

'Then it remains only to fix an official enquiry. Epaphroditus, would you go at once to the senate and have them investigate the incident? There is little point in waiting for memories to fog before looking in to such matters. At the very least, I expect to see the sponsor of the show and any fellow instigators exiled - and Pompeii must be forbidden to hold shows for a period of ten years.' He paused, considering. 'I was going to call for Phaon and see what funds could be made available for the injured. But it would seem that there are few innocent parties in this sorry affair and they may live with their own consequences.'

His eye fell on Sporus, who sat beside the two dogs and gazed at him just as adoringly.

'Come here, my little Sabina, and grant me a hug,' he requested, using Poppaea's family name which had already become his pet name for the boy. 'It would seem that whenever my faith in human nature wanes I have only to look upon your face to have that faith restored.'

He received his embrace, and bent to pet the two dogs, who longed to join in but were already too mature and portly to leap up in their former puppyish fashion. He allowed Sporus a gentle kiss as he straightened; the boy pressed so tightly against him that he could feel the physical effect the kiss had on him. He sighed.

'Already my arms are full. How can I embrace still more?'

He spoke softly, as though to himself, and Sporus could neither understand his words nor answer.

'Already I have Acte and Poppaea and Doryphorus,' he said now to the boy, 'and I must confess to more than a mere casual passion for Silia and Messalina. Do I have room in my heart for you as well, my little Sabina?'

Sporus said nothing, but clung to Nero still more tightly.

'It is your very good fortune that the great ladies I have mentioned are as fond of you as I,' Nero continued, 'for you would not otherwise be tolerated. And that, my Sabina, is something I could not bear.'

Chapter Thirty-Seven

MAY A.D. 60

'Tigellinus seeks an audience.'

Epaphroditus sat down beside Nero on the bed, watching him browse the documents left in by Phaon.

'Should you not be showing him in?' Nero enquired, without looking up.

'I knew you'd see him. I told him to wait a few moments and follow me in. He has come to discuss horses.'

'And so we shall both settle back and enjoy his company!' Nero pushed aside the documents and held out a hand in welcome to his guest.

'Tigellinus! A pleasure to see you again. The mare you fetched up from the South is the best in my stable and a personal favourite with Acte. Have you any others from the same family? I've two young boys who need decent animals of their own.'

Tigellinus sighed and sat down beside them.

'Nothing from that family. But it is my best racing strain that I have come here to lament. My foundation mare died and leaves only colts of her bloodline. The stud was barely profitable before her successes and I cannot afford another mare of her quality. And so I come here, my Lord, to seek employment - perhaps at the Circus, or in your own stables.'

'How much do you need?' Nero asked, 'You must not give up the stud for mere want of money.'

Tigellinus laughed. 'Mere want of money? Line up every broodmare in the Empire and set a price of one gold piece on each. I could spend the entire Treasury and still not buy the right mare! How can anyone predict what she will produce?' He shook his head. 'No; the stud is gone. Already sold.'

'But I need horses for Sporus and Crispinus.'

'I have my contacts still, that's no problem. How old is the youngest boy? I fetched up a quiet gelding for Vitellius, but it would suit an older child with some ability.'

'I need an older horse with no ability to suit my youngest child!' Nero laughed. 'The boy is reckless and no horse can stay quiet in his company! For him, a small pony - less far to fall!'

'And the other?'

'My young friend Sporus. Fifteen, at a guess, and not overly confident. Acte's mare suits him well, but I would prefer him to have one of his own.'

'I'll do my best, Nero. Now, what will you do for me?'

'What position would you like?'

'I lack the funds for a praetorship.'

Nero laughed. 'Funds I can give, but not office. And certainly not such an office!'

'Your horses must be particularly demanding that you didn't hear the trouble we had with praetors!' Epaphroditus joked. 'The senate somehow contrived to arrange fifteen candidates for the twelve praetorships! Nero had to step in to restore harmony.'

'Yes, that's a point,' Nero said, sidetracked, 'I appointed the three extra men to brigade commands. I have a watch command still available and it requires no particular skill or experience. Would you be interested, my friend?'

'Commander of the Watch,' Tigellinus said, sampling the title, 'yes, that would suit me well. Thank you, my Lord.'

'What did you do before horses?' Epaphroditus enquired.

Tigellinus smiled. 'You need ask? Then I am, indeed, old news.'

'If it was newsworthy then I would like to hear all!' the secretary begged.

'I cannot speak of the past, for fear of offending the emperor.'

'I know that you were exiled by Caligula - and I suspect the reason why,' Nero said, 'so you may continue without fear of embarrassment to me. I confess to being interested myself!'

'I was raised here in the Palace with your late mother and her sisters; who, shall we say, found me much to their liking. Caligula, of course, was never an advocate of sharing and so I took up a very prosperous career as a fisherman in Greece, which paid for the stud when once I could return from exile.'

'What a sordid little tale!' Nero laughed, 'And all the more interesting for it! Do you think I inherit a certain insatiability from the Augusta, I wonder?!'

'From her and her sisters and brother combined!' Epaphroditus laughed. 'Tigellinus, never let our friend here call you sordid. The effeminate young rider for whom he seeks a horse is yet another addition to his bed!'

'So I have heard,' Tigellinus said, 'I trust my appointment comes without strings?!'

Nero laughed. 'From me you are safe, but there are some very demanding women in the vicinity of Augustus' Lake should the fancy take you!'

'We have already met!'

'Good! Then you shall fit in nicely, Tigellinus!' Nero rose from the bed. 'Let us take a look at this gelding you have for Vitellius. I think too well of him to deprive him of the beast - but then again he thinks too well of me to begrudge me!'

Later that day, Nero met with Patrobius and Phaon to finalise the details of the Neronia, a new five-yearly competition based on examples from Greece and celebrating the art forms of oratory, poetry and music, as well as horsemanship and gymnastics. Such had been the success of the Youth Games, held within Nero's own Gardens, that the emperor had seized upon the opportunity to capitalise on this new public passion.

'How far forward are we with the new baths and gymnasium?' he asked of Patrobius.

'Complete, Nero, barring the few interior decoration details still in progress. They should take no more than a few weeks.'

'Well then I may put back the opening to coincide with the Neronia,' Nero decided, 'it can be a simultaneous affair - the one opening in celebration of the other.'

'And judges for the competitions, Nero? Have you come to any decision?' Patrobius asked.

'Our ex-consuls; a worthy honour, don't you think? They may draw lots for each contest, which will also solve the matter of too few prizes and too many ex-consuls!'

Patrobius and Phaon exchanged glances, which did not go unnoticed by Nero.

'You believe they will feel obliged to award every prize to their emperor?' He shook his head, smiling ruefully. 'I won't even be allowed to enter. My only appearance on a 'public' stage to date was still a fairly private affair, after all. The entire audience was invited.'

'As a matter of fact,' Phaon admitted, 'Seneca has already called a number of meetings to discuss the prevention of your entry into any of the competitions.'

'If he had spoken with me first I could have spared him the effort.'

'If it is any consolation to you at all, Nero, he no longer believes he can talk to you; talk you out of things, that is. Or into them, for that matter.'

Nero smiled. 'He knows me too well. But, perhaps, one day I may surprise him.'

When Nero fell ill, later that month, he and his staff retired to his mansion at Sublaqueum, just to the east of the city near the Simbruine Lakes. The fever was mild and soon passed, but was notable simply because Nero so rarely suffered illness, seeming to be immune to the common coughs and sneezes which so frequently swept through the city.

'It comes of bathing in the source of the Marcian Aqueduct,' Poppaea told him crossly as she tended him, 'those waters are holy and you had no right to desecrate them in such manner.'

'Well I can see precious little evidence of their healing properties,' Nero teased.

'Holy, not healing. And you have received your just punishment.'

'I caught a chill,' Nero scoffed, 'and will simply be more careful next time.'

'There will be no next time,' Poppaea warned, 'not even the Emperor of Rome is allowed a second opportunity to mock God.'

'It is utter nonsense, Poppaea! Why do you delight in vexing me so? You are never more happy than when driving me to argument, even as you nurse me on my sick bed. Am I to have no respite from your malice?'

'And so now it is I the instigator of all our fights!' Poppaea rounded on him indignantly. 'I ask that you respect the beliefs of your people, but in place of simple acquiescence you must abuse me with a string of arguments in your favour! I ask that you marry me, and again I become the scold, while listening to your torrent of excuses!'

'And so it comes back to that! I am already married, Poppaea.'

'The Augusta is gone; who is there to prevent your divorce but yourself?'

'I made my vows once and they proved a costly mistake. I need not make them again. We are happy, Poppaea, and need no ceremony to make it so.'

'And when I give birth to your son, will you be content to see him without title, at the mercy of those with the legitimate blood of Caesar in their veins?'

'When you fall pregnant then of course we shall marry at once.'

'Then why not now, Nero? How many years has it been with Octavia? Who would not now agree that the woman is barren? You have every right to divorce her on such grounds and no one would deny you.'

'It is a matter of public opinion,' Nero explained wearily, 'how many times must I go through this? She is worshipped by the people. Their cheers are as great for her as they are for me. You may trade in husbands with whatever frequency you see fit, for it is your life alone. But I have an image to maintain, an example to set. My public wife was chosen for me and I must keep her. But love is my own choice and I need no ceremonial vows to prove my love for you.'

'And what if Acte falls pregnant before me? Am I then to remain forever your mistress, my children by you shunned from decent society?'

'Why do you torment me so?! I can never marry Acte, yet always you goad me with such impossible examples!'

Poppaea's frustration became unbearable. Tears of anger welled in her eyes as she advanced on him.

'Because it hurts you! Because it causes you pain! Pain that I feel, knowing that I cannot marry you!'

She lashed out at him in fury and he fought back just as violently, despite his weakness from fever. And, as always, the physical contact soon gave way to passion of a different nature.

Dinner that evening was a subdued affair, overshadowed by a violent thunderstorm that threatened menacingly overhead. It was a humid night and as yet no fall of rain, so dinner was served out in the courtyard, the storm rumbling above all conversation. Under the circumstances, talk soon fell to darker matters, of magic and mysterious forces of nature.

'I am sorry now that I ever took a dip in those waters!' Nero confessed, holding up his hands in defeat to his many accusers, 'And sorrier still that I relieved myself in them!' He laughed at the instant uproar his words caused. 'It's a joke, it's a joke!'

'Your disregard of serious portents is no joke,' Seneca rebuked him. 'While there are none of the signs that so accurately foretold your accession, there are omens to suggest that there may be a change of emperor this year.'

'Alas for your omens, I am recovered from my fever,' Nero chided.

'How then do you explain the comet?' Vitellius asked. 'Comets always denote a new emperor - the last one was seen shortly before the death of Claudius. You are living on borrowed time, my young friend!'

'There have been others since!' Nero laughed, 'You are all so easily taken in by tales surrounding nothing more mysterious than the weather!'

'Perhaps there *is* nothing more mysterious than the weather,' Seneca suggested; much to his emperor's amusement.

'They say Rubellius Plautus is the most likely candidate,' Vitellius continued, 'he had his supporters when Agrippina first put him forward a few years ago.'

'I've heard him favoured, too,' Poppaea agreed, 'most people would agree that he is bred for the role.'

'You should have dealt with him when you had the chance, five years ago,' Vitellius told Nero.

'Had he true designs on the throne he would have dealt with me over these past five years!' Nero laughed.

The laughter stopped abruptly and the ladies present screamed in terror. The two heavy dogs lumbered to their feet and ran yelping to the loggia, scattering the men and slaves who hurried to the aid of Nero. The table at which he dined lay broken in two, the blinding flash of lightning that had split it gone just as instantly as it had struck, leaving no more than a plume of smoke and a clinging smell of burning.

The incident took but a few seconds; the shock it caused a great deal longer to set in. The party followed the prudent example of the dogs and retired to Nero's chamber, making the most of the limited seating and talking furiously of the lightning strike. Then, gradually, conversation died away, as each in turn considered just how lucky to escape injury they had been.

'You know, Nero, the lightning cut through our conversation at a particular moment, would you not agree?' Seneca said seriously.

'My last words - which so nearly might have been, at that - are very much forgotten, Seneca. Do not ask me to continue whatever discourse in which we were involved at the time.'

'At the time we were discussing Plautus. Plautus lives but a few miles from this very spot. What do you think now of my omens, Nero?'

'No more than I thought of them previously! Now please, let me hear no more.'

By the following afternoon, Nero had heard nothing but. Already the talk in Rome was of the portent, the lightning having struck near what was now said to be the birthplace of Plautus' father. While Nero could not comprehend the willingness of so many seemingly reasonable people to believe so firmly in gods and omens, he could well understand the outcome of such views.

He sat quietly at his desk and wrote a letter to Plautus, requesting him in the interests of the city's peace to withdraw from malevolent gossip and to retire to his family estates in Asia.

The Neronia proved a resounding success. The many distinguished competitors, by unanimous vote, reserved the Wreath for Latin Oratory and Verse for Nero, in view of his absence from the competition, and he descended to the orchestra in order to collect so treasured an honour.

The judges also accorded him the Wreath for the Lyre Solo, but he knew well that it was no more than a sycophantic gesture. Nevertheless, he accepted it with good grace and bowed reverently to them.

'Pray lay it on the ground before Augustus' statue,' he requested, and returned to his seat to enjoy the remainder of the competitions.

Chapter Thirty-Eight

APRIL A.D. 61

The small Roman force allowed to remain in Britain, in honour of Claudius, had for many years been troubled by Queen Boadicea, but now at last came the news that she had finally met defeat at their hands and was dead. There were various celebrations throughout Rome, but none equalled the party thrown by City Prefect Lucius Secundus. It was to prove his last.

It was Epaphroditus who broke the news to Nero.

'Have you heard? Secundus has been murdered!'

'Secundus! Who by?'

'One of his slaves. It seems they agreed on a particular price, but when the slave came up with the money Secundus went back on his word and refused to grant him freedom. It's a scandalous affair, Nero. By law, every slave in the household must die with their guilty colleague - and Secundus has four hundred or more.'

'No, no, that cannot be,' Nero protested, 'the law exists because it is not possible for a slave to plot murder without another of his colleagues finding out. But in a household of that size less than a handful could have known his intention. There must be a way to avoid this.'

He set off immediately for the senate, which had already convened, but was as powerless to find a solution as the hundred or so members gathered with him.

'It's appalling,' remarked Julius Vestinus, beside him, 'the slave could have taken his complaint to officials. There was no need for such drastic action, knowing, as he did, that it would bring death to the entire household. Just what price was his freedom?'

'It was never a matter of freedom,' Vitellius interposed, 'we all know the sort of household Secundus kept. He and the slave were rivals for the affections of a certain senator who sits not a million miles from this row. The slave could not tolerate competition from his master and killed him. I could name names, if it came to it.'

'It makes a great deal more sense than a mere matter of money,' Nero agreed, 'but the outcome is no less sensational. What are we to do about the remainder of the slaves?'

'What is there to be done but condemn them?' Vitellius replied.

'We cannot condemn four hundred men and women for the crime of just one man.'

'A pity you are not once again consul this year, Nero. As it is, much depends on their decision and that of the senate - and very little depends on you.'

'I can veto their decision.'

'A majority vote in favour of one of our most long-standing laws? Would that be just?'

'Let us hope that it does not come to such,' Nero said.

'I know which way my vote will go,' Vitellius told him, 'and I would feel bitter indeed if you intervened against the majority - whether in my favour or against.'

'You possess a cruel streak, Spintria. I trust you are alone in that among the members.'

The debate proved a lengthy one. Cassius Longinus, the eminent lawyer and consul, pointed out that Roman society had a large submerged slave population held down by force, which would collapse altogether if such crimes were not ruthlessly punished.

'Nowadays our huge households are international,' he stated in his opening speech, 'They include every alien religion or none at all. The only way to keep this sum down is by intimidation. Innocent people will die, you say. Yes! And when in a defeated army every tenth man is flogged to death, the brave have to draw lots with the others. Exemplary punishment always contains an element of injustice. For individual wrongs are outweighed by the advantage of the community.'

Although there was strong feeling against such severity, the majority eventually voted against altering the existing law, which offered such obvious protection to all slave owners.

By this stage a large crowd had gathered outside, eager to save the lives of so many innocent people. The gathering soon turned to a riot at news of the verdict and the senate house was besieged.

'Listen to that!' Nero protested, 'That is your majority!'

'You can veto our ruling,' Vitellius warned, 'but if you side with the mob outside, then you have turned against us for the final time. Would you really see this law revoked, with so many slaves of your own - and so many enemies eager to influence them?' 'I trust my own household, as all slave owners should.'

'Nero, you know barely half your slaves. If you really felt this law should be changed then you would have done so. Your inaction says more than your words.'

On the day of the execution, great crowds with stones and torches prevented the order from being carried out. Nero was forced to issue an edict to rebuke the population, and lined troops along the entire route that the condemned were to be taken for execution.

To relieve his mind of such matters Nero threw himself increasingly into his music. He composed a vast number of songs that became popular with the commons and could be heard sung in every town throughout the empire. The Palace was filled ever more with musicians and poets and the breath-takingly beautiful male ballet dancers, of which Paris was considered the finest.

They danced and mimed in exquisite gold-embroidered tunics, purple cloaks, flowing silks and beautiful tight-lipped masks. For each successive role they changed both costume and mask, often during a single piece. Their total silence as they danced seemed to add to their mystique.

Huge orchestras and massed choirs were regularly gathered to accompany the dancers. Seneca's nephew, the noted poet Lucan, wrote fourteen librettos for these choirs.

As they sat one evening, lost as always in the story of the ballet, Nero leaned across to Seneca.

'I had an interesting letter today from a prince of Pontus in Asia Minor,' he whispered to Seneca, 'he asked me to present him with a dancer he had seen in Rome. He said the man's expressive gestures would enable interpreters to be dispensed with at the Pontic Court.'

'I do not doubt it, Nero. You will remember, perhaps, one of my earliest poems, that I once taught you at school?'

' "Their gestures flowed as fast as words".'

Seneca smiled. 'I had not expected you to remember individual lines.'

'I recite it to myself regularly; in my head, as I watch them dance.'

'Will you send the prince his dancer?'

'How could I not?'

When the entertainment finally drew to a close, Nero and his friends retired to his chamber to throw dice. It was a popular choice with all bar one; Sporus preferring to sit at Nero's feet as a mere spectator and rest his cheek against a knee, carelessly stroking his hand up and down the inside of Nero's thigh. In such occupation he was content; but the others, it seemed, were not.

'Come, Sporus! Take a turn with the dice,' Doryphorus insisted. 'You can't lull there all night like a hand-maiden!'

'Here; let us raise the stakes,' Nero suggested, handing out gold pieces to all, lest Sporus be embarrassed by his charity. 'We already have the advantage on you, Little Sabina, so you had better take part of my pile, too.'

'I am content simply to watch.'

'Nonsense!' Nero clapped him amiably across the shoulder and patted the couch beside him. 'Come; sit up beside me and test your skill while you have nothing to lose.'

Sporus pulled away from him in irritation. 'I have no interest in playing. I would prefer to retire to my own room.'

His statement met with desultory tuts.

'You are becoming a bore, Sporus!' Petronius complained. 'The only thing you show any enthusiasm for these days is sulking! Swoon at your lover's feet once more, if that is your wish, and we shall not press you again to join our fun.'

Sporus bristled with indignation, but said nothing; turning instead for the door and making a hasty retreat. Nero made as if to follow him, but Petronius put a cautionary hand on his leg.

'Leave him, Nero. He is at an awkward age; it will pass.'

'I will go to him,' Poppaea announced wearily, raising herself up from the bed, where she had been reading.

Nero smiled at her in gratitude; then continued his game.

In his room, Sporus sat, naked, at the foot of his bed, silently staring at the opposite wall. His eyelids flickered from time to time and the muscle in his jaw tensed and relaxed, tensed and relaxed, as though he were in the throws of a heated exchange somewhere deep within himself. His lips moved faintly; but his eyes continued to stare blankly at the wall.

There was hatred in them. A violent, undisguised loathing that seethed from within. Poppaea, he knew, saw it as jealousy towards herself. Nero took it simply to be jealousy towards all his other bedfellows. But none of them knew. Not one of them understood. None of them understood that which he was only just coming to realise himself.

He hated Nero's comradely embraces. He hated the tousling of hair and friendly punches. The camaraderie and invitations to join in this rowdy exercise or that. He hated the crudeness of their sex together, of Nero's taste for variation depriving him of his passive role. He hated himself and his very existence.

He wept now, with the bitter loathing of it all. And he took up the dagger that had lain impassive in his lap, against such sensitive and vulnerable flesh. His unseeing eyes looked straight through the warm blade; seeing only its promised relief.

Without hesitation he sliced through his flesh.

Chapter Thirty-Nine

'My Lord! You must come immediately!'

A slave was calling urgently from some way off, his voice breathless and full of panic. Nero rose at once and ran out into the corridor to meet him.

'Quickly, my Lord! Sporus' room!'

'Andromachus! Get Andromachus!' Nero shouted to him, as he broke into a sprint.

'He has already been summoned.'

'Poppaea?'

'She is there, my Lord, and unharmed.'

They raced towards Sporus' private rooms, his cries clearly audible above the sounds of panic emanating from his bedchamber.

Poppaea was outside, visibly shaken by whatever calamity had befallen the young Greek boy, and accepting support from two distressed slaves.

'What's happened, what's wrong?' Nero asked quickly. Poppaea shook her head, too nauseous to speak.

'Nero! Get in here - fast!' called Andromachus, hearing his voice.

The emperor pushed his way through the bustle of slaves, who served as clerks to the doctor. Sporus lay writhing on the blood-soaked bed, the strip of leather clenched between his teeth barely inhibiting his screams. At the sight of Nero his arms flew out to cling to him; one hand bitten through almost to the bone in what could only have been a self-inflicted wound.

Nero embraced him protectively, reduced to tears by the boy's agony.

'What have you done, Sporus? What have you done to yourself?'

'Hold him well, Nero. I must cauterise the wound.'

'What wound? What has he done?' Nero pleaded with Andromachus desperately.

The indefinable aroma of red hot metal blending with charcoal filled the room, as the doctor pulled the glowing iron out of the fire and steadied himself for the application.

'He castrated himself,' Andromachus said; and applied the iron.

Nero felt the scream erupt from the depths of the body in his arms; but it died with Sporus' consciousness without ever reaching his lips. The arms, which only seconds ago had threatened to crush his ribcage, fell limply away from him; the indentations left between his shoulder blades suddenly burning all the hotter now that the desperate fingernails had been withdrawn.

Nero screamed for him, and collapsed onto his knees on the floor beside the bed. He vomited repeatedly until the sweat drenched his hair and his body trembled, every muscle rebelling against the strain.

Andromachus tended him perfunctorily and restored him to his position at the edge of the bed.

'You must hold on to him,' he advised the emperor, 'don't let him slip away. More than that, we cannot do.'

He began to usher out his clerks and clear the room.

'We will leave you alone now, Nero. Call me if he wakes.'

'Where will you be?' Nero demanded, his voice rising once more in panic.

Andromachus gently patted his shoulder. 'Only in the next room. Far enough not to hear your words; close enough to hear him wake. You must try to remain calm, Nero. The boy is quite clearly strong-minded, which is enough to pull him through. While you, my Lord...' Andromachus smiled ruefully. 'One patient will be enough for me this evening.'

Nero sat in the sudden silence and closed his eyes, desperate to quell the maelstrom of fear that still churned within, but the darkness brought only visions of blood. He gulped back the rising panic and reached for a cloth, dowsing it liberally with the pitcher and gently wiping Sporus' face. A determination to cleanse the boy swept through him, shutting out all else. With concentrated effort, he set about his task; wringing out the cloth without thought on the floor and drenching it again and again with the pitcher. Only when he had folded the silk mantle down to the boy's hips did he stop; brought back with a sudden jolt at the sight of the hollows which fell away from the stark hip bones and the longing to trace his fingers down those curves, as always.

His earlier fear receded.

He gently unfolded the mantle back up to Sporus' neck and smoothed it down around him, calmed by the boy's serenity. As he sat back against the wall, he saw Sporus' eyes flicker and open, wide with disorientation.

'Be calm, Sporus; you are safe. You are safe.'

'I'm bleeding!'

'No, you're not. Andromachus has dealt with it.'

'But I can feel it - I can feel the blood!'

'It isn't there, Sporus.' Nero grimaced wryly. 'Please!'

Sporus managed to raise a smile, though it quickly faded.

'A wonder you stayed with me,' he remarked weakly.

'What else would I do?'

Nero picked up the damp cloth and wiped away the sweat standing on the boy's brow, then dabbed at his neck and shoulders.

He stopped. 'Apart from all else, it brought back my visions of her.'

Sporus regarded him, uncomprehending.

'Pale slender arms - not yours at all. Nor hers. Just limp; lifeless. I sat there kissing them, though she was gone. And you, still alive before me, I could not touch.'

'I never meant to kill myself,' Sporus said, as though in apology. 'I didn't mean to cause all this. I just...' he hesitated.

Nero smiled in understanding. 'You just didn't want to throw dice.'

'I had a slave burn all my clothes.'

'Now that was a pity. There are many who could have benefited from such charity. Still; it is not a problem. Supposing we have Messalina take you in hand, when you are feeling much better, and clothe you from her own wardrobe?'

Sporus' eyes widened. 'You would allow that?'

'I am always willing to accept a new mistress into my bed! If only you had spoken up sooner, you would have saved me much suffering!'

'It is no joke, Nero. What will they say?'

'I am the emperor of Rome. They will not dare say a word against you. Nor will they wish to. I shall be the victim of their tongues, not you - and it bothers me not in the least.'

He took Sporus' hand and held it in both his own. The ensuing break in conversation gave Andromachus the opportunity he had been awaiting to enter the room.

'Ah! I see the patient is back with us. And how are you feeling, my boy? Sore, no doubt, sore; but it will pass. Not going to miss the little chaps now, are you?' He buzzed around Sporus, as though merely occupying himself. 'No sign of a fever. The only serious danger now, I would say, is to your tongue - unless our emperor retires for what is left of the evening and cares to allow it rest.'

Nero stood up and kissed Sporus gently on the forehead.

'Sleep well, my little one.'

Poppaea was sitting up in bed, waiting for him.

'How is he?'

'He will be fine. It seems he wished to be my mistress, not my boyfriend.'

'I could have told you that.'

'Then why didn't you?!'

'Your lovers are of no concern to me. And I certainly had no idea he would ever attempt anything so drastic.'

'You should still have said something.'

Poppaea glared at him. 'You should have seen it yourself. He is your lover, not mine. I am expected to turn a blind eye to your liaisons, not offer advice where it shouldn't even be needed. But then, I forget, Nero - we are here only for your benefit; you cannot be expected to spare a thought for our needs and desires.'

'You know that is not so!'

'How? Have you sent me an edict to that effect, which I have somehow overlooked?! Was an errant slave, perhaps, sent with the message?! How else, then, am I expected to know?!'

'The pleasure must be a shared one to be any pleasure at all!'

'So if I am not satisfied, neither are you?'

'I don't know how you have the audacity to argue otherwise!'

'Do you not? Tell me, Nero - for, unlike you, I find it hard to keep up - is Acte satisfied, alone tonight in Neapolis? And as you pander to the whims of Doryphorus - for I am sure they are not your own, my selfless one - is Sporus satisfied?'

'How can you throw this at me now?! Has there ever been a time when I've not been there for you? I would give them all up if you asked it, you know that.'

'Oh yes! How I know that! Am I never allowed forget it? Am I never to be forgiven for your sacrifices?'

'Don't bait me, Poppaea, for you use the wrong spur. Never have I blamed you; never have I laid regret at your door. I did what I thought best, don't flatter yourself otherwise. And now you challenge me to prove that I care more for you than for Sporus! I am permitted to roll on the floor in shallow pleasures, but I am not allowed to fret over them, when I should be thinking only of you! My entire private life is no more than a pandering to your own whims, Poppaea - and now you dare to throw that back in my face!'

'Do my whims include competing with an ever-growing list of mistresses?! You delude yourself in your selflessness! Acte has never been in my way; and Sporus and Doryphorus posed no threat. But then you take Messalina, who would look to my title if she were free! And now Sporus has set his sights and demands higher! And still you claim to be there for us - when you are not even here for me on race days! You do not even pretend to give me preference over the Circus!'

'I don't even know what we are fighting about!' Nero cried out in consternation. 'First you accuse me of using my lovers - then you accuse me of loving them too much! Which is it to be? And why now?'

'Because you are so *blind*!' Poppaea screamed in rage. 'Because this evening Sporus mutilated himself and you didn't see it coming! Because you can tell me when your favourite racemares are due in season, but didn't even notice that I have missed two of mine! Because I am with child, Nero - and you need me to tell you!'

Chapter Forty

MAY A.D. 62

Poppaea's pregnancy proved to be a false alarm. Nero wondered privately just how definite it had ever been, but had heavier concerns than Poppaea's attention seeking. Sporus was enjoying a remarkably speedy recovery, his doctors at Court in touch by letter with the noted Greek practitioner Thessalus. The boy was soon allowed out of bed and was permitted to dress from the wardrobe of former wives of emperors; the same wardrobe that had once been denied to Agrippina. To prevent any repetition of the problems that had led to his self-mutilation he was indulged in his every whim and Nero could not be separated from him. They were seen kissing amorously in the Street of the Sigillaria by every casual passer-by and Seneca was forced to intervene, in the face of public criticism.

'I must urge you to be more discreet,' he warned Nero, 'no one looks unkindly upon the poor boy, but it is unacceptable to display such affections in public. You are a married man, after all, and every man on the street is currently voicing an opinion on your outrageous and flagrant breach of convention.'

'Would it be acceptable to kiss my wife in public?' Nero enquired bitterly.

'If that you would! You would instantly heal every wound you had ever inflicted!'

'Then I shall, dear friend. Arrange for my divorce and I will marry one whom I love. We will kiss long and hard for our adoring public - and indulge them in any other display of affection they may demand. I am not shy, Seneca, and am ever willing to please.'

Seneca bristled with anger at such mockery. 'When will you ever learn obeyance?'

'When will you ever learn that I will not tolerate being told what to do? If you ask me to refrain from kissing Sporus quite so amorously in public then I might try. If you tell me I must cease then you will only goad me into more outrageous behaviour. I refuse to live my life in obeyance with rules and traditions with which I have never and will never agree.'

'You cannot seek divorce, Nero. I would gladly see you free of Octavia and I have never spoken against your private affairs. But I speak now to protect you. I speak for the commons, not as a friend. I speak for the senate and the troops and every decent man in Rome whom you seek to offend.'

'Every decent man in Rome? Every decent man who will pay five hundred denarii for a slave, but two thousand denarii for a pretty young boy or girl, whether that slave be to please himself or his wife? This decent society in which it is acceptable to sleep with whom we choose in the privacy of our own household, but makes it a capital offence to commit adultery? What standards are you endeavouring to set, Seneca?'

'They are not of my choosing, Nero. But it is your duty to comply by them.'

'They are not of my choosing, either! According to private behaviour, they are not of anyone's choosing! And you say it is my duty to comply?'

'Nero, please, be reasonable,' Seneca pleaded, 'a single unfortunate lapse caused a huge public outcry and I seek only to avoid a repetition.'

'A lapse? To betray myself as human is a lapse? Do they not yet realise that I am but one of them? For all my efforts to the contrary, do they still see me as some inhuman creature far above their feelings and common habits?'

'Nero! There is no talking to you!'

'No, Seneca, you have spoken, and I have heard. And I understand that this fight is not with you.'

He reached out a hand and drew Seneca to him, embracing him tightly in friendship. Yet Seneca suspected a deeper motive behind the act and left his company with a feeling of great unease.

'We are to have a wedding!' Nero declared cheerfully later that day.

'Oh? And who are the happy couple?' Doryphorus asked.

'I thought I might ask for the hand of Sporus,' Nero told him casually, 'since I would not then require a divorce.'

The group of friends at once burst into laughter.

'But you do not approve of marriage or its vows,' Poppaea reminded him wryly.

'No, and so I am happy to go through the ceremony as often as I wish, with whomsoever I choose. And when they realise that no further scandal can shame the imperial house, I might indeed be granted my divorce and can celebrate with a legal marriage to you, my love.'

'I am not so stupid as to believe you would go through such humiliation for me alone,' Poppaea assured him, 'and what makes you suppose that Sporus is foolish enough to be humiliated merely to outrage the senate?'

'It is not a question of outraging the senate,' Nero insisted earnestly, 'but a question of raising the public's awareness in matters of morality. I guarantee that we will suffer no humiliation, no condemnation - only goodwill and a shared sense of fun. And devilment, too, if you like. I admit to that - but see how many others will also do so. And then we shall find out the true outraged parties, the true so-called protectors of public morality. I believe I know Sporus well enough to be certain that he will join me in this... what will we call it, Little Sabina?'

'A statement!' Sporus suggested without hesitation.

'Yes, exactly.'

'So, when is your marriage to be?' Poppaea asked.

'As soon as I've had a dress made?' Sporus suggested hopefully.

'Why not,' Nero agreed. 'Perhaps we can ask Vitellius to give you away. He did the job fairly well on the last occasion and I can hardly hold him responsible for his unfortunate choice!'

'Silia and Messalina and I must be your bridesmaids,' Poppaea insisted.

Sporus consented happily.

'May I carry the hawthorn torch?' Doryphorus asked, much to the amusement of his companions.

'Why not?' consented Nero, 'Why worry that you are a might too old, when the bride herself is of the wrong sex!'

'I won't have Crispinus involved,' Poppaea interrupted more seriously.

'No, of course not, I would not have it myself,' Nero agreed, 'we will find Doryphorus two other companions, perhaps from the household. There are two fine boys in the stables whom I'm sure would be happy to oblige.'

'Let me find my own boys,' Sporus insisted, 'it is my wedding, after all. I am to be the Empress of Rome!'

'You only pave the way for me,' Poppaea reminded him curtly.

'Burrus is already ill,' Doryphorus pointed out, 'so if this has the desired effect and causes Seneca heart failure then you may be fortunate, Poppaea.'

She scowled at him icily.

The wedding took place just a few days later, Nero and his entourage arriving at the city mansion of Vitellius, where the formal ceremony was held in exact accordance with custom. Sporus wore a tunic of ivory silk, coupled with the traditional cloak of saffron and flaming orange veil. Nero also wore silk, in a hemmed tunic of bright Greek style, a pale orange complimenting the bridal gown.

The ceremony over, the wedding procession set off for the Palace, followed by an enormous crowd who cheered and clapped and fully entered into the spirit of the occasion.

'Did I not tell you so?' Nero called to Poppaea ahead of him, 'my detractors are not to be found here in the street.'

'You have drawn too great a crowd to turn them away from the nuptial bed,' Poppaea called back, 'will you give them the desired show and really draw out your detractors?'

'This is no mere pantomime,' Sporus reminded her.

'No? I think you may be mistaken, my little namesake.'

'This is a true wedding,' Nero insisted, 'and my guests will retreat respectfully at the appropriate moment, as at every wedding.'

But, when the time came, only a handful of the guests admitted to the Palace were turned away from the nuptials. The bridesmaids and torch bearer were allowed to remain and, indeed, participate; while various other members of the emperor's intimate circle stayed on as spectators, Tigellinus, Vitellius and Petronius among them.

The bizarre ceremony was repeated just a few days later, Nero keen to emphasise the mockery of it all. This time he left the Palace in the role of the bride, Doryphorus his chosen groom. An even larger procession accompanied them to the grounds of Tigellinus' villa, where the nuptials were conducted in the open and no one was turned away. The performance was straight from a stage and no one was left in any doubt as to the true statement made. Nero's public popularity soared, which was no more than he had expected, but members of the senate no longer hid behind the House as a collective and were open in their individual condemnation of their emperor.

In the light of these events, the praetor Antistius wrote a series of crude and satirical verses against him and read them aloud at a dinner party.
The senator Capito found them to be far more vile and distasteful than the events themselves and took his complaint to Nero, bringing charges against Antistius for treason.

'I am not happy at this renewal of the Treason Law,' Nero confessed to Vitellius as they discussed the matter before it came up before the senate. 'It is so open to abuse, as Tiberius and Caligula contemptuously proved. And yet I cannot merely laugh off so personal an attack. I admit to deliberately laying myself open to such criticism, but Antistius has grossly over-stepped the mark and must be severely punished. Nevertheless, I shall over-ride the senate's verdict and veto his execution, and see that he is comfortably banished instead.' He smiled regretfully. 'You know, Spintria, he has cut me to the quick with his words. They say that words alone cannot hurt a man, but I can hereby prove them wrong. I wish for all concerned that Capito had said nothing and this sordid case had never come to light.'

As expected, Antistius was found guilty, though the members seemed to take a cruel delight in the repetition of his verses. But before any sentence could be agreed, Thrasea took the stand and proposed leniency, suggesting that Antistius merely have his property confiscated and that he be banished to an island. This was readily agreed and the sentence duly passed.

Nero was furious. The hurt inflicted by Antistius' words was nothing in comparison to the senate's condonement.

'Thrasea, you say?' he verified, as Vitellius recounted events, 'His proposal has caused me more pain than any of Antistius' verses. How could such a sentence come to pass?'

'You wanted nothing more severe yourself!' Vitellius reminded him.

'Not from the senate! I wanted to know who spoke against me; identify my enemies and know how to overcome their opposition. I did not expect to see the whole House condone so personal an attack on their emperor! I am in their hands, Spintria. Have you any comprehension of how frightening that is?'

'I lived through the reigns of Tiberius, Caligula and Claudius,' Vitellius said in reply.

Nero looked at him. 'But they were your friends, Spintria. I have no such safeguard.'

Nero wasted no time in voicing his indignation, immediately writing a letter to the senate which, in the heat of the moment, perfectly conveyed his feelings.

"Antistius, unprovoked, has greatly abused the emperor. The senate was asked to punish him. It ought to have fixed a punishment fitting the enormity of the crime. But I will not amend your leniency. Indeed, I should not have allowed anything else. Decide as you please. You could have acquitted him if you wished."

The bitter petulance was hard to overlook and his displeasure plain. The issue here was no longer Antistius, but the enmity of the senate.

Nero's anxiety over the renewal of the Treason Law proved justified. A nobleman by the name of Veiento almost immediately fell to a similar charge as that of Antistius, namely the known inclusion in his will of numerous insults against senators and priests. It was the custom at Rome to read out the wills of newly deceased noblemen in the senate, ostensibly as a mark of respect though in reality it served only to satisfy curiosity, revealing as it did the extent of the dead man's estate and his various wishes.

He was also charged with accepting bribes in return for his supposed influence with Nero regarding official promotions. For this reason Nero dealt with the case himself and found Veiento guilty. Veiento was expelled from Italy and Nero ordered his writings to be burnt.

Throughout this trial Burrus had been absent, confined to bed with an ever-worsening throat infection. Nero went straight to him from court and sat by his bedside to recount the day's events.

'I suppose I should really have acquitted him!' Nero joked. 'And, you know, if it had only been a matter of his will, I believe I would have done.'

Burrus endeavoured to speak, but found it too great a strain.

'I think churlish is the word you are looking for,' Nero quipped, 'though why, I cannot imagine!' He poured the commander some water and watched with some distress as Burrus struggled to take the smallest sips.

'I would sing you my latest composition if I thought it would be appreciated,' Nero continued, setting the goblet down, 'but I know a poem by Petronius you might enjoy:

"There's some use in everything, sometime, somehow -
In trouble, what you've thrown away seems so useful now;
When the boat goes down and the strongroom bullion too,
It's the floating oars that save the drowning crew;
When the trumpet sounds, the sword's at the rich man's throat,
And the poor man stands there safe, in his ragged coat."

'I like that very much, don't you? Most people would not give a second thought to worthless items.' He smiled, pre-empting the commander's reply. 'Yes, I know, Petronius does not give any thought to them either!'

When Burrus began to doze, Nero left him to his slumber and went outside to consult the younger Andromachus.

'It's a tumour in his throat, I'm afraid,' the doctor told him, 'there is nothing that we can do for him.'

'Nothing? How long does he have?'

'A matter of weeks, no more. The tumour will gradually increase and eventually prevent him from breathing.' He shrugged helplessly.

'Does he know?'

'I think he must, Nero.'

AUGUST A.D. 62

In the end, Burrus' death came as a blessing to all concerned. Nero had already mourned his loss and wasted no time in appointing a successor.

'No one can replace Burrus,' he told Epaphroditus, 'which is why I am reverting to the appointment of two commanders. On a personal level, I need a particular replacement for Burrus. A friend, a protector and an advisor. I hope Tigellinus will fit that bill.

'But there is also an element of distrust. My mother opted for single command because she knew that it would be hard to control two commanders. And for that same reason I wish to revert to a joint command. All the time I have two commanders I am free from the perils of plots and corruption.

'Therefore I have selected Faenius Rufus to join Tigellinus. He is honest and sober, and popular with both guardsmen and civilians. I have here their letters of appointment. I would be grateful if you would see that they are delivered and arrange an early audience.'

'A pleasure, Nero. By the way, Poppaea asked to see you the moment you have a spare moment.'

'Why the urgency, Phaon? Did she say?'

'I have no idea, but clearly she cannot wait until your day's business is concluded.'

Nero sighed. 'I shall see her now.' He turned to Sporus. 'You wait here with the dogs; there is no point in us all incurring her wrath, though I can't for the life of me imagine how I've offended her.'

He found her in her own chamber, attended by Ecloge who was dismissed at once. Nero watched her leave, wondering.

'I am with child, Nero,' Poppaea said at once.

'Are you certain?'

'Of course I'm certain. That's why I have waited this long to tell you. It certainly wasn't in the vain hope that you might notice for yourself.'

'How would I notice? You look no different, not even fuller of figure. How long has it been?'

'The child is due in February. And as to how long it has been, I would have expected you to notice that it has been business as usual for three months now without the customary interruption.'

Nero grinned. 'Really? I hadn't noticed. And there'll be no interruption now for the next six months, either! This is marvellous news, my darling!'

Poppaea accepted his embrace. 'The fact that we are to have a baby is quite good news, too.'

He laughed and hugged her more tightly. 'That is the best news in the world. How long have I waited for this...'

'We must spend a few weeks at Neapolis,' Poppaea suggested, 'you'll be eager to see Acte and I may not be fit to travel for much more of the summer.'

'Oh, this is wonderful, Poppaea! Last time there was too much going on, it was just one more worry on top of many and over before I had even grasped it. But this time it's just perfect, and we have nothing to worry about, do we?'

'Well... Crispinus was not an easy child. And, as you say, the last was over before it had gone too far. We are not worry free, my love. But other women survive and I don't see why I shouldn't.'

'You must tell Andromachus. And Ecloge and Alexandria must attend you night and day. And no riding. No physical exertion at all.'

'Nero! You sound like a doctor! I am pregnant, not sick! And we have more important things to arrange than nurses and doctors. There must be a wedding - and this time it must entail a divorce.'

Doryphorus was horrified when Nero told him the news.

'It is just another of her tricks, Nero. She has waited barely a month before capitalising on Burrus' death. You know he would never have allowed you a divorce. And she knew it too. A little too well-timed, this child, wouldn't you say?'

'Don't speak rot, Doryphorus. You are jealous. You have always been jealous of her.'

'Jealousy doesn't enter into it. It took you years to escape your mother - and barely any time at all to find just as deadly a replacement! Poppaea has all the cunning of the Augusta - and if you ask me I believe that to be the only attraction.'

'You're a fool, Doryphorus, and you tread a dangerous path.'

'I'm a fool? She has played you for one since she banished Otho!'

'I refuse to listen to this! Get out of my sight!'

'Gladly! And don't think divorce will be easily won - I'll join Seneca to fight you in this. She will be the ruin of you, Nero.'

'She's already the ruin of you,' Nero said coldly. 'Take your things and get out.'

Chapter Forty-One

OCTOBER A.D. 62

Divorcing Octavia on the grounds that she was barren, Nero married Poppaea just twelve days later, despite the active opposition of Doryphorus. The people of Rome were outraged, just as Seneca had predicted.

'Your opposition to the wedding was conspicuous by its absence,' Tigellinus said accusingly, as he and Seneca met by the lake.

Seneca tried at first to ignore him.

'Were you enjoying the pleasure of the local ladies?' Tigellinus enquired.

'I am content with my own good wife. Unlike some.'

'But you would not dare preach so to Nero, old man,' the commander sneered. 'It seems to me that you hardly dare preach to him at all these days.'

'You may fancy you have some influence, Commander; but Nero will do as I bid.'

'Will he, indeed? That surprises me. You see, old man, you mock his voice training and openly abhor his acting. You do your utmost to prevent his racing; while I, on the other hand, publicly encourage him in all three. It seems to me that he is beginning to see you in no better light than the senate.'

'It seems to me, Commander, that you actively push him in such a direction. But you bargain without love.'

'Love! A driving passion, I agree. But not nearly as strong a force as fear.'

'You can't frighten me, Tigellinus.'

'No; but I frighten Nero so very easily! He has a tendency to kill, when backed up against a wall. Be sure not to cross him, old man.'

'Name me one who has been condemned!' Seneca retorted crossly, impatient with his companion's petty threats.

'I'll name you a hundred if you wish, by the end of my tenure! Shall we start with... say... Octavia! There, old man! You will not admit to fear, yet you spoke not a word to save her marriage. Perhaps you suspect that I have you marked first in my bloody reign! Or your precious Nero's, for, after all, I only carry out his instructions.'

'So that's the way it is to be, is it, Commander?'

Tigellinus smiled. 'I'm glad we understand one another. Continue to hold your tongue, allow the boy the freedom he needs, and you will live a long and peaceful life. I am a man of high ambition, Seneca, and I do not tolerate rivals.'

In Velitrae, at Acte's villa, Nero sat with Acte in the garden, while Poppaea took a nap. It was a rare opportunity to be alone and they made the most of it.

'You're not too disappointed about the baby, are you?' Nero asked gently.

'Disappointed? I'm delighted for you both!'

'But we've tried so hard for such a long time, Acte. Even if you don't feel it, I do.'

She squeezed his hand.

'It's for the best, Nero. Our child would always have to contend with your legitimate children. It's a dangerous world for them, Nero. You have only to look at your own family for evidence!'

'Poppaea would not allow me to adopt Crispinus, for the same reason. She said that rivalry for the empire had wiped out nearly every member of my house!'

'She's right, though, isn't she? I don't know too much about history, but I know there have been more adopted heirs than emperors!'

'Drusus, Nero, Gemelus - all were once assured of accession. Britannicus, too. Who knows? Gemelus may have succeeded Tiberius had Caligula not murdered them both.'

'Your grandfather would have been the greatest emperor of all, had Tiberius not poisoned him.'

'It was never proved, Acte. In fact, Mother always hinted that Tiberius was innocent in his death. She said Caligula would have killed him anyway! She said if he could not wait the precious few years Tiberius had left, then how could he have waited for the full length of his father's reign before succeeding him as emperor?!' He laughed. 'I hope that we are not all such bad stock. If I have a son I shall name him after my grandfather. Germanicus Caesar.'

'Oh, he would be worshipped then, Nero!'

'As I am, I believe. Were it not for my grandfather, I am convinced I would already have been deposed!' He smiled. 'I will never be the hero Germanicus was, nor remembered in my own right. But it would be nice to think that I might be remembered as the father of the great Germanicus Caesar, don't you think?'

'You will be remembered, Nero. You are already loved just as much as your grandfather ever was.'

'Not at the moment!' he reminded her, 'I am the loathsome scoundrel who cast the daughter of Claudius out into the street! And she a niece of Germanicus!'

'It will pass,' Acte assured him. 'No one likes to see a wife passed over for a mistress. It has nothing really to do with her ancestry. We hold similar councils of war every market day about this woman and that. It's just much more interesting when the victim happens to be an empress!'

'Epaphroditus tells me that it's quite serious in Rome.' He hesitated.

'Nero?'

He lowered his head. 'It isn't my wish. It was never my wish to hurt Octavia; and nor would I do anything to hurt Poppaea. But I didn't even want this wretched divorce.' He stood up, agitated. 'Public feeling is quite strong in Rome. Last night I could think of nothing else. I am seriously considering an immediate divorce and marrying Octavia once more. Allow things to be as they were. We were all happy then.'

'You've only been married a few weeks! And I hardly think Octavia would be any more happy than Poppaea at such a suggestion! At least now she is free to remarry and live her life.'

'Who is free to remarry?' Poppaea asked, joining them in time to catch the end of the discussion.

'That was a short rest,' Nero said, kissing her, 'don't do too much, will you?'

'Who were you talking about?'

'Octavia. I felt sorry for her, I suppose. The public sees it as an end to her life, but Acte is right; it's the beginning.'

Poppaea was dismissive. 'Who would have her? She's barren.'

'I don't suppose anyone truly believes that. And she is from the finest family in Rome.'

'Of course she's barren! Maybe you didn't put it to the test yourself, but where are all her little bastards from her handsome young slaves?'

Nero laughed. 'Not every woman possesses your appetite, Poppaea!'

'Every woman possesses it, but few care to admit it. Octavia had her lovers, it's a wonder you don't prosecute her for adultery.'

Nero considered it a wonderful joke. 'You prove it, Poppaea, and I'll prosecute! But I'm telling you, my love, there was never a man nor a woman who once turned her head.'

'In your presence. What a fool she will make you look when you discover you were the only one in the Palace who didn't know.'

'Don't let's argue,' Acte protested, 'Nero is likely to be called away by Phaon at any moment. We should go for a walk together and enjoy ourselves while we can.'

'The girl is quite right,' Poppaea agreed, 'and I need all the exercise I can get. This buffoon barely allows me to rise from my bed! We should only be grateful that Epaphroditus did not accompany us, or we should never get any time with our loved one.'

'It's very unlike him,' Acte remarked, 'why didn't he come?'

'Detained in Rome,' Nero said simply, and strode ahead.

Poppaea smiled. 'In truth, Acte, he has assumed the duties of the Foreign Minister, because the Foreign Minister will not speak to Nero and Nero, in turn, will not permit him entry to the Palace!'

'No wonder he's so edgy.'

'I suspect he only wants Octavia back because he believes he will win Doryphorus back at the same time.'

Acte looked at Poppaea. 'You heard him say that, then?'

'Of course I did. And be sure he will pay for it, too.'

The freedwoman smiled. 'He meant no offence, Poppaea. He gets these wild ideas, you know yourself. He never thinks things through.'

'You defend him far too easily, my dear. If he were made to suffer the consequences he might begin to consider them first.'

They allowed him to walk on ahead and went, instead, to look at Poppaea's donkeys, fifty of which she had brought with her from Rome. They had been shod in golden shoes, especially for the journey, and the light occasionally reflected from the little upturned feet as the animals moved about.

'Your face cream is wonderful,' Acte told Poppaea admiringly, 'even here in the provinces I don't know of any woman who doesn't use it.'

'It pays for their shoes!' Poppaea laughed. 'They must be kept in foal to produce their milk and the damned things simply multiplied! I had far too much moisturiser for my own use, so it was pure necessity rather than genius that led me to market it. Besides, the secret of making moisturiser from asses' milk is not new. One simply requires a wealthy husband to ensure a ready supply of it! And Nero likes the animals. He likes to see them out grazing in the gardens and even talks of introducing deer and more exotic species.'

'I warned you about his mad ideas,' Acte laughed, 'he'll have wild beasts running loose in the gardens before you know it!'

When Nero returned to the Palace after his short break, Seneca was among the first to request an audience.

'I grow old, Nero,' he complained, 'and weary of my position. I am dogged by neurosis and this is hardly an office to ease such complaint. I come before you now to request permission to retire from duty.'

'But you can't, Seneca. I have already lost Burrus; I cannot lose you.' He looked at Seneca searchingly. 'It's Tigellinus, isn't it? If you think for a moment I pay heed to the gossip he relays...'

'No, Nero, it has nothing to do with Tigellinus. He would be the first to wish me gone, it is true, but I need this for myself. I am too old, Nero. Too old.'

'Nonsense!' Nero tried to laugh it off, but could see at once that Seneca could not be swayed. 'Please, Seneca, don't do this to me,' he pleaded.

Seneca smiled. 'You plead with me only for the sake of your own selfishness. The fact is, Nero, I am no longer equal to the burden of my wealth. Order your agents to take over my property and incorporate it in yours. I do not suggest plunging myself into poverty, but giving up the things that are too brilliant and dazzle me. The time now spent on gardens and mansions shall be devoted to the mind. You have abundant strength. For years the supreme power has been familiar to you.'

Nero stared at him, horrified by his words. 'You expect to have your estate stolen and give it up merely to save your life. Someone is trying to prosecute you. Tell me who and I shall see them in exile!'

'No, Nero! The reasons I lay before you are the truth. Let me go.'

'How can I, Seneca? How can I not?' Nero rose in agitation and stood before Seneca. 'My first debt to you is that I can reply impromptu to your premeditated speech. For you taught me to improvise as well as to make prepared orations. If my life had been warlike, you would have fought for me. But you gave what our situation demanded: wisdom, advice, philosophy, to support me as boy and youth. Your gifts to me will endure as long as life itself. My gifts to you, gardens and mansions and revenues, are liable to circumstances.

'They may seem extensive. But many people far less deserving than you have had more. I omit, from shame, to mention ex-slaves who flaunt greater wealth. I am even ashamed that you, my dearest friend, are not the richest of all men. You are still vigorous and fit for state affairs and their rewards. My reign is only beginning.

'If youth's slippery paths lead me astray, be at hand to call me back. You equipped my manhood; devote even greater care to guiding it. If you return my gifts and desert your emperor, it is not your unpretentiousness, your retirement that will be on everyone's lips, but my meanness, your dread of my brutality.'

So saying, he clasped Seneca tightly and kissed him.

Yet his impassioned speech was to no avail. While Seneca did not officially retire, he curtailed his large receptions, dismissed most of his household and rarely visited Rome. It was publicly suggested, much to Nero's sorrow, that he had been driven from the emperor's company. In his absence, Nero grew increasingly dependant upon Tigellinus.

They were frequently to be found at the Circus, allowing no official business to interrupt a day at the races, however important.

'Rufus should join us,' Tigellinus remarked as they sat together in the imperial box, 'he isn't particularly fond of horses, but he does enjoy gambling. Constantly in and out of debt as a result, of course.'

'Is he in any difficulty at the moment?'

'No, I don't think so. There are always places available within the Praetorian Guard and plenty of people willing to pay for them, so I suspect. Just as one of his bad debts is paid off, so another recruit joins us!'

Nero chose to disregard the remark. 'I would always help him out, if necessary.'

'An old allegiance to him, Nero?'

'What do you mean? I barely knew him before his appointment.'

'No? I thought you might have run into him, whenever he was with the Augusta.'

'I don't believe he knew the Augusta.'

'Perhaps I am mistaken. I always thought she was the one thing we shared in common; though my relationship with her was too far in the past to warrant the comparison of notes!'

'He claims to have slept with her?' Nero asked, somewhat incredulously, privately wondering what benefits he had fetched with him to her bed.

'So I have heard.'

Nero continued to watch the activity in the arena, unconcerned.

'Who is it I see about foreign affairs?' Tigellinus asked after a short break in conversation. 'Epaphroditus suggested I should by-pass Doryphorus altogether and go straight to him, but I hardly like to do so when it could be of a highly delicate nature.'

'Epaphroditus is competent and trustworthy. Is it anything I should be made aware of?'

'I hope that it won't be. But it's not a decision I feel able to make on my own.'

Nero smiled, pleased that the commander was willing to seek advice. It was clear that he regarded Rufus as a rival, but perhaps understandable.

'I appreciate the fact that you have no wish to trouble me unnecessarily. But I may as well hear what is to be said now rather than later. And you may as well know, Tigellinus, that I preside over all councils of war and my ministers answer directly to me. That isn't a warning; just letting you know where you stand. I don't simply leave matters in the hands of my ministers.'

'But it is worrying, Nero. Truly worrying. You are already aware of two of your greatest rivals for the throne. Plautus you had removed to Asia; Sulla was banished to Gaul.' Tigellinus allowed himself a smile. 'If you will forgive me for saying so, it is quite obvious you make all decisions yourself. Any commander worth half his pay would have recommended against such dangerous placements.[1]

'So whom else do I need fear?' Nero asked with some urgency.

'No one else, Nero. And perhaps not even Sulla or Plautus. But their close proximity to the armies of the East and of Germany is positively dangerous. I was greatly alarmed even before I heard rumours of their activity.'

'What activity?' Nero interrupted.

'The Gauls regard Sulla as a great dictator. We need not wonder who gave them that idea. The Asians are excited by Plautus as a grandson of Drusus. With the troops in their pay and their great ancestry, these men are capable of ripping the empire asunder. And it is clear from their endeavours to win over the troops that they intend to make some attempt at power.'

Nero was visibly alarmed.

'I need more evidence,' Tigellinus reassured him, 'perhaps they merely test the water. Perhaps they are making preparations for a waiting game, ready to make a legitimate move when the opportunity arises. I need to confer first with someone with more experience in these matters, with more expert knowledge and better details to hand.' Tigellinus shook his head. 'I really had no wish to worry you with a threat of civil war which may ultimately come to nothing.'

'Civil war? Are they in collusion?'

'I am doing my utmost to find out. They are certainly in contact with each other. But as friends or foes, I do not know. And, to be honest, I don't even know if that's good or bad. Two bodies of troops marching on Rome and each other - or the one group united.'

'They must be denounced as agitators, immediately,' Nero said at once. 'You have laid enough evidence before me to take such action and we need not wait for this to go further. Banished at once as agitators, they are removed from access to power. Wrongly accused or not, they can be accused of no such attempts in the future.'

'Banishment? Are you not reacting too hastily, Nero?'

'Do I first wait for them to win over the armies in their region?'

'Wait just long enough for harder evidence and they can be condemned!'

'I will not wait,' Nero said adamantly, 'they are to be banished. And more sensibly, this time. Arrange it, Commander.'

Tigellinus smiled. 'I shall see to it at once.'

Nero paid the price for a day at the races and was inundated with official business on his return to duty, later that week.

'Firstly, deaths,' Epaphroditus began, smiling already at the news to impart. 'With great sorrow I must report the passing of Pallas, my Lord.'

Nero grinned. 'Why with great sorrow? Did he stipulate it in his will?!'

'His will has already been read and proved as dull and arrogant as he was! He left you nothing, incidentally.'

'I expected nothing. Well, well, well, old Pallas gone at last. The gods must already be suffering!'

'Plautus and Sulla are also dead.'

Nero sat up at once.

'Dead? What do you mean, dead?'

'No longer with us, Nero. Sulla resisted arrest and severely injured two of Tigellinus' men. He was quickly overcome and put to death.' He referred to his notes. 'Plautus took his own life when the Guards entered. Tigellinus believes he had already received word of Sulla's death.'

'Unfortunate.'

'They were agitators, Nero. I think their deaths merely prove that point.' Epaphroditus looked back to his papers. 'We have through the final report of the earthquake in Pompeii, I'll leave it with you. Deaths not as high as we first estimated, but the town has been largely demolished. Phaon has all the relevant financial details and I believe he is currently working on the figures for the rebuild.

'I have also a detailed report from Paetus in Parthia. I had a quick look through it with Doryphorus and it's basically a lot of unspecific nonsense. He concludes that the current situation is inconclusive - which, frankly, Doryphorus doubts.'

'Thank you, Epaphroditus, leave it with me.'

'Phaon says that including your plans up to the Saturnalia, your gifts to the nation for this year stand at sixty million sesterces.'

'Does he say that with relief, or disapproval?'

'It's only fair to warn you, Nero, that it was said with great disapproval. I think you're a denarii short of becoming a beggar, according to the great Phaon!'

'He worries unnecessarily.'

'Yes, well there is the small matter of Pompeii, and your beautiful new gymnasium.'

The gymnasium, still in only its infancy and already considered to be one of the finest ever erected, had been struck by lightning and completely burnt down.

'You'll remember my statue inside melted to a shapeless bronze mass?' Nero reminded his secretary. 'Tell Phaon half his work has already been done for him. He can melt it down into coins and build the new gymnasium out of that!'

'I'll leave that pleasure to you, Nero! And now Poppaea awaits an audience.'

'About what, do you know?'

'A prosecution.'

'A prosecution! That woman chills my heart whenever she seeks audience on official business. Why can't she amuse herself with music and fashion, like Sporus?'

'Chill you to the heart?' Poppaea repeated, entering without knocking. 'At least I don't make a public fool out of you, as your previous wife has done. Oh how the commons weep for her! If they but knew the scandal she could have brought to your house over the years.'

'Epaphroditus, you had better remain and take notes,' Nero instructed him, as he backed carefully out of the door. 'Well, Poppaea, tell me what you know.'

'I was of course right in accusing her of affairs with her slaves. But it transpires to have been only one in particular, among your own household and so not departed with her. And one of her own slaves, a rival for her affections, is now so bitter and jealous he brings charges of adultery against her.'

'This is an outrage! How can it be avoided?'

'It cannot. The slave has already spoken out against her.'

'Can it be proved?'

'We'll leave that for the courts to decide. Personally, I have no doubt it can be.'

'Never mind the courts, have her banished to Campania and put under military surveillance. It is enough to show the crime does not go unpunished and we can wait for this whole thing to blow over. I wish to the gods I had never divorced the woman, she brings me nothing but trouble.'

'I agree,' Poppaea said sharply, 'only I wish that you had never married her in the first place.' She turned abruptly and left.

Keeping her anger in check, she immediately sought out Anicetus, Commander of the Fleet, who was at Rome for the recent racing. She invited him to her own room and dismissed her attendants.

'Anicetus, let me blunt. The Augusta was a grave threat to me and you dealt with her admirably.'

'My Lady, she was a threat to Nero and I failed to deal with her at all. That honour must go to poor Burrus.'

'Your 'poor' Burrus waited for legal methods - and then only when he was faced with no alternative. You were willing to use some initiative. I need some more of it.'

'My Lady, I serve Nero. He was my pupil as a child and my friend now.'

'And you think I don't?! I'm his wife, you imbecile!' Poppaea struggled to keep her temper. 'Anicetus, it is well known among the household that Octavia had an affair with a slave. Now that she has been removed from the Palace the affair is likely to be made public. I do not think Nero is in the least concerned, but I certainly have no wish to be made a public laughing stock. I want her suitably punished and I need your help.'

Anicetus shifted uncomfortably. 'With respect, my Lady, I hope that I did not save Nero from the Augusta, only to see him threatened by another.'

Poppaea laughed. 'I have no interest whatsoever in power struggles. My interests are far more shallow. Octavia has constantly insulted me and, quite simply, I want revenge. I don't want to see her settled comfortably in Campania. I want to see her brought to trial for adultery.'

'And what exactly can I do about it?'

'The slave loves her. He won't betray her under torture.'

'How can you be so sure?' Anicetus asked carefully. 'Is there, in fact, a slave?'

Poppaea successfully feigned indignation.

'If I intended to accuse her falsely, do you not think I might have done so much sooner?' She sighed. 'I admit, Anicetus, that I was often tempted. But I resisted the urge. Which makes her guilt all the more pleasurable to me and her likely acquittal all the more painful. She is not to be acquitted. Do you understand me, Commander?'

'Plainly. I am to see that the slave confesses and that Octavia is condemned.'

'No, no, no! I have already told you, the slave will not confess.'

'Because he is innocent?'

Poppaea lost patience. 'Question him yourself! My own request is that you admit to sleeping with her.'

'*What*?'

'Tell Nero you have been having an affair with her. You're his friend - he'll believe you. And forgive you.'

'Poppaea! Octavia is noted for her virtue. What manner of fool do you take Nero for? First you ask him to believe that she sleeps with her slaves...'

'Who doesn't?!'

'And then,' he continued firmly, 'you expect him to believe that she had an affair with me! During my infrequent visits to Rome, I suppose?'

'During her forthcoming detainment in Campania.'

'My Lady, have you actually thought this through?' Anicetus smiled. 'What, exactly, is the current situation? Tell me the facts and I shall tell you a solution.'

'I told Nero of her affair and he is sending her to Campania, under military surveillance until the scandal blows over.'

'So she will have quite an alibi, won't she?' Anicetus grinned at her reaction. 'Do not fret, Poppaea. I am Commander of the Fleet. I can be part of the surveillance team. I can visit her as and when I choose, in complete privacy, and be a familiar face, a shoulder to cry on. And possibly more.'

'Perfect!'

'Umm. If I can seduce her.'

'Even if you can't. It's her word against yours.' Poppaea was delighted. 'Can I get you anything, Commander?'

He rose and shook his head. 'Don't trouble yourself, Poppaea. Octavia was a burden to him as a wife and a liability as an ex-wife. I do Nero a justice, though he won't thank me for it. For you, my Lady, I do no favours.' He bowed and took his leave.

NOVEMBER A.D. 62

It was with genuine shame that Anicetus confessed his affair to Nero. The emperor found it hard to believe, but there were plenty willing to agree with Poppaea's explanation.

'It is quite obvious that she felt public spirit was behind her,' she insisted. 'She has always regarded you as a usurper - a thief of her brother's birthright. Quite possibly she believes you murdered him, too. And now she has the perfect opportunity to claim justice. By seducing Anicetus she can win over the Fleet and make an attempt to overthrow you.'

'Poppaea is right,' Epaphroditus agreed, 'for years she lived in solitude, whatever gossip would have us believe. Why would she only now take a lover - and such a one as Anicetus?'

'She has full public sympathy,' Tigellinus pointed out, 'and once again in your leniency you placed her too near to temptation.'

'Allow Tigellinus to decide upon a place of exile,' Poppaea suggested firmly, 'a suitably nauseous isle to which not even the most loyal friend would wish to visit. Let your enemies plot to depose you with no allies to hand!' She looked sharply at Tigellinus. 'They might even prefer suicide to such a fate, and then you are truly rid of them, without damage to your conscience.'

Nero ignored her remark. 'And where would you suggest, Commander?'

'The island of Pandateria. Under strictest military surveillance. She has tested the water a little too successfully and is now a serious threat.'

'So be it.'

Chapter Forty-Two

It was Poppaea who gave the order to have Octavia executed. The soldiers guarding her would have been reluctant to carry out their orders had they not taken such pity on Octavia and seen her death as a mercy. There was also the no small point that her death meant their own release from the hell hole that was Pandateria. Octavia had been just twenty-three.

The exact details of the death were contrived between Poppaea and Tigellinus. Tigellinus insisted he had been given orders from the Empress and, since Octavia's execution seemed more than sensible, he had acted upon them. Poppaea, however, was equally adamant that she believed her orders would not be taken seriously and that she had never genuinely expected Octavia's death. Both stood before Nero, indignant that he should accuse them of any impropriety.

'I have received no special instruction as an Empress,' Poppaea protested, 'and have been your mistress - overlooked and ignored by all - for a great deal longer. How am I expected to know that the least little remark I make is taken as official instructions!'

'The Lady is quite right,' Tigellinus agreed. 'I am entirely at fault for not checking with you first, my Lord. But I believed I was accepting orders from the Empress and, at the time, had no reason to question them. I know that you rarely condone executions, but in this instance it seemed the best course of action to take. Octavia was a serious threat to you, my Lord.'

Nero sighed. 'I have no wish to undermine you, Poppaea. But I must know what is going on and therefore have no option but to have Tigellinus report to me first, before carrying out any of your orders. I promise you that I will not veto them without good reason - and without first consulting you. But I cannot have events of this nature occurring without my knowledge.'

'I understand that, my darling, and I'm sorry,' Poppaea wept.

Nero embraced her and offered what comfort he could, his outrage already forgotten.

Tigellinus bowed his head.

'I am sorry, too, my Lord. I acted with only your best interests in mind.'

'I know that, Tigellinus. You have my complete trust. Now perhaps you had best leave us.'

It was Epaphroditus who finally disturbed them and it was clear at once that his news caused him great distress.

'What is it?' Nero asked with concern, 'If you bring me news of Octavia then I may save you the effort. Tigellinus has already confessed his crime.'

'Octavia was never loved in this Palace and will never be missed,' Epaphroditus said bitterly. 'It is Doryphorus. He is dead, Nero.'

'Dead?' Nero sat back, releasing Poppaea from his embrace. 'No, that can't be. That can't be.'

'He collapsed in the street,' the secretary said numbly. 'The doctor attending him said that he had been habitually ill. He can give no cause, only to say that Doryphorus had carried a disease from his earliest youth. Perhaps a heart condition. I don't really know, Nero, I could hardly take it in.'

'He was always so deathly pale,' Poppaea murmured. 'Sporus and I often wish our lives away... wished... for such a complexion.' She shook her head.

'He gave me no chance to apologise,' Nero said through his tears. 'How can I tell him I'm sorry? He can't be dead, Epaphroditus, he can't be.'

The funeral was a simple affair, and the Saturnalia was once again a shallow festivity within the Palace; Nero doing no more than going through the motions during a season that seemed to evoke more sorrow than joy. The friends and family with whom the festivities were traditionally enjoyed were becoming painfully fewer.

Once more, the tradition of presenting gifts by patron to client was broken at the Palace; the household slaves giving Nero the carefully chosen and saved for gifts which never ceased to overwhelm him. Yet still he yearned for the festivities to end and the old Year to be finished. It had, once again, brought him too much sorrow.

JANUARY A.D. 63

Throughout the winter the general Paetus had sent hopeful reports from Armenia, which gave Nero the impression that the situation remained inconclusive. It was doubtful that the reports were entirely trustworthy and it was with great interest that Nero received a Parthian delegation, bringing a message from Vologeses himself.

One of the delegates stood before Nero to read the letter written by Vologeses.

"I say nothing now about my frequently repeated claim to Armenia, since the gods, who direct the fates even of the greatest nations, have handed the country to the Parthians, not without Roman ignominy. When, recently, I besieged Tigranes, I could have destroyed Lucius Paetus and his army. But I let them go free. I have sufficiently demonstrated my power; and I have also given proof of my clemency. Tiridates, too, would not decline to come to Rome and receive his diadem, if this were not prevented by taboos connected with his priesthood. He would attend the emperor's Standards and statues, and inaugurate his reign before the Roman army."

Nero sat back on his couch and smiled gently to himself.

'Thank you, my friends. Your report reads quite differently to those I have been receiving. You will forgive me if I withdraw and consult with my council.'

He rose and bowed to them, before nodding to the escorting staff-officer to join him outside.

'And you are?' he asked briskly.

'Granius, my Lord.'

'Well, Granius, how am I to reconcile this message with the reports I have been receiving from Paetus? Just how 'inconclusive', exactly, is our position?'

'I know nothing of my general's reports, my Lord. But all Romans have long since left Armenia.'

'So Vologeses is requesting from me that which he has already seized?' Nero laughed at the ludicrousness of the situation. 'Thank the gods that Vologeses is a man of honour - unlike our good general Paetus.' He looked around him, at Tigellinus and Rufus, at Epaphroditus, now the official Foreign Minister, and the various staff-officers gathered. 'So, gentlemen, what do we do now? Do we declare war against an army who have already stolen victory? Or do we accept peace under these humiliating circumstances?'

The unanimous decision was war.

'Very well,' Nero agreed, 'but to prevent any further disgrace sole command is to be given to Corbulo. He is to have unlimited power.'

He returned to the Parthian delegates and dismissed them with a multitude of gifts.

'Though our countries are at war, I ask you to accept these gifts as my friends not my enemies. If Tiridates makes the same appeal to me in person it will be favourably received.'

Paetus was summoned to Rome and no doubt feared the worst. But he was already a laughing stock at Rome and Nero felt he had been punished enough. He contented himself with a sarcastic rebuke, issuing the declaration that he was pardoning Paetus immediately because prolonged suspense would damage so timid a person's health.

Corbulo sent Paetus' brigades to Syria, feeling that they would be too demoralised to fight. He addressed his soldiers and blamed all past defeats on the inexperience of Paetus, listing his own worthy achievements to boost confidence. When envoys were sent by Tiridates and Vologeses to discuss peace, Corbulo was ready with an answer.

'Matters have not reached the point when war to the finish is unavoidable,' he told them. 'Rome's many successes, Parthia's successes, too, are warnings against arrogance. To accept his kingdom as a gift, undevastated, is to Tiridates' advantage. Vologeses, too, will serve Parthian interests better by alliance with Rome than by a policy of mutual injury. I know the internal dissentions of your kingdom, with its formidable, lawless nations - a contrast to my emperor, whose territories are uniformly peaceful. This is his only war.'

Vologeses duly requested a truce in certain provinces, while Tiridates requested a conference, which was duly arranged.

Tiridates met with Corbulo and laid his royal diadem at the feet of Nero's statue.

'I will resume it only from Nero's own hand,' he declared, and embraced Corbulo to signify their friendship.

Peace having been formally declared, both armies were collected and paraded in magnificent array. Troop after troop of Parthian cavalry lined up with their national ensigns. The Roman brigades stood opposite, with their glittering Eagles and Standards. In the centre a Roman official chair was placed on a dais, bearing an effigy of Nero. Tiridates advanced to the dais and, when the customary sacrifices had been made, took the diadem from his head and placed it at the feet of the statue.

The news of these events was lost upon Nero, however, who had a greater event of his own to concern him. As Poppaea's time fast approached, they travelled to his own birthplace of Antium, where she could begin her confinement.

On the twenty-first of January of that year, Poppaea gave birth to a baby girl.

Nero's joy knew no bounds and both mother and child were honoured with the title 'Augusta'. The entire members of the senate travelled to Antium, to pay their respects to the emperor's daughter, but Thrasea was the single notable exception.

'I forbid him to attend,' Nero announced hotly.

'Enough time has elapsed to forget this silly quarrel,' Seneca urged, but his words were lost on Nero.

'They all wish me dead,' Nero insisted, 'but Thrasea wears his colours openly. I will not have him near my child.' He smiled at Seneca, grateful to him for making the journey. 'He made me feel an outcast, Seneca. Well now I may reciprocate.'

'Never mind Thrasea, let me see little Claudia Augusta!' Seneca's wife Paulina insisted. They both fussed over the tiny infant and declared her to be as beautiful as her mother.

'She has your fair skin and amber hair,' Paulina told Poppaea, 'she will break hearts within just a few years. Cherish her, Poppaea; they grow so fast.'

'You are far too old to go broody on me!' Seneca laughed, 'Come away now and let the poor mother have her rest.'

'Take Nero with you, if you can!' Poppaea pleaded, 'He will not let the poor child alone!'

'Since the senate is gathered in all but its entirety, you may take the opportunity to address it,' Seneca told Nero firmly.

Nero stood before them with only minor reluctance. He was far too euphoric to remember their malice and wished only to share his euphoria.

'I decree that Poppaea and Claudia Augusta are to be honoured with the title 'Augusta',' he announced, 'And I decree a temple of fertility to them. Golden statues of the Two Fortunes of Antium are to be placed on the throne of the Capitoline Jupiter. Antium is to have Circus Games in honour of the Claudian and Domitian Houses, just as Bovillae honour the Julian House. And I will inaugurate a new competition, to be modelled on the Victory Festival established here by Augustus.'

Though he didn't yet know it, none of these plans would be implemented.

Nero stepped down and returned at once to his family, unwilling to be separated from baby Claudia for more than a moment. Though Acte and Sporus were with them, he preferred to be alone with Poppaea and they rarely intruded.

'I love you so much, Poppaea,' he told her, as they lay together, cradling Claudia between them, 'She is the best thing we've ever done. She's so perfect, Poppaea!' He sounded incredulous, still marvelling at this tiny being who was so dependent upon them.

'Crispinus was once perfect, too!' Poppaea warned.

'This tiny? This fragile?'

For a moment, concern flickered across Poppaea's face. 'No,' she said softly, 'not nearly so small and fragile.'

'A proper little girl; a delicate flower. Our flower.' He brushed her tiny cheek with a gentle finger and nestled his face against Poppaea. 'I have never been happier.' He sighed. 'I don't believe I could ever be happier.'

'That baby is not right,' Paulina told Seneca that same evening, 'far too pale to be healthy.'

'Her mother is fair skinned. As is her father, for that matter.'

'No, no. Nothing to do with complexion. She isn't well.'

'The doctors have given her a clean bill of health, my dear.'

'That's as maybe. But still, there's something not right.'

MAY A.D. 63

For a while, Paulina's fears proved unjustified. It was some time before mother and daughter were fit enough to travel, but by mid-April the emperor and his family were back in Rome.

Claudia quickly settled into the routine of Palace life. There were fewer visitors to wake her at odd hours and she could be left for longer in the company of Ecloge and Alexandria, now that both her parents were better able to cope with separation from her. She slept for long intervals and rarely cried, earning great praise from Nero, but giving some cause for concern to Poppaea and the two nurses. Though none of them would dare voice such suspicions, they all felt that her lack of energy was unnatural.

It was no surprise to Ecloge, therefore, when the child could not be disturbed from her slumber at the usual hour, shortly before the slaves awoke Nero and Poppaea.

'Has Ecloge not taken Claudia for her breakfast?' Poppaea asked Helos, as the slave returned with the dogs from their walk and the baby still lay in the cradle beside the bed.

'She left her sleeping this morning, Augusta. The little Augusta was not ready to wake.'

'She looks no more ready now,' Poppaea smiled. 'Where is my cat?'

'I believe Crispinus has her down by the lake, Augusta.'

'Good.' Poppaea had all but banished her pet cheetah, since the birth of Claudia, anxious that the animal could not be trusted. 'Go summon Ecloge now. I am getting up and have no wish to be disturbed.'

'Yes, Augusta.'

Poppaea leaned across and stroked the child's head.

'Nero! She's cold!'

Nero turned over, only half awake.

'She can't be cold,' he assured her, 'you have her wrapped in too many blankets as it is and the room is stifling.'

'No!' Poppaea said in despair, 'She's cold! Cold to the touch! Icy!'

Both were out of the bed in an instant, Poppaea snatching up the lifeless infant and cradling her to her breast.

'Oh! She's gone, Nero! She's gone!' Poppaea wailed, grasping the child tighter as Nero tried to take her.

He took up the tiny hand and rubbed it desperately, as though trying to restore warmth.

Slaves had already come running, alerted by Poppaea's cries, and Ecloge was soon with them. All present sobbed uncontrollably; Nero still trying to prise the baby free of its mother, convinced he could revive her.

'Get Andromachus!' he screamed, 'And Xenophon! And Alexandria!'

Tubero ran for help, taking the dogs with him as they sought a hiding place from the turmoil and only succeeded in getting even more under foot.

'No! Don't take them!' Nero cried instantly, seeing them leave, 'they must stay with me. I want them with me.' He slid down onto the floor, against the bed, and put his arms around the dogs, who sniffed at his tears in fascination and licked his face. He sobbed wildly against them, while Poppaea paced in front of him, nursing Claudia hopelessly.

When Alexandria appeared, the tears streaming down her face, he deserted the comfort of his dogs and flung himself into her arms, clinging to her as though his life depended upon it and crying until his face ached with the pain.

'Bring her back, Alexandria, bring her back. Please bring her back.'

Claudia Augusta, who had lived for less than four months, was declared a goddess and voted a place on the ceremonial couch of the gods, receiving her own shrine and priest.

Nero's grief far exceeded human measure, earning him widespread condemnation for his 'excessive' mourning. While his staff and household wondered if he would ever survive the loss, Poppaea took strength from his weakness. It was, in the end, her calm resignation that saw him through.

Chapter Forty-Three

FEBRUARY A.D. 64

It had been a miserable winter, with a Saturnalia again best left forgotten, and little to look forward to in the coming year. As each passing month signified Poppaea's failure to fall pregnant, both she and Nero began to lose hope that she would ever again conceive.

Matters were made considerably worse by Messalina's announcement of marriage to Vestinus. She had become an integral part of leisure time at the Palace and was as much a favoured sexual partner of Poppaea as she was of Nero. Neither quite knew how they would cope without her.

'Why Vestinus!' Nero protested, 'He is a loathsome reptile!'

'And you are jealous!' Messalina argued. 'I have no wish to remain a spinster and he is as good an offer as I am ever likely to get. He is not afraid of offending you by asking for my hand, unlike all other men in Rome. And he keeps a most commendable staff of handsome young men which should keep me amply satisfied.'

'Not afraid to offend me?!' Nero repeated. 'Why else did he ask for your hand?! He is not content with making me the butt of all his jokes, he must now steal my lovers, too.'

'He could have been your lover and we could have all continued as we are in great contentment,' Messalina insisted. 'But you were the one who excluded him from your circle. He could never have written such crude jokes if he hadn't once been a party to your activities, Nero.'

Nero looked to Poppaea for moral support, but she merely threw up her arms in despair.

'I did not want him as my lover!' Nero protested. 'I allowed him to join in with our games, but you cannot expect me to tolerate his forced intimacy merely to indulge you! Poppaea finds him repulsive, and my little Sabina is afraid of him! It is a wonder I tolerated his presence for as long as I did; and I find it a greater wonder that you now rebuke me for sending him away! Marry him, Messalina, but not with our blessing.'

'But you will of course attend our wedding?'

'We will do no such thing!' This time it was Poppaea who gave vent to her feelings. 'We love you, Messalina. But we will not honour Vestinus, not even for you. Come back to us freely, we will always welcome you. But not with that accursed man in tow. Nero is right. He marries you only to cause him offence.'

Messalina smiled. 'I don't even want to question his motives. I am just happy to have secured a husband. And happy not to have lost either of you in the process.'

They kissed and hugged; but, still, Messalina was gone.

Sporus missed her more acutely than anyone and his depression seemed to infect the Palace like a disease. She sent him her wedding gown, which he wore to the exclusion of all others; but it served only to increase the dark mood.

Nero could tolerate the oppressive atmosphere no longer and had already resolved to leave Rome and embark on a grand tour, when word of fresh tragedy reached him. There had been a boating accident on the lake. Though the two slaves who had accompanied young Crispinus on his fishing excursion had fought desperately to find him, he had been lost beneath the surface and drowned.

'We are definitely leaving on a tour of Greece,' Nero insisted, as he sat with Poppaea beside the lake. 'I care nothing for your arguments now - we need to be free of this place, free of this dark cloud that haunts us. I refuse to have any more mourning.'

Poppaea leaned against him quietly. 'If we run away, we have to return again at some point.'

'But then it will be different. We will do things to lift our spirits. We will return with new memories.'

'I don't want new memories, Nero. I want my old ones. I want my Claudia, and my Crispinus, even if they are only memories now. They are all I have of them.'

They both wept silently.

Nero returned to the lake's edge once more with Acte, shortly before their departure. She had come to Rome for the funeral and had stayed on, to see the large party off on their journey.

'It is such a beautiful and serene place,' Nero remarked, 'yet none of my memories of it reflect that.'

'Don't dwell on them, Nero,' Acte advised.

'No, it's not unpleasant. I like to recall the good times. A farewell gesture to them, perhaps. But my good times here were never in keeping with the settings.

'Senecio and I used to set up a market with our little gang, just over there, complete with all the banter and even brothels! And now I am too old for such things.

'Just across there, near that tree, is where Otho and I used to walk our horses and stop to water them. And we had our one and only fight there, too. And now, he is gone and we're not even on speaking terms.'

Nero sighed, but continued.

'Right here, where we sit now, is where Doryphorus and I often played our games. He would tie the girls to posts and I would be wrapped in some animal skin or other. He would release me from a makeshift cage and I would ravage the girls accordingly! Be it tiger or wolf, it was generally the same result! Much indecent pawing and nibbling! Such screams and laughter! I would tease the girls criminally and Doryphorus would... despatch me, shall we say. And that's all gone, too. No Doryphorus, no Messalina. And I never even had the chance to tell him I was sorry.'

'He made no attempt at reconciliation either,' Acte pointed out.

'What would it have mattered anyway? Friends or enemies, still he is gone. And Crispinus - what a nuisance he was! Always lurking on these shores. How he ever squeezed the dogs into his little boats, I don't know! I was convinced he'd drown both them and himself! Yet it was when he was in the charge of two of my most trusted slaves that he met his death. If life is unpredictable, then death is more so.'

He looked about him, with more appreciation than sorrow.

'We can find here tranquillity when we need it. But this spot will never be tranquil for me. It's too full of life and colour and sounds. I don't want to come back home to them, Acte. I don't know what I'm going to fetch back with me, but I won't return to this.'

The emperor and his massive entourage left Rome a few days later, travelling first to his beloved Neapolis, where he had planned his official public stage debut.

The immense theatre was filled to capacity, despite the murmurings of an earthquake. The ground tremor increased throughout the performance, but Nero sang his piece through to the very end. Only after the large crowd had left the theatre did it succumb to the violent tremors and collapsed totally. Miraculously, there were no casualties and Nero immediately composed a poem, thanking the gods for the happy outcome of the event.

'I want to go home,' Poppaea insisted, seeing the collapse as an ill omen rather than a lucky escape.

'Nonsense! Things are already looking bright. The gods have smiled upon us, our tour is blessed.'

'The dark cloud has merely followed us,' Poppaea corrected him, 'and the theatre has fallen in proof of its power. We cannot run from it, Nero. Let us just go home.'

'Not until I have sung my songs on every stage in Greece! I am going to win the wreath of their Games and nothing else matters to me.'

'Nothing else may matter to you, but I agree with Poppaea,' Sporus pleaded, 'the theatre collapsed! What greater omen do you need?!'

Their pleas were lost on Nero and the vast mule train moved on once more after a few days, towards the Adriatic. They stopped at Beneventum en route, to attend a gladiatorial display given by the notorious degenerate Vatinius.

Nero mingled freely with the crowd and joined in heartily with the boisterous encouragement of the combatants. During the intervals he sat with those in the cheap tiers and joined in with the games they had chalked onto the seats. Talk was mainly of the contests, or of trivial local gossip, but Nero chanced to overhear a name he knew well and it immediately seized his attention.

'Torquatus, did you say?' he asked of the merchant alongside him, 'I know him well. What news do you have of him?'

'I was just telling my good friend here, he has died.'

'Died? But that's terrible!'

'I had many dealings with the man and I always found him to be fair. My freedman brought me the news only just now. He has been fetching goods back from Torquatus, the gods have mercy on the poor man.'

'Watch your words, in the present company,' his companion warned.

The merchant looked at Nero. 'I'm sorry, my Lord. I mean no offence.' He looked at his companion in confusion; as did Nero.

'Well, you know... the circumstances and all that,' the other man said vaguely, as though Nero should be the one to clarify his remarks.

'I'm afraid I don't know,' Nero told him, 'perhaps you would care to fill in further details? My first news of this is from our friend here.'

'My freedman knows only that Torquatus is dead. His slaves say he took his own life,' the merchant said.

'Oh, he did,' his companion agreed, 'but only to dodge standing trial. Our Lord here must know, surely?'

'Nero, please; and, no, I know nothing of which you speak,' Nero insisted, alarmed by the man's news, 'please tell me everything you know.'

'Well, it's only hearsay, my Lord. But I've just come from a tavern and a group of merchants from Rome were in. They seemed to know what they were talking about. They were saying he'd been charged with treason. Having designs on the throne, they said. You know, that's why I thought you'd know all about it.'

'This is the first I've heard of it!'

Nero rose in panic and sought out Vatinius at once.

'Have you heard any news from Rome?' he demanded, 'They say Torquatus is dead!'

Vatinius shrugged. 'I've heard nothing.'

'Neither have I!' Nero said angrily. 'The gossip all around me is of how he plotted to overthrow me and took his own life rather than stand trial - and I have been told nothing!'

Vatinius could not care less. 'But he's dead, anyway. It hardly matters now whether he plotted against you.'

'Of course it matters! Had he stood trial I would have acquitted him! I know the man, Vatinius. How was this case ever allowed to go this far without my knowledge?'

'Don't look to me, Nero! I know as much about this as you! Besides which, you haven't been in Rome. Perhaps there are messengers on their way at this very minute, with every detail you seek.'

'I'm sorry, Vatinius, but I am going to have to return to Rome.'

Slaves were sent in search of his immediate travelling companions and a coach was prepared at once.

'I don't know what has shocked me more,' Nero told Poppaea and Sporus as they travelled back to Rome together, 'Torquatus' death, the fact that he was charged with treason, or my lack of knowledge in any of this.'

'Rufus and Tigellinus are well able to cope in your absence,' Poppaea assured him.

But Nero had his doubts.

Once back in Rome, Nero found that there were few facts to become acquainted with. Torquatus had committed suicide before word could be sent of the charges brought against him.

'However guilty he had been, if he had only waited for the mercy of the judge he would have lived,' Nero told Tigellinus regretfully.

Rufus shot his colleague a glance.

'I'm very sorry this forced your return to Rome,' Tigellinus apologised, 'had the situation been in any way serious I would of course have summoned you. But as it was, it hardly necessitated the abandonment of your trip.'

'Perhaps it was ill-omened after all,' Nero sighed, 'Greece may wait. I think I shall go instead to Egypt and visit Alexandria. While I cannot face repeating the journey to the Adriatic once more, I certainly cannot face the prospect of remaining at Rome.'

'You will not leave immediately?' Rufus asked with concern.

'And why not? But for this incident, I would already be away. I am sure Poppaea and Sporus will be grateful for a few days of rest, but we will set off again as soon as possible. I trust you can cope in my absence?'

'Of course, my Lord,' Tigellinus insisted, 'in fact, we see it as a sleight that you saw fit to curtail your trip on this occasion.'

'I meant no insult to you both,' Nero assured them, 'but in future I would prefer to hear of plots and charges in the customary manner, rather than as common gossip. And I would like to see at least one person brought to trial to experience my leniency - which may put an end to these unnecessary suicides!' He laughed, but his humour was forced.

Tigellinus smiled grimly.

Once more, a day of departure was set and, at Poppaea's insistence, Nero embarked on a farewell tour of the city temples. His final visit before leaving for Alexandria was to the shrine of Vesta, but as he stood up to leave the shrine he became dizzy, overcome by a sudden blindness. It was too swift to cause panic and he sat down once more, Sporus finding that the hem of his robe had been caught on his seat and had perhaps pulled him back.

'Are you okay?' he asked Nero anxiously, loosening the scarf at his throat.

'I don't know,' Nero said vaguely, 'I couldn't see a thing. But I'm fine now; perfectly well.'

They returned to the Palace, where Nero was passed fit by his doctors. Yet the incident left him uneasy and he cancelled the arranged trip.

'I for one am glad,' Poppaea told him, 'we should simply get on with our life as best we can, in surroundings that are familiar and with people we know.'

'I must concede at last that you are right,' Nero agreed, 'but instead of my tour we will have feast days here in Rome - a whole succession of them, throughout the city, to which everyone is invited.'

Having made the decision to remain in Rome he was true to his word and quickly made the entire city his home. He threw banquets in public places throughout the city, which lasted from noon till midnight and beyond; with only occasional breaks for diving into warm baths in the late evening or snow-cooled water in the heat of the afternoon.

The artificial lakes in the Campus Martius, and that in the Circus, were frequently drained to accommodate Nero's large public parties, at which dancing girls and prostitutes mingled freely with knights and senators.

There were many outraged by such behaviour, but still more who were grateful for the diversion and who strove to outdo one another in the battle for Nero's approval. His own hospitality was returned fourfold, his friends going out of their way to throw bigger and wilder parties than the last.

Vitellius succeeded in spending forty thousand gold pieces on a turban party; while Petronius doubled that figure on a rose banquet. As a result, roses became the height of fashion, particularly winter roses, shipped in from Egypt, which commanded ridiculous prices.

Not to be outdone, Tigellinus threw a party on the lake of Agrippa, on a raft towed by boats fitted entirely with gold and ivory. He stocked the lake with exotic sea creatures especially for the occasion and the raft was filled with foreign birds and animals. Yet the most noteworthy feature of his notorious party was the inclusion of naked prostitutes, who lined the banks opposite; while the brothels on the quays were given over to any noblewomen who chose to make use of them.

Such was the scale of these parties that detractors soon came up with a new lampoon that found its way onto city walls:

"The Palace is spreading and swallowing Rome,
Let us all flee to Veii and make it our home,
Yet the Palace is growing so damnably fast,
That it threatens to gobble up Veii at last."

As with all lampoons, Nero ignored it and tolerated all insults he encountered as he mixed freely on the city streets. While crossing the street in front of the market one afternoon, in the company of some friends, he was abused by the Cynic, Isidorous, who shouted after him,

'In your song about Nauplius you make good use of ancient ills, but in all practical matters you make ill use of modern goods!'

Nero laughed it off, but his friends were incensed on his behalf and brought charges of treason against Isidorous, as well as the actor Datus. Datus, during an Atellan farce, had illustrated the first line of the song "Goodbye Father, goodbye Mother," with gestures of drinking and swimming, with clear reference to Claudius, known to have been poisoned, and Agrippina. He accompanied the final line, "Hell guides your feet," with a wave of the hand towards the senators. For these insults the senate was ready to condemn both men, but Nero intervened and saw that they were merely exiled.

'How can you afford to be so tolerant?' Senecio complained to Nero, 'when you lay yourself open to this sort of abuse, you lay the senate wide open to criticism, too.'

'In what way?' Nero demanded with amusement.

'You represent the ultimate power of Rome, but it is a mockery. And so the public mocks all things powerful. Not just you, but the senate, and the tribunes and city prefects who maintain law and order.'

'The public does not mock me,' Nero pointed out mildly, 'or were you only referring to the wealthier members of the public, perhaps?'

'These were public insults, Nero. Directed at you in front of rich and poor alike. Not just some hurtful remarks over a dinner table in a more exclusive setting. The crimes of Datus and Isidorous are far more serious than those of Antistius, whom you would have been happy to see condemned.'

'I wanted him exiled!' Nero argued. 'What I wanted in his case was the support of the senate. In these instances, I personally would have acquitted them both. Let them stir up public feeling against Roman nobility. It matters not to me.'

'That much is clear,' Senecio said bitterly.

The series of feasts came to an end and by mid-summer Nero was seeking fresh diversion. He moved his Court to Antium for the summer break, already distanced from the sad memories it held.

Chapter Forty-Four

19TH JULY A.D. 64

It was late afternoon when Epaphroditus fetched an urgent despatch from Rome. He found Nero in his chamber, packing away the remaining business of the day and preparing to bathe before dinner.

'Oh, Nero,' he cried, 'I have terrible news from Rome, terrible! A fire is sweeping through the city and there is nothing that can be done to stop it. It destroys everything in its path and gains strength by the hour.'

'Has a fire officer been sent?'

'They send only a note, with details.'

Nero took the note, to read for himself.

'The fate of the city is in the lap of the gods, there is precious little we can do, Epaphroditus. But make arrangements at once for our return. We'll travel first light tomorrow.'

He sought out Poppaea and Sporus and they joined him in the bath, alarmed by his news.

'What casualties?' Poppaea asked, 'Oh, the gods! I hope Silia and Messalina are safe.'

'There is no word of casualties. People are being evacuated, it seems the fire-fighters have everything under control except the fire,' Nero assured her. 'They believe it began at the Circus Maximus, where it adjoins the Palatine and Caelian Hills. It isn't the usual town fire; there are no walled mansions or temples in its immediate path to arrest its progress. It spread at once threw the little shops along the Circus itself, and the strong wind has merely fanned it. The Circus is gone, and much of its vicinity. And no sign of any abatement.'

'Oh, Nero, what can we do?'

'We can do nothing. You and Sporus must remain here. Everyone is leaving Rome.'

'But what about you?' Sporus asked immediately.

'I have to go back, my little one. They are my people - what else can I do?'

'He will be quite safe,' Poppaea reassured him, 'the Guards will not allow him too close to the flames or the people.' She turned her attention to Nero. 'You do realise there will be looters and cut-throats in abundance?'

'I promise to keep well away from the fire and not mingle with the crowd,' Nero assured her.

'I only hope you love us enough to keep that promise.'

Nero kissed her tenderly.

At first light the following morning he set off with only the minimum escort for Rome. The traffic out of the city was immense and they made slow progress, pushing their way through the evacuees who filled both sides of the road. Carts were piled high with personal possessions, the noblemen of Rome unwilling to leave anything of value for either flames or looters. Nero became increasingly incensed as the morning wore on.

'You! Aemilius! That poor beast cannot pull all that on its own. What are you thinking of?' he called to one of the many he recognised, who had harnessed an inadequate riding horse and endeavoured to salvage the entire contents of his city mansion. 'Where are your slaves? Could you spare no room for them amid your bronze couches?'

'They follow on foot, Nero. And where are you heading?'

'The city, of course.'

'You waste your time! No one remains. All roads out are blocked by carts such as mine. Everyone is escaping to their country villas - I recommend you do the same.'

'Everyone, Aemilius? Does everyone in Rome have a country villa to escape to?'

Aemilius shrugged. 'Perhaps there's the odd merchant in need of lodging, but there'll be no shortage of friends to offer such, I'm sure.' He moved off once more, content in his ignorance.

'Fool!' Nero cursed bitterly. 'Look at them all, rescuing their precious jewelled couches. One man to each cart; and I'll warrant the carriages contain no more than a noblewoman and a single handmaid. What of those with no country villas? They are left in Rome with neither homes nor possessions to rescue. Where are they, on this trail of salvation?'

'There is nothing we can do,' Epaphroditus told him, 'but the quicker we reach Rome, the sooner we may be able to give some help.'

They pushed on, deserting the road when the traffic reached standstill and travelling across country. By the time they reached Rome, the fire had engulfed the whole of the Palatine district, including the Palace. Nero watched in fascination from the Tower of Maecenas, in the gardens.

'Such destruction; and, yet, such beauty,' he confessed, enraptured by the flames, ' "Their gestures flowed as fast as words." '

A large crowd had already gathered at the foot of the tower and now called for a speech. Nero looked down at them desperately.

'What can I say to these people?' he asked of Epaphroditus. 'They have nothing more than the charred clothes in which they stand. What words of comfort can I offer?'

'That you are here is enough, Nero,' the secretary told him.

After some consideration, Nero decided to sing the famous 'Sack Of Ilium' as a mark of respect, recalling, as it did, a similar disaster and the courage such tragedy evoked. It was a poignant choice, against the backdrop of flames and smouldering rubble. 'I'll send the Guards in now to move the crowd on,' Epaphroditus suggested, when the song had ended.

'Move them on to where, exactly?'

'They can hardly be permitted to remain in your own Gardens!'

'And why not?' Nero looked about him, already formulating a course of action. 'Epaphroditus, gather who you can and throw open my Gardens for the relief of the destitute. Have the Field of Mars designated for them, too. Have the Guards throw up makeshift canvases to form some sort of shelter. And the public buildings of Agrippa must also be given over to the homeless. I'll gather what slaves I can and arrange food and clothing. Send to Actium for all members of staff, so that food and clothing can be properly distributed and the shelters managed. Sporus must ransack every wardrobe in the house and see that adequate supplies of clothing are sent.'

Epaphroditus did as he was told at once and within a short time some order had returned to the city, though the fire still raged throughout each district, fed by the narrow winding streets and irregular buildings. Gangs of looters hampered fire-fighters, but Nero's own men were sent in to restore harmony and Nero himself worked among the destitute in the Maecenas Gardens, erecting temporary accommodation and handing out rations.

Two days passed in this fashion, the emperor tireless in his support of the victims. Food supplies were brought in from Ostia and neighbouring towns, and Nero reduced the price of corn by a sixth, to less than a quarter sesterce a pound; subsidising the price from his private purse.

By the twenty-fourth of July, six days into the inferno, the flames had been stamped out, but started up again on part of an estate belonging to Tigellinus, in the Aemilian district. Rumours were rife that the fire was deliberate, since fire-fighters were called to at least a dozen fires daily but none before had ever got out of hand.

'I think that is reason enough to show the fire was not deliberate,' Nero told Epaphroditus, as they discussed the gossip on the streets during a welcome respite from the shelters. 'With so many fires breaking out constantly, it was only a matter of time before a disaster on this scale occurred. I have seen five storey wooden buildings, with no stone in sight - and each apartment home to a charcoal fire.'

'The Christians were preaching about fire ending the world and marking the return of their Messiah,' Epaphroditus said, 'there's more than one of them in the shelters claiming responsibility for it.'

'The fact that my own men were seen out with the looters already points the finger of blame in my direction!' Nero laughed. 'Vitellius sent word that the senate is of the opinion I destroyed the existing city in order to name the new one after myself! Apparently, they cite the fact that I sang a song in celebration while the fire raged - not to mention the fact that it was Tigellinus who rekindled the accursed flames, though they know nothing of that outside the city as yet!'

'Tigellinus was boasting of divine intervention that his estate was spared!' Epaphroditus laughed, 'the Guards Camp was a joyous place this morning when they learned of this new intervention by the gods!'

'Was that deliberate, do you think, against him?'

'He's not well loved, Nero, but neither is he that much hated. I for one have taken an interest in this story put out by the Christians. Whether they mean to cash in on an accident and merely make use of the publicity, I don't know. But I've come across some fanatics at the temple, looking for their Messiah. They're convinced he'll come, as a result of the fire. They feel they've driven all evil from the city. And they seem to feel strongly enough about it that they could well have lit the first torches themselves. They are certainly more than happy to claim they did so.'

'Who exactly are they? Not that sect Senecio was thinking of joining a while ago?'

'They preach free love and incest. Their meetings invariably end in orgies, apparently. But so far they have attracted only the rougher citizens and Senecio lacked the courage to sign up! He says now that they are no better than the followers of Isis and drink human blood and eat the flesh of their leaders in cannibalistic rituals.'

'Sour grapes, no doubt, because they would not let him in!'

'No, I've seen their preachings, Nero, and it's all love thy brother and thy neighbour - and anything that drops its underwear keenly enough!'

They both laughed, though the sinister aspect of the sect gave credence to the current gossip.

'Round up a few of the professed incendiaries and see if there is any truth in their tale,' Nero suggested.

They returned to their duties in the shelters erected in the Gardens and news soon arrived that the fire had finally been stamped out. But such news brought little to celebrate. Of the fourteen districts of Rome, only four were left undamaged. Three had been levelled to the ground; the remainder nothing more than scorched and mangled ruins. Countless ancient treasures were lost; valuable libraries filled with irreplaceable manuscripts; mansions that had belonged to famous generals and were decorated with their triumphal trophies; temples, vowed and dedicated by the kings; ancient monuments of historical interest. All destroyed.

Scholars noted that the fire had started on the same day that the Senonian Gauls had captured and burnt the city four hundred and fifty-four years earlier. They even went to elaborate lengths to work out that the two fires were separated by four hundred and eighteen years, four hundred and eighteen months and four hundred and eighteen days. Nero took no interest in their findings, being too preoccupied in the clearance and rebuilding of the city.

The architects Severus and Celer were summoned, but found that they had been left with little to do.

'I have drawn up some designs,' Nero informed them, spreading vast sheets out over his bed. 'I have given much thought to the ancient style of building, which so easily fuelled the fire, and the alternatives to its design.' He showed them his detailed drawings, his days in the classroom sketching horses no longer wasted. 'Do you see here, porches are built out from the fronts of apartments and private houses, to serve as fire-fighting platforms. The street fronts are to be of regular alignment and their heights to be restricted to four storeys. All houses are to be built around courtyards and the streets themselves must be of a minimum width. Semi-detached houses are forbidden - every building must have its own walls. Broad, uncluttered streets cannot conduct a fire.'

He rolled up his plans and referred to his notes.

'I am introducing a law, with immediate affect, that a fixed proportion of every building must be of untimbered stone from Gabii or Alba; such stones being fireproof, of course. I leave it to you both to decide on the exact proportion to be fixed, according to building regulations.'

Both Celer and Severus were impressed, and happy to work from the plans given. Nero next summoned the city prefect, to discuss security arrangements with regard to the city's water supply.

'I have heard it said by many who have lost their homes that their water supply had been fenced off and used by wealthier home-owners in villas alongside. Tales of restricted access are rife. Some individuals have even been accused of selling rights to water access. A new brigade must be formed to see that this practise is stamped out and free access is enforced and properly maintained. See to it.'

Over the coming months, all work centred upon the rebuilding of Rome. Nero erected the new apartment blocks at his own expense and personally paid for the clearance of debris from building sites before transferring them to their owners. The empty corn-ships returning down the Tiber were used to dump the rubbish in the Ostian marshes. He also gave substantial bonuses for the completion of houses and apartment blocks before a given date.

Neither were Celer nor Severus allowed a free hand in the rebuilding of the Palace. Nero designed it, not on the usual luxurious scale, but in a provincial rustic style. In keeping with this theme, he had the gardens landscaped in faked rusticity, complete with ploughed fields, vineyards, pastures and woodlands, where every variety of domestic animal roamed freely; and even several species of wild animal.

He called in his architects, however, for a more traditional approach when the time came for the rebuilding of his own mansion, which had once linked the Gardens of Maecenas to the Palatine.

'This is from my own private purse and no expense is to be spared,' he told them. 'It is to be called The Golden House. I want the entrance hall large enough to accommodate a statue of myself I have commissioned from Zenodorus.'

'And how big might that be?' Celer enquired.

Nero grinned. 'One hundred and twenty feet tall. Impressive, don't you think? The pillared arcade is to run for a mile, in keeping with the size and splendour of the building overall. I want this House to be a national monument, replacing every ancient treasure lost to us. There is to be a huge pool, surrounded by dressing rooms designed in such a way that they represent a city-scape of all the great capitals of the world.' He paused to consider further aspects of his proposed Golden House. 'The anterooms are to be overlaid with gold and studded with jewels and mother-of-pearl. Famulus will be commissioned for the designs. And, for Acte, ceilings of fretted ivory in each of the dining rooms. I would like the ceiling of the main dining room to be circular, so that it might revolve day and night in time with the sky itself. Visitors will come from all over the empire to witness the wonders of modern technology and the beauty of our contemporary artists, so that, in time, all that we lost to the Fire will not be missed.'

'In time. I'm glad you said that,' Celer remarked, 'because I can't see this project being completed in less than five years.'

'I would not expect it in less,' Nero agreed, 'this is for future generations to enjoy. And to be started only when builders become available once more. We have far more important things to attend to before monuments such as The Golden House.'

Of pre-eminent importance was the arrest of those responsible for the Fire. Rumours had intensified as to its deliberate cause and, while many senators still pointed an accusing finger at their emperor, public opinion centred on the underground religious sect calling themselves Christians. Several members of the sect came forward voluntarily to claim responsibility, declaring it their intention to cleanse the city of evil and to pave the way for the return of their Messiah. These individuals readily divulged the names of others, until a large number had been rounded up and imprisoned.

'They must be put to death,' Vitellius insisted, as he sat with Nero and Senecio at dice. 'The magnitude of their crime deserves nothing less.'

'Then you agree that they are indeed the perpetrators of this crime?'

Vitellius shook his head. 'I think it was an act of the gods! But these Christians are the perpetrators of every other crime in Rome. They deserve death anyway, if only for the cowardly manner in which they so readily poured out the names of their co-conspirators!'

Nero laughed. 'But hardly a reason for condemning a man to death, Spintria?'

'Being the latest new sect in town, every known cutthroat has been quick to sign up. They are already proving a menace to society, causing all manner of public nuisance and disturbance. Good enough reason, Nero. There'll be few so quick to sign up when once you have made an example of these criminals. Burn them, Nero! Make human torches of them in the arena! That would be suitable punishment indeed!'

'Throw them to the dogs,' Senecio suggested hopefully, 'we've had no sport of that nature for many a year now. After the horrors we've endured this summer, we're deserving of some festival days and Games.'

'A few genuine gladiatorial combats,' Vitellius agreed, 'pitch them to the death against our finest swordsmen. Wrap a few in animal skins and have the wild dogs tear them apart in the arena, as Senecio suggests. And make human torches of the frailer ones, who can provide no sport.' He became quite enthusiastic, as did Senecio, and was ready to summon Patrobius to finalise arrangements.

'And if I disagree?' Nero asked.

'How can you, Nero? The senate already knows you hate it! You desecrate the public buildings and gardens of Rome to accommodate homeless rabble! You rushed to the city to watch it burn and sing songs in celebration! To veto a few days of Games would not only be a final crime against the senate, but against your rabble, too! Don't you think they want these Games as much as the rest of us? We need only to be comforted in our loss of town houses. Your rabble, as you so often tell us, have lost everything. Surely, for their sake alone, you will permit just three days of Games?'

'It would redeem you in the eyes of the senate,' Senecio pressed.

'Redeem you?' Vitellius laughed, 'They would deify you if you allowed this!'

Patrobius, when summoned, could only agree.

'The people have been deprived of true Games for too long,' he told Nero, 'how can our children learn to respect life when they are allowed to witness only fights of honour? It is only when combatants are fighting for their lives that the spectator understands the true value of life.'

Nero smiled. 'It would be pleasant to be popular, if only for a short spell!'

'Then let us fix a date for the Games!' Patrobius declared. 'Shall we say, three days?'

'Have we enough victims for longer?' Nero queried sarcastically.

'Barely enough for three days, but we must make the most of the limited opportunities you allow, my Lord!'

'Then three days holiday it is, Patrobius. I leave it all in your capable hands.'

'Official reason for death?' Patrobius asked, before leaving.

Nero considered it. 'Record them as being condemned because of illegal association potentially guilty of violence or subversiveness.'

DECEMBER A.D. 64

The Games had been predictably well received, Nero adding horse racing to the shows held in his own Gardens and mixing with the crowd in his chosen attire of a charioteer.

The building work throughout Rome advanced at a furious pace, with the enlisting of prisoners from every corner of the empire brought to Rome, and Nero took advantage of the ready availability of contractors and labourers to begin several projects of his own.

Celer and Severus were set to building a shipping canal that stretched the full one hundred and seventy-two miles from Lake Avernus to the Tiber estuary at Ostia, broad enough for two of the largest galleys in the fleet to pass.

Men were also set to work on an immense covered bath, surrounded by colonnades, that spread from Misenum to Lake Avernus. Each of the hot springs within the district of Baiae were canalised in order to feed it.

Though Nero had undertaken much of this work at his own expense, Phaon was driven to distraction by the lack of funds in the Treasury. Breaking point arrived in the shape of a naval disaster, the fleet largely destroyed as it returned to Campania for the winter. Rounding Cape Misenum, a south-westerly gale drove them ashore near Cumae and numerous warships were lost.

'We are as good as bankrupt,' Phaon told Nero in a private audience with him, shortly after his birthday. 'The building renewals have already bled us dry.'

'Then I will foot the bills personally until we receive fresh revenue.'

'Nero! You have already footed most of the bills! You have precious little money left yourself! Continued spending is not an option.'

'What other option is there? It will be at least two years before every home lost to the Fire has been replaced. I can hardly call a halt now!'

'I agree, Nero, but we need fresh resources. Current revenue is totally inadequate.'

'Well what do you suggest? I will not curb spending and now you tell me I have no money left of my own! Find some! It's your job!'

'In the name of the gods, Nero, I cannot conjure it up out of thin air! I deserve honours untold for keeping you afloat thus far! If Otho ever taught you anything it was how to spend money!'

Nero laughed desultorily. 'I need no feckless playboy to teach me that! Money has no other use but to be spent. How is the Fire Fund progressing?'

'Spent in advance; and still bleeding the provinces dry.'

'And what of our dependent nations? They would be willing to contribute towards the Fire Fund, I am sure. Send agents to collect what they can.'

'Who shall I send?'

'Well Carrinas, obviously. And I have a promising freedman in need of good office - Acratus. I had hoped to send them abroad anyway to buy artwork for The Golden House. Appoint them as my agents and send them to Greece and Asia Minor. They are to beg, steal and borrow all that they can.' He smiled grimly. 'Lives depend upon them, Phaon.'

Chapter Forty-Five

MARCH A.D. 65

'The emperor grows more dangerous by the day,' Senecio said, as he sat with the knight, Natalis, and Flavus, a colonel of the Guard, at the Circus. 'He threatens to destroy the very order of society. His slave Acratus is now an imperial agent, plundering the treasures of Greece to fill Nero's purse, while people like ourselves, of good family, are over-looked year after year for office.'

'Our opinions are not so easily bought,' Natalis pointed out, 'his slaves are pitifully grateful and unlikely to speak a word against him. Nor are they likely to seek the salary we would expect.'

'Easily bought, there you have it in a nutshell,' Flavus agreed. 'He will tolerate only those who worship the very ground he walks on and who hang on his every word!'

'They're ignorant and uneducated, ready to do whatever he suggests,' Senecio complained, 'and they are in office!' He paused to cheer home, in vain, his choice in the third race. 'I have been Nero's closest friend since childhood; yet I am left to scrape a living from my father's business.'

'Scrape a living?' Natalis raised an eyebrow, 'my friend, you will be able to buy Nero himself fairly soon! The hurricane that ravaged Campania will line your pockets handsomely!'

Senecio smiled. 'Well, yes, it is true, I admit. But the emperor's dearest friend should be a man of importance, not a merchant.'

'What price corn this week?' Flavus asked. 'You must surely be naming any figure you like with such a shortage.'

'Too much and we'll have no customers!' Senecio laughed. 'Two hundred and forty denarii, which has comfortably trebled its value. Of course, we haven't the usual quantities to sell, that's the whole point! So we're not making a vast amount.'

His companions laughed.

'You're selling as much as you ever were! It filled your warehouses all winter and was bought at last year's prices, too!' Natalis scoffed, 'don't plead poverty to us!'

'We're the ones paying your inflated prices!' Flavus reminded him.

'What would you have us do? Sell it at it's usual price until it is gone?! At least this way, the majority of our customers are priced out. Only the better families can afford it and we'll suffer no shortage ourselves. There are too many beggars on our streets as it is. A famine will thin the numbers, which is no bad thing.'

'The Fire should have cleansed the city,' Natalis agreed, 'but for Nero's intervention. It was a disgrace, the way in which he defiled our public buildings and gardens. The filth and utter dregs given shelter! I shudder even now at the thought! The man is criminally insane and has no thought for his people.'

'At least some good came of it,' Flavus pointed out, 'the Games were the best in living memory.'

'Three days of Games!' Senecio scoffed. 'Is that the best he can be credited with? He defiles the city and the Palace; he drives chariots and performs on a public stage and all that can be said in his redemption is that he put a handful of criminals spectacularly to death! You forget that we enjoyed Games of that nature a hundred times a year before his intervention - don't praise him now for a paltry three days!'

'There speaks a true friend!' Flavus jeered.

'Well, what friend has he been to me? A few country villas and a well-stocked stable - no more than any one slave in his household! That lyre-player has been given finer houses than I for his services.'

'Ah, but what exactly were his services?!' Natalis laughed.

Nero was watching the races from his box, but he, too, was distracted by the current corn shortage.

'It is fairly clear what will happen,' he told Petronius, 'the merchants will meet every ship at port and sell what little there is at an extortionate rate.'

'I know,' Petronius sighed, 'but what can one do? We must put food on the table, after all. We are simply at their mercy.'

'What of those who cannot pay the prices?'

'And what of them, Nero? In times of shortage some must starve. A cruel fact of life, I'm afraid.' Petronius looked down into the arena, attracted by the line-up for the final race of the day. 'Excuse me, Nero, but I think I shall wander out and see if I can't find an easy way to put food on the table!' He nodded his farewell and left the box.

'What do you say about it?' Nero asked Phaon.

'What? This race? I've barely seen them, Nero - you're a better judge than I.'

'No, no; the corn shortage. Exactly how bad is it?'

'Not as bad as in Claudius' time. Are you old enough to remember the time he was mobbed in the market?'

'If sensibly rationed, we would have enough?'

'It isn't that drastic, Nero. Rationing won't be necessary. The ships will be in from Egypt long before we actually run out.'

'And by paying extortionate prices, we will be ensuring a comfortable supply until that time. Those who can afford it will not go short - those who depend solely upon it will be forced to go without, so that our own supplies never actually diminish.'

Phaon looked at him. 'What, then, do you propose?'

'I propose to buy all of the corn myself. I can well afford to subsidise its price and see that it sells for less than the normal price. Everyone will go short - but no one will starve.'

Phaon laughed. 'Go ahead, beggar yourself! I don't know where you dream up these schemes but at least no sane man will ever blame your poor Financial Minister! Though they'll wonder why you ever employ one!'

'I'm serious, Phaon. Deadly serious.'

'They'll throw you in the Tiber, Nero.'

'No. They'll *want* to throw me in the Tiber. They may even call for my prosecution. But they won't do it, Phaon. I, on the other hand, will.'

'Nero,' Phaon protested in panic, 'there are merchants who have already invested their projected profits! There is far more resting on this shortage than the chance of starvation!'

'What can be more important than starvation, Phaon? Supposing you could not afford to feed your family? Would you so readily protect the poor merchants who stand to lose their investments?'

'And who will protect you?'

'Tigellinus and Rufus.'

'Tigellinus! I'd trust him no further than I could throw him.'

'He is so hated, Phaon, that his own survival depends entirely on mine. I trust him implicitly. My Mother taught me that one invaluable piece of advice.'

Nero's agents were employed to ration out the corn supplies, according to size of family. Everyone publicly commended Nero on his handling of the situation; but privately there was not a noble family who did not abhor his action. When a plague swept through Rome and devastated the population, they cited it as nature's way of amending Nero's wrongs.

A fire destroyed Lugdunum and was alleviated by an imperial gift of four million sesterces. It fell to Phaon to remind Nero that he did not have four million sesterces to give.

'It is no more than the sum they raised for us after the Great Fire,' Nero pointed out.

'But that was spent, Nero!'

'Then take it from my own purse.'

'A small matter of subsidised corn, Nero?'

'I must have some money left!'

'I struggled to bring the Treasury back in line and continually struggle to keep your own purse in order,' Phaon argued, 'but you continually over-stretch yourself.'

'Take funds from The Golden House, then.'

'There are no funds. Work is at a standstill. You cannot even afford to pay the soldiers or give the veterans their benefits - you have just handed that to Lugdunum!'

'Remove the gold and silver images of the household gods from the temples and have them melted down for coins. The Neronian Games are due for renewal this year, they'll generate enough revenue to replace them. It will be enough to tide us over, Phaon.'

'So it will, Nero, but we cannot continue in this fashion.'

'Fire, famine, plague! How many more disasters can there be?!' Nero laughed. 'I sincerely hope that we will not be continuing in such fashion, my friend!'

When once Phaon had been dismissed, he readied himself for dinner and met with Senecio and the ever-increasing members of his social circle. They made quite a group as they sat back to enjoy the after-dinner entertainment, provided by Seneca's popular nephew, Lucan, who read from his latest collection of poetry.

'He lacks your lyricism,' Petronius whispered to Nero, 'yet he repeatedly veers toward the subjects you favour. He would do well to find his own niche and avoid comparison.'

'I prefer Lucilius,' Senecio remarked, 'I don't personally like this love affair with all things ancient.'

'Seneca is writing a book of natural history, did I tell you?' Nero said, as a matter of interest, 'he retired from Rome because of pressure of work and is now under even greater pressure to complete some five volumes, so he believes!'

'And is it near completion?' Senecio asked.

'I have no idea, he speaks with me rarely these days. The book, I imagine, takes up all his time.' He saw that Lucan was about to take his seat once more and called out to him. 'Has Seneca finished his Natural History yet?'

Lucan looked wounded. 'I believe so, yes,' he replied stiffly.

Petronius grinned. 'You have much to learn about poets, my boy,' he scolded Nero, 'when they have stood before you for an hour, reciting their work, it is not the done thing to respond with a question about another author. A simple 'well done' would have been a little less hurtful!'

Nero smiled. 'Had his poetry been better, we would not have been distracted by his uncle's pastimes!'

The dinner party soon broke up and the guests travelling home began to make arrangements to share carriages.

Senecio found himself offering a seat in his own coach to Lucan and took great delight in repeating Nero's cutting comments to him. They apparently came as no surprise to the poet.

'He despises me as a rival,' Lucan complained, 'I shall never gain recognition while he makes such a habit of stealing my pet subjects.'

'He despises us all,' Senecio said bitterly, 'don't think that you are any exception.'

'He showed that last year,' Lucan agreed. 'We had such a summer! One social round after another. It was a pure delight to escape the confines of Rome. Yet Nero snubbed us all. Granted, many of the country villas were some way short of the luxury of a town house, but even so! - the man dwelt under canvas with peasants in preference! I was not alone in taking it as a personal insult.'

'You're still smarting over last summer?' Senecio complained. 'There are others at Rome who have far more recent grievances. My father stood to gain a fortune from the corn shortage. Nero robbed him of every penny.'

'The famine should have wiped out the beggars on the street, but instead they were left to struggle on. Now they have infected us all with their filthy plague. The plague is no respecter of class. It claims the likes of you and me just as readily as the scum who should have been eradicated by famine. Nero has upset the balance of nature, not just society.'

'We were only discussing the same thing yesterday!' Senecio declared, happy to have found a new soul mate. 'How his meddling has made him a public danger. Piso is refined and eloquent - many of us are of the opinion that he would make a perfect emperor.' 'Calpurnius Piso? I know him well! Ah, yes, he is a man of impressive stature indeed and high morals! I would back him any day against Nero.'

'Perhaps you would like to meet with a few of my friends?' Senecio asked eagerly, 'we like to sit in taverns and right the wrongs of this world! You would be a welcome addition to our group.'

'I'm staying with Piso himself at Baiae at the weekend - fetch your friends along.'

'Several of us are already under invitation,' Senecio thanked him, 'it will make quite an interesting house party!'

APRIL A.D. 65

Lucan had for long been in the habit of meeting privately with Flavus, a colonel of the Guard, and Asper, a company-commander; together with one or two other loyal friends. On this occasion he wasted no time in calling them all together, anxious to impart the information he had gained from Senecio.

'We have a replacement!' he declared triumphantly, 'it's a wonder we hadn't looked to him sooner - Piso.'

'In point of disgrace,' Flavus objected, 'it makes little difference to remove a lyre-player and replace him by a performer in tragedies. I would put forward Annaeus Seneca.'

'A very respected figure,' Lateranus agreed, 'but would he agree to join us?'

'Rumour has it that Nero has more or less banished him from Rome. He hides in the country, in fear of his life.'

'Piso is more certain to join us,' Lucan informed them, 'I understand that he is open to persuasion.'

'Most men are open to persuasion!' Scaevinus pointed out, 'but does he have the courage to carry it through?'

'Everyone loathes Nero,' Afranius, the other member of their group, spoke up, 'what courage does it take to rebel? We'll have the whole of Rome behind us!'

'We don't have the Guard,' Asper reminded them.

Flavus smiled. 'Oh, but we might, Asper. I have been speaking with Rufus - carefully, of course - but I think he would join us, if asked.'

'Rufus?!'

'He fears for his life,' Flavus continued, 'Tigellinus blackens his name at every opportunity. He believes it to be no more than a matter of time before he is accused of a crime and is forced to take his own life.'

'A great many noblemen have chosen to take their own life,' Afranius said, 'since Tigellinus came to power!'

'That is the whole point,' Flavus agreed, 'we did not choose Tigellinus as 'emperor' any more than we chose that degenerate Nero. With Rufus behind us, we can keep the Guard - and our heads with them!'

'Natalis is a close friend of Senecio,' Lucan stepped in, 'and is also the trusted confidante of Piso. The person we actually need to enlist is Senecio. He will bring with him both Piso and Natalis. I met with his friends at Baiae, and they include no less than six knights who already embrace treason: Natalis himself, of course; Proculus; Araricus; Augurinus; Gratus and Festus. How can we find an accomplice closer to the emperor than Senecio?! And bringing with him enough names to sway Rufus!'

'The plot is hatched, then?' Flavus said simply.

Lucan smiled. 'The plot is indeed hatched.'

Chapter Forty-Six

APRIL A.D. 65

The conspirators were happy to continue meeting regularly and discuss the many ideal opportunities to murder their emperor. They were less happy to agree on an actual time and place for the crime. Flavus remained unconvinced of Piso's suitability and met secretly with Natalis, in an attempt to win over Seneca. Natalis agreed to visit Seneca and attempt to enlist him.

Senecio had been easily recruited, bringing with him the promised support. Flavus and Asper had first recruited two colonels of the Guard, Silvanus and Proxumus, and had then been joined by two company-commanders, Scaurus and Paulus. This was more than enough to tempt Rufus, who joined them without qualms. As a result, the conspirators now numbered eighteen and it was becoming increasingly difficult to find convenient and discreet meeting places.

Epicharis, a freedwoman living beside Proculus, was quick to pick up on the clandestine meetings and had soon contrived a place in the group. She at once grew impatient with their cowardice and urged them to act.

'You've been plotting for at least six weeks, that I'm aware of!' she complained, 'when will just one of you be man enough to name a date?!'

'It is not something that can be rushed,' Lucan told her.

'Then you'll simply wait for others to uncover your plot, as I did.'

'It isn't a matter of merely killing the emperor,' Flavus tried to explain, in their defence, 'we must also survive the attack ourselves. We need to depose the emperor's men and replace them with those of our choosing. Any madman could rush up and stab Nero. But that would serve no purpose at all.'

'You've had long enough to plan it now,' Epicharis criticised, 'why don't you enlist the Fleet? I'm going to Neapolis next week, I'd be more than willing to sound them out for you.'

'Don't be mad, woman!' Lucan snapped, 'You'll have us all condemned!'

'Why? The loyalty at Misenum is questionable. Didn't Octavia manage to win over Anicetus.'

'And he betrayed her,' Flavus reminded her.

'Perhaps she picked the wrong man.'

'Leave well alone, Epicharis,' Lucan warned.

But Epicharis could not leave it alone. While in Campania she visited Misenum and made an attempt to implicate the naval officers. Few would hear any word spoken against Nero, but Rear-Admiral Volusius sided with her in her complaints against the emperor.

'I did more than Anicetus in the plot against Agrippina,' he told her, 'but I received no thanks from Nero. Anicetus drew up the designs, but I had to implement the whole scheme - ensure the co-operation of the oarsmen; keep the tongues of the ship-builders from wagging. Anicetus did well out of Agrippina's death. I didn't even get a thank you. That's the emperor I know - not this mythical philanthropist the men here are so keen to praise.'

'You should be at Rome more often,' Epicharis said, 'your tale of woe pales in comparison to the stories of most. I know of a group who even plot to depose him, so strong are their feelings against him. I was thinking of joining them myself. Would you be interested?'

Volusius was taken aback. 'I hadn't thought quite that far.'

'You've not yet had cause to,' she pressed. 'But with Tigellinus running the show, mere ingratitude could be the least of your worries. We could do with men of your stature in our little club.'

'And who is in your club?' he asked carefully.

'To be frank, I wouldn't know,' Epicharis lied, 'we never exchange names. But they are men of influence, certainly. This is no ill-thought up scheme.'

'Soldiers? Officers?'

Epicharis shrugged. 'I honestly don't know. I imagine some of them must be, simply because of the suggestions they make.'

Volusius smiled. 'My dear lady, I am not so foolish as to enter into a conspiracy without first learning the names of my co-conspirators! You could be an agent of Nero's, for all I know, sent to trick me!'

'I can't prove otherwise. But it's a risk the others have all been willing to take.'

Volusius shook his head. 'No, madam. My small complaint is not worth such a risk. But I wish you well, all the same.' He bowed to her politely and went about his business.

When Epicharis had left Misenum, Volusius immediately made plans to see Nero, who was staying with Acte in Puteoli. He was granted an audience that same evening.

'What may I do for you, Admiral?' Nero asked.

'I believe I have information of a conspiracy against you, Nero.'

Nero at once summoned Tigellinus.

'Names and addresses?' the Commander demanded.

'I'm afraid I have none,' Volusius admitted. 'A freedwoman calling herself Epicharis approached my men and aired a few minor complaints against you, Nero. I can truthfully say that most of my men turned their backs on her. But I was interested in what she had to say and confessed to a few grievances myself. She told me of a conspiracy and invited me to join. But even when I refused to join without names, she refused to give them. She hinted that they included officers of the Guard.'

'Go with Tigellinus, find this woman and bring her before me,' Nero ordered, 'we'll see what truth there is in her tale.'

Epicharis proved easy to trace, having made herself well known to the sailors at Misenum. She seemed unconcerned at facing the emperor.

'I have it on good authority that you know details of a conspiracy,' Nero confronted her, 'tell me the names of all those involved and I shall see that you are handsomely rewarded.'

Epicharis laughed. 'Who told you that?! I don't know anything about conspiracies!'

'I happen to have been told otherwise.'

'Then your source is not the good authority you think!' She paused to consider. 'It wasn't that stuffy admiral, was it? I don't remember his name, but he got so excited when I was having a bit of a moan about you with some of the sailors. You know the sort of thing, not enough pay, no Games, all the usual gripes. I said you should be deposed and I knew some people who'd do the job. All a big joke, of course, but he didn't see the funny side of it. I didn't think he'd take it this seriously, though!'

Nero looked at her assessingly.

'A misunderstanding, then?'

She laughed at the understatement. 'I should say so! Here I am, nearly condemned for treason, because of some silly facetious remark! He's not too bright, is he, your Admiral of the Fleet?'

'Perhaps not,' Nero agreed mildly, 'but neither are your manners very desirable. We all have our faults.' He looked to Tigellinus. 'Both stories are convincing, Commander; but only one is dangerous to ignore. Detain Epicharis in custody.'

By the end of the month, Nero had more on his mind than the conspiracy. Even the delay of a few days in Poppaea's cycle raised their hearts in hope, only to be repeatedly quashed. This time she was already a week late and neither could concentrate on anything else.

'It is far too soon to be certain,' Poppaea tried to caution him, 'I have got this far too many times now to recall.'

'Then for goodness sake retire to your bed!' Nero insisted. 'Time and again you claim false alarms, but never once do you rest and do anything to save our child!'

'What child?!' Poppaea snapped angrily. 'How many other women retreat to their beds on a monthly basis?! There may not be any child - don't you dare accuse me of murder without even a victim!'

'How many more victims do you need before you start to take better care?!' Nero fought back, 'What does it take to remain in bed for a few weeks?'

'You remain in bed for a few weeks! See how you like it!' Poppaea stormed.

She fetched him a smart slap across his shoulder in frustration and walked out. His companions grinned.

'Does this mean we must suffer her time of the month for the next nine?!' Epaphroditus enquired. 'I may hand in my resignation now!'

'She'll come round,' Sporus assured them both, 'she always does. One moment she has her hands tightly about his throat, the next they have dropped to a considerably lower location!'

Epaphroditus laughed. 'There were never such domestic disturbances when Octavia was your wife!'

'Never such enjoyment or pleasure, either,' Nero smiled.

They were interrupted by a slave, who brought word that someone sought audience with Nero. Epaphroditus went off to check the rights of the claimant and Sporus took the dogs out, leaving Nero alone with whatever business of the day now presented itself.

At Piso's villa in Baiae, a hasty meeting of conspirators was convened. News had now reached all members of the arrest of Epicharis and they gathered anxiously in Piso's private rooms.

'We have no choice but to act immediately,' Rufus urged, 'Epicharis will betray us at any moment. We can no longer even think in terms of days.'

'Has she been charged or interrogated?' Lucan asked.

'I don't know,' Rufus confessed miserably, 'Tigellinus maintains silence on the subject, which can only mean that he suspects his own men. He will not even confide in me.'

'Then we must bring this to an immediate close,' Lucan insisted. 'Piso, invite Nero here. He always visits you alone and unarmed. It would be a perfect opportunity for us.'

'I can't be so directly involved!' Piso protested in alarm. 'Nero has a good many sympathisers and there are any number of men they could choose to take my place! His replacement is to be innocent in this crime - I would have thought that went without saying.'

'It's true,' Rufus agreed, 'the Guards alone would refuse to accept anyone who played a part in this, never mind Nero's sympathisers.'

'Well, where, then?' Lucan demanded.

'The Circus,' Senecio suggested. 'Nero generally escapes his escort and we can confront him when he is alone.'

'And if he draws his sword?' Rufus enquired. 'I know that I cannot claim to be any match for him. Who among us would be prepared to take him on?'

There was a general murmur of refusals.

'Then we must first distract him,' Lucan recommended, 'take him by the arm to go and look at horses, Senecio, while someone stabs him in the back.'

'I've already done my part,' Senecio insisted, 'I have brought support and a party leader. I need do no more.'

'Natalis, then. You can engage him in conversation.'

'Lateranus is always looking to him for handouts,' Natalis said in response, 'let him prostrate himself at Nero's feet and beg for assistance. The scene will cause such commotion, not even the crowd around us will see who commits the crime itself.'

'An excellent idea!' all bar Lateranus agreed.

Lateranus himself aired his doubts. 'I usually catch him alone and request a small purse.'

'And has he ever refused you?'

'No. Although he barely gave me enough to cover my debts last time. He claimed he had little money himself!'

'Well, there's your excuse!' Lucan declared, 'Beg him for his full mercy, let him know that he failed you on the previous occasion. Kiss his feet or some such gesture, so that he might bend down to you. Scaevinus can then rush up and stab him, then disappear into the crowd unseen. No one will even suspect a plot!'

'Why me?!' Scaevinus protested. 'The Guards will remove the dagger and identify it as mine! I refuse to be the martyr for your cause!'

'Steal a dagger from a temple,' Lucan told him, 'it will only add to the theory that it was merely an attack by some racegoer - which, incidentally, is exactly why I chose you.'

'And what is that supposed to imply?'

'That you have very plain and ordinary features. You would never be identified.'

'The same must go for any one of us,' Scaevinus argued.

'It doesn't. And someone must do the deed. If we sit here trying to choose a man, we'll be here all night. And, if I might say so Scaevinus, you are the only one among us who can be depended upon to keep his head in times of crisis. So, is everyone in favour of this proposal?'

Every hand rose; including that of Scaevinus, albeit late and with obvious reluctance.

'May I just add that Piso should wait at the temple of Ceres,' Rufus suggested, 'and from there I shall collect him and take him to the Guards Camp to be declared emperor.'

'Then the matter is settled. Next race day in Rome, Nero meets his death.'

The day before the races, Scaevinus met with Natalis and together they stole a dagger. Scaevinus then returned home and wrote his will, giving the dagger to his freedman, Milichus, to sharpen. Convinced that he would meet his death the following day, he threw a lavish party for his household and freed his favourite slaves. To the others he gave large presents of money. Before retiring to bed he took the added precaution of asking Milichus to prepare bandages for wounds. Satisfied that his affairs were in order, he settled back for a fitful night.

Milichus was puzzled by his behaviour.

'Don't worry about it,' his colleagues advised, 'the emperor has probably found out about all these secret meetings he keeps hosting and Tigellinus will be here on the morrow to enforce his suicide!'

'Our master take his own life?' Milichus scoffed, 'He is too much of a coward! But you have a good point about the meetings. What could they have been about?'

He passed a fitful night himself, pre-occupied by the odd behaviour of his patron and the possible implications of the meetings. It occurred to him that the one thing connecting the group of friends who often called was that they all detested the emperor he so loved. A sudden fear chilled him and he rose at first light to seek an audience with the emperor.

He had never been in the area of Nero's mansion, in the Servilian Gardens, and it took him a good while to locate an entrance. Even then, the officiousness of the guards almost caused him to give up on his mission and return home.

'I must see the emperor!' he begged; a plea which met with nothing but derision.

'Let me at least speak to one of the Guard,' he pleaded desperately, ready to give up. But a young company-commander overheard him and came across to see him.

'What is your problem?'

'I believe there is a plot against the emperor!'

'And what gives you that idea? Did your master dock you a few sesterces pay and now you feel the need to accuse him of treason?'

'I have no proof,' Milichus responded, ignoring the insult, 'but I feel that if the emperor hears me he would know if I was right to suspect a plot. I'm a freedman from the house of Scaevinus. Please let me see him.'

The officer called a slave and sent him to fetch Epaphroditus. The imperial secretary listened to Milichus' story with interest and considered it to be worth an audience.

Within an hour, Milichus stood before Nero and presented him with the dagger he had been asked to sharpen.

Nero shrank from it.

'Does it belong to Scaevinus?' he asked.

'I had never seen it before yesterday, my Lord.'

'Have you ever seen one like it?' Nero pressed.

'I've seen such daggers in temples, my Lord, but Scaevinus does not collect such things.'

'Umm.' Nero turned to a slave. 'Have the Commander Rufus take a company and search the temples. He is to report back if he finds a dagger missing.' He returned his attention to Milichus. 'What is unusual about Scaevinus throwing a party to free his best slaves?'

Milichus was nonplussed.

'Why did it arouse suspicion?' Nero pressed.

'Well... he would not normally dream of throwing such a party. We've never received gifts from him. The only freedmen in his household have worked hard to buy their freedom.'

Nero sat back, considering. 'He plans suicide, do you think?'

'No. I don't believe him capable, my Lord. I grew up with him. I believe he intends to commit murder, my Lord, and he has been meeting with men I know to despise you.'

'Can you name them?'

'They meet privately, my Lord, but I've seen them in the market and overheard their complaints. I would know most of them by sight.'

'Thank you Milichus, you have been of great help. Who knows? You may even have saved my life!' Nero turned to Epaphroditus. 'Take Milichus to Phaon and see that he is well rewarded. Then have the soldiers sent to arrest Scaevinus.'

Scaevinus was fetched before Nero almost immediately, but managed to remain calm and composed. In his own mind he was secure in the knowledge that he had not committed any crime, least of all murder.

'The weapon concerned in this charge is a venerated heirloom kept in my bedroom,' he told Nero in response to the accusations, 'This ex-slave Milichus has stolen it. As to my will, I have often signed new clauses without particularly noting the date. I have given slaves their freedom and money-gifts before. This time the scale was larger because, with reduced means and pressing creditors, I feared my will would be rejected. My table has always been generous, my life comfortable - too comfortable for austere critics. Bandages for wounds I did not order. But the man's allegations of patent untruths are so unconvincing that he has added this charge merely because it rests wholly on his own evidence.'

Nero found it hard to disbelieve him in the face of such composure.

'He does not strike me as a man guilty of treason,' he said quietly to Epaphroditus, 'I begin to think that we were a little hasty in listening to Milichus. Fetch him back and this time let us switch the charges.'

Milichus returned and stood uncomfortably beside Scaevinus.

'I shall be frank with you, Milichus,' Nero told him, 'I seriously doubt your earlier statement. Is there anything at all that you can remember that might back your allegations? Think very carefully.'

Milichus' nerves betrayed him. He began to repeat his story, stammering nervously, while Scaevinus stood smugly beside him.

'We know the allegations,' Nero reminded Milichus impatiently, 'I simply ask you now for a little extra evidence. Perhaps something you have omitted? The names of those you say met with Scaevinus?'

Milichus struggled desperately to picture the faces of those who had so regularly visited the house. Scaevinus gloated unashamedly, sharing glances with Nero that suggested they both felt the accusations were beneath their contempt.

'Antonius Natalis!' Milichus suddenly exclaimed, his immense relief obvious, 'Natalis! I have seen him in the seats reserved for knights at the Circus and I have heard him introducing himself at the market.'

'Natalis is a friend of mine, of course the man knows him!' Scaevinus smirked.

'Nevertheless, it is only fair to question him,' Nero said mildly. 'Have him brought in.' He signalled to the company-commander present and took him to one side. 'I want both Natalis and Scaevinus questioned about their last conversation - they are not to meet and are to be questioned separately.'

It proved the decisive factor.

The discrepancy between their replies aroused immediate suspicion and they were put in chains at once. At the threat of torture they broke down and confessed all. Natalis broke first and denounced Piso. To Nero's horror he also denounced Seneca, but was so vague in his details that Nero suspected him of naming Seneca for no better reason than spite.

When told of Natalis' confession, Scaevinus named several more conspirators. The names cut through Nero more searingly than the dagger could ever have done.

'Fetch them all in,' he said grimly, 'with the obvious exception of Seneca. He isn't even at Rome.'

Most of the conspirators broke down upon arrest and begged for Nero's mercy. Only Lucan, Afranius and Senecio steadfastly refused to incriminate themselves.

'You were not named out of spite,' Nero told them bitterly, 'and your refusal to admit to your guilt only lowers you still further in my eyes. Afranius, perhaps occasionally I have been rude about you in my poems. But we share the same vices, how can you take my insults so personally? And Lucan, I can think of no reason why you should now stand before me. What did I do to you which could warrant my death?' He met Senecio's eye. 'What can I say?'

'I am innocent.'

'Too many of your friends say you are guilty. If you would only admit the truth it would go some way in redeeming you in my eyes. You owe me that much, Senecio.'

Senecio's shame betrayed his guilt. He avoided Nero's eyes.

'If I were to grant you impunity in exchange for names?' Nero suggested.

'And if we refuse it?' Senecio asked.

'Death.'

All three confessed. Senecio denounced two of his closest friends; Lucan denounced his mother, who had done no more than offer her home for their meetings. Nero chose not to act on their information and left those named by them unharmed.

After the long and draining day, he could hardly contemplate bed.

'Conspiracy I can understand,' he told Epaphroditus wearily, 'but the involvement of my own friends? Senecio and I went riding together only the day before yesterday. I told him that Poppaea might be pregnant. I've told no one else, until now. And he already knew that I was to die.' A sudden memory came to him. 'Do you remember, at Puteoli? Volusius accused Epicharis of enlisting sailors for a conspiracy? Could there be a connection, do you think?' His mind already raced ahead of his words. 'Piso! He claimed she named Piso as my replacement - and he is a close friend of Natalis! Quick! Summon Rufus or Tigellinus and have her fetched up to Rome and interrogated!'

Epicharis maintained her innocence under the most severe interrogation. Knowing her to be lying, Nero ordered her to be tortured, assuming that she would break at once. But in shielding virtual strangers she showed the immense courage that her fellow conspirators had lacked. Neither the lash not branding could weaken her denials. On only the second day her limbs could no longer support her and she was taken from her cell by chair. On the way, she tore off her breast band, fastened it in a noose to the canopy of the chair and strangled herself.

Chapter Forty-Seven

MAY A.D. 65

Nero redoubled his guard, while troops manned the city walls and blockaded the city by sea and river. The public squares of even neighbouring towns and districts were invaded by infantry and cavalry. Principle among them at Rome were Germans, who Nero particularly trusted.

Those accused of conspiracy were dragged in chains to the Servilian Gardens, where they were interrogated fiercely by Nero and his two commanders. As though to disguise his own guilt, Rufus was particularly savage in his attacks on the accused, but amazingly no one yet denounced him. Just as bad was Flavus, who was among those soldiers standing by. In this manner the trials began.

Wary of old soldiers, Nero selected new or recent recruits to work under him as executioners. Lateranus, who had been elected to serve the next consulship, was first to die. As he faced his accusers, Flavus signalled to Rufus that he would cut Nero down. Rufus shook his head frantically, as Flavus' hand went for his sword, and the incident passed unnoticed by all except Lateranus. He said nothing to betray them. Taken to the spot reserved for the execution of slaves, Lateranus was dispatched by the Guard Colonel Proxumus and died without divulging Proxumus' equal guilt.

Next to face trial was Scaevinus. Rufus' fear of betrayal increased his brutality and he pressed Scaevinus all the more savagely.

'But no one is better informed than yourself,' Scaevinus sneered, 'you should demonstrate your gratitude voluntarily to your excellent emperor.'

If words failed Rufus, then so too did silence. A stammering utterance betrayed his terror and he was immediately seized and bound. He was executed soon after Scaevinus.

Proculus now came before them and showed no hesitation in denouncing Flavus. For his information he received a pardon.

'You have stood alongside me, interrogating your fellow conspirators,' Nero said in disgust, 'what reason can you give for forgetting your military oath?'

'Because I detest you! I was as loyal as any of your soldiers as long as you deserved affection. I began detesting you when you murdered your mother and wife and became charioteer, actor and incendiary!'

Nero turned away from him, sickened by his words.

Colonel Niger was detailed to execute Flavus and ordered a grave to be dug in a field nearby.

'I hope that isn't intended for me?' Flavus objected, 'it's far too shallow and narrow.' He looked across at the soldiers present. 'More bad discipline,' he remarked.

'Offer your neck firmly!' Niger instructed him impatiently.

'You strike equally firmly!'

But Niger only just managed to sever his head with two blows.

Nero had next to deal with the statement from Natalis and the implication of Seneca. Natalis swore that he had recruited him during a visit and the Colonel of the Guard, Silvanus, was sent to Seneca to convey this report. He returned with a statement from Seneca, which he read to Nero in the presence of Poppaea and Tigellinus.

"Natalis was sent to me to protest, on Piso's behalf, because I would not let him visit me. I answered excusing myself on grounds of health and love of quiet. I could have no reason to value any private person's welfare above my own. Nor am I a flatterer. Nero knows this exceptionally well. He has had more frankness than servility from Seneca!"

'He lies,' Nero said quietly, as though to himself.

'How do you know?' Poppaea asked.

'Because Natalis has already given a report of their conversation. Why did he not simply say that Natalis sought support and was denied?'

'He would never plot against you, never!'

'I know that. But I cannot understand this response.' He turned to Silvanus. 'Did you notice any fear or sorrow in his words or features?' he asked him.

'I'm not sure, my Lord.'

'He is always prone to melancholy,' Nero said softly. 'Go back to him, Silvanus, and find out if he is preparing for suicide.'

'Yes, my Lord.'

Seneca's death was lingering. He and Paulina cut their arms together, but his blood failed to flow freely enough. He took hemlock, but his limbs were too cold and numbed for it to take affect. Instead he plunged himself into a vapour bath and suffocated. Word had already reached Nero, by runner, and the distraught emperor ordered that Paulina be saved. Slaves bound her arms and tended her, until she was out of danger.

Messalina's husband, Vestinus, was next to die. He had been cited by several of the conspirators, but no accuser had come forward against him.

'Silvanus, take a battalion of the Guard, seize his citadel and over power his picked young followers!' Nero ordered, with reference to the handsome young slaves Vestinus kept in his house over-looking the Forum.

Vestinus was giving a dinner party when the soldiers entered, but immediately shut himself in his bedroom and took his own life.

One by one the remaining conspirators met their fate. Lucan, despite having been granted impunity, cut his veins; Silvanus, who had himself enforced the deaths of his fellow conspirators, was acquitted, but committed suicide. Proxumus, too, took his own life, only hours before he would have received news of his pardon. Natalis was pardoned for his prompt information and the remaining conspirators were exiled.

There followed thank-offerings on the Capitol and every home in Rome was decorated with laurel. People threw themselves at Nero's feet and kissed his hands incessantly whenever he appeared in public. He addressed the Guard and presented each man with two thousand sesterces and the right to free corn. He then awarded honorary Triumphs to the ex-consul Turpilianus, the young praetor-designate Nerva, and to Tigellinus. In gratitude to their loyalty, both Nerva and Tigellinus were awarded statues in the Palace, as well as triumphal effigies in the Forum. An honorary consulship was bestowed on Nymphidius, who replaced Rufus as joint-commander of the Guard.

In addition, the Circus Games of Ceres were enlarged by extra horse races. Nero dedicated the fateful dagger on the Capitol, to Jupiter the Avenger. Then followed the usual sycophantic proposals from the senate, in particular that the month of April be renamed Neroneus, that a temple of Welfare be built and that a temple be erected to the Divine Nero, a proposal vetoed by Nero himself.

MAY A.D. 65

Unnerved by the plot, Nero allowed several race days to go by without his attendance, but this only increased his enthusiasm when he did return to the Circus. He kept habitually late hours, incurring the physical wrath of Poppaea whenever he returned.

'It's your own fault,' Phaon told him, 'you have increased the number of races in a day to a ridiculous level. Team managers will no longer bring their teams out unless it is well worth their while. Poppaea is not the only abandoned wife in Rome on Circus days!'

'Well I'm certainly not going to linger in the Palace, watching her abuse our unborn child,' Nero complained. 'Time and again I have warned her to take better care of herself, but instead she indulges in full scale boxing matches with me whenever I do or say the wrong thing.'

'In all honesty, Nero, you deserve it. Leave her be, she knows what's best for her. You cannot even be certain that she is expecting yet! And all these arguments are doing more harm than any of her own activities. One moment you're ordering her to remain in bed, the next the pair of you are fighting like cat and dog! Fists flying, kicks aimed with vicious intent...'

'You need tell me?' Nero said ruefully, still painfully aware of those that had made contact, 'but it is well worth the results!'

Phaon grinned. 'Yes, we hear those, too! I sometimes think the pair of you deserve each other!'

'You didn't come here to lecture me on domestic violence,' Nero reminded him, 'exactly how do we stand financially?'

'We plug along, Nero. Providing you don't over-do your usual extravagance, we will have a reasonable year. You gave far too much to Milichus from your own purse...'

'What you gave him was an insult!'

'Well, from both of us he eventually did very nicely! These gifts must stop, Nero. Your private funds are quickly exhausted and not so easily replenished. None of your friends and acquaintances are short of houses or horses. I feel it is safe to suggest calling a halt to additional bestowals of such gifts! Unless you increase the number of days in a year, they will hardly have use of further villas anyway!'

Nero smiled. 'You exaggerate unmercifully, Phaon, but I do get your point. The Games this summer will bring in a rich revenue and by next year it should be business as usual. The Golden House progresses well and should be completed within three years. The new Palace is almost ready to move in to and Rome itself is beginning to look less of a building site and more of a city. However much we over stretched ourselves, we are now at least reaping the benefits.'

Epaphroditus entered and apologised for interrupting them.

'A man by the name of Bassus is seeking audience with you, Nero. He has travelled from Carthage to see you and has bribed his way this far. I felt he deserved some response, after going to such lengths. He refuses to state his business, but insists it is of great national importance.'

Nero sighed. 'Send him in.'

The Carthagian was fetched in and stood nervously before the emperor and his companions.

'My Lord, my Lady,' he bowed respectfully, believing Sporus to be Poppaea, 'I have found a great treasure. No one but the emperor has the wealth and resources to excavate it, but if you are willing to supply the men then I am willing to lead you to the exact spot where it lies.'

'Exactly how great is this treasure?' Nero asked in interest. 'If it is worth such manpower, how is it that it has not been taken sooner?'

'I stumbled upon it quite by chance, my Lord. My mule broke loose and I wandered into a remote area in search of him. It is on my own land, so has never been explored freely. I chanced upon a land slippage and found that it led to an immense cave. The cave was far too deep for me to safely enter on my own, but I could quite clearly see that it was filled with ancient unworked gold bullion. When I returned to the spot with tools, earth movement had filled it in.'

'But this is quite incredible!' Nero exclaimed, 'How did this treasure come to be there?'

'I have a theory,' Bassus explained, 'that it is the treasure of the Phoenician Queen Dido, hidden after her flight from Troy, when she founded Carthage. The entire cave is filled with giant ingots, standing upright like columns.'

'I know the legend,' Nero confirmed, 'she was afraid that too much wealth would corrupt her young nation and that the hostile kings of Numidia might go to war to steal it.'

'Then you also know the vastness of this treasure. And I know its exact location.'

Nero looked at Phaon.

'The answer to our prayers,' Phaon said quietly, 'give him all the backing he requires.'

Nero at once made arrangements to recover the treasure. Warships were allocated with picked rowers to speed the journey and soldiers were assigned to the task of excavation.

The whole of Rome was soon in a state of great excitement, conversation everywhere was of the treasure. Nero's excessive generosity increased and he persisted in giving a variety of free distributions to the commons.

'All of our existing sources have been squandered,' Phaon warned, 'if the soldiers do not excavate the treasure quickly we will be in financial ruin. You must stop these excesses until the gold is fetched back from Carthage.'

Meanwhile in Carthage Bassus had set the soldiers to work, digging vast areas of land without success. After a period of several weeks they grew disgruntled and it began to be apparent that there was no treasure.

'What exactly is going on here?' Nymphidius demanded of Bassus, as he tried to oversee the project while Bassus picked fresh locations daily.

'I know it's here,' Bassus argued, 'I just can't identify the exact spot.'

'We have dug in fields and rough ground, beside streams and beside hills,' Nymphidius pointed out, 'we've dug to the east of your house and now you send us to the west. There is a limit to how vague your memory can be! Tell me the truth, Bassus - is this story pure invention?'

'No, I swear!' Bassus protested.

'Then tell me where you found this treasure and put a stop to this ridiculous wild goose chase!'

Bassus hung his head in shame. 'I didn't actually find it,' he was forced to admit, 'I had a dream which revealed the cave and all its treasures.'

'A *dream*?!' Nymphidius repeated incredulously. 'We have come all this way because you had a *dream*?!'

'I often have dreams,' Bassus said frantically, 'ask anyone in the neighbourhood, I'm renowned for my gift. They never fail to come true, never!'

'Except this time!'

'You give up too soon!'

'We have dug over every square inch of your land! Short of digging up the whole of Carthage, when would you suggest we call a halt?!'

Bassus fell to his knees. 'I have always been right in the past,' he wept, 'I was so certain I was doing a good deed. You must have mercy on me, I beg of you!'

The commander sneered. 'Ask my men to have mercy! I will only ask them to arrest you!'

When word reached Nero, he ordered that Bassus be released.

'He meant well,' he told Phaon, 'but we shall confiscate his entire estate, in compensation for the lack of promised treasure. That is punishment enough.'

'It is not compensation enough,' Phaon said realistically, 'we have been faced with bankruptcy before. This time there is no way out.'

'What can we do?'

'Resort to the old methods - treason trials, seizing the estates of those who fail to name the emperor in their will, raising taxes.'

'Those are the very things I have struggled to stamp out!'

'Those are the very things that kept your predecessors going.'

'I refuse to raise taxes. As to treason trials and wills, such laws are insignificant to most. Most of my people do not have enough money to worry about wills or being accused of treason.' The bitterness in his tone was plain.

'So then it is agreed?'

'It will have to be, won't it, Phaon?'

Discussing it later with Poppaea and Sporus, Nero consoled himself with the fact that his victims were more than deserving.

'They need only leave me a small percentage of their estates and if they have any sense they would already have given away fortunes to their chosen recipients before their deaths. The sums involved mean nothing to them.'

'And treason trials?' Poppaea asked. 'All of Rome lives in fear of their neighbour. The accuser gets half the estate while you get the other! Soon everyone will turn accuser! There'll be no one left to accuse!'

'The case must first be proven,' Nero reminded her. 'If the accuser is found guilty of bringing false charges against the accused, it will be he who loses his estate.'

'And what do you care?' Poppaea remarked, 'Either way you win.'

'And why should I care?' Nero retorted, 'What do I owe any of them?'

'There were little more than a dozen who conspired against you.'

'And a little more than nine hundred ready to back them.'

'Some of your friends are senators,' Poppaea reminded him gently.

He looked at her. 'And some of my friends were conspirators.'

The following day, when it fell upon him to appoint a new magistrate, the full enormity of the situation overwhelmed him.

'You know my needs,' he told him simply, 'let us see to it that nobody is left with anything.'

And as the appointment ended and the magistrate was shown out, Nero realised with pain that he felt no guilt. The enthusiasm and ideals he had fetched with him to office already seemed a lifetime away.

Chapter Forty-Eight

JUNE A.D. 65

With the Neronian Games fast approaching, Nero concentrated all his energies on constant rehearsals. Whenever a Greek city held Games, the sponsors made a point of presenting him with an honorary prize for lyre-playing. He in turn made sure that the delegates were given the earliest audience of the day and took great pleasure in inviting them to private dinners.

Just such a group were his guests that evening and, as usual, they begged him to sing for them after their meal.

'With pleasure!' he consented, 'The Greeks alone are worthy of my efforts, they really listen to music!'

He sang one of his own compositions to rapturous applause, which increased his confidence for the forthcoming competitions. He stepped carefully over Palamedes to return to his couch and reclined once more beside Sporus.

'Fine dogs,' Theophrastus, one of the delegates, remarked. 'I keep Salukis at home. Your own two seem less energetic!'

'They were very energetic once upon a time,' Nero laughed, 'but Palamedes here is a little stiff in his legs and it is easier to step over him than wait for him to move! Mysticus is sulking under the couch because I scolded him earlier for stealing food from a plate. Something he hasn't done since he was a puppy, which perhaps speaks volumes for the chef!'

'And the Augusta? We have missed her this evening,' Theophrastus asked.

'She is ill, I'm afraid, and cannot join us. But she sends you her regards, as always.'

'I'm sorry to hear that. Nothing serious, I hope?'

Nero smiled proudly. 'She is expecting a child in the New Year. We haven't even had time to make a public announcement, so you are among the first to know. But this time it is very hard on her. She has been constantly sick for the past couple of weeks.'

'My wife suffered similarly with our third,' another of the delegates remarked, 'and we have all suffered from him ever since!'

They all laughed. Conversation soon returned to the Neronian and Nero confessed his nerves.

'I suffer greatly from stage fright,' he admitted, 'but it seems there is no cure. It doesn't help matters that I am not actually permitted to enter of my own choosing. Etiquette and protocol and other such nonsense. I must rely on my friend Vitellius to lead the audience in their request to see me perform, and I am always afraid, as I pace back stage with my fellow competitors, that he will be delayed and I won't get my call! Terrifying!'

'I imagine it must be. And when will the Greeks - by your own admission so worthy of your talents! - be allowed to see you perform?'

'Obviously I will be unable to travel until the end of next year. But it is my dearest wish to compete in your Olympiad.'

The delegates nodded approvingly.

All too soon came the Neronian itself. The senate again did its best to avert the scandal of the emperor appearing on stage and offered him prizes for song and eloquence in advance of the competition.

'There is no need for favouritism,' Nero insisted, 'I will compete on equal terms and rely on the consciences of the judges to award the prizes to those most deserving.'

He addressed the judges with great deference and astonished them all with his obvious fear.

'Anyone would believe that his victory was in doubt!' Rubrius, one of the judges, remarked.

Any remaining doubts they might have had as to his conviction of being treated on an equal basis with his rivals were soon quashed by his performance. He adhered strictly to the rules, never daring to clear his throat and wiping the profuse sweat from his brow with his arm, since handkerchiefs were not permitted.

The first discipline was acting and Nero's natural aptitude shone through. However, midway through his piece he dropped his sceptre and was at once struck by the terror of disqualification.

'They haven't noticed!' his accompanist hissed, 'Keep going!'

By the time he left the stage, to await the verdict of the judges, he was shaking with nerves.

'Calm down, no one noticed,' Vitellius assured him.

'How could they fail to!'

'I was out there, Nero! The audience was listening with such rapt attention that not one spotted the mistake!'

Nero's relief was obvious. He took a few deep breaths to calm himself. 'Are you sure?'

'You weren't disqualified, were you?'

The trembling grew worse. 'Oh thank the gods, thank the gods!' He sat down quickly and tried to collect himself.

As the results were announced he could hardly bear to listen. When he was not called for either of the runner-up medals he sighed in relief and smiled at Vitellius.

'Oh well, better luck next time, perhaps,' he said without sorrow, 'I'm just relieved it's over!'

'But it isn't over! They're calling the winner!'

Nero raised his head in interest, not expecting to hear his own name called. And yet the first prize of the competition was his.

He accepted the medal in stunned silence, too shocked and too deeply moved for even the briefest of speeches.

'Had his acting been so convincing in the contest I might have genuinely granted him first prize!' Rubrius joked to his colleagues.

When it came to the lyre-playing, Nero was in a state of serious nerves and was allowed to be accompanied on stage by a group of friends, a Guards prefect carrying his lyre for him.

He had chosen to sing Niobe and soon lost himself in the beauty of the melody, forgetting the importance of the occasion and relaxing for the first time. He sang on until two hours before dusk and earned the Winner's Crown for his effort.

He returned to his villa in a state of absolute elation and could not wait to show his prizes to Poppaea.

'Oh, I wish you had been there,' he told her.

'When I was well you wouldn't allow me out of my bed!' Poppaea said bitterly, 'and now you would have me rise from my sick bed merely to hear you sing.'

'I would have no such thing! It is only that I wanted you there, to set the seal.'

'It is only that you think I am milking this sickness! I suppose you think I have hit upon a great excuse to lounge in bed all day and that it is high time I was up and about once more!'

'Of course not! I would have insisted on this sooner,' Nero protested.

'And you did insist! You would have left me rotting in this bed since last month! What does it matter to you, when you have Silia and Sporus to attend to your needs! And did you rush back with your prizes? Did it occur to you that I might be lying here wondering how you got on? Did any such thought cross your mind, as you celebrated your wins until the small hours!'

'It is hardly late, Poppaea! Why must you ruin my finest hour! You are so shrivelled and embittered with spite and envy, you cannot bear to see me happy!'

'Back to that! You were happy with Octavia, you were happy with Otho, you were happy with Doryphorus. And I destroyed every happiness you ever knew. You didn't turn Otho out, you didn't turn Doryphorus out. You pleaded with Octavia to stay, I suppose! And it was I, the wicked bitch, who cast them from your society!'

Nero hurled his crown at her and she dodged deftly, picking up her perfume box from beside the bed with the intent to launch it at him in retaliation. But she immediately doubled over, a cramp wrenching at her stomach.

'Poppaea! Are you alright?'

He was by her side in an instant, holding her close to him and gently rubbing her stomach.

'Just cramp,' she gasped, 'just cramp. It's passing.'

They sat quietly for a moment and the dogs re-emerged from under the bed, where they had retreated the moment the first voice had been raised. Nero patted them absently.

'I wish we didn't fight, Poppaea.'

She smiled and held him tighter. 'I don't believe anything I say. But you're so easy to wound! And I feel frustrated, stuck here all day by myself.'

'You've plenty of friends to sit with you.'

'They're our friends, Nero! And they were all at the Games to watch you perform! The dogs and cat have been my only companions these past few days; and frankly their conversation is wearing thin!'

'Until you are well enough to come with me I shall not leave these walls,' he promised.

JULY A.D. 65

The call of the stage proved too strong and his promise to Poppaea was quickly and frequently broken. He stayed with Acte at Puteoli for several days in order to perform in Neapolis, singing in tragedies and reading his own poetry. He had written an epic poem on the Trojan War and had chosen as his hero not the brave and virtuous Hector but the traditional weakling Paris, in which Paris anonymously entered a wrestling contest and defeated all comers, including Hector. Nero's performance so delighted the public that a thanksgiving was voted him, as though he had won a great victory. Passages from the poem were printed in letters of gold on plaques dedicated to Capitoline Jupiter.

A fleet had put in from Alexandria and the sailors attended one of the performances. Nero was so captivated by their unique rhythmic applause that he sent to Alexandria for more and fetched them back with him to Rome. There he selected a team of youths whom he divided into groups and taught the Alexandrian method.

'The Bees make a loud humming noise,' he explained to Sporus, as he lined up his team for a demonstration, 'the Roof-Tiles clap with hollow hands and the Bricks with flat hands. I am calling them the Augustiani and paying them four hundred gold pieces each for every performance. Not only barristers can have hired applause!'

'They sound glorious!' Sporus said approvingly.

'They merely draw attention to your disgrace!' Petronius joked.

'Singing is sacred to Apollo,' Nero reminded him, 'that glorious and provident god is represented in a musician's dress in Greek cities - and in Roman temples as well.'

'When can we go to Greece?' Sporus asked, 'You did say that the tour was only deferred, not cancelled.'

'Greece! I cannot even go to Neapolis!' Nero complained. 'You'll note that she is not here for the demonstration.'

'We heard as much!' Petronius told him.

'I never once left her side,' Sporus said defensively, 'and Silia and Messalina have been here almost permanently.'

'I entertained the good lady myself,' Petronius agreed, 'but it is no substitute for a husband! Brave her fists, Nero, and suffer their reward!'

Nero smiled and dismissed his applauders.

When he returned home late from the races later on that week, he was unprepared for the force of Poppaea's anger.

'You have only been home a matter of days!' she cursed him, 'Is this swollen body so disgusting that you must avoid it at all cost?!'

'Fat it may be, but it's not nearly so revolting as the person within it!' he retorted spitefully.

The ensuing battle was more violent than usual, sending the animals running for cover and the slaves into hasty retreat. As Nero straightened after receiving a particularly malicious blow and aimed a retaliating kick at Poppaea's shin, so she dropped suddenly to the floor. He had kicked her before even realising that she was down.

'Quickly! Help me!' he called, dropping down beside her and slapping her face to bring her round.

There was no response.

'Is it a cramp again?' he asked her, rubbing her back soothingly. 'Talk to me, Poppaea; tell me what's wrong.'

The first of the slaves to arrive on the scene cried out in alarm and immediately ran to fetch the doctors. Nero could get no response from Poppaea and was suddenly aware that he sat cradling her in a pool of blood. He looked down at the pale arm hanging limply against him, bringing back visions of the cold lifeless body of his mother, and he dropped her in horror; jumping back against the far wall and fighting for breath.

It seemed the entire household had been roused by the commotion. One of the doctors Andromachus ran to Nero's aid, trying to calm him, while the other tended Poppaea. She was already dead - the victim of a haemorrhage probably induced by the dead child within her.

Alexandria and Ecloge were already on the scene, but the two doctors kept them away from Nero, who was in need of more expert medical attention. Lack of breath had made him physically sick and he snatched blindly at the air around him, unaware of those who had come to his aid.

Sporus fought to be by his side, more distraught at the sight of his emperor than at the death of Poppaea. Silia knelt weeping beside the empress and slaves struggled to keep the two lumbering dogs at bay. Vitellius alone stood back from the situation and began to issue orders, sending some slaves out into the gardens with the dogs, while others were instructed to prepare a pyre and lay out the empress on a couch with fresh linen and her finest silks.

'He won't survive this,' Petronius said grimly, standing beside Vitellius. 'On top of everything else that has befallen him since Claudia's death, this will finish him.'

'It's just a panic attack,' Vitellius disagreed, 'he has always been prone to them. I thought he would collapse during the recent Games, such was his fear.'

Petronius shook his head. 'No, Spintria; this is the end of him. When a man lives on his nerves they can't afford to be as brittle as his.'

By the following morning Nero had recovered his senses. Though the doctors told him repeatedly that the baby had probably been dead for several weeks and had poisoned her system, Nero blamed himself totally for her death. Arrangements for her funeral were made hastily, in an effort to speed his own recovery, but he would hear none of it.

'She is not to be cremated,' he insisted, 'I want her embalmed and laid to rest in her tomb, as they do in the East. I won't see her burn.'

He took over the arrangements of her state funeral himself, sending to the orient for spices to burn at the funeral and ordering a coffin of purest white porphyry. No detail was deemed too small to warrant his attention, no workload too great.

'Let him do as much as he wants,' Petronius told Epaphroditus, when the secretary complained of Nero's involvement, 'the activity clearly compensates for her loss.'

Indeed, Nero appeared to be coping so well that neither doctor raised any objection when he insisted upon reading the funeral oration himself. The whole of Rome turned out for the occasion, and many from the far reaches of the empire had converged on the city, bringing it to a standstill. The strength of public feeling overwhelmed Nero, but he retained his composure and drew strength from the support of his close friends as he prepared himself mentally for the ordeal ahead.

Nero mounted the dais, his blue eyes blinking back the tears and sparing him the clear vision of the immense crowd before him. He was aware of the coffin of white porphyry beside him; though he dared not look upon it. All around him burned the fragrant spices, which represented the entire year's supply from Arabia. Yet there was no pyre for Poppaea; embalmed within her coffin in the manner of a great Eastern potentate. No flames to consume her beauty; her soul; that part of him that lay there with her. No flames to destroy their unborn child, who had lost life before living it.

He knew nothing of the oration he gave. He remembered speaking at length of her beauty; though his words were lost to him amid the visions in his mind of her soft amber hair and flawless skin. He had spoken, too, of her bearing him Claudia - a child so perfect that the gods themselves could not bear to be parted from her, and reclaimed her after only three months. He remembered speaking of them both as though they were still alive; as though he were not so completely alone and helpless; struggling to address the crowd before him with words he could not himself hear; while within him his voice rose in a silent scream of all-consuming grief.

It was as Nero stepped down from the dais, the oration coming to an end only just before his forced composure, that his eyes were drawn to the figure at the rear of the mourners. The lowered face could not be seen, but the elegant, stylish robes were as recognisable to Nero as the form that he knew lay beneath them. That same pristine body that now filled his mind and sent an inexcusable longing coursing through his veins.

Nero had wondered if he would come. In his darkest moments of grief he had cried out a prayer to bring him rushing to his side. But with the drying of each final tear he had hoped that he would stay away. His feelings, even now, were of despair and elation. He had never hated him so much; nor needed him so badly.

He stood alone, waiting; brushing off with uncharacteristic anger the attendants who fretted over him. They slowly backed off, leaving him to his private grief.

Though he did not look up, he knew when the nobleman finally stood before him.

'We are even, now, my friend,' said a quiet voice, without rancour.

Weeping, Nero raised his head; almost afraid to look upon the face before him. But the features were still the same - languid and affable; a casual observer of the chaos of life, who could jump in or ignore as the fancy took him. His Otho. His own dear Otho.

He raised a hand to Otho's face, as though doubting its very existence. Fingertips gently remembering each line of bone, each crease and hollow; turning his hand now to tenderly stroke the back of his wrist against the warm softness of Otho's cheek.

Otho stood silently by and allowed him such liberties, as the young emperor's hand traced the hard outline of his shoulder through the silk robe. He leaned forward and kissed him lightly on the lips.

'She is gone; and we can never go back.'

'I could not bear to be parted from her,' Nero sobbed now, uncontrollably. It was an apology, a plea.

Otho sighed wearily. 'So many tears, Nero. You were always too sensitive, too emotional. You used to cry so often.'

Nero met his eyes.

'It was the only way I knew to make you hold me.'

Otho held him now, suddenly and tightly; gathering him up in his arms with an all-consuming strength that threatened his facade of cool detachment.

'I am so sorry; so very sorry,' murmured Nero.

'For what? That she chose you instead of me? She used me simply as a piece on a game board, a means to an end. To you. If any apology is owed, it is not from you, my friend.'

'You cannot hate her. You would not have come today if you did not still feel some love for her. And you must know that I killed her!'

'I know only that you could not have killed her. I know nothing of the circumstances of her death; but I know you, Nero. Only too well.' Otho put his hands on Nero's waist and stood back from him momentarily; running his eyes over his old friend and rival. 'Besides,' he added, 'it was not love for Poppaea that brought me here today.'

'You'll stay, of course?'

'It is better that I don't. I left once in bitterness; I have no wish to do so a second time.'

Nero regarded him carefully.

'You fear me, Otho.'

Otho shook his head regretfully. 'Not you, my friend. But there are those at Court who cannot tolerate rivals. It is better to relinquish your friendship than my life.'

Nero said nothing; already knowing the truth of his words. He felt Otho's grip on his waist lessen and the pain engulfed him. He felt his knees buckle as though involuntarily forcing him back into the security of Otho's arms. And at once he felt Otho's hand slip around his back and under his arm in support; and he surrendered himself completely to the emotions that would keep him there.

Otho gently brushed the locks back from Nero's eyes and kissed his eyelids. It was an act of compassion, no more. Yet the tender kisses strayed to the nape of his neck; the smooth skin of his shoulder; the soft creases in the crook of his arm as it hung with such familiarity around his neck, washing away the years as though they had never come between them.

It was a parting gesture, they both knew. And when the moment came, Nero could utter no protest. Otho simply turned away and walked back to his awaiting sedan chair. He looked back, as he reached it, and gave a casual wave of farewell, that Nero returned. Then the chair was gone.

Nero remembered nothing more.

Chapter Forty-Nine

JANUARY A.D. 66

The crowd roared as a four-horse chariot pulled clear of its rivals and raced up to the finishing line in the tightly packed Circus. The victorious charioteer saluted to the cheering crowd and Nero waved back heartily from the imperial box.

'Ah; how I wish I had but half his talent,' Nero sighed, brushing the ever-lengthening blonde locks back from his face.

Petronius, leaning back on a couch and picking lazily at sweetmeats, glanced across at him.

'You are either modest or stupid! You could ride rings around that damned fool.'

The bright blue eyes of the emperor clouded visibly with disappointment.

'Not you as well, Petronius? I thought that I could at least rely upon my friends to be honest with me. If I am useless at something, then please have the decency to tell me. I find all this false flattery very depressing.'

Nero sank onto his couch once more and casually brushed the locks from his eyes. The enthusiasm he usually showed at the races was strangely lacking.

Petronius finished the last of the sweetmeats and clicked his fingers for more.

'There is very little false flattery directed at you,' he remarked between mouthfuls, 'you put enough effort into your pursuits - why shouldn't you be accomplished?'

'I fell from the chariot less than halfway round this morning and was still awarded the race,' Nero protested. But he lacked the spirit to be angry.

Until that astonishing morning, he had believed that all of his cherished prizes had been won on merit. Now, they were rendered invalid.

The slave offered him the dish of sweetmeats and he shook his head.

'No thank you, Helios, you may leave them with my guest. Thank you.'

Petronius glanced across at him with concern, the emperor's unhappy frame of mind once so out of character that it would have been remarkable. Yet, since his recovery from his collapse at the funeral, the events of the past year had finally taken their toll.

'You cannot pretend that a few false awards are all that distress you, my friend,' Petronius said lightly. 'You are still blaming yourself over Poppaea. It was not a good pregnancy from the outset. You know yourself how ill she was throughout. One almighty row was not enough to kill her - she would still have died had you spent all your moments whispering sweet-nothings in her ear.'

'But instead we fought... and I kicked her...'

'But you didn't kill her, Nero. Don't punish yourself with this needless guilt. It comes too soon on top of everything else.' He shook his head despairingly. 'The Fire, the plot, her death - all of these things require time from which to recover. And instead you continue to work yourself to the point of exhaustion!'

'I do no more than my duty.'

'The rebuilding of the city is not your duty! You have architects and builders for such things. But no, you have to take control yourself, as always. Throwing open the Palace grounds to the destitute! Feeding them, clothing them, housing them! You have defiled your name and title in the eyes of the senate. They even whisper that you were responsible for the fire in the first place, so eager were you to cleanse your conscience! Such is their hatred. Why didn't you remain in the country, like the rest of us, and leave the mob to clean up their own mess?'

'They are my people - I'm responsible for them,' Nero said in irritation, flicking at his hair crossly. 'How I wish to the gods that I wasn't.'

'Huh! Few people would agree with you there, my friend. Even the senate concedes that without you at our helm we might suffer under another despot, like your bloody predecessors.'

'Why, then, did Senecio and his friends conspire against me?'

Petronius waved a hand in the air at the triviality of the question.

'You were not quick enough to accept their sycophantic praises and hand out equally false promotions, so they decided to take their own honours. Their greed casts no reflection on your leadership.'

Nero rested his head in his hands.

'I have been emperor since I was sixteen,' he said unhappily, 'and all it has brought me is heartache. I have worked myself to exhaustion, as you say. And for what thanks? I have laboured under some idealistic sense of duty, endeavouring to work for my people and to help them. But what people? The senate blocks my every move to help the commons; and the Patricians need no help. Every reform has had to be fought for, tooth and nail. As for our own class, they are never satisfied. They have everything, yet I cannot do enough for them. Well, no more. No more.' His last words were spoken with such vehemence that Petronius began to take notice.

'What are you planning to do?' he enquired sarcastically, 'Incite a revolution?!'

Nero's eyes twinkled as he raised his head. 'If the commons were literate, we could incite them to revolt tomorrow.'

'Do you still live in the past?' Petronius asked. 'The commons are literate. They may not have their own tutors, but one cannot walk along the street without hearing a schoolmaster and his noisy class of brats sheltered somewhere under a shop's awning.'

Nero shook his head. 'You miss my point. They can read and write. But they cannot afford to buy books any more than they can afford the time to sit and read them.'

Petronius grunted. 'You have an understanding of their problems with which the rest of us do not trouble ourselves. And how would you propose to incite this revolution of yours, anyway?'

'With books and art. Your smutty stories of decrepit old men still bedding young beauties are only popular because they give hope. We read a book and become part of it. We look at a painting and become totally absorbed. Art, in all its forms, takes our dreams into new dimensions. If you can inspire hope in the heart of a seventy-year-old, then you can give hope of a different sort to others. Write, Petronius! Tell them how it should be. Let them see the dream and urge them to take it.'

'A beautiful sentiment,' Petronius sneered, 'but what dream? Slaughter and destruction?'

'For us, perhaps. But don't you think we deserve it? Look at the list of the dead conspirators. Great men, who had everything, but wanted more. Greed drives our hearts, while need drives the instincts of the poor. The ruling classes are so distant from the commons that they have no understanding of the needs of those they are supposed to be ruling. Look at us, here in the luxury of this box. Is it not absurd to entrust to me the fate of so many people? Just as we entrusted my father Claudius and my uncle Caligula?'

Petronius laughed. 'With the utmost respect, my dear Nero, I am quite content for my fate to remain in your hands. I hardly think I could maintain such comfort and luxury with a commoner at the head of state!'

'Luxury, no - but comfort, by all means. Every citizen on equal status, working together for the common good. Every business, every occupation, every property state-owned. No one getting rich on the backs of others.'

'Dangerous words,' Petronius said stiffly, 'and familiar actions, too. When you bought up every consignment of corn during the famine and sold it at a subsidised price, you gained no thanks from the merchants, did you? And by your decree, all lawyers must be paid a fixed fee, so that rich and poor alike can avail of the services of the very best of them. Yet more noses out of joint! And the only thing you have incited thus far is anger - among your own class! Isn't one plot against your life enough?'

'Unfortunately, yes. And so I bow to cowardice. But you are against me, Petronius? You, who wrote:

' "What uses are laws where money is king?
  Where poverty's helpless and can't win a thing?" '

'Even cynics who sneer are rarely averse
To selling their scruples to fill up their purse.
There's no justice at law - it's the bidding that counts;
And the job of the judge is to fix the amounts.' Petronius completed the poem for him. 'Mere words, Nero, to sell a book.' He fidgeted crossly on his couch. 'I'm your Arbiter of Taste - I enjoy fine things. To give all men equality one must lessen the great divide. While your commoners gain in wealth and comfort, we must in turn lose a little of ours. The very idea is totally abhorrent! In fact, Nero, with such thoughts in your mind you will only invite another plot against your life - perhaps this time successful.' Petronius rose and adjusted his toga with ill-concealed irritation. 'With your permission, my Lord, I shall take my leave,' he announced curtly, and left without waiting for a reply.

As he stepped outside, he brushed past Epaphroditus and paused to exchange a few words.

'How is he?' the secretary enquired, 'still in low spirits?'

'Epaphroditus, your master is a dangerous man. I have survived the bloody reigns of Tiberius, Caligula and Claudius. But Nero, with his good heart and good intentions, is the greatest menace of them all! He'll bring us all down, mark my words, for he has what the rest of his family lacked - a conscience.'

Petronius glanced back at the door to the box with a heavy pang of regret. With reluctant decisiveness he said, 'Well, it will be his downfall, but it won't be mine. I wash my hands of him - and his dangerous games. You will see no more of me at the Palace. I take my leave.'

Epaphroditus stared at his departing back in bemusement, then passed by the Guards, into the box.

'Whatever is the matter with Petronius?!' he asked Nero lightly.

'I fear we have fallen out. A disagreement over politics.'

'So! Your spirit has returned! What, then, are your plans?'

Nero stretched out on the couch and sifted through a bowl of fruit.

'To retire from public life, my dear friend. As emperor, I am unwanted. The senate would fare better without my unwelcome interference.'

'Fare better for whom?! You're needed; you can't give in now.'

'I'm a coward, Epaphroditus. I have no taste for bloodshed of any kind - least of all my own. My interference in matters of state is dangerous and will henceforth cease. Let me now devote time to my own pleasures. Cancel all my appointments; as of tomorrow I shall be dining at noon - until midnight and beyond! Why the disapproving scowl, Epaphroditus? Is it not time that I had a little fun?'

'Are your appointments to be cancelled? Or merely postponed?'

'Cancelled. I am washing my hands of affairs of state. And, as my secretary, you are now free of the burdens of office, too. So wipe that disagreeable scowl from your face and join the party!'

FEBRUARY A.D. 66

'This is welcome news!' Petronius said, as he sat with Tigellinus and Epaphroditus in Nero's chamber, waiting for the emperor to return from a walk with the dogs. 'The gods know we can do with a good year - the past few have been disastrous.'

'Hardly good news,' Tigellinus said, 'I cannot see how Nero will meet the necessary costs.'

'We will all have to pull together to see that he can,' Petronius insisted, 'and teach that damnable Phaon to keep his mouth shut! This is just what Nero needs, to bring him out of himself.'

'He recovered quickly enough after the funeral,' Tigellinus argued, as though for the sake of it.

'I would hardly call a matter of weeks 'quickly', Commander! And it is a point of argument as to whether he is fully recovered even now. A state visit of this sort will be a welcome tonic; if it has got me back to the Palace, then it will surely rekindle his interest in state affairs! I can hardly wait to break the news.'

'Is it your place to tell him?' Tigellinus asked bluntly.

Petronius was aware of the Commander's jealousy, but remained deliberately obtuse.

'As his official Arbiter of Taste I would say that the right is mine alone,' Petronius informed him, 'it may be a matter of State, but the social aspect is of far greater importance. In fact, I wonder at your need to be here at all, Commander.'

Epaphroditus could not conceal his amusement, which only added to Tigellinus' annoyance. Nero had come to rely increasingly on Petronius, but during his brief absence had transferred much of that dependency to Tigellinus. It was not a privilege he would easily relinquish.

The door opened and Nero entered, the two dogs panting in his wake. Gone were the days when they would burst in several minutes ahead of him. Palamedes took his favoured spot beneath the bed, while Mysticus managed a final piece of athleticism and sprawled out on the bed itself.

'Well, gentlemen, this is quite a gathering. Are we at war?' Nero enquired. 'Petronius! You too! Have you that book I requested?'

'It would be inappropriate to suggest that it would be written over my dead body - when it is your neck on the line,' Petronius replied.

Nero laughed.

'We have just received word that Tiridates is on his way to Rome,' Tigellinus told him quickly, before Petronius could announce the news.

'Excellent!' Nero declared happily, 'We must redouble our efforts to have The Golden House in some way presentable and declare some feast days in his honour. How long do we have? Does he require fast ships to be sent?'

'Apparently he is forbidden to cross by sea,' Epaphroditus explained.

'Oh, that's right, he's a Magian priest, is he not? They have some belief about polluting the sea by travelling on its surface. The gods! It will be some journey for him, then! Assign a body guard of Roman troops to accompany him, would you, Tigellinus.' 'I have taken the liberty of already doing so,' the Commander replied.

'Phaon estimates the trip to take some eight or nine months,' Epaphroditus added, 'and the entourage is impressive. He already has Parthian troops guarding him. Phaon is of the opinion the entire journey will be at a cost of eight hundred thousand sesterces a day.'

'But the fact that he is not here, advising against such expense, means that we can afford it?' Nero checked.

'Comfortably,' Epaphroditus assured him, 'the many visitors we welcomed to the city last year spent handsomely.'

'Then we have nine months in which to prepare ourselves!' Nero enthused. 'What do you suggest, Petronius?'

'You must meet him at Neapolis and perhaps we will hold gladiatorial Games at Puteoli, before moving on to Rome; I'll arrange it with Patrobius. More Games, in the Theatre of Pompey, and, of course, a public presentation of the Crown.'

'Get together with Patrobius and Phaon and see what else we can do,' Nero suggested, 'it isn't every day, after all, that we are visited by a foreign king!'

'Well I had already thought of guilding the Theatre of Pompey for the occasion,' Petronius told him, 'and commissioning an awning for it.'

'Oh yes! A false sky, perhaps! Midnight blue - no, purple! - covered with gold stars in shining silk thread! That would be perfect.'

'Perhaps an embroidery of our emperor driving a chariot?' Petronius suggested.

'A Magian priest might find that offensive,' Tigellinus warned.

'Nonsense!' Nero told him, 'Chariot racing was an accomplishment of ancient kings and leaders - it was honoured by poets, and closely associated with divine worship.' He stood up, ready to end the meeting. 'I shall go and tell Sabina of our royal visit, it will cheer him no end. In fact, if Tiridates can make so arduous a journey, then I can certainly put off my visit to Greece no longer! The Olympiad are next year, we will depart as soon as we have seen off our honoured guest!'

He left them, to go in search of Sporus.

'So much for his return to office!' Epaphroditus said, 'This is merely just an additional excuse to party! And what is our Magian priest and king to make of the young Sabina, I wonder?!'

'We need a new consort,' Petronius agreed, 'I shall have a word with our young widow Messalina. This time they are both free and I cannot see either of them objecting to marriage. Sporus will welcome it, too.'

'Not at your suggestion,' Epaphroditus warned. 'Nero can be contrary when it comes to receiving instruction. Put the idea in Silia's head, not Messalina's. She will soon talk them into a wedding!'

So it was that Nero found himself enjoying his fifth wedding, albeit it to only his third wife. He had been opposed to the idea, but not seriously enough to stand up to Messalina's pleas.

'I need to be married,' she had insisted, when he argued that Sporus was his chosen wife, 'I married Vestinus - and I shall marry again if you do not claim me!'

'Very well, I shall claim you, then!' Nero finally consented, 'But Sabina remains my official consort.'

Messalina had no interest in public life and readily agreed.

Not long after the ceremony, Nero received a letter from Antistius, who had been exiled after his acidic comments on Nero's marriage to Sporus and Doryphorus.

'Let us see what he has to say on this occasion!' Nero grinned, opening the letter with interest.

'What does he say?' Sporus asked, seeing Nero's expression turn instantly to alarm.

'He claims to have information vital to my safety.'

'Another plot?'

'And another and another. I will not be free of fear until they finally drive me to my grave.' He called Tigellinus. 'Send our fastest ship to collect Antistius and fetch him to Rome. I must see him.'

Antistius was delighted to receive word of his impending freedom. He had spent many months contriving his return to Rome and cared not the slightest for those he would bring down in the process.

He arrived at the Palace and duly brought his case before Nero.

'I happened to befriend a fellow-exile by the name of Pammenes,' he told Nero, 'you may of heard of him? A famous astrologer. Anyway, I noticed that messengers were constantly arriving from Rome to consult him and he happened to let slip that he was in receipt of a handsome annual subsidy from Publius Anteius.

'That name struck a chord. He was once a lover of the old Augusta, was he not? I seemed to remember, too, that you greatly disliked him, my Lord. So I intercepted a letter from him, to Pammenes, and stole some files from Pammenes office. Included with those of Publius were also documents belonging to Ostorius.

'I am afraid, my Lord, that Ostorius and Publius are studying their own destinies - as well as your own astrological charts. I believe, in so doing, they are endangering the empire.'

'And what do you owe either me or the empire?' Nero asked.

'I owe you nothing,' Antistius confessed frankly, 'but I hate living in exile. I trade you this information for my freedom.'

Nero looked to Tigellinus.

'Have them both arrested and see what they have to say about these charges.'

Neither of the accused, as it turned out, had any answer to the accusations. Both Ostorius and Publius took their own lives as soon as their denunciation became known.

JULY A.D. 66

Though far from complete, The Golden house was deemed fit for dedication by mid-summer. It consisted, not of a single building, but of many separate ones and the gardens, open freely to the general public and spanning nearly three hundred and seventy acres, were the finest ever seen.

Petronius opened the dedication with a poem in tribute to the magnificent park, much to Nero's pleasure.

'The tall plane-tree disposes summer shade,
Metamorphosed Daphne nearby, crowned with berries.
Cypresses tremulous, clipped pines around
Shuddering at their tops.

Playing among them
A stream with wandering waters,
Spume-flecked, worrying the stones
With a querulous spray.
A place fit for love.'

The grounds included a lake built on the site of a large swamp at the bottom of a valley. To the right, on the Caelian Hill, was a picturesque colonnaded retreat, filled with flowers, running water, statues and grottoes. On the left, along the Oppian spur of the Esquiline Hill, stood the main residential section.

This in itself was an architectural marvel. Celer and Severus had outdone themselves, using designs and innovations never before used in building. The two residential sections were of unequal asymmetrical west and east wings, two and three storeys high. They contained rows of small rooms facing onto a long straight portico, opening into a five-sided colonnaded courtyard at the junction of the two wings, with a sixth side open to the majestic parkland.

The east wing was split by a domed hall, which had used in its construction, for the very first time, the revolutionary new invention - concrete. So, too, was the interior of The Golden House filled with the latest gadgets. The baths were served by a flow of both salt and sulphurous water, while the music room contained the largest and most powerful hydraulic organ ever made.

Nero's agents, Carrinas and Acratus, had spent nearly two years collecting art from Asia Minor and Greece, which now graced every room. Statues by the famed Greek Praxiteles stood alongside those of Zenodorus, while the predominantly white walls were filled with the work of Famulus, who specialised in the combination of painting and stucco.

'Good,' Nero declared, when he had been shown around the completed rooms, 'now I can at last begin to live like a human being!'

Yet it was not enough to keep Nero in Rome.

He spent the summer in Campania, returning to the city only for racedays. And in his absence Tigellinus took the opportunity to expel another rival.

Chapter Fifty

AUGUST A.D. 66

The first course had just been finished and Nero and his dinner guests were now plunging freely into the warm baths provided for their pleasure. The bathing would take an hour or more, depending upon the opportunities it presented for further, more intimate pleasures. Music and poetry recitals were planned for the late afternoon, before returning to the dining tables once more. Such was the daily routine of the emperor, since cutting himself off from the senate and his ministers.

He sat on the edge of the pool, enjoying a brief respite from the energetic frolics of his companions, and sipped at a goblet of wine. He was interrupted by the arrival of a slave, who announced that the Commander of the Guards had urgent business to discuss.

'Then send him in, Gaius, and thank you.'

Nero awaited the commander resignedly and greeted him with his usual warmth.

'Tigellinus! What news do you bring? I fear it must be bad to warrant this intrusion.'

Tigellinus removed his helmet and tucked it under his arm.

'Grievous, my Lord. It concerns Petronius.'

Nero raised his eyes heavenward. 'Petronius! My dear Tigellinus, I fear that his crude jokes about me hurt you more than they do me!' he complained, with exaggerated patience. 'I am well aware that I am the subject of his witty and lurid after-dinner speeches. But I urge you to ignore the man. He cannot be the only person in Rome who mocks me behind my back. Leave him be, Tigellinus.'

'That I cannot do while his talk endangers your life. My Lord, he has been saying that the incestuous attempts upon you by your mother were not only successful, but welcomed by you. I need hardly remind you that the Guards will not tolerate a sacrilegious emperor.'

The depths to which Nero's heart had plummeted were reflected in his expression.

'Dear gods,' he groaned, as though to himself, 'must she haunt me forever?' He stared into his goblet, then emptied it in one gulp and faced Tigellinus. 'Why is he suggesting such things? He saw to it that I was never left alone in her company.'

'Perhaps his funds are running short. There would be fresh opportunities for advancement under a new emperor. Forgive me, Nero; I know how much this must grieve you.'

'Her actions grieved me more than his talk of them. He has opened up old wounds.' Nero considered the situation for a moment. 'Send the Guards to Petronius. Inform him that I shall not hesitate to bring him to trial should he continue to slander my name.'

'With the greatest respect, my Lord, your leniency in this instance is sheer lunacy!'

'I find it hard enough to sign the death warrants of hardened criminals, as well you know. I shall not condemn a man to death simply for making fun of his emperor, however cruelly. Give him my message and let it be known that I am angered. My leniency may aggravate you, Tigellinus, but I assure you that I will see him in exile if he dares to defy me in this. Now go.'

Petronius was entertaining a small party of dinner guests when the Guards burst in. Intrusions of this sort had become a regular occurrence in Rome and it was known that there could be only one outcome. Tigellinus stepped forward with cruel delight and prevented Petronius and his guests from rising from their couches.

'Petronius, I bring a message from your emperor. He is preparing to bring you to trial as a traitor. But, in honour of your past friendship, he is willing to spare you the humiliation of standing trial. He has therefore granted you enough time to arrange a more honourable alternative, before any case is brought against you.'

'You are telling me to take my own life?'

'I merely deliver the message.'

'Do you, I wonder?'

Tigellinus overlooked the insinuation. 'I will leave a company of Guards outside your house, to prevent any of you from leaving. If you carry out the request before nightfall, I will see to it that none of your guests come to any harm.'

Petronius successfully retained his composure, but his voice betrayed his fear and sorrow. 'You owe me nothing, but at least tell me this - what did you tell him, to warrant this visit?'

'He heard of your talk of his incestuous liaisons with his mother.'

'His *what*? You know full well that we succeeded in protecting the boy from her. Go away, Tigellinus, the mere sight of you makes me sick; now more than ever.'

'I have been instructed to remain.'

'Then at least grant me privacy to write my will.'

Petronius left the dining room and returned some time later, his wrists discreetly bound with blood-soaked bandages.

Nero had not yet risen when Tigellinus was shown into his bedchamber by Epaphroditus.

'My Lord, forgive this disturbance. I have fetched you a copy of the will of Petronius. I have already dispatched a copy to the senate, to be read out this morning as a mark of respect.'

Nero nodded and accepted the scroll in silence. Respect did not enter in to the customary reading of wills at the senate. He regarded it as simply a distasteful way of finding out the business of others. Who had what, who got what.

He ushered Tigellinus away with a wave of his hand, without looking up. He had no wish to look at the man he now knew to be little short of a murderer. He heard the door click shut and slowly opened the final work of Petronius...

'Gentlemen of the House, I read you now the will of Petronius, a good friend to us all, who will be sadly missed.' Vitellius stood in front of the packed senate and unrolled the scroll.

' "I am a writer, an artist," ' he read, ' "therefore, I will not bore you with the tedious wishes of a dead man. I will instead amuse you with the antics of one still living - your own emperor, Nero!" ' Vitellius paused and grinned at his audience. 'Well, well, well! A wit to the very end! It would seem that this document is not a will, but possibly Petronius' finest work yet!' He scanned the scroll rapidly and continued.

' "For amusement, where better place to turn than the emperor's bedchamber. A place where your head of state dons animal skins and molests his similarly attired lovers accordingly! The same man who abhors the spectacle of wild animal shows in the arena is happy to take the arena to his bedchamber!

' "His bedfellows have been that affected youth, Sporus; the ex-slave, Doryphorus; and the Governor, Marcus Otho; the subsequent empress Poppaea - but while still married to Otho!; the slave girl, Acte; the noblewoman, Silia..." ' Vitellius stopped, aghast, and all heads turned to the senator whose wife had just been named.

Vitellius returned to the scroll and proceeded with caution. The list of lovers preceded a list of Nero's diverse and inventive sexual activities, described in the same witty and lurid detail that had made the books of Petronius so popular. As amused as his audience, Vitellius finally rolled up the scroll and stepped down from the dais.

Nero slowly rolled up the damning scroll and handed it numbly to Epaphroditus, who read it through in stunned silence.

'I must have upset him badly to provoke such spite,' Nero said, with heavy regret, 'though I cannot remember ever doing so. Well, it is done, and cannot be undone. By publicising these intimacies he is asking the people to judge my public life by my private conduct. He has dragged my affairs into the open, and there they must now remain. Well, so be it. Discretion shall be a thing of the past. Call Tigellinus and wait outside.'

Epaphroditus left the room and a moment later Tigellinus entered. Nero addressed him coldly.

'Commander, Petronius is not the first person to receive a warning from me and to have immediately taken his own life.'

'With respect, my...'

Nero raised his hand. 'Have no fear, Commander, this is not a reprimand. Let us just say that my messages are losing a little in translation. I have come to understand now why so trusted a friend and advisor as Seneca grew to fear me, and cut his wrists.

'I am no fool; although perhaps I have behaved like one of late. I know that, of all my friends, you alone have only my best interests at heart. You are so hated by all that your very survival depends upon mine. You are aware that I no longer concern myself with the burdens of office, and yet you come running to me with the least triviality.

'Well, then. Let me now spare you that chore. Let me spare you the need to twist my words inventively to suit your own purpose. As of now, my dear Tigellinus, you have supreme command. You may use my seal as and when you please; put my name to your commands; deal with traitors as you see fit. Indeed, deal with 'suspected traitors' as you wish, since that suits your needs far more.'

Nero removed a ring from his finger and tossed it with disdain to Tigellinus.

'My seal; take it. I shall wear just this one ring, a gift from Sporus, as you - and all others - must now be well aware. It is far dearer to my heart than that with which you are now burdened. Now go; leave me to my amusements. The gods know that I can have but little time left for the pleasures of the living.'

Tigellinus studied the power in his hand for a moment, before slipping it onto his finger, with a callous smile, and leaving the room.

Nero watched him go, gently twisting the ring engraved with the Rape of Proserpine round his finger, considering the chore of living up to the reputation created for him by Petronius, aware that if he did so it would be the end of him; as it had been the end of those before him.

SEPTEMBER A.D. 66

Spending much of his time in Neapolis, Nero returned to Rome briefly in order to hear the charges against the senator Thrasea, accused of party-warfare against the government by Cossutianus. The arguments presented by Cossutianus only reminded him why he had turned his back on State affairs, and he bore them only because he so loathed Thrasea.

'At the New Year, Thrasea evaded the regular oath. Though a member of the Board of Fifteen for Religious Ceremonies, he absented himself from the national vows,' Cossutianus told Nero, remembering how Thrasea had once convicted him of extortion and at last seeing vengeance in his grasp. 'He has never sacrificed for the emperor's welfare or his divine voice. Once an indefatigable and invariable participant in the senate's discussions - taking sides on even the most trivial proposal - now, for three years, he has not entered the senate.' Cossutianus listed various incidences of absenteeism. 'This is party-warfare against the government,' he continued, 'it is secession. If many more have the same impudence, it is war. As this faction-loving country once talked of Caesar versus Cato, so now, Nero, it talks of you versus Thrasea. And he has his followers - or his courtiers rather. They do not yet imitate his treasonable voting. But they copy his grim and gloomy manner and expression: they rebuke your amusements. He is the one man to whom your safety is immaterial, your talents unadmired. He dislikes the emperor to be happy. But even your unhappiness, your bereavements, do not appease him. Disbelief in Poppaea's divinity shows the same spirit as refusing allegiance to the acts of the divine Augustus and divine Julius. Thrasea rejects religion, abrogates law.

'In every province and army the official Gazette is read with special care - to see what Thrasea has refused to do. If his principles are better, let us adopt them. Otherwise, let us deprive these revolutionaries of their chief and champion.' He continued on at great length about Cassius and Brutus and the end of Liberty, before suggesting, 'Write no instructions about Thrasea yourself. Leave the senate to decide between us.'

'I can do little else,' Nero said wearily, 'I have been given insufficient time to convene the senate. King Tiridates already approaches Italy and I must return to Neapolis to welcome him. But I will give consideration to your charges and will convene the senate after the State visit.' He shot a glance at Tigellinus. 'Always supposing I need to, of course.'

When Cossutianus had left, Nero instructed Epaphroditus to forbid Thrasea's attendance in Rome during the royal visit.

'If he cannot bother himself to attend the senate, then he need not bother himself to welcome King Tiridates either.'

Back in Campania, Nero sent a two-horse carriage for the royal party, to transport them from the Italian border to his villa at Neapolis. There they were greeted by Nero's select circle, Petronius' contributions sorely missed.

'My consort, Sporus,' Nero said, introducing the house guests, 'my wife, Messalina; my mistress, Acte; my Minister of Leisure, Patrobius; and last, but by no means least, my secretary and Foreign Minister, Epaphroditus.'

Tiridates bowed and held out a hand for his wife to step forward. She wore a visor of gold to hide her face, in keeping with the custom of her country.

'My wife, Doris,' Tiridates announced.

Nero grasped her hand firmly and kissed her fingers. 'May I congratulate you on your exquisite visor!' he exclaimed. 'Do you keep many?'

Tiridates smiled. 'Colours to suit her mood and expressions to match!'

'Then you must give me the name of your goldsmith and permit me to commission just such a mask as you wear today. I would wear it with pride on stage.'

'You may have this very one,' Doris consented, 'your hospitaly so far is worth far greater gifts.'

'On the proviso,' Tiridates added, 'that we are to see it for ourselves in one of your famed performances.'

'A pleasure to grant!' Nero laughed.

They formed a relaxed and comradely party at dinner; neither Tiridates nor Doris in the least perturbed by Nero's companions. Their idle chatter at once identified them as kindred spirits and Nero and Tiridates struck up an immediate friendship, which kept them up in conversation until the early hours of the morning.

After a welcome rest in Neapolis, the party moved on to Puteoli, where they stayed at Acte's villa. Patrobius had arranged Games on an elaborate scale, importing Nile sand for the gymnastics.

Tiridates was impressed with both the spectacle and his host's enthusiasm.

'I plan to compete in the Greek Olympiad next Spring,' Nero told him, in explanation of his detailed knowledge of wrestling.

'And why not here?' Tiridates asked.

Nero smiled. 'Hardly acceptable, Tiridates - I am your host, after all!'

'And emperor! As King of Armenia, I shall expect to do anything I wish! The one thing I find difficult to understand in this strange country are your peculiar and complicated laws of etiquette.'

'Believe me, you are not alone!'

'Would you raise any objection to my own participation, Nero?'

Nero was taken aback. 'The gods, no! I should be honoured that you deem our Games so worthy.'

'Then I fancy taking a shot at the wild animals. I am a much respected archer at home.'

He proved his skill in amazing fashion, bringing down two bulls with a single arrow.

It was a highly animated party that set off on their final journey, to Rome. Nero and Tiridates discussed the finer points of wrestling, while Doris gave presents of exotic robes to Sporus, who had coveted a visor until finding it too uncomfortable to wear.

'One gets used to them,' she told him kindly, 'and I am not so often in public. At home, there is no need to wear one at all.'

As they approached Rome they could see that the entire populace had turned out to greet them. The broad streets were alive with colour, every window underlined by its brightly-planted window box, always a feature of Rome but now more noticeable than ever; the bright holiday clothes of the people accentuating the colours.

Tiridates was taken to the Palace, where Doris fell in love at once with the natural parkland and its quietly grazing animals.

'Are those antelope? Here, in Rome?'

'Three varieties,' Nero told her, 'and zebra and deer. I even kept a very small pack of wolves, to keep down the numbers, but they proved far too timid and my dogs saw them off! The most exotic member of my menagerie at present is a young lion. I am having him trained to perform on stage with me and I hope to be able to safely wrestle him by the time we tour Greece.'

The royal couple were equally impressed with The Golden House and only sorry that it wasn't yet open for residence.

'When would you hope to move in?' Tiridates asked.

'Perhaps the year after next. There is still so much to do. The rooms you see now were only completed for your visit.'

'Then we must make a point of returning to Rome in a few years time, to see it in its full glory!'

The weather for the remainder of the week took a turn for the worse and Tiridates could not be displayed to the people on the assigned day. But he was brought out as soon as possible afterwards, to be overwhelmed once more by the enthusiasm of the populace.

The Guards cohorts were drawn up in full armour round the temples of the Forum, while Nero sat in his curule chair on the rostrum, wearing triumphal dress and surrounded by military insignia and standards.

Tiridates walked up a ramp and prostrated himself at the feet of the emperor. Nero stretched out his hand, drew him to his feet and kissed him.

'You have done well in coming here in person to enjoy my presence yourself,' Nero announced. 'Your father did not leave you this kingdom; your brothers, though they gave it to you, could not guard it for you; but that is my gracious grant to you, and I make you King of Armenia, in order that both you and they may learn that I have the power both to take away kingdoms and to bestow them.'

He then removed Tiridates' turban and replaced it with the diadem.

The people then hailed Nero as Imperator and he dedicated a laurel-wreath in the Capitol; closing the double doors of the temple of Janus, as a sign that all war was at an end. Tiridates gave a humble speech, which was translated publicly, before being taken to the Theatre of Pompey and offered a seat on Nero's right.

After seating his guest, Nero drove a four-horse chariot in a race and then played the lyre, before rejoining the king to enjoy the remainder of the performances.

All too soon the visit came to an end. Having already spent eight thousand gold pieces a day on his newfound friend, Nero now gave him a parting gift of more than a million.

'What can I say of your hospitality!' Tiridates said, embracing Nero for a final time. 'Your newly built city has inspired me to rebuild Artaxata on a magnificent scale - and it shall be renamed Neronia, in honour not of your gifts, but of your friendship.'

The entourage returning with the king, therefore, was swelled considerably by large numbers of skilled workmen, as well as bearers of the many gifts presented by Nero.

Chapter Fifty-One

SEPTEMBER A.D. 66

Nero's proposed trip to Greece was delayed temporarily in order to deal with the accusations against Thrasea. During Tiridates stay Thrasea had written to the emperor to enquire about the exact charges and to insist he could clear his name if granted the opportunity. Nero now convened the senate, but Thrasea failed to attend.

The following morning, Nero drew up two battalions of the Guard in the temple of Venus, in the Forum of Julius Caesar. He lined the approach to the senate house with Guards in civilian dress, displaying their swords, and further troops were arrayed around the principal forums and law courts. Under this surveillance the senators entered the House.

Having made his point, Nero went one step further and had a quaestor read his address, refusing to speak to the members himself. Without mentioning any names, Nero's address rebuked members for neglecting their official duties and setting knights a slovenly example.

'What wonder if senators from distant provinces stayed away, when many ex-consuls and priests showed greater devotion to the embellishment of their gardens?' the quaestor read.

At once Cossutianus seized the opportunity to attack Thrasea; and Marcellus followed up with biting eloquence, claiming that the issue was one of prime national importance. Thrasea was condemned, but was allowed to choose his own death and severed his veins.

Now at last Nero was free to leave for Greece, on a tour that would take a year. He left the two dogs and Poppaea's cat with Acte and it proved a tearful farewell.

'Come with us,' he urged.

Acte shook her head. 'Someone must mind the animals. Palamedes isn't fit enough for such a journey.'

'We all got on so well,' Nero pleaded.

'But not for a year, Nero.' She smiled. 'Who else is going with you, anyway?'

'All of my ministers. Tigellinus, because I would not feel safe leaving him in Rome. Vitellius. And Sabina and Messalina, of course. My little Sabina has a new handmaid to attend his wardrobe - no less than Calvia Crispinilla! And his wardrobe is such that it will take all of Poppaea's donkeys to carry it!'

'Then I will not be missed! Now go, and enjoy yourself!'

Left at Rome in charge of State affairs were just two Greek freedmen - Helius, who had previously been in charge of Asian estates, and Polyclitus, who had been the very successful British envoy. The members of the senate believed themselves deserted by their emperor and were insulted to find they had been entrusted to foreign ex-slaves.

Meanwhile, Nero and his immense entourage stopped first at Corcyra and Actium to attend festivals, then travelled on to Corinth, where they spent the winter. Here, Nero began work on the Isthmus Canal project. Each year the stormy sea route round Cape Matapan took a heavy toll on lives and property, so it was hoped the canal could eventually offer an alternative route. Nero dug the first spadeful, arranging a musical programme for the inauguration of the project, and Vespasian, the commander in Judaea, sent six thousand prisoners to work on it.

The Greeks had altered the dates of their four national Games to enable Nero to compete in all four during the year and in the spring he made his first appearance on a Greek stage, in a festival at Argos. He then entered the first of the national Games, the Pythian at Delphi, where he sang a short song about the divinities of the sea and then took first prize for his acting in a Greek tragedy.

These successes were repeated in the Nemean Games, before the culmination of his near life-long ambition at Olympia. Though he had practised long and hard, Nero did not yet consider himself ready for the Olympic wrestling contests, but watched them like a judge, squatting on the ground and personally pushing back any pair of competitors who worked away from the centre of the ring.

'I have four years in which to improve my standard,' he assured his hosts, promising his return for the next renewals. In the meantime he won first prize in the tragic acting; singing; oration and lyre playing, defeating the great Terpnus, to his immense satisfaction. He so enjoyed announcing his own victories that he decided to enter the contest for heralds, too, and cherished that victory above all others.

'It matters not that these prizes are false,' he told Vitellius privately during a break in competitions, 'I cannot begin to describe to you the pleasure in performing here in Greece. Win or lose, to compete is reward enough. And these prizes are accepted in the spirit in which they were awarded. As a mark of respect and gratitude, not to buy my favour.'

The most popular of the Olympic Games was the chariot racing and Nero drove two teams of four horses to victory. He was less fortunate in his handling of a ten-horse team and fell from the chariot at the halfway point. He was too dazed and shaken to continue, but was awarded the gold medal for his abortive efforts.

JULY A.D. 67

Throughout the tour Helius had sent repeated messages urging Nero to return to Rome. He now surprised the emperor by making his plea in person.

'What the goodness are you doing here?' Nero demanded, 'how necessary can my presence in Rome be when you yourself believe that Polyclitus can cope alone!'

'There are rumours of revolt in every province,' Helius warned, 'and the citizens at Rome are restless in your absence. Remember how badly your absence was felt after the old Augusta's death?'

'Yes, you have made yourself quite plain,' Nero responded, 'I am aware that you want me to go home; you will do far better, however, if you encourage me to stay until I have proved myself worthy of Nero.'

'In other words, you mean to please only yourself?' Helius said bitterly.

'You are stubborn, Helius, but at least you are not stupid. Now return to Rome and deal with matters yourself. That is what you are employed for.'

'Are you having misgivings?' Epaphroditus enquired, after Helius had left.

Nero smiled ruefully. 'I have heard tales of treason and conspiracy so often now that I should have grown immune to the fear they induce. But it isn't fear of rebellion that bothers me now.'

'It can hardly be fear of losing!' Vitellius laughed, 'you have so far won over a thousand prizes!'

'It is fear of Athens itself,' Nero confessed. 'Since my mother's death I have been plagued almost nightly by the same nightmare. Remember how the Furies chased Orestes? Foolish though it sounds, I am terrified of entering the city.'

'It's Athens!' Epaphroditus laughed, 'Surely not even the Furies can keep you away!'

By chance, they arrived in Athens during the Eleusinian Mysteries. Nero was reluctant to join the audience, but was left with little option for fear of offending his hosts. However, when a herald ordered all impious and criminal persons to withdraw prior to the start of the ceremonies, Nero promptly withdrew, not daring to participate.

'Now you carry guilt too far,' both Phaon and Epaphroditus scolded, as they sat out the ceremonies, 'remind us again of your crime?'

'The death of one Augusta was not enough for me.'

'And the deaths of two were nothing to do with you! Why can we not convince you of your innocence?'

'You are only bitter because I have forced you to miss the Mysteries,' Nero told them, 'Sabina, Messalina and Vitellius will report every incident in the fullest detail, believe me. We might just as well have ringside seats!'

'Vitellius will describe the food served, or the food they failed to serve, while your two wives will argue over the costumes!' Phaon joked disdainfully.

'My two wives,' Nero repeated with pleasure, 'I think perhaps that has been the best part of this tour. How willingly the Greeks accept Sabina as my consort. He has been granted every honour of an empress and treated with equal respect and courtesy. And isn't he thriving on it?'

'Our Sporus has never been better!' Epaphroditus agreed, 'will we bother to return to Rome at all, Nero?'

Nero sighed. 'Nero says no; but I am also emperor of Rome. It is my destiny and I cannot run from it.'

All too soon came the last of the national Games, the Isthmian at Corinth. On the twenty-eighth of November, the eve of his departure, Nero stood in the centre of the stadium and announced the liberation of Greece, declaring it free and exempt from Roman tribute.

'Unexpected is the gift, men of Greece, with which I present you - though perhaps nothing can be thought unexpected from munificence such as mine - and so vast that you could not hope to ask for it. Would that I could have made this grant when Hellas was in its prime, so that there might have been more men to enjoy my grace. Not through pity, however, but through goodwill I now make you this benefaction, and I thank your gods, whose watchful providence I have always experienced both on sea and land, that they have afforded me the opportunity of so great a benefaction. Other emperors have freed cities; Nero alone a whole province!'

Nero now started back across the Adriatic, setting out in a storm that nearly wrecked his ship, so eager was he to return to Neapolis. He entered his beloved city in a white chariot and ordered part of the city wall to be razed, a Greek custom whenever the victor in any of the Sacred Games returned home. He repeated this at Antium, Albanum and, finally, Rome.

At Rome he staged a triumphal procession.

'A procession of peace, not war; of arts, not arms,' he announced publicly, 'My supreme jubilation - the conversion of the blood-thirsty Triumph to a procession of peace.'

Wearing a purple robe and cloak glittering with gold stars, Nero stood in the guilded chariot used by Augustus in his Triumph, with the lyre-player Diodurus, one of his famous defeated rivals. He wore the wild olive crown of the Olympic Games and carried the bay leaves of the Pythian Games, while men marched behind carrying each of his prizes, with banners listing the victories.

The procession swept down the Sacred Way and onto the Forum, the crowd cheering and hailing him victor. He proceeded to the Capitol, the traditional end of all triumphal processions, then on to the Palatine Hill, where his chosen end was the magnificent shrine of Apollo, patron of the arts. Here he dedicated all his wreaths, though he could not bear to be parted from those that held special significance for him.

He stayed on in Rome for only a few weeks before retiring once more to Neapolis; convinced, this time, that it was for good.

MARCH A.D. 68

Nero had ceased to enjoy the Festival of Minerva, but spent it at Baiae each year more through force of habit than any great love of tradition. He had planned to watch an exhibition of gymnastics on the anniversary of Agrippina's death, but was called to an urgent audience with Epaphroditus.

'Nero, the news is grave,' the secretary informed him, 'Vindex, the governor of Gaul, has revolted.'

'He has no legionaries under his command,' Nero pointed out.

'He claims royal Gallic origin and has enlisted several Gallic tribes. They number a hundred thousand, Nero.'

'Do they really? Gaul is a long way from Rome, Epaphroditus, and right now my only interest is in seeing the gymnastics.'

He departed quite calmly for the gymnasium, with Sporus and Acte, leaving Epaphroditus in a highly agitated state.

'Why does he do nothing to act on this?' Epaphroditus asked of Phaon, 'Does he not realise the full enormity of the revolt?'

'Perhaps we have cried wolf too often,' Phaon suggested; though they both knew in their hearts that Nero welcomed his downfall.

When a despatch arrived the following week from Vindex himself, Nero's ministers hoped that he would at last take the threat seriously.

'Vindex has issued a public proclamation,' Epaphroditus told him, 'He has denounced your Greek victories and public appearances, and your so-called extravagances, and has put forward Galba, the governor of Nearer Spain.'

'Galba! The man is long past retirement. He was sixty-two when I appointed him governor, and that was eight years ago! What support can he have?'

'Never mind his support - what of his attackers! What do you propose to do, Nero?'

'A simple craft will keep a man from want,' Nero replied, 'I shall retire to Greece and earn a living playing the lyre.'

'And how many of your predecessors were ever allowed to retire?' Phaon warned.

A further letter arrived from the governor of Aquitania, begging Nero's help against Vindex, which was ignored. On the second of April, Galba made a proclamation at Carthago Nova, declaring himself an ally of Vindex. He had few men and enrolled a legion among the Spaniards, before turning to his neighbouring governor for additional support.

'Otho has now joined forces with Galba,' Epaphroditus informed Nero, when word first reached them.

Nero showed no surprise.

'How can it be?!' Sporus demanded, 'They lie! They lie to break his will!'

Nero put out a calming hand, resting Sporus back beside him.

'I know Otho just as well as it seems he knows me,' he told him, 'and it is no lie. He already knows I do not intend to fight this. And in my defeat all those I have claimed as friends will perish, too.' He smiled gently to himself. 'And do you know, my Sabina? I had almost made my mind up to fight.'

'But you must fight!' Sporus insisted in panic.

'For what?' Nero demanded. 'I would lay down my life for you; but for the empire?'

Yet his calm detachment could not last. He returned to Rome to demonstrate the workings of the hydraulic organ in The Golden House and chanced to read the proclamation by Galba. He collapsed at once.

The armies in the Rhine were now called into action. The commander Verginius of Upper Germany made his move at once and marched with three legions on Vindex. At the end of May they fought at Vesontio, where Vindex was defeated and killed.

Verginius returned to his own province, where Galba sent him a letter of appeal for co-operation. Galba was now declared a public enemy and Nero once more assumed the rank of consul, this time serving on his own. For a short while he raised armies and prepared to march against Galba. He recruited a new legion from sailors at Misenum and sent three legions to Gaul, under the commands of Turpilianus, governor of Britain, and ex-consul Rubrius.

By the time news arrived of the defeat of Vindex, the loyalty of Verginius was already in question.

'You have only to pledge your support and send him the additional legions and he is yours!' Epaphroditus urged. 'Galba will be destroyed as easily as Vindex. Hesitate, and Galba enlists the best ally he could ever hope for. You cannot expect loyalty if you desert him, Nero.'

'I do not want loyalty!' Nero cried out, 'I do not want these troops or this empire! Let them end it now, for one rebellion will surely follow on another, and another. This is not how I wish to live out my life. This is not what the Triumph of peace advocated!'

'Nero, they will kill you! You cannot slip away quietly and hand over your crown to the first general to arrive in Rome!'

'I shall go to Gaul and throw myself unarmed and weeping at the feet of the enemy. They will take pity on me and exile me.'

Epaphroditus could only throw up his hands in despair, but worse news was to come. Tigellinus and Nymphidius had left Rome, deserting the emperor. The Praetorian Guard now left Nero to his fate, feeling that he had already abandoned them to theirs. The legions under Rubrius quickly followed suit and revolted.

Only now did Nero panic. He sent his freedmen and slaves to Ostia to prepare a ship and made immediate plans to take flight to Egypt. He ransacked the Palace in search of the gold snakeskin bracelet once given to him by Agrippina for protection. And when he could find no trace of it, he gave in to superstition, convinced that all hope of salvation was gone.

'We have no time for despair,' Epaphroditus urged him, 'you must pull yourself together and make ready for your escape. The soldiers are nearing Rome and we have only days, if that.'

'I cannot be murdered,' Nero sobbed, 'I must die peacefully, painlessly.'

'You won't die at all if you do as we say and make haste!'

'Summon Locusta! Locusta can brew me a potion! Send Tubero to her at once!'

Epaphroditus did as he was asked, not wishing to cause Nero any further distress than he already suffered. Tubero returned the following day with an exquisite gold trinket box, which contained a lethal pill. But it had already cost them a valuable day.

'Put it beside your bed,' Epaphroditus advised him, 'but I promise you, you will not need it. We shall be out of Rome in the morning.'

Chapter Fifty-Two

8TH JUNE A.D. 68

The silence woke him.

He sat up instantly; his heart thumping at an absurd volume, audible to him as he strained to pick up the familiar sounds that were not forthcoming. The exaggerated pounding made him feel flushed and faint. In the cold sweat of a nightmare, he concentrated on the tremor in his limbs and tried to regather his wits.

No quiet movements of slaves at work in the corridors. No hushed conversations from the Guards outside his door. He knew that they were gone. The unnatural stillness of the Palace terrified him and he shook with deep, silent sobs - contained for the sake of Sporus, who still slept so peacefully beside him.

Slipping gently from the boy's embrace, Nero crept hesitantly to his desk; filled with a deep dread of what lay there. Yet even before he neared it, he could see by the shadows that it was not as he had left it. The drawers were hanging open, the top of the desk cleared of all contents. He let out a low moan of agony, but made no further sound; trembling as his hands groped desperately in the half-light for Locusta's missing box. His sobs became uncontrolled and all the more audible as he searched frenziedly for the little golden box. But even as he shook out the empty drawers, he knew that the box had been taken. Stolen for its own apparent value and not for the priceless treasure within. Yet still he searched; unable to face up to this final destruction of hope.

He was choking now and a new fear took hold. He sank onto his haunches and buried his face in his arms; stifling his tears and trying so hard to steady the heavy gulps of his breathing. Only the two elderly dogs heard him, and neither bothered to move from their place of slumber at the foot of his bed. Nor too had they paid any attention to the seemingly familiar movements of the slaves who had robbed him.

Dreading the thought of waking Sporus and the painful explanations that would ensue, Nero bade the dogs stay and ran out into the corridor, finding it to be like his own room - stripped bare of all movable contents. In renewed panic, he ran down the corridor, beating frantically at the doors of his friends' apartments, which were all locked and seemingly empty.

'Spiculus! SPICULUS!' he screamed, tearing at his hair which was sticking to his face. 'Spiculus? *Anyone*! Any trained executioner to put an end to me!' He fell, sobbing wildly, to his knees and vomited on the polished marble, which reflected only the bare, gold-painted walls.

He rose up shakily and ran from the scenes of desertion, out into the gardens, crying, 'What? Have I then neither friends nor enemies left?' The idea came to him to throw himself into the Tiber, but he could do no more than fling himself down onto the soft cushion of turf at the realisation that he lacked even the courage for this pitiful end.

It was here that Phaon and Sporus found him, having been woken by his cries.

'I thought you had forsaken me,' Nero admitted, as they ran to his aid.

Phaon shook his head and took Nero up into his arms. 'I bolted my door against intruders when I heard the Guard depart. That was sometime around midnight. The slaves have had a merry time of it since then.'

Sporus, unable to mask his distress, added that Epaphroditus had also been to Nero's room and was now rousing a slave in readiness for escape.

'He will no doubt find us soon; in the meantime we could prepare some horses, perhaps?'

Nero stared dazedly at them both. 'I need only a secluded spot where I can hide and collect myself.'

'There is my own villa,' Phaon suggested, 'just four miles from here, between the Nomentan and Salaria roads. We have an hour yet before full light - ample time to escape unseen.'

'I'll make ready five horses,' Sporus said decisively; and had already brought them up when Epaphroditus, in the company of the slave Tubero, located them at last.

Nero was wearing only a thin under-tunic and was bare-footed. Tubero gave him his own faded cloak and hat to wear, and the emperor took the added precaution of covering his face with a handkerchief. The party moved off in silence, the ominous approach of a thunderstorm appropriate to their mood.

They had gone only a short way when an earth-tremor was felt, and a flash of lightning split the sky. The horses were naturally unsettled, and Nero himself gave way to his terror, upsetting his own mount all the more. It took all the collective powers of persuasion of his friends to pacify him, and his horse remained dangerously skittish.

They passed by a soldiers' camp, where even at this early hour the inhabitants were up and about. The soldiers could be heard shouting to one another about the impending battle, and the defeat Galba would inflict upon Nero. It was only a matter of moments before the riders were spotted by some of the troops.

'Look! Those people are in pursuit of the emperor!'

'What's the latest of him in town?'

The five horsemen kept their heads low and made no attempt to reply, but the horses became alarmed by the stench of a dead body lying by the roadside and gave their riders some trouble in going past. Already nervous, Nero's mount reared up and tried to swing round. Nero succeeded in holding him together, but dropped the handkerchief concealing his face and was immediately recognised and saluted by a veteran of the Guard.

They came at last to the lane leading to Phaon's villa and abandoned the horses, following a path on foot which ran through the bushes bordering the grounds. The going was difficult, winding through briars and a plantation of reeds. After just a short time Nero's feet were torn and bleeding, so his companions spread their cloaks on the ground for him to walk on.

'There is a gravel pit, completely hidden, just to our left,' Phaon said, as they paused to lay out the cloaks again. 'Please, Nero - you must rest. Hide within it and catch your breath for a while.'

For a moment, Nero's eyes glazed with fear; but he shook his head and said quite calmly, 'No, I refuse to go underground before I die.'

At this, Sporus collapsed completely and Nero was too occupied in soothing the boy to dwell on his own misfortune. They continued on with an air of calm resignation, Sporus supported by Nero, who very quickly began to feel the strain of this added burden. He remembered that he had neither eaten nor drunk since collapsing into bed the night before, and that thought alone was enough to increase his hunger and thirst. For the final few yards of their trek, these discomforts served to take his mind off the pain of his feet - and the inexorable fate that awaited him.

'We're at the rear of the house,' Phaon said at long last, 'but we dare not enter by any means that would betray us. There is a little cellar door, long since overgrown and forgotten, just across there. With a little effort, it can be our secret entrance. Nero, you wait here while we dig it out.'

Too exhausted to protest, Nero sank gratefully down by the side of a carp pool and scooped up some of the dirty water in his cupped hands and drank it. Then he occupied his mind by carefully picking out the thorns from his cloak, until the time came to crawl through the makeshift tunnel into the house.

Once inside, he refused to go any further than the first room into which they came, a disused lobby sparsely furnished with the casts-off from the rest of the house. There he sank down onto a tattered old couch with a poor mattress, much to the consternation of Phaon.

'I'll go and find us some bread and warm a little water,' Phaon told him gently, but when he returned he found that, despite Nero's hunger, the emperor could not eat the bread, and could only sip at the warmed water. His companions found their own appetites little better.

'We were seen leaving the city,' Epaphroditus remarked grimly. 'I think it would be best if you at least, Phaon, returned to the Palace. We shall need someone there to send word of any changes in the situation - and your own absence would only lead them here that much faster.'

'Perhaps.' Phaon glanced across to where Nero lay on the couch with Sporus, the latter still not yet recovered from the fit of distress which had overwhelmed him at the gravel pit. 'Can you manage here on your own?'

'I have Tubero. I'll cope, if I have to.' And so it was tacitly agreed.

Phaon could not say goodbye. He shied from taking his leave of them and instead wandered out under the pretence of fetching more water. He didn't come back.

'There is no escape, is there?' Nero said after a while, his tone one of calm acceptance.

Epaphroditus shook his head.

'Then might I simply await the soldiers?'

Sporus let out a scream. '*NO*! No! You cannot accept so degrading a death when you have lived such a life.'

'He's right,' Epaphroditus concurred, 'you must take your own life before the soldiers arrive.'

Nero trembled. He looked at Epaphroditus, and did not have to voice the words that he lacked the courage for such action.

'There are practicalities to be considered,' Epaphroditus said bluntly, 'arrangements to be made. However painful, they cannot be ignored.'

Nero nodded and swallowed. For a moment, he failed to find his voice. 'We must prepare a grave,' he said at last, as though arranging a pleasant evening's entertainment, 'and gather pieces of marble to line it. And wood, to dispose of... the body. And perfumed water, for the pyre. I should like perfumed water.' He struggled to raise a smile. 'Come, Sporus, it will be like a scavenger hunt! We can occupy ourselves until Phaon sends word.'

They busied themselves collecting together all the items Nero felt necessary, bustling about in the garden and ransacking the other rooms of the house, until Nero was satisfied with the macabre collection. As they dug out a grave, he tried hard to raise a smile and declared, almost jovially, 'Dead! And so great an artist!'

When Tubero and Epaphroditus began work on the pyre, Nero took the distraught Sporus back in to the lobby, where they fell weeping into each other's arms on the shabby couch. Nero was conscious of the grotesque surroundings in which he was inevitably to die, but he closed his mind to such thoughts and cried all the harder for Acte, and Messalina, and Sporus.

They both jumped violently at a sudden rap on the door, out in the main hall. Nero ran to answer it, without heed to danger. It was a runner, sent by Phaon.

'I have a message for the slaves of the house, from their master,' the runner stammered nervously, recognising the emperor at once.

Nero snatched the note from his grasp and read it immediately.

'It says that I have been declared a public enemy by the senate and will be punished in ancient style when arrested. What is 'ancient style'? What does it mean?' His voice rose in panic, and Tubero and Epaphroditus came running in alarm. They dismissed the runner, with pleas for his silence.

'What does this mean?' Nero cried again, and Epaphroditus could see no reason for avoiding an answer.

'Ancient style,' he said frankly, 'is when the executioner strips his victim naked, thrusts the victim's head into a wooden fork and flogs him to death with rods.'

Nero blanched. In terror, he snatched up the two daggers fetched by Phaon and tested their points. But his courage failed him and he threw them down once more.

'No! My hour has not yet come! My hour has not yet come.'

He fell, sobbing, to the floor and clutched at Sporus, who had found renewed strength in the face of Nero's sudden distress.

'Don't let them cut off my head,' Nero sobbed, 'please don't let them cut off my head. Let me buried in one piece.'

Though Sporus did his best, Nero could not be consoled.

'Promise to mourn me, Sporus - weep for me when I am gone.' His sobs came in great choking gulps, so that he found it difficult to speak; yet he could not be silent. 'Oh! Such cowardice!' he sobbed bitterly, 'How ugly and vulgar my life has become.'

Clinging to the emperor's neck and unable to face him, Sporus broke down once more and Epaphroditus, no less visibly distressed himself, tried to ease the boy's pain.

'This certainly is no credit to Nero, no credit at all,' Nero cried to himself in Greek, trying vainly to curb his own tears. 'Come, pull yourself together.' Yet his tears only increased.

Suddenly, he sat up quite sharply and his face glazed with joy.

'Hark! Hark to the sound I hear! It is hooves of galloping horses.'

He could hear, as could his companions, the steady rhythmic beat of an approaching troop of cavalry, sent out from the city with orders to take him alive. He took comfort in this familiar sound, fancying he could smell the leather and horseflesh; feel the warmth and softness of the animals. They were galloping not to his death, but to the final turn at the Circus Maximus. And he guided them.

He reached calmly for a dagger and raised it steadily to his throat, pushing it against his skin. More than that, he could not do. His hand began to shake and he looked imploringly to Epaphroditus.

Neither spoke.

Epaphroditus gently placed his hand over Nero's; and the dagger was driven home.

He was already at the point of death when the first of the soldiers burst in. A centurion, under strict instructions to return Nero alive to the city for punishment, took in the scene at once and rushed to the emperor's aid, staunching the gaping wound with his cloak. Nero reached out and grasped his hand in gratitude, misunderstanding the reason for such action.

'Too late! But, ah, such fidelity!'

And he said no more.

EPILOGUE

The commons wept for him as they had wept for his grandfather Germanicus. His edicts were circulated as though he were still alive, many hoping that he would return to confound his enemies. The senate, having done so much during his lifetime to turn them against him, now dared not besmirch his name in death and lose the commons in uprising. When a united body of foreign heads of state, led by King Vologeses of Parthia, and Tiridates, urged the senate to honour his name, the request was grudgingly granted. Galba greeted the news of Nero's death with an invitation to his freedman Icelus to have sex with him, there and then, by way of celebration. And so began the short reign of Galba, his six months in power earning him universal hatred for his greed and cruelty. Icelus, meanwhile, had been present at Nero's passing and had granted his final wish, to be buried in one piece.

So it was that the hastily dug hole in the grounds of Phaon's villa was left unfilled. In a funeral costing two thousand gold pieces, Nero was laid on his scented pyre, dressed in the gold-embroidered white robes that he had worn on 1st January. Acte, Ecloge and Alexandria carried his remains to the Pincian Hill, where a coffin of purest white porphyry awaited him in the family tomb. Enclosed by a balustrade of stone from Thasos, and with an altar of Luna marble standing over it, the grave was decorated further by fresh flowers that were laid daily for more than thirty years after his death, by the commons who so loved him. Those in the city also placed statues of him, dressed in his fringed toga, on the Rostra. For each one removed, there was always a replacement, for many years after.

The army, abandoned by Nero and deserting him in turn, was the first to turn against the atrocities of Galba. After less than seven months, as he made his way to the Forum, a troop of cavalry ran him down and butchered him. His body was left rotting where it lay, until a soldier decapitated the corpse and took the head to Otho. It was placed on a spear at the Guards' camp, Otho having been already carried there, high on the shoulders of common citizens, to be hailed as emperor, some considerable time before Galba's death.

Several times during the preceding months Otho had planned to assassinate Galba, but by strange coincidence the same cohort of Guards who had abandoned both Caligula and Nero to their fate were again on duty on each occasion. He felt reluctant to sully their reputation still further and instead waited his moment. He had already won the confidence of the troops in Rome and his accession had been assured even before Galba's death.

But the armies in Germany refused to vow allegiance to him and gave their loyalty instead to Vitellius. Though he had risen against Galba only because he had been assured a bloodless victory, Otho had now to march on the dissenters, a prospect he abhorred deeply. Though his armies won three battles at the Alps, en route, he loathed the victories for the deaths they had caused. Vitellius therefore arranged for peace talks at Betriacum, but it proved an act of treachery. The deceived troops on both sides had fraternised during the day, but Vitellius, staying well clear of all danger, did not meet Otho. Instead he had his generals lead his men into battle against Otho's troops, who met their first defeat.

The needless bloodshed and the circumstances of this battle destroyed Otho. That same day, the ninety-fifth of his reign, he plunged a dagger through his heart. He had been about to marry Nero's widow, Messalina, and had restored all of Nero's freedmen and ministers to their former positions, with the notable exception of Tigellinus, whom he put to death for his crimes. He had also completed The Golden House, which Nero hadn't lived to see finished.

As emperor, Vitellius fared little better. He was abhorred for his gluttony and cruelty and he derived pleasure from having even friends and noblemen tortured or killed on only the slightest of pretexts. After eight months of these atrocities the army rebelled and swore allegiance to Vespasian, former governor of Judaea. The Palace was invaded and Vitellius taken prisoner. With a noose about his neck, he was stripped and paraded at the Forum, where the populace threw dung and filth in his face. The soldiers then put him through the torture of 'the little cuts' before finally killing him and throwing his body in the Tiber.

Vespasian throughout this time had remained in his African provinces. But letters from both Otho and King Vologeses urged him to march on Rome. Otho had written at the time of his suicide, looking to Vespasian to avenge his death. But only when the Prefect of Egypt had sworn his armies over in allegiance to Vespasian, did Vespasian himself make any attempt at civil war. When he did begin his march, Vologeses sent him forty thousand archers.

Upon assuming the role of emperor, Vespasian punished a great many of Vitellius' men and set about establishing himself as a strict disciplinarian. Yet he proved fair and moderate, in a reign lasting ten years. He died at the age of sixty-nine, on 23rd June, A.D. 79, and was deified. His sons Titus and Domitian, both once included in Nero's circle, followed him as subsequent emperors; and Domitian was succeeded in A.D. 96 by Nerva, who had himself won honours from Nero as a young general.

Sadly, one of Domitian's final acts in A.D. 96 was to have the long serving imperial secretary, Epaphroditus, put to death. He declared it to be a gesture, to show that a freedman must never have a hand in the death of an emperor, no matter how extenuating the circumstances – referring, of course, to Epaphroditus' final act of compassion for Nero, twenty-nine years earlier. The following day Domitian was assassinated.

Some twenty years after Nero's death, a man emerged in Parthia claiming to be Nero. The Parthians at once gave him their support and were willing to do their utmost to restore him to his throne. It was only with the greatest of reluctance did they accept the evidence that he was no more than a confidence trickster, and unwillingly surrendered him to Rome. The people of Rome, their hopes cruelly raised, mourned his loss for a second time.

Such was the magic of his name.

Printed in Great Britain
by Amazon